Retribution

Retribution

Susanne Beck

Renaissance Alliance Publishing, Inc.
Nederland, Texas

ISBN 1-930928-24-6

First Printing 2001

9 8 7 6 5 4 3 2 1

Cover art and design by Mary Draganis

Published by:

Renaissance Alliance Publishing, Inc.
PMB 238, 8691 9th Avenue
Port Arthur, Texas 77642-8025

Find us on the World Wide Web at
http://www.rapbooks.com

Printed in the United States of America

Special thanks to the following people for believing in my dream: Kricket and Pudderbear, Elizabeth "Four" Baldwin, Linda "Lola" Lynch, Lisa "Sulli/Slurpee" Sullivan, Carol Stephens, Judi Mair, Missy Good, Mary D, Lunacy, Candace Chellew, Mom, Dad, Paul, Stephanie, Julia and Alex, Alex and Kelly Moore, everyone at My Sisters Room, everyone at RAP for their fantastic work, and a special thanks to Lucy Lawless, Renee O'Connor, Robert Tapert, Stephen Sears, RJ Stewart, and all the cast and crew of Xena:Warrior Princess for six years of joy, angst and inspiration!

For

Sheri Jo Hardwick

---Forever love

Chapter 1

It was cold. So cold.

And dark, like the bottom of a newly dug grave.

My whole body was numb; my heart, encased in a block of ice which promised never to thaw.

I could feel the rain around me, pelting down in almost horizontal sheets of stinging fire, driven on by the frenzy of an unholy wind.

A wooden shutter, torn askew by the power of the storm, slammed repeatedly against the weathered wooden siding, sounding a death-knell which rose even over the howling of the wind and the wailing of sirens. Sirens which, like the fog, crept closer and closer, not on cat's feet, but on dragon's bloody claws.

Lightning drew its spiky graph onto the sky, imprinting itself on my retinas.

Thunder cracked and rolled, pulling an inane thought to the forefront of my brain. *God's bowling with the angels again*, my father's voice said from somewhere beyond the grave.

And still I waited, blind and frozen like some immortal statue. Waited for the wind to cease its unending fury. Waited for the rain to part its opaque curtain.

Waited for a vision my eyes could not see. A vision my soul could not forget.

As if drawn into the clearing by the force of my unvoiced plea, still more cars came, their churning tires flinging muddy fans into the air. Their powerful headlights broke through the cloak of mist, illuminating the scene I wished so desperately to see from my frozen perch on the porch of the home I'd helped to build.

A home, a dream, that I would willingly leave, never stopping once to look back upon it, if only someone would take these scales from my eyes.

If only.

She stood there straight and tall, backlit by the artificial lighting; my lover, my heart, my soul. Proud back unbowed, head held high, eyes blazing fire.

Proud, yes. But helpless.

Not against the arms which held her, nor the cuffs which bound her strong arms, nor even the guns that pointed at every vulnerable spot in an otherwise invulnerable body.

No, not that. Never that.

Helpless, instead, against the weight of a past which had, once again, come home to roost.

Helpless against the weight of a love she had sold her very soul to nurture and cherish.

The look in her eyes is something I'll take with me to the grave. A grave that, God willing, will not be long in coming.

Anger at her past for intruding. Rage at the arms which held her, at the guns which nudged her with their hollow silver noses. Sorrow, that the chance we had had ended much too soon.

And love.

Always love.

Her full lips parted, and I strained to hear her words over the storm's redoubled fury. But even they were taken from me, just as surely as she would be, drawn away into the mist from which only endings came.

But still, I watched as those lips formed words only my heart could hear.

I love you

And then a word came which shattered my soul.

Goodbye.

"*No!*" I screamed, bolting up and grabbing at my chest as the breath gusted from my lungs. My heart beat rapidly against fingers which trembled from the intensity of emotion welling up in me.

I blinked my eyes once, and then again, my pupils dilating to accept the feeble light from the window. Managing to relax the panic-induced lock of my muscles, I turned my head slightly, taking in the warm familiarity of the room around me. *Oh, thank God. It's just a dream. Just a dream.*

Nestled, sleep-warm, beside me, the object of my terrified

thoughts mumbled, yawned, and stretched slightly, pale eyes blinking fuzzily open. "Are you ok?"

A smile rose unbidden to my face as I lowered my hand to stroke sleep-tousled hair. "Yes," I whispered. "It was just a dream."

Burrowing closer, she lifted a hand and laid it against my thigh, resting her forehead against my hip. She cleared her throat. "Wanna talk about it?"

I reveled in the warmth of the simple contact and slowly shook my head. "No. I'm fine." I didn't have the heart to tell her that this same dream, which had haunted my sleep for the last year or more, had become nearly a nightly occurrence, tearing at my soul bit by merciless bit and leaving me drained and aching every morning. "Just go back to sleep, love. I know how tired you are."

Blue eyes narrowed, their gaze sharpening as she inspected my expression.

Consciously softening my face, I reached out and gently grasped her hand, my thumb tenderly rubbing against the harshly chapped flesh so stained with oil from her labors that it seemed it would never be clean again. Blinking back fresh tears, I somehow managed to keep my expression unguarded and relaxed.

She saw right through my attempt and pulled her hand away from mine, reaching up to capture a tear on her finger. "Why are you crying?"

The answer to that was easy. "Because I love you."

She looked as if she were about to argue the point, but the weight of many nights of little or no sleep caught up to her and she yawned once again. "Love you, too," she mumbled, her heavy eyelids already drifting down over her stunning eyes. "My angel."

I caught her hand once again as it drifted down from my face and brought it to my lips as I gave my tears permission to fall. "I love you, Morgan," I whispered around her warm flesh. "More than you will ever know."

Placing her hand back into my lap, I turned my gaze to the rain-speckled window, watching with idle interest as fat raindrops heralded yet another mid-summer storm. My vision trebled with my tears as I thought back over the rapidly fleeing remnants of my nightmare, wondering for perhaps the thousandth time if it was just a subconscious reaction to stress, as my dreams often were, or if it served to portend something infinitely more ominous.

Pushing the thoughts as down deep as possible, I leaned my head back against the wall and gazed out at the winter landscape, allowing my mind to go where it would. It chose a simpler time, where the scope of our world was narrowed down to just one word.

Survival.

I stooped behind Ice's broad back, desperately needing to pee, my muscles stiffened by the cold, mountain air and the need to stay absolutely still, my teeth chattering away like castanets in the hands of an insane Spaniard.

The sun was setting to the west, stealing the last feeble warmth from the early spring sky, and the wind redoubled its efforts to slip inside the painfully thin jacket I'd donned that morning.

Ice had sold her bike to a friend of hers earlier, leaving her with a small wad of cash which, when added to my own pitiful sum, didn't amount to much. We'd made a quick trip to the local thrift store to stock up on meager supplies, painfully aware that the money we had would be all we had to live on until God knew when.

We'd walked from there, carefully keeping off the main roads, even when the urge to hook an easy ride from a passing trucker seemed almost overwhelming, especially given the screaming of my irritated and quickly blistering feet.

It was hours later before we finally made it to what Ice pronounced as the border. I didn't ask her how she knew, a map most definitely not being one of our meager purchases. It wouldn't have done me any good anyway. Ice was never the most talkative woman in the world, and I was sure her mind was occupied with far weightier matters than my simple, if nagging, curiosity.

At least that's what I told myself when my fifth question in a row was answered by a low grunt and a gesture to "hush."

So, I kept quiet and contented myself with memorizing our route as best I could, my mind's eye already in some warm room somewhere jotting down the day's adventures in the journal I was determined to keep writing in.

If I had expected some grand pronouncement, a sign, perhaps, announcing that we were leaving the "land of the brave" and entering the "home of the Canucks," I was sorely disappointed. The stretch of thickly wooded forest was much the same as the hundreds of others we'd passed on our journey to freedom.

But when Ice suddenly halted and pulled me down behind a

thick hedgerow, I realized that we were probably close to our destination.

And so we waited as the sun blazed out its last in a riot of color. We waited as the moon rose and the stars came out to watch over us, no doubt wondering, as I most surely did, exactly what it was that we were waiting for.

All I knew was that the stillness, the waiting, and the cold were not doing kind things to my bladder, and I was at the point where we either moved, and quickly, or I was going to do something I hadn't done since I was two.

To take my mind off my rather urgent need, I turned my thoughts to other things. Like this wonderful feeling called "freedom" and what it meant to me, even this far out in the middle of nowhere. I was still in that blissful honeymoon phase, I think, where even the most annoying of circumstances seemed to be viewed through a pair of those proverbial rose-colored glasses.

Everything around me seemed so impossibly vast and open without the constant specter of bars to mar the view and remind me where my place was at any given moment. To remind me that society considered me beneath contempt; unfit to make even the smallest decision for myself.

Even such a mundane task as needing to pee took on a whole new meaning when one realized that you could simply...well...*do* it, without having to ask permission from anyone but your own body.

I was shaken out of my quiet thoughts by what appeared to me to be oncoming headlights. I stiffened, placing a hand on Ice's back and peering over her shoulder, determined to face what was coming, be it friend or foe, with as much courage as was mine to possess.

Moments later, my suspicions were confirmed as several pick-up trucks, blazing with lights, bounced over the rugged terrain and into my view. I could easily hear the shouts of drunken men over the roar of the engines. Several large deer were tied down to the hoods of the trucks.

The trucks pulled to a stop some yards from our hiding place, and one of the men jumped out, resplendent in his "hunter orange" vest and cap. He drunkenly weaved his way over to a tree quite near us, his breath huffing out in frosty plumes, and proceeded to do what I'd been needing to for the past several hours.

I turned my head away in disgust, leaning it against Ice's back. I nearly jumped out of my skin as her voice rumbled through her chest and into my ear. "Better put that away before somebody hurts you with it," she said in a menacing voice.

The big man squeaked and spun toward our position, his round eyes the size of saucers. "Who's there?"

"Ya got a license to be jacking deer out here, buddy?"

He paled under his thick beard and, for a second, I thought he was going to faint. Then his eyes narrowed and he took several determined steps toward us, apparently forgetting that a more sensitive part of his anatomy was left hanging, so to speak, in the breeze. "That you, Morgan?"

"Could be," came the taunting answer.

Behind her, I stiffened in surprise. *These* were our escorts? "Ice?" I asked, tugging at the back of her jacket.

Her head turned slowly, amused eyes meeting mine. "Yes?"

I gestured to the man still standing opposite us. "A marching band and a neon sign would probably be more subtle, you know."

She winked at me, then turned her head back around. "So, ya gonna just stand there all night with your little friend hanging out or what?"

The man's blush was vivid, lit up as it was by the blazing lights of the trucks off to the side. He quickly reached down and attended to business, before stepping closer and reaching a hand down to pull Ice from her hiding place.

Ice raised an eyebrow and looked at the proffered hand, then back at her friend.

He cleared his throat, blushed again, and wiped his hands off on his bloodstained trousers. "Jesus, Morgan, you nearly scared the shit outta me, hiding there like that!"

Rising to her feet with a grace I envied, my partner grinned and clapped her friend on the back. "Sorry about that, Bull. Thanks for meeting us out here."

The man's eyes widened again. "'Us?'"

Turning, Ice reached down and helped me to my feet, pulling me to stand beside her. "Us. Bull, meet Angel. Angel, this is my friend Albert. 'Bull' to his drunken, deer jacking buddies."

This time, his blush was truly spectacular, as he reached up and snatched his cap off his head and stood, wringing it in his hands. "I'm sorry, ma'am. I didn't.... Oh, God."

Grinning to ease his discomfort, I stepped forward and laid a hand on his arm. "I'm very pleased to meet you, Bull. Thank you for helping us out like this."

"Oh...um...it wasn't anything much, ma'am. Really. H-happy to do it."

Breaking through the man's embarrassment in a way so typical of her, Ice clapped Bull on the shoulder once more and gestured to the waiting trucks, their drivers and passengers staring at us with open-mouthed drunkenness. "Shall we?"

After a moment, Bull dragged his eyes away from me and slapped the cap down on top of his head. "Yeah. Right this way, ladies."

And, just like that, we were in Canada.

After a drive that seemed like an eternity over rutted wannabe roads that had my fillings, and the teeth they were attached to, rolling around like dice in my head, a small shanty came into sudden view, a welcoming curl of smoke rising gracefully from the brick chimney.

Gratefully escaping from a truck cab that smelled like a distillery, I hugged my arms to myself as the cold conspired against me, again, and looked at the tiny shack that was, apparently, to be a rest stop on our journey.

It look sturdy enough, but much smaller than I had expected, hardly more than a crude lean-to with four walls and a roof to hold it all together.

I shrugged mentally. I could do "tiny." I'd been in smaller spaces, after all. The green-painted walls of my cell came into my mind's eye and I shivered, just slightly. *No more of that, Angel. You're free now. Start acting like it.*

Mustering up a smile, I looked up at Ice, who put a careful arm around my shoulders and guided me into the cabin. Warmth from a blazing fire and the wonderful smells of grilling meat enveloped my senses immediately. My stomach, of course, growled its impatience, but the crowd around us was too boisterous to pay any notice.

Ice, of course, *did* notice and quirked me a half-grin before turning and accepting a quick kiss on the cheek from a tall, handsome man with smiling dark eyes and a bushy moustache that almost covered his mouth. He waved a greeting to me as well before being pulled back to his cooking duties by the men who demanded food, and right now, if you please.

"Andre," Ice commented softly by way of introduction. "Not much of a hunter, but he cooks a mean venison steak. I think you'll enjoy it."

I laughed. "After five years of jail food, I'd enjoy a cardboard box if it had something more than pepper on it."

My lover smiled back in wry acknowledgement as Bull once again made his presence known, gesturing around the cabin with one massive arm. "Well, this is it. It's not much, I know. But at least it's warm."

"And that's more than we could ever ask for," I replied quickly, looking around the tiny shack, which was, essentially, just one large room. Bunk beds were pushed up against three of the four walls. A couch, having seen better days around the time Lincoln was President, sat off to one side. A fireplace dominated the fourth wall, with a decent sized stove and a small refrigerator completing the ensemble. A rough-hewn table sat in the center of the room, loaded down with clothing, ammunition, gun-oil, and several objects which remained mysteries to me.

At a shout from Andre, several of the men began clearing the table, grumbling drunkenly if good naturedly, while Bull walked to the only door in the cabin and pulled it open.

An unbelievably tiny room was displayed. A narrow cot sat off to one side with a window above it. A three-cornered stool, a rather pornographic lamp sitting atop it, was the only other furniture that could have fit there. Ice could have easily reached across the entire space with both arms outstretched.

Thoughts of prison came to me once again, but I pushed them away, grateful for any bit of hospitality I was given.

"It's small, but the door closes, so you'll have some privacy, at least."

"It's perfect," I pronounced, walking inside and laying my backpack on the bed. "Thank you, Bull."

Blushing again, he looked down at his feet before mumbling something unintelligible and backing away into the main room.

Shaking her head in mock exasperation, Ice stepped past the retreating man and joined me in the cramped room, looking around. "Not exactly the Ritz, but it'll do in a pinch, I suppose."

I flopped down on the bed, crossed my legs, and grinned up at her. "I'm not complaining. It's warm, the food smells heavenly, and I get to spend all night in this tiny bed with you. What more could a girl ask for?"

She smiled that heart-stopping grin at me, then ducked down and brushed a soft, warm kiss against my lips before straightening again. "I'd give you a palace if I could, Angel."

"I don't need a palace, Ice. I just need you."

We might have gone on for years staring into one another's eyes if my bladder hadn't chosen just that moment to announce its final summons. I jumped up from the bed. "Where's the bathroom?" I asked out of the corner of my mouth, not wanting to be overheard.

"There isn't one," Ice responded in like fashion.

My eyes, I'm sure, widened dramatically. "*What*? Then

where do you...?"

Taking pity on my desperate condition, Ice leaned over the bed, pulling the tattered window shade out of the way. "Out-house."

"Great." I sighed.

My bladder twinged again, and I shrugged. *Oh well, any port in a storm, I suppose.*

Dinner was a loud, boisterous, but delicious affair. We ate pressed close together, Ice on my right, Andre on my left, and the rest of the men trading outrageous hunting tales that went into the realm of science fiction rather quickly.

Though grateful for the kindnesses shown me, I couldn't help but feel slightly uncomfortable as the night wore on. After spending five years in the sole company of women and, in addition, having a bit of a sore spot when it came to drunken males, given my past history with at least one of their species, I felt myself gradually begin to close off as a means, I suppose, of self preservation. Ice was warmly supportive, but there were still places deep within me that even she couldn't reach, and this was one of them.

Giving my hand a warm squeeze under the table, Ice turned her head and brought her lips down to brush against my ear, sending a wonderful shiver throughout my entire body. "Why don't you bow out? Try and relax and get some sleep. I'll be back shortly."

That sent a great deal more than a shiver though me and I concentrated on keeping my breathing steady as I whispered back. "Are you sure?"

"Yeah. I have a couple of things to discuss with these brutes before they all pass out. Then I'll come back and join you. Sound good?"

I could feel my eyes closing against my will at the tickle of her warm breath against my neck. "Oh, it sounds *better* than good."

Though unseen, I could still feel her smile as she squeezed my hand once more before releasing it.

Taking another moment to compose myself and make sure my legs would hold my weight, I slowly pushed my chair back and rose to my feet, smiling at my hosts. "I hate to be a party-pooper, but all that walking and the wonderful dinner about did me in. I think it's time I went to bed. Goodnight, guys. And thanks."

I entered the bedroom to the sounds of cheery "goodnights" and closed the door with a sense of profound relief as the sturdy wood drowned out the loudest of the noises.

Running my hands through my hair, I breathed out a sigh of relief and sat down on the narrow cot, picking up my knapsack and digging out my journal and pen, thinking to put the day's adventures down on paper.

But the words wouldn't come right away and, leaning back against one wall, I gazed around the tiny room, wondering at the paradox that something so reminiscent of my time in the Bog, a room no larger than my home for five years, could bring with it such a feeling of security.

There's an old jailhouse maxim that says that an inmate spends all of his time thinking of ways to get out of prison, while an ex-convict spends all of his time thinking of ways to get back *in*.

While not entirely true in my case (or at least I hoped not), I couldn't ignore the fact that there was a certain sense of security that came with being told when to get up, when to eat, what to wear, where to go, what to do, and when to sleep. Freedom meant owning up to those decisions once again, and sometimes the choices seemed too many to reach an easy decision on.

I wondered, briefly, what Ice's thoughts were on the subject, having spent many more years behind bars than I. Then I grinned and just shook my head at my own foolishness. The woman had truly blossomed outside the prison's imposing walls, giving me insights into her personality that could never have come if we were still trapped within the Bog's confines.

No, Ice caged was like a wild animal in a zoo. Pretty to look at, dangerous, but dying by slow inches inside, where it counted. I doubted if she spared even one passing thought about the place we'd left behind, and if she did, words like "comfort" and "security" probably weren't in her vocabulary.

Drawing my knees up to my chest, I wrapped my arms around them, rested my chin atop them, and stared blankly at an empty wall, thinking about the people, the friends, I'd left behind, never realizing when I nodded off.

I awoke from a hazy dream of having tea in the library with Corinne and blinked the sleep from my eyes to take in the vision of Ice standing against the door, looking down at me with an expression of such loving tenderness that my heart swelled in pure, emotional reaction.

"Hey," she said softly, pushing herself away from the wall and coming to stand beside the cot. "Didn't mean to wake you up."

"That's ok," I replied, yawning and stretching the kinks from my neck and back. "I didn't plan on falling asleep."

"You needed it."

I could feel my eyebrow rise as I stared back at her. "So do you."

She smiled slightly. "Touché."

I grinned right back at her, scoring one for myself.

Her expression turned more sober. "Sorry about dinner. I knew you were starting to get a little uncomfortable."

I gave her a nonchalant shrug. "That's ok. They're really nice." I couldn't help giggling a little. "I think Bull has a crush on me."

Ice grinned. "Bull's a mountain man. He doesn't get to see women very often. Especially not one as beautiful as you."

I was sure the blush on my face could have lit up the room. I cleared my throat a bit awkwardly, still unused, even after all this time, to receiving compliments, especially from Ice. "Where did you meet them, anyway?"

Sitting with casual grace on the bed, Ice copied my position, drawing her knees up and resting her head on the wall next to the window ledge. "They're friends of my father's, actually. He used to come up here on occasion to get away from it all. Most of these guys are white collar types who like to work off their stress by getting drunk and going up against the savage, razor-toothed deer." Her lips curled in a wry smile. "Bull's been their guide for as long as I can remember."

As I watched, her gaze became distant and a trifle sad. "My father brought me up here sometimes. It was fun, hanging out with them. Roughing it in the wilderness." She smiled again, sadly, this time. "He wouldn't let me handle a rifle, but then again, he wasn't much into them himself. So he taught me to bow hunt instead." She sighed. "It was right here, in these woods, where I deliberately took the life of another creature for the first time." She looked down at her hands, squeezing them into tight fists and releasing them. "And it's never been the same since."

Reaching out, I covered her knee with my hand and squeezed gently. Her face became more relaxed as she reached down and covered it with her own. "Anyway, they're usually up here around this time of the year. I managed to contact Andre at his restaurant yesterday and set this whole thing up." She blinked and then turned her head to face me. "They really are good guys. Give you the shirt off their backs. Just a little too rowdy for their own good sometimes."

I returned her tender look. "Thanks for sharing that with me. I know remembering those times is hard for you."

She shrugged. "Nah. It's alright. You deserved to know, anyway. I didn't tell you before because I couldn't be sure it'd work out, and I didn't want you to be disappointed if it didn't."

Smiling, I grasped her hand tighter and pulled it against my chest. "You haven't disappointed me yet, my love."

She raised an eyebrow at that, clearly disbelieving, then tugged her hand back and me along with it. I fell across her lap in an untidy sprawl, which she immediately corrected by pulling me up to sit beside her, my head tucked down against her chest and beneath her chin. Her warm hand made slow circles on my back and I felt my eyelids grow heavy once again, my sigh of contentment ruffling the denim fabric of her shirt.

One of the buttons on said shirt, right at my eye level, seemed to be a bit constricted, so I eased its burden by releasing it from its cloth prison. The soft skin bared by my labors begged for a kiss.

I obliged, smiling as the slowly circling hand on my back hesitated briefly before continuing on its way.

Because the lone button seemed so unhappy without its mates, I decided to give it some company and liberated another, smoothing my hand inside the opening I'd made and pressing another kiss, a bit lower, against warm, fragrant flesh.

"Smooth, Angel." Her amused voice rumbled through her chest and into my ear, sending a flush of warmth through my body.

"Like butter," I replied, grinning into her chest before tracing the line of her sternum with the very tip of my tongue. My fingers reached under her bra to cup a firm breast. "Like silk."

The world spun a bit, then, and when I opened my eyes finally, I found myself straddling a taut waist, indigo eyes staring into mine with well-loved and unmistakable intent. Her bent knees provided a solid support for my back and I couldn't help but cry out softly as the front of my shirt was torn open in a scattering of buttons.

I was more than grateful that I'd had the foresight to forgo a bra that morning when warm lips nuzzled into the valley of my breasts and a teasing tongue darted out to taste my suddenly sweating skin.

Her strong, beautiful hands slipped behind my back as her fingers slid down past the waistband of my jeans, pulling me closer to her body. Turning her head suddenly, she took a nipple into her mouth, and I responded sharply, thrusting against the strong, flat plane of her belly. The inseam of my jeans rode snugly against me with the move I'd made and, groaning softly, I closed my eyes as my head lolled back over her knees.

She encouraged the motion of my body, using her strong legs to help guide me in time with her suckling lips, teeth, and tongue.

When she switched to my other breast, my orgasm came so quickly that I didn't have time to even draw a breath before I stiffened and shook against her, rolling helplessly with the waves of intense passion that flowed through me, into my lover, and back again.

I barely had time to catch my spent breath before my back met a warm, slightly scratchy, woolen cover. Opening my eyes, I saw Ice above me, still gently thrusting her hips into my widely spread legs, her eyes dark and half-lidded, her hair swinging free, the smile on her face a wild, feral thing.

Ducking her head down, she captured my lips in a kiss full of fire and passionate promise. Her deft tongue glided over my teeth, then into my mouth, filling me with the taste of her. I responded in kind, lifting leaden arms to tangle in her hair and bring her closer to me.

Our twin growls sounded softly in the tiny room, spurring my arousal even higher.

Then I whimpered as her sharp teeth grasped my lower lip and she swirled her tongue over the captured flesh, each sensual move a promise of things yet to come.

She pulled away finally and smiled again, fiercely, before trailing kisses and tiny bites down my supremely sensitized flesh. Her hands reached down between our bodies, and within seconds, my jeans and underwear became a swiftly fading memory, as did hers before she lay back down to claim her spot between my legs.

The first touch of her warm, soft skin was almost enough to send me over the edge yet again and I gritted my teeth against the possibility. Chuckling softly, Ice simply smirked at me, determined to push me to my limits and beyond.

Another smoldering kiss to my already swollen lips and she began a slow glide down my body, aided, no doubt, by the ample evidence of my arousal coating her skin.

Her merciless attentions didn't stop when she finally, after what seemed several eternities at least, arrived at what I hoped was her final destination. She nipped at the insides of both thighs while her hands contented themselves skimming lightly over my breasts, never settling in one place for more than a heartbeat, and serving only to crank my excitement up yet another notch.

When I was almost beyond the point of thinking, let alone begging, one hand left my breast and a bare, breathless second later, she filled me completely while her mouth covered me, hot and wet and oh, so very needed.

Her tongue and fingers began their slow duet, my breathless pants keeping time, her low moans adding depth to the dance.

Together we moved, one into the other, sometimes quickly, sometimes slowly, sometimes hard, sometimes achingly soft, reaching the crescendo, where I was finally emancipated, borne up on the sweetest of currents, reaching out to the sky and the sea and the stars.

Reaching out and making them my own.

I collapsed back against the bed, completely drained, and unbelievably happy. Ice rose up slightly, then covered my body with her own, gently stroking my sweaty bangs from their tangled nest on my forehead. The look on her face was so tender and so loving that tears pricked at my eyes, gilding her in a diamond haze.

"Don't cry," she whispered. Her face was soft and totally open.

"I can't help it," I whispered back.

Closing my eyes, I felt the warm touch of her lips on my lids, drying my tears and replacing them with kisses. Then she lowered herself the rest of the way down and gathered me up in a tender embrace, molding our bodies along their entire lengths, one long leg thrown casually over mine.

Then she turned so that we were lying belly to belly, pulling her head away just enough to stare deeply into my eyes. Her expression was deadly serious. "I love you, Angel."

Burying my flushed face against her damp neck, I hugged her with every ounce of strength in me. "I love you, too, Morgan. More than I ever thought I was capable of loving another person." I smiled, snuffling against her neck. "I just wish I could tell you how much."

"Ya just did," she murmured into my hair as she tightened her grip around my pliant body. One large hand stroked my hair until I, with the ease of going from one breath to the next, fell asleep in her warm and loving arms.

Sometimes words are overrated.

I sat up quickly, my heart lodged somewhere in the vicinity

of my throat. Only the years spent living in one of the most dangerous places on earth and the resulting need to keep from showing fear at all costs, kept me from screaming out my fear.

I looked around wildly, my eyes slow to adjust to the near total blackness of the tiny room. Ice's comforting presence was nowhere to be found and I swallowed down my fear, wondering just what was going on.

The savage pounding that had awoken me sounded again, and I jumped slightly, gathering the sheet up to my chest, still staring blindly at nothing. "Ice?" I whispered soft as I could.

A warm hand to my naked back almost shot me through the ceiling, and another hand covered my mouth, muffling the wheezing gasp that came up from my lungs. Fortunately, the touch was one I knew intimately, and I nodded, signifying I was alright.

Ice removed her hand and slipped into bed beside me.

"Jesus, Ice," I whispered, "you scared the hell out of me there."

"Sorry. I didn't mean to."

"What's going on?"

"I don't know."

That particular piece of information made me more nervous than all the racket still going on outside our door. "You don't ...know?"

"Not yet. But I will." Leaning across my body, she pulled the shade slightly away from the window. The room was suddenly bathed in flashing red lights.

Leaving it's temporary home in my throat, my heart then sunk down to my knees, convulsing rapidly as I twisted the sheet in my hands. *No! Not already! We just got here! Please, we just need more time!*

Releasing the shade to lay flat against the window once more, Ice relaxed slightly and leaned back against the wall. "It's alright," she said in a low voice.

"It is?"

"Yeah. It's just the game warden."

"The game warden?"

Yes, it seemed that I was back to being Ice's parrot, a habit I thought I'd broken some years ago, but apparently had remained content to hide out until it was faced with a situation just like this one before jumping cheerily into the fray once again. *C'mon, Angel. Try and think of something intelligent to say, huh?* "Why would the game warden be here at this time of night?" While not a question Einstein might have asked, it was the best I could do under the circumstances.

"Well, normally, the local law doesn't look too kindly on people jacking deer out of these woods. But the way the natural predators have been run off lately, the herds have grown out of control, so there really isn't a problem, as long as you've got a license."

I nodded sagely. Then another question popped into my mind. "Ice?"

"Mmmm?"

"Bull *does* have a license, doesn't he?"

"Yeah."

I breathed a sigh of relief.

"I hope," she muttered, half under her breath.

Oh boy.

Ice stiffened beside me.

"What?"

"They're coming this way."

Before I could think to do anything but duck down, as if that action would somehow make me invisible to prying eyes, the door was thrown open and bright light spilled into our room, illuminating it quite thoroughly.

Dead silence.

Not able to help myself, I slowly poked my head around Ice's broad shoulder, almost unable to prevent myself from collapsing into gales of laughter at the look on the warden's face; a face that was currently staring at my naked lover in all her magnificent glory.

I didn't even have to look at said naked and magnificent lover to know she was treating the man to one of her famous raised eyebrow stares. "Yes?" she drawled, managing to sound dangerous and sultry at the same time.

The man's Adam's apple bobbed as he swallowed convulsively, his eyes round and shiny as newly minted coins.

"Is there a problem?"

Looking acutely uncomfortable, the game warden rocked back on his heels. "Um...no. I...err...was just making sure things were...ok...in here."

Unable to pass up such a wonderful opening, I stuck my head out further and grinned. "They're just fine, thanks. No problems here."

The poor man looked to be about a second from fainting. He cleared his throat, fingering his collar and loosening it from its no-doubt tight grip around his neck. "Err...ok then. As long as there aren't any problems."

I pretended to think about it. "Nope. Can't think of a one. We do appreciate your checking, though. Don't we, Ice?" I nudged my partner with a gentle elbow to the ribs.

Ice pasted on her best imitation of a sincere smile, which, to be truthful, needed a bit of work. "Indeed we do," she replied in a tone that was just a hair short of smug.

"Well, then. I guess I'll just...leave you two alone." Clearing his throat one last time, the beleaguered game warden slowly backed out of the room, pulling the door shut once he'd fully cleared the threshold.

As the room became dark once again, I gave into my insane craving and collapsed back on the bed, shaking with laughter. After a moment, Ice joined me, though her mirth, typically, was reduced to just a few wry chuckles.

As someone or other has been known to say throughout the ages, "Laughter is the best medicine." And, indeed, for me, it was, banishing all my doubts and fears into a place too deep within me to notice, at least right then.

And, for the second time that night, I fell asleep with a happy heart.

It often times seems that the closer you get to your final destination, the longer the trip seems to take. That was certainly the truth in my case those first weeks of early spring. We traveled for what seemed like years over rutted mountain roads, some so deeply packed with snow that I despaired of ever seeing civilization again and pictured us all frozen like statues and waiting for some summer hiker to come along and discover our bodies.

True to his word, though, Bull was an excellent guide and never once lost that cheery—if half-embarrassed—good nature that kept my usually natural optimism close to the surface.

We took sleep and food where we could find it, often taking turns navigating or driving while another slept in the cramped cab of Bull's heavy truck. As I've never been one for driving in heavy snow, and Bull seemed to share Ice's aversion to maps, I spent most of my time smashed between two large bodies, staring out into the Canadian wilderness and counting trees.

And sleeping.

A lot.

And so it was with a great sense of relief that I spied the tall church spire that marked the entrance to the little town where I had spent so many happy summers. It stood as I'd always remembered it, straight, tall, and proud; pointing the way to Heaven for those with no sense of direction, as my father would say every time it came into his view.

The cold air was biting on my face as I accepted Ice's help and stepped down from the high cab, coming to stand in a snowdrift that reached almost to my hips. I shivered and pulled the down jacket Bull had so chivalrously offered me tight around my chest, digging my cold-numbed hands deep into the pockets.

Ice, true to her nick, stood relaxed, as if standing in drifts of snow half again her height was all in a day's work for her. I wanted to envy her cool attitude but, upon thinking about the price she had paid for it, reconsidered my thoughts.

I'd settle for shivering any day.

Bull stepped from his side of the truck and came over to say his good-byes, smiling broadly and looking for all the world like a friendly grizzly begging for treats by the roadside.

"Are you sure you don't want to stop, just for a couple minutes?" I asked. "I know the town doesn't look like much, but the café's bound to be open and the coffee's really good." Though at that point, they could have served turpentine in a mug and I would have pronounced it delicious, as long as it was hot.

Bull smiled, though it had a touch of sadness to it. "I'm gonna have to take a rain check on that, if you don't mind, ma'am. I've got a bunch of hunters waiting for me back at the cabin, and my paycheck's with 'em."

I nodded in commiseration. Needing money was something I could certainly understand, much as I sometimes wished that that particular lesson wasn't quite so easily learned, especially now. "Thank you, Bull. I don't know what we would have done without your help. You're a great person."

The resulting blush melted all the snow in a ten-mile radius and, unkind though it might have been, I couldn't keep myself from grinning, then enveloping him in a heartfelt hug. "Take care of yourself, Bull," I said, pulling away. "I mean it."

"You do the same," he replied in kind, squeezing the stuffing out of me one last time for good measure. He jerked his head toward Ice, his eyes never leaving mine. "Take care of her, too, ok?"

"Promise."

After Bull and Ice had said their farewells and the big man climbed back in his truck, he waved one last time and pulled away in a plume of white exhaust. I sighed a little, watching until the truck had disappeared back into the endless forest, then pulled myself out of the deep drift and onto the moderately paved road leading into the town.

A small tendril of melancholy wove its way through my soul as I looked down the road and into the town proper. It stood there, desolate and seemingly empty. If green is the color of despair and red, rage, then gray is desolation's hue. The whole town seemed to be painted with it, as if some suicidal artist had drawn a brush over the entire scene, preserving it forever for entombment in some museum's misery exhibit.

Summer towns were always like this off-season, I reminded myself. Always waiting, like an inattentive man's pining pet, for a loving touch and the summer sun to restore color and life to the land.

"You alright?" Ice's voice came from very close beside me, and I started a bit before settling back down.

"Yeah. Just thinking." *And hoping. Praying.* During our long flight to freedom, I hadn't had the time to wonder if this place that I had banked all my dreams on would, in fact, be what I needed for it to be. Seeing it like this, watching as a mournful wind whipped through the towering pines and chased faerie swirls of snow down the empty street, I wondered, for just a moment, if my dream was slowly turning into a nightmare.

Were the dreams of a lonely child enough to build an adult's life upon? And what right did I have to drag Ice into them with me? A woman who was here, not because she had no place else to go, but rather because she had made the choice to try and build a life wherever it was that I wanted to be.

It suddenly became too much responsibility for me to bear. Deep inside, the child who had always lived for the sight of this place suddenly turned away, sobbing in fear.

I almost gave in to the insane urge to run screaming after Bull's departed truck and beg him to take us away. Far away from this place of empty promises and broken dreams.

I might have done it, too, such was my need to escape, if a long, denim-clad body hadn't chosen that exact second to interpose itself between me and my view of the village beyond. A strong hand, reddened and chapped by wind and cold, reached out and tipped my chin so that I was staring into eyes the exact color of the sky above. "We're in this together, Angel. No matter what."

I took only a moment to wonder at her sudden telepathic skills before opening my mouth to respond, watching as my breath plumed into the frosty air upon leaving my lungs. "I know. And that's what scares me. What if this isn't right for us? What if I'm just taking us away from one prison and throwing us into another? What if it's," I dropped my eyes, staring at the blurred lines in her palm, "not like I remember?"

"Things in life rarely are, Angel," she replied with her typical, and sometimes brutal, honesty. I looked up to see a slight, sad smile briefly curve her lips. "But if we didn't take chances, we wouldn't need dreams. And without dreams..."

As her words sunk in, I couldn't help but return her smile, remembering the evening she told me how her own dreams, dreams of a life with me outside prison walls, had kept her from killing one of her greatest enemies. "Where would we be?" I murmured softly, finishing her phrase.

Tipping me a wink, Ice removed her hand and settled her thin jacket around her trim, well-muscled form. "Where would we be indeed." Hooking a hand 'round my upper arm, she carefully guided me down the ice-slicked road and forward into whatever future this lonely, bleak town portended.

Chapter 2

"Homey," Ice remarked dryly as she took in the sights around her with an amused half-smile.

"I think the word you're looking for is 'creepy.'" I could feel the weight of a dozen pairs of unseen eyes on my back; waiting, assessing, judging.

Directly in front of me, the town's only Bed and Breakfast, *The Silver Pine*, stood in a huge bank of snow. That name had always intrigued me when I was younger. The "pine" part of the name was a given, surrounded as it was by hundreds if not thousands of the species and huddled among them like a Lilliputian in a land of Gulliver's.

"Silver," however, was a bit of a misnomer, given that I've never in my life seen a silver pine tree, unless you counted those spray painted plastic deals they sell at those cut-rate department stores around Christmas time.

I got up the nerve to ask my mother one day. She smiled that infuriating smile that is the patent of mothers everywhere, patted me on the head like a none-too-bright puppy and said, "Poetic license, dear."

And, of course, left me with *two* questions where only one had existed before.

Despite the incongruity of its name, however, *The Silver Pine* was a place that I'd remembered with great fondness, not only because of the delicious cookies the owner, Mrs. Carmody, would sneak into my hand when my parents weren't looking, but also because of the huge old rooms, the exploration of which would take up most of a rainy summer's day.

It now looked like the hotel straight out of *The Shining*.

Or perhaps *Psycho.*

Cassandra's girlish, malicious giggle bubbled in my mind, adding to the macabre feel of the place. "Shut up," I muttered, chasing down an attack of the shivers. "Just shut up."

"Pardon me?" Ice asked, swinging her head in my direction.

"Sorry. Just talking to myself." *As usual. C'mon, Angel, snap out of it or she's gonna think you've gone completely 'round the bend, alright?* "This isn't exactly how I remembered it," I remarked, sharing my brilliant insight with my smirking lover.

"I don't doubt that." She shrugged, seemingly unconcerned. "The season probably has a lot to do with it, though."

"Yeah, I guess you're right." I commenced looking around, taking in the combination gas station-auto body shop. It, too, appeared to be deserted; the only sign of life being the neon "Drink Coca Cola" sign winking on and off like some enraged Cyclops' eye.

Across from that, the small, one story schoolhouse stood, its walk shoveled and carefully salted. And, next to the school, the church, seeming all the more imposing with its gigantic stained glass windows displaying colors never seen except in others of its ilk, stood sternly. Churches like this didn't invite worship. They *demanded* it.

The only building that displayed at least a modicum of warmth was the long, low-slung café, which also doubled as the town's only grocery store. The windows were fogged from the inside and ghostly light filtered out into the darkening day. "I kinda feel like I stepped into the middle of a Stephen King novel."

Snorting softly, Ice turned to face the café. "I think the natives are getting restless. Let's go assuage their curiosity."

"Sounds good to me," I replied, craving some warmth. "I hope they still serve coffee."

Softly humming the theme from *The Twilight Zone*, Ice once again took my arm and escorted me to the café.

The blast of heat, which came at us as I opened the door, almost sent me rushing right back outside again to escape the sudden suffocation. But the smell of coffee, as tantalizing as I remembered, as well as Ice's firm grip on my arm, spurred me onward.

The café was sparsely populated, even given its relatively small size, and stony faces with mistrustful eyes followed us to the counter, making me feel acutely uncomfortable. Screwing on my brightest smile, I slid onto a stool and caught the attention of the café's waitress, a bleached-blonde with a generous figure and the stub of a slowly smoldering cigarette dangling from her garishly painted lips.

I grinned internally, thinking that if Pony were here with us, she'd be immediately smitten. She always did have a soft spot for "cheap and easy."

"Two coffees, please," I said in my most friendly voice.

The haggard woman eyed us through the blue haze of smoke from her cigarette. "You got money? We don't give hand-outs here."

"Sure we do," I replied, digging into the pocket of my jeans and coming up with several wadded bills and an odd smattering of lint-covered coins. "It's American, though. Do you accept that here?" I asked, knowing darn well they did. Come summer, these people would be taking every Abe Lincoln, George Washington, and Andrew Jackson that came across their path.

After a moment's contemplation, the woman nodded, then turned away to pour us two cups of steaming coffee from the glass pots sitting on the hotplate near the kitchen door. Turning once again, she slid the cups over to us indifferently, the liquid inside sloshing over the rim to pool on the cracked, cigarette-burned Formica that made up the counter top.

I shot a quick glance over to my partner, who was staring placidly into the mirror behind the counter, seemingly unconcerned about the way we were being treated.

We're gonna have to have a little talk, Ice. After all, what good was it to have the "Beast of the Bog" sitting beside you if she refused to intimidate an incredibly rude waitress into giving better service?

Grunting and stubbing her cigarette out in a nearby ashtray, the waitress grabbed my bills and went to the cash register, returning with a few scattered Canadian coins which she tossed onto the counter.

"Give her the rest of it," came a cool, calm, and oh so deathly soft voice to my right.

The waitress spun, a sharp retort, I'm sure, on her lips. It froze unuttered as she blanched through several shades of pale before finally deciding on "I-think-I-just-wet-myself" white. Looking up into the mirror, I didn't even bother to hide my smug grin. *Ahh, that's more like it.*

"Now."

"I...don't know what you're talking about," the waitress replied, sounding more fearful than ferocious.

From my view in the mirror, I watched Ice's eyes as they moved from the sign displaying the prices, toward the two coffees sitting on the counter, and back to the waitress. Her face remained completely expressionless.

To give credit where it's due, the woman didn't back down from my partner's intimidating stare until Ice made as if to stand. Then she spun as if all the demons of Hell were at her heels, punched open the cash register, and gave me back the correct change in record time.

"Thank you," I said sweetly, finally sipping my hard-earned coffee.

It tasted even better than I remembered.

After an hour or so of enduring the coldness of strangers, I'd finally had enough. Even the hot coffee didn't thaw the chill sitting in my belly at the eyes following my every move, as if my drink was expected somehow to materialize into a deadly weapon with which to kill them all where they sat.

I was decidedly relieved when Ice caught my eye and gave a short nod. Pushing forward a tip that was in no way deserved, I slipped from my stool and grabbed my heavy pack, slipping it over my shoulders and settling it more comfortably onto my back.

Ice did the same and, with a final, measuring look at each and every one of our watchers, letting them know in no uncertain terms that she had a very long and a very good memory, led the way to the door and our escape from the stultifying atmosphere of the café.

Though well below freezing, the chill outside seemed warmer, somehow, than what we had just endured. I stuffed my hands inside the roomy pockets of my borrowed jacket and turned to look at Ice. "Well, wasn't *that* just a day at the beach?"

Ice shrugged, settling her pack across her shoulders. "Guess they don't get paid to be nice to strangers in the off-season."

"Guess not." Sighing, I turned to look back at The Silver Pine, which looked as closed and remote as it had earlier. It had been my plan to secure a room there until we could at least get the cabin started, but given my earlier thoughts, even if it had been open for business I don't think that even a team of horses, wild or otherwise, could have dragged me in there.

Though it was just past mid-day, the sky continued to darken. A huge cloudbank slowly advanced from the west, promising yet more snow. I shivered again, then turned to look at my partner, who was standing calmly in the middle of the deserted street, returning my gaze. The heavy weight of responsibility settled itself on my shoulders once again, a feeling at definite odds with the sense of blissful freedom I'd felt here as a child. Maybe what they said was right. Maybe you never really *could* go home again.

Smiling slightly, Ice came forward and enveloped me in a warm hug, heedless of the stares I could feel all around us. Pulling back, she looked down at me, capturing my gaze effortlessly. "C'mon. Let's see what we have to work with, hmm?"

Though a woman of relatively few words, Ice well knew how to make the best out of what she had. She somehow managed, as always it seemed, to take my mind off my guilt and put it where it belonged.

Our future.

I hugged her to me tightly in thanks, then pulled away, turning determined eyes toward our destination, seeing the obstacles before me for what they truly were, not impossible chasms, but rather challenges to be met and exceeded.

Nodding to myself, I struck off down the road, Ice casually making her way behind me. When the buildings of the town faded into the mist, I made an abrupt right, stepping off the road and into knee-deep snow. "Shortcut," I explained without turning to see my companion's no doubt amused reaction to the sudden detour.

I felt my heart begin to grow lighter as I walked through the friendly and well loved forest surrounding me. The further I traveled down the game trail, my body instinctively knowing the way without my mind having to shout directions, the younger, it seemed, I became. The trees grew taller somehow. The snow was replaced by a fresh layer of pine needles. The smell of sap was heavy in the air. The birds chorused cheerfully as the light from the slowly setting sun slanted through the woods, warming my skin and putting a smile on my face.

If I closed my eyes, I could just hear the far-off chatter of children playing on the tiny beach down by the sparkling blue lake. I could feel the light, but important, weight of penny candies in my hand as I dodged the shadows and played tag with the sun.

I would have walked right into a deadfall, and likely broken my neck on the sharp and somehow ominous branches, if Ice hadn't pulled me out of my dream and back into reality with a sharp tug to the back of my jacket.

"Watch yourself," Ice commented mildly as she surveyed the tangle of fallen pines, hands on her hips.

I blinked, feeling the cold and my adult body and responsibilities, close in around me once again. But somehow, after the gift I'd just been given, neither seemed quite so harsh as before. "This ...wasn't here before," I replied, feeling a slight blush warming cheeks gone numb with the cold.

Ice just shot me a look, doubtless choosing silence as the better part of valor, especially given my brilliant observation, before returning her attention to the large deadfall blocking our path. "Looks like a detour is in order."

"No problem. C'mon."

It only took a few minutes to return to the trail I'd been following and before I knew it, I could just see the lake past the last of the trees sheltering it. Instead of being the deep, friendly blue I remembered, however, it was landlocked and gray with ice. Great sections of it had been cleared of snow and a huge bonfire blazed near its center. A smattering of children glided back and forth on the ice, most playing what I guessed to be hockey. The sounds of their sticks hitting the ice echoed across the lake.

Making a quick left, I followed the tree line until the first of the cottages, more like huge houses than simple shacks, came into view. I passed the first two cottages, then stopped. Even my breathing halted, as I saw with my own eyes what my heart refused to believe.

The cottage, that place where I'd spent so many wonderful summers, the place whose memories led me through the hardest years of my life, was gone.

Only a blanket of pristine snow marked its grave.

I felt tears well up; tears which even Ice's warm and steady presence at my side failed to banish. All these years, some part of my heart still held out hope that the news of its burning had been some sort of cruel joke, played upon me by a merciless god.

It appeared that the joke was on me.

"You ok?" Ice asked after a moment, no-doubt wondering just what it was that was making me cry *this* time.

"It's gone," I whispered. Then I laughed in self-deprecation. "Really stupid, I know. I shouldn't be surprised, right? I mean, I *knew* it was gone. I just didn't expect it to be so..."

"Empty?"

I sighed. "Yeah. Empty."

"Do you remember what it looked like?"

I turned to her. "Do I? Of course I do! I think I've memorized every single timber and shingle on it. The way the roof used to sag a little, right in the middle. The back entrance with the screen door that always looked like it needed a new coat of paint. The windows that always had cobwebs in them. The wooden furniture on the front porch. The tire swing. Everything."

"And can you picture it in your mind now?"

I smiled through my tears, remembering. "Yeah."

Ice returned my smile. "Good. Because it'll look like that again. All we need is a little time and a little sweat."

I looked at the utter conviction in her eyes and, for the second time that day, believed. A grin blossomed on my face, erasing the tears. "What are we waiting for then? I've got the time, if you've got the sweat."

And, bounding away like a snowshoe hare, I scampered through the snow toward the flat rectangle of snow-covered ground that would one day be the cabin I remembered.

Only better, because I would have Ice to share it with me.

It was close to sunset when we returned, cold and hungry, from our impromptu exploration of the area. We had spent most of the day, Ice following complacently as I cheerfully led her around to take in the sights of my former haunts: the little green dock which sat tottering on the small stretch of sand beach that the entire community trucked in load by laborious load (and illegally, I might add just for veracity's sake); the rushes where the summer frogs waited, loudly chirping for their mates; the tiny inlet where the water was always warm and where you could always find thousands of tiny tadpoles squirming around in the algae and water-smoothed, if slightly slimy, rocks perfect for skimming.

I even prodded her up into my favorite tree, a friendly old pine with limbs just right for the shortened tread of tiny legs and a smooth crotch which nestled a child's bottom cozily while said child watched the sailboats race around the lake in a rainbow of color.

Just as we arrived at the empty lot, the snowflakes began to spit from the sky, fat and wet with the promise of a sizable accumulation. I sighed, dejected. I was cold, soaked to the skin, hungry, and had the beginnings of a headache that promised to reach horse-felling proportions before it was through digging itself into my brain from behind my eyelids.

"Guess we might as well set up for the night, huh?" I asked in a tone which even a soon-to-be-hanged man would find disheartening.

Grunting in reply, she set her heavy pack down and started to unload our gear, which included a two-man mountain tent and three lightweight, but cold rated, sleeping bags which we had accepted from Bull over Ice's vociferous objections.

I stood off to the side, momentarily entranced by the white snow dusting the dark fall of her hair before finally realizing that our camp wouldn't set itself up.

I took a step in Ice's direction before a breaking twig caused me to whirl to my right, my hands up in a defensive posture that would do exactly nothing if our evening visitor was a grizzly or something as equally deadly.

However, instead of a grizzly, or a wolf, or even a rabbit investigating the funny looking strangers intruding on its habitat, I saw a small, slight figure wrapped in a heavy parka and standing atop the short rise that separated our property from the neighboring plot of land. I raised my hand higher in a hesitant wave, hoping that whoever our silent watcher was, he wasn't hiding something more than his hands in the pockets of his jacket.

A feminine and slightly wavering voice came from within the furred confines of the parka's hood, and if I hadn't had the heavy pack still strapped to my back, I might have sagged with relief and toppled gleefully right into the snow. "Who are you?" the woman asked, making no move to come closer. "That's private property, you know. I'll call the police if I have to."

A disbelieving grin broke over my face as I recognized the broad Massachusetts accent that I'd so loved to try and decipher—and imitate—as a child. "Mrs. Anderson? Is that you?"

"Who are you?" the voice repeated, no more friendly for my having guessed her name.

I winced, hesitated a split-second longer than society deemed polite, then bit the proverbial bullet and opened my mouth, hoping that perhaps an avalanche from a non-existent mountain, or perhaps that woman-eating grizzly I'd envisioned, would have the foresight to swallow me up.

No such luck.

You see, back in that little slice of hell called the Bog, an inordinate amount of time—or so it seemed to me—was spent, particularly by the Amazons, in playing a little game called "Guess Angel's real name." Oh, they knew my *last* name, of course. Everyone did. The guards shouted it at least four times a day, at headcount. More, if I'd committed an infraction or was needed somewhere.

But my *first* name... Well, I kept the door to *that* little secret closed tighter than Fort Knox, thank you very much. And for good reason, too, having endured more than a little teasing over it in the tender years of my youth and beyond.

What surprised me the most, though, was that Corinne, for all her long and many tentacles dipping in and out of all aspects of prison life, hadn't found out. Thinking back on it now, though, I figure she probably knew what it was within the first several seconds of my confinement in the Bog, but had never had the need, or perhaps the opportunity, to pull out that particular weapon to use on me. For which I was and will forever be profoundly grateful.

And as for Ice, I asked her about her seeming lack of curiosity one evening when the game was going on especially fast and furious, leaving me blushing to the roots of my hair and the tips of my toes over some of the more...inventive...guesses.

She's shrugged and, in her typical blunt style, said, "If Angel's what you want to be called, then that's what I'll call ya."

Simple as that.

I blinked my eyes at the softly cleared throat behind me, and realized that not only was our watcher waiting for my answer, Ice was, too.

Damn.

Double damn.

"It's Tyler, Mrs. Anderson," I said finally, probably more softly than I should have, but much more loudly, by several decibels, than I would have wished.

"Tyler?" the woman repeated. The hood of the parka cocked sideways in that birdlike little head tilt of curiosity I remembered so well. "Tyler Moore? It that really you?"

I smiled, though it probably wasn't one of my more encouraging ones.

It must have been good enough for her, however, because she began to make her way down the hill toward us, moving with the sure-footed grace of one well accustomed to wading through deep drifts of snow.

"Don't say it," I warned softly to the steady presence at my back. "Don't even *think* it."

A beat of silence.

"Wouldn't dream of it."

Thank you, God.

"Mary."

If I wasn't absolutely positive, with every single fiber of my being, that Ice could turn me into fish flakes before I even thought to blink, I would have been on her faster than a wolf on a rabbit. As it was, however, I contented myself with simply turning my head and shooting her a look which, I was sure, was searing enough to melt glass, had there been any about waiting to be liquefied by my powers of intimidation.

Unfortunately, even the snow beneath us refused to so much as melt under the heat of my stare. And as for the object of my pitiful attempt at wrath, she looked just as calm and collected as ever—*Darn her. Couldn't she at least* try *to look scared?*—her face expressionless, but her eyes twinkling smugly.

You just wait, Miss High and Mighty. Paybacks are a real bitch.

That was all I had time to think before I felt myself engulfed in a hug, its strength belying the slight body of the woman embracing me. I returned the hug, though without as much vigor as I would have used to hug, say, Ice, knowing well the brittleness of elderly bones.

We both pulled away after a long moment and I felt my numb cheeks being cupped by a pair of warm, gloved hands. "By God in His mercy, child, it really *is* you! You've grown so much I hardly recognize you!"

I smiled and, of course, blushed. "Yes, well, the years have a way of doing that to you." I could barely see her face, but her smile shone through the darkness of her hood like a beacon, bathing me in the warmth of her welcome.

She laughed, a very musical and well-loved sound, before stepping away. "I wish the years would have a way of doing that to me. I wake up every morning and swear I've shrunk a little in the night."

Then she pulled back her hood, giving me my first glimpse of a face I remembered so well that it could have been just a day ago that I'd seen her. Her hair was a little grayer, her face a little more lined, but looking at her was like stepping back in time once again, just another step through the Twilight Zone on a day that had been filled with déjà vu.

"It's so wonderful to see you," I said, probably looking like an absolute idiot as I stood there, snow melting on my shoulders, grinning at her.

Gently grasping my arm, she returned my smile. "It's wonderful to see you, too, sweetheart. I thought maybe I never would. Your mother's been a bit reticent in telling me your goings on whenever we speak, which lately, hasn't been very often at all."

While I made sure to keep the smile firmly affixed to my face, inside I was cringing.

All thoughts of paybacks flew right out of the proverbial window when Ice, obviously sensing my acute discomfort with the situation I suddenly found myself in, picked up her pack and pretended to search for something in it, making a bit more noise than she was generally wont to do.

My grin became more natural with the apparent success of the diversionary tactic. "Mrs. Anderson, I'd like you to meet my friend, Morgan. Morgan, this is Mrs. Anderson, my neighbor."

"Pleased to meet you, ma'am," Ice replied, gently shaking the older woman's hand in greeting.

"Enough of that," she said, pumping my lover's hand firmly. "I've been Ruby for going on seventy-five years, and that's the name I'll thank you to call me, Morgan." Turning her head, she tipped a wink at me. "The same goes for you as well, Tyler."

I firmly believe that there are times in every adult's life when the weight of the years melt away and we find ourselves seven again, being chastised by the second grade teacher we've spent the entire school year developing a serious crush on.

This was one of those times.

I stood there, sure that the heat of my cheeks would set the forest ablaze, and tried desperately not to let on how small I felt beneath the weight of her gentle rebuke.

There was a moment of awkward silence before Mrs. Anderson—*Ruby*—released Ice's hand and smiled at me. "Well, you've certainly picked the perfect season to do some visiting, Tyler. No crowds."

I laughed, put immediately at ease by the warmth of her smile. "Yeah, well the water's probably a little cold."

"And quite hard, to boot, I'd imagine," she teased.

"That, too. On the plus side, though, I probably don't have to worry about getting a sunburn." My attempt at lighthearted conversation ground to a halt and I looked down at my hands, the smile slipping from my face like a Halloween mask after the last treat has been passed out.

While telling a lie might have been a poor way to say hello, telling the truth just might mean a permanent goodbye. Insecure about all the changes in my life as I was, the one thing I couldn't afford was to lose someone like Ruby, who could be a desperately needed link to the townspeople as well as being a much-needed friend.

"I'm ...not here just to visit," I began, hoping that my well-rehearsed speech would come out better than it sounded in my head. I avoided looking at Ice, though it was hard. I really needed her support with this. I took in a deep breath, then let it out slowly. "I needed a break, from where I was. I was tired of the violence around me," which was, in fact, true. "The beatings. The stabbings. The shootings." And here, I looked up at Ice, who closed her eyes briefly in silent acknowledgement before opening them again to meet my gaze steadily. I wanted to reach out to her but didn't dare.

The memory of seeing her bleeding into the ground was a wound still much too fresh to withstand a deep inspection of it.

To this day, it haunts my dreams with distressing regularity, leaving me sweating and breathless each time it crawls up from the hole I've dug for it in my mind.

Tearing my eyes from those of my partner, I resumed looking at Ruby, who looked back, a compassionate expression on her face. I summoned up a smile from somewhere. "The memory of this place has gotten me through a lot of hard times in my life. And so I figured that if I just came back here and tried to turn the dream into a reality once again, maybe things would start making sense again."

I sighed again. I could feel my shoulders slump beneath the weight of the need I had to make the words I'd just spoken come to fruition. "I don't know if it's just wishful thinking on my part, but I *do* know that I have to try."

Ruby smiled and placed a gentle hand on my shoulder. "You always were a dreamer, Tyler. From the first time I saw you, sitting on that porch swing staring into the sunset. It used to drive your mother to distraction. She never really understood you, I don't think. But I always believed that if someone could dream so sweetly and so well, they deserved a chance to have those dreams come true. And if living here is all it takes to make that dream of yours come true, then I'll help in any way I can."

Tears stung my eyes as a little part of my heart fell in love all over again with the woman who'd been a young, friendless girl's only confidant all those years ago. "Thank you," I whispered with all the sincerity in my heart.

"You're welcome," she replied in kind, smiling tenderly at me, maybe remembering, as I did, how it was between us all those years ago.

Removing her hand from my shoulder, Ruby turned and fixed Ice with an inquisitive stare. "And you? You don't seem the dreaming type, Morgan."

Ice smiled, and I could see just the faintest touch of danger in the white gleam of her teeth. "I might be."

From the corner of my eye, I could see Ruby react, stiffening just slightly before nodding. "Yes. You just might be, at that."

Then she turned and looked down, eyes widening in surprise. "Surely you aren't planning on spending the night camping out here in the cold, are you?"

I sighed. "That wasn't my first choice, no. I had planned to grab a room at The Silver Pine, but it's closed for the season." I could feel my cheeks heating again and I looked up at her with what I'm sure was a child-like expression on my face. "Guess I should have figured that, huh?"

Ruby shook her head in negation. "Not really. Margaret Carmody kept that place open the year around. She did good business, even in the middle of the winter, what with all the hunters around here. But when she passed on, her niece took over. Pleasant woman, but a little...," she paused, obviously searching for the right word, "eccentric is, I suppose, the best way to put it."

I laughed. "Crazy, huh?"

"As a bedbug," Ruby replied primly.

"I'm sorry to hear that Mrs. Carmody died. She was a very sweet person."

"Indeed she was." She looked down at our gear, then back up at me, a no-nonsense expression on her face. "Now, I suggest you pack all of those supplies back up again and come with me. You'll stay with me in my home until the cabin gets rebuilt."

Swallowing hard, I chanced a look in Ice's direction. Sure enough, my lover was staring at Ruby, her eyes narrowed to the barest of slits. I could almost feel her simmering anger from where I stood.

This wasn't good.

"Is there a problem?" Ruby asked, looking from Ice, to me, and back again, obviously noting that we weren't jumping at her rather enforced invitation.

"Um, no. No problem at all. Right, I...Morgan?"

My mother's voice chose exactly that moment to shuffle through my consciousness. *When in doubt, beg.*

And so I did. Not with words, no. But given the choice between sleeping in a tiny, cold tent and sleeping in a nice, warm house, in a nice, warm bed, well, it wasn't difficult to come to a decision.

The only thing that remained was to convince my proud partner, for whom the receipt of any type of charity was seen as a major character weakness. Even if said charity could help save us from an early death, or, at the very least, the loss of several appendages from frostbite.

If I sound a bit melodramatic, you have to remember that I was really, *really* cold. And really, *really* tired. And that headache had gone past what my father always called the "hosskick" stage. It now resembled the stomp of a mule, and a feisty one at that.

I continued to look at Ice, putting every ounce of pleading into my expression, hoping against hope it would work.

After a time, which seemed like an eternity but was in reality only a matter of a few short seconds, I saw her expression soften slightly and her shoulders slump. A wry smile curved her lips and I thought I saw her eyes roll, but by then it was too dark to be sure.

Carefully concealing the joy in my small victory, I turned to Ruby and gave what I hoped was a gracious nod—graciousness having been pretty much pounded out of me during my stay in prison to the point where I wasn't even sure if I could *act* gracious, let alone look that way. "If you're sure it won't be too much trouble, Ruby, we'd be happy to accept your invitation."

"Good. Then it's settled. Gather your things and follow me."

The inside of Ruby's home was exactly as I'd remembered; warm, comforting, smelling of cedar and freshly burned wood. I sighed happily, my tension melting like the snow on my clothes as she led us over to the massive stone fireplace that dominated one wall of the living room.

Smells have always had the power to relax or invigorate me, even as a small child. I can remember, on cold winter mornings, going into the bathroom and uncapping a bottle of suntan oil, fingering the sand that still clung to the neck, and taking in the scent, my mind instantly transported back to a sunny day at the beach and swearing that if I could just listen hard enough, I'd be able to hear the crashing of the waves and the high-pitched screech of the seagulls as they wheeled over the sand, looking for a handout through beady brown eyes.

Just as a certain song might bring back memories of a sadly ended love affair, or the sight of the sunlight slanting through the trees a certain way might cause you to remember a wonderful day, the smell of Ruby's home, with its merrily blazing fire, made me feel happy and young and free in a way nothing else ever could.

"Warm yourselves by the fire while I get you some dry clothes. You'll fit nicely into one of my robes, Tyler. You," Ruby paused, looking at my tall companion, "I think I have one of Jack's old robes stored away somewhere. Stay right here. I'll be back in a flash."

As she strode away with that brisk walk that had always been hers, I looked over at Ice, who was warming her hands in the fire's friendly heat and rubbing them briskly. "Sorry," I offered softly, not particularly sorry at all, but needing to say something to break the tension I felt between us.

She returned my look, her eyes shadowed with secrets, and shrugged. "'s alright." Then she turned her gaze back to the fire, seemingly absorbed in its flickering images.

Meaning, I could tell, that it wasn't "alright" at all. Meaning that I'd stepped over yet another invisible boundary that she put up to protect herself from the outside world. Meaning that as well as I thought I knew her, I came to find, yet again, that I didn't really know her at all.

Oh, Corinne, I wish you were here right now. I sure could use some of your advice.

Though I missed the friends I'd made in the Bog and thought of them often, there was no one I missed as much as Corinne, whose motherly affection, gentle flirtation, and sage, if sarcastic, advice had never failed to put me at ease, almost always giving me the answers I sought.

Corinne, however, was still safely ensconced in the Bog, and probably would be until the day she breathed her last. That thought twisted my guts inside me into a painful knot, the feeling at jarring odds with the warmth and security surrounding me.

Plus, there was still Ice to deal with.

That particular problem would have to wait, however, because the sounds of Ruby's staccato footsteps resonated on the wood floors of the hallway, coming closer at a brisk pace.

Ruby Anderson did everything quickly. Reading. Eating. Talking. I remember spending wondrous rainy day hours watching her knit, the needles flying so fast that I swore I could see sparks when they struck together. Scarves fit for giants would flow, like multi-colored waterfalls, from those needles in what seemed to be a matter of seconds.

She was a wonder to behold.

She came into the room, smiling and bearing two plush robes. Handing one to each of us, she placed a hand on my shoulder. "You remember where the bathroom is, Tyler. Take Morgan with you and get out of those wet clothes. Bring them back with you and we'll put them up on these quilt racks by the fire. I'll go make us some coffee."

With that, she was gone, rapidly retreating into the kitchen as I stared after her dumbly. After a moment, I turned back to Ice. "C'mon. Let's go get dry."

She followed after me without hesitation or complaint, and for that, I was profoundly relieved.

Ruby's bathroom was a typical example of *genus grandmotherus.* Little soaps you didn't dare use lest you ruin their cunningly crafted shapes, the tastefully disguised denture cup (and for this, I was grateful. My own grandmother used to store her dentures in the tissue box. Great for avoiding looking at someone's teeth sitting in a Polydent bath. Bad if you had allergies.). Tiny little washcloths that matched tiny little hand towels that matched bath towels, rugs, toilet tank covers, and the shower curtain, all done up in that "Antique Rose" color that, it seems, only women over the age of sixty five are moved to buy.

I stripped down to my birthday suit in no time flat and was briskly rubbing my cold-numbed body with a thick, fluffy—not to mention rose—bath towel when I noticed Ice uncharacteristically fumble with the buttons on her cotton shirt.

While I had had the relative luxury of a thick down jacket to protect me somewhat from the elements, Ice had made do with her denim jacket and little else. She was soaked to the skin, and while the vision of her standing so close to me, her shirt plastered against her magnificent body, caused my hormones to jump up and start clapping, the more rational and clinical part of my mind worried about the pneumonia my dark lover was sure to catch if she didn't divest herself of her clothing immediately.

"Let me help you with that," I urged softly, dropping my towel and reaching for her shirt.

Scowling, she stepped back so quickly that she almost backed into the tub as she turned a shoulder away from me, not relinquishing the fumbling hold she had on her shirt. "I'll take care of it."

As I may have told you before, one of the most unwelcome gifts my father ever gave me was his penchant for sarcasm. It was a lesson of his that I learned well and often, and, as his was wont to do; it came out at the worst times imaginable.

Like now.

"Sure you'll take care of it, Ice," I replied, my voice positively dripping with ridicule. "At the rate you're going, it'll be summer before you even get half of your buttons undone. Just let me help you, alright?"

Her teeth flashed, but it wasn't a smile she was offering me. Or maybe it was. Just not the kind you associate with the happier emotions. "I said I'd handle it."

I blinked, then backed up a step in unconscious reaction.

Sometimes, with Ice, it's so easy to forget exactly who I'm dealing with. Her absolute devotion, her utter tenderness with me causes me to sometimes overlook the dangerous, wild woman that lay beneath the trappings of civility she'd learned to pull on, like a coat, in order to survive in what we call society.

But then there are times, like this one, where it all comes back to me, with the rushing speed of a southbound freight, just who and what this woman I love with all my heart truly is.

A cold-blooded killer.

A hot-blooded lover.

An icy reserve.

A loving tenderness.

Ice is all of those things and so many more. A contradiction wrapped up in an enigma, as someone somewhere has been known to say.

I finally let out a long held breath and forced myself to meet her icy gaze, pushing my fear down deep where she couldn't sense it. "I'm sorry I pushed you," I began softly. "I'm sorry I made this decision for both of us."

Frustrated by the lack of emotion in her eyes, I clenched my fists and slammed them down on my thighs. "Damnit, Ice! I'm cold, wet, tired, and hungry. And I really didn't want to face the prospect of spending a cold, wet, tired, and hungry night outside. Not when the answer to all of those problems was standing not three feet from me and being kind enough to offer up her home to us."

I sighed, still not able to break through the thick wall thrown up in my path. "Look. I know how much you hate charity. I also know that Ruby can be a bit of a martinet at times. But she's a good woman with a good heart and I couldn't see any reason to turn down what she was so generously offering."

Bending down, I gathered up my wet clothing, clutching it to my chest and wincing at the chill of the fabric against my naked skin. "I can understand how uncomfortable this makes you. If you really want to spend the night in our tent, then let's go. I'll think up some excuse to tell her."

My peace said, I spun from her and took a step toward the door, not even caring that I was still completely naked save for my clothes pressed up against the front of my body.

"Wait."

I stopped, but didn't turn, knowing instinctively that whatever my partner had to say, she would be more comfortable expressing it without having to look at me directly.

"This ...really means a lot to you, doesn't it?"

The hesitation in her voice drew me back around and I took in the almost lost expression on her face, my heart breaking, just a little. "Yes. It does."

She closed her eyes for a long moment, and when they reopened, the stone wall was gone and in its place stood the woman I loved. "Alright, then. If it's what you want, we'll stay."

I nodded, unable to keep the smile from overspreading my face. "Thank you."

Saying nothing, she returned my nod. Her fingers had apparently warmed up enough during our small argument, because she removed her shirt without much trouble, her other clothes following quickly. Taking the towel I offered her, she dried her body thoroughly, then put on the old robe and belted it securely, hiding her wonderful body from my appreciative gaze once again.

Then, reaching out, she gently removed the wet clothes from my hand and replaced them with a thick, terrycloth robe, which I gratefully slid over my shoulders and belted closed. Then I simply stood there, arms loose at my sides, still unsure where we stood after all this.

As if reading my mind, she reached out and clasped my right hand, squeezing it tightly and bestowing upon me the tiniest hint of a smile. "G'wan now. Let's get you warmed up, hmm?"

Tugging, I brought Ice's hand up to my lips, a smile in my eyes. "I love you, too, Ice."

Maybe we *were* ok, after all.

Chapter 3

I rolled in the bed once again, kicking at the covers which wound themselves around my legs like some earthbound octopus, and punched the pillow lying complacently beneath my head. The sigh that gusted from my lungs would have been nominated for an Academy Award, had anyone but the walls been around to hear it.

Flipping to my back again, I put one arm up across my forehead and stared at the ceiling with morose eyes.

I wasn't having fun.

Oh, the visit had gone well enough, with Ruby and I catching up on old times while she filled me full of the local gossip. Or as much gossip as a town this size could have, anyway.

Which wasn't much.

For her part, Ice seemed content to sit silently, sipping her coffee and taking in the sights of the tastefully decorated den in which we were sitting. When Ruby saw her gaze land upon some of the trophies that decorated the large fireplace mantel, she launched into the story of her husband, Jack, dead many years, and how they had met and married.

I didn't remember much about her husband, but what I did remember, I liked. Jack Anderson had been a golf pro way back when. No one of special note, really, but he won enough tournaments to, as Ruby was prone to say, "pay the rent in style."

They had met when he competed in a tournament that her company was sponsoring. Her knowledge of golf was nil; she likened it to watching the grass grow or the chickens molt. But the big, strapping man with the easy grin and the handsome face assured her interest in the sport for good.

Theirs was a whirlwind courtship, played out on the shores of Nantucket, her home. And when he asked her to marry him, she said yes without a second thought, and made her life with him in the very house in which we were sitting; a house he had built with his own hands.

Having heard that particular tale a time or ten in my life, I allowed my thoughts to wander, and before I realized it, was being shaken awake by a warm hand and looked upon by Ruby's twinkling eyes.

After a suitable period of utter mortification, my small, if unintentional, bit of rudeness was brushed off as just being one of those things, and Ice and I were led to our rooms.

And therein lay the problem.

Rooms.

Plural.

That was most definitely something I hadn't thought about during my quest to make Ice see the wisdom of choosing a warm house over a cold tent. And believe me when I tell you that when I realized that particular blunder, words which would scorch the paper this is being written on screamed through my head, though thankfully, they refrained from passing my lips and giving our gracious host a stroke.

You see, while in the Bog, one of my deepest regrets—only one of many, but still—was that I couldn't spend even one night sleeping in the arms of the person I loved. Yes, there was that wonderful, exhilarating night in the trailer. A night that even now arouses me just thinking about it, but aside from that, nighttime in prison meant battling your personal demons alone.

I swore to myself that if we were ever able to make it out of that particular hell, I would never spend another night apart from her again.

Yet here I was, not a month into freedom, sleeping without her. And trapped by my own cunning, no less!

"Congratulations, Angel. You've just won the *Idiot of the Year* award. Where are you going to celebrate?"

Not Disneyland.

I sighed again, my rebellious mind gleefully providing me a fantasy in which Ice and I had done things her way and we were, right this very moment, sleeping in that tent I had, up until an hour ago, so despised. Wound together like mummies in a single sleeping bag to conserve body heat.

Maybe doing a little something else to *generate* body heat.

I groaned and turned again, punching a pillow that, if it hadn't been a mere ball of feathers, would surely have punched me back in payment for the abuse I was heaping on it.

Great. Just great.

It was then that I heard the faintest scraping of my door easing open. A fractured beam of low light played through the crack, illuminating the edge of the curtain covering the window to my right.

The light was cut off almost immediately as the door silently closed, leaving me in darkness once again.

But not alone.

With instincts well honed by years in prison, I could feel another's presence in the room with me. I tensed automatically, my hands gripping at the blankets, which covered my body.

My ears strained for any sound at all, even the slightest breath, but silence held its reign over the small room. I could feel my heart picking up its pace even though the more rational part of my mind assured me that there was nothing to fear. This wasn't the Bog. This wasn't Pittsburgh. This was just a simple country home in the middle of the backwoods, miles from anyone who would want to do me harm.

Or so I hoped.

"Show yourself. I know you're in here." My voice surprised me with its absolute steadiness.

Silence, still. The pregnant kind, where you could literally hear the hairs on the back of your neck come to attention.

I opened my eyes wider, trying to take in any light there might have been, and almost fainted when a low rumble bathed over my heightened senses from mere inches away.

"Move over. You're hoggin' the bed."

It was the most wonderful-terrible scare I've ever had and I grinned like a kid as I scrambled back against the wall, making room for the larger body of my partner, then snuggling into her open arms with a joy that is reserved for well-answered prayers.

"You have absolutely no idea how happy I am to see you," I murmured into the flesh of her gloriously naked chest. Then I stopped. "Well, not see you exactly. Mmm. But feel you. And smell you. And taste you. Definitely taste you."

A cleared throat stopped my effusive utterings. I turned my head up to where I knew her face would be. "Yes?"

"It's probably best if we don't go down this particular road right now."

"Why not?" I asked, knowing that I sounded like a petulant child being denied her favorite toy.

"Give ya a hint." There was a smile in her voice. "She's about your height, gray hair, and ears she probably fine tunes every night before bed so she'll have something new to tell the sewing circle in the morning."

"Oh."

Drat. Outmaneuvered.

"Well," I tried, "we could be really quiet."

A soft snort. "That would be great. If it were possible. Which we know it isn't."

"Hey!" I didn't know whether to be indignant or embarrassed.

She hugged me close briefly before loosening her arms. "You could be quiet as a church mouse, Angel, and we'd still have a problem."

"Oh yeah? And what might that be?"

I felt her stomach muscles clench beneath my thigh, then she bounced several times on the mattress.

The room was filled with the sounds of protesting bedsprings squeaking their displeasure.

"Oh," I said again, feeling my face heat. "That's not a good thing."

"Well," she replied, sounding as if she were reconsidering the offer, "I wouldn't have a problem with it. It *is* your room, after all."

She bounced again, slowly, rhythmically, then steadily picking up speed until I was ready to just fall through floor in embarrassment.

I put a hand on her firm belly and pushed down. "Stop. Just stop."

Squeak. Squeak.

"Please?"

Squeak-squeak-squeak.

"Ice!"

Silence.

Absolute, total, and *blessed* silence.

Groaning, I plopped my head back down on her chest. "You're an evil woman, Morgan Steele. Truly, heartlessly, evil."

Her long body stretched beneath me before settling back once again. "That's what they tell me." She sounded quite, quite pleased with herself.

The payback list was getting longer.

I awoke to bright sunshine streaming through the window, putting a smile on my face before I even opened my eyes. The bed was empty and I spared a brief moment of wondering if the events of the night before had been just a dream when Ice's scent came to me from the pillow I'd cradled in lieu of her body.

My smile broadened as I treated myself to a healthy stretch, my muscles complaining only mildly over having shared sleeping quarters with a woman half again my size. The rest of me was just a happy puddle.

The tantalizing smells of breakfast cooking wafted gently into my awakening senses and I rolled over onto my back, finally thinking to open my eyes and take in the newly dawning day.

Well, perhaps *dawning* wasn't the best word for it. From the looks of things, the sun had been up for a good while, rising slowly in the sky as I slept on, blissfully unaware.

That thought gave me a moment's pause. For more than five years, I'd awoken at five thirty every morning to the sounds of guards' shouts, bells ringing, and batons sliding against metal bars. The habit was so ingrained within me that even after I'd left the Bog for good, not a morning had passed where I hadn't awoken in the dark, coming to my feet before my body even realized that my mind had given it a command.

Until today.

"Well, whadda ya know," I said to the patiently waiting ceiling. "Maybe there's hope for me yet, huh?"

After another healthy stretch and a good, long yawn, I rolled out of bed and briefly debated pulling some clothes on. Tossing out that thought like yesterday's bathwater, I shrugged into Ruby's comfortable robe and padded silently through the room, reaching out to touch a tiny figurine of a unicorn that had always enchanted me as a child. "For luck," I whispered before opening the door and letting myself out of the room, which in itself was a wonderful feeling, let me tell you.

I walked quickly down the stairs, the scents of breakfast leading me on like those smoky fingers you see on Saturday morning cartoons hooked through some character's nostrils.

Ruby turned from her place at the stove as she spied me coming into the kitchen. A wide smile of welcome creased her almost unlined face. "I *thought* this might tempt you into waking up. Good to see I haven't lost my touch."

"Oh, you most definitely haven't," I replied, walking over to help her with the plates.

"Just sit yourself down at the table, Tyler. I've got this all taken care of."

"Are you sure?"

"Positive. Just go sit down."

Resisting the urge to snap off a salute, I pulled out a chair and sat down at the table. Within seconds, a steaming plate piled high with food was placed in front of me. My mouth watering, I dug in without a second's pause.

Ruby joined me at the table, cupping a coffee mug in her hands and taking small sips from it as she smiled at my talent for laying waste to vast armies of food, a trait I'd had since I was a small child. "Your friend is certainly the industrious sort."

My fork paused halfway to my mouth. I shot her a questioning look, wondering whether I had cause to be nervous or not.

She gestured with her coffee mug toward the kitchen window, and I found myself slowly rising to my feet, curiosity pulling at me like a fish lure.

"Wow," was all I could say as I looked down at the scene laid out before me. The walk had been shoveled and salted, as had the long, winding driveway that led out to the main road. Snowdrifts, which had covered the first floor windows, were completely cleared away, down to the grass. Trees near the house, which had almost been bent double with the weight of the snow, now were free of their chilly burden and standing straight and proud once again. "Unbelievable." My breath fogged the window as I spoke, misting the icy clarity of the incredible scene outside.

"I agree. Is she always like this?"

Turning back toward the table, I gave my host a smile. "Pretty much, yeah."

"Quite handy to have around then, I'd say. Where did you meet her?"

I paused again, my thoughts running rapidly, if uselessly, through my brain. "It's a long story."

Which it was. Five years long, to be exact. Just not a story I was comfortable telling to the woman who was housing us, for obvious reasons.

The smile she gave me brought to mind pictures of dinosaurs I'd seen in textbooks when I was in school. A predator's grin, full of slashing teeth, topped by beady brown eyes.

Or maybe it was the way the light hit her face.

"I'm an old woman, Tyler. Time is one thing I have plenty of."

Strike one.

I smiled, weakly. "You're not *that* old."

The grin widened, recognizing, no doubt, my pitiful delaying tactic. "Old enough."

Strike two!

I took in a deep breath, the breakfast I'd consumed sitting like a leaden ball in my stomach. My fingers were pressed white against the polished wood of the tabletop.

As I opened my mouth to speak, there was a brisk rapping on the front door, followed by a "Yoo hoo! Ruby! Are you home, dear?"

Yes!

As Ruby slowly moved to her feet, the look she gave me let me know in no uncertain terms that this conversation was far from being over.

Oh, well. I'd take a rain delay any day.

I walked outside, feeling the warmth of the sun on my face and smiling into the perfect blue sky. The snow the night before seemed a sort of harbinger of spring and the temperature rose to lend strength to my supposition. The air was filled with the sounds of overburdened trees and rooftops dropping their heavy loads to the ground. Birdsong wove its way intermittently through the low percussion of the falling mounds of snow, and when I looked up, I spied a sizable flock of ducks circling the lake and looking for a nice, wet place to land.

My grin broadened as I walked down the shoveled path, my boots crunching the salt beneath my feet. It was a glorious day. The kind that made you believe in God, if you didn't already. And right then, I most certainly did.

Looking down the small hill that led to the lake, I saw Ice standing on the little green dock on our beach, looking out over the frozen water, her dark hair blown off her brow by a gentle spring breeze. Her posture was attentive, alert, but relaxed in a way I didn't often get to see.

I stopped, taken by the sight.

At that moment, I wished I were a painter so I could capture the beauty of what my eyes were seeing.

Because I wasn't and still am not, I settled for a long, comfortable stare, capturing in my mind what my hands refused to render.

As if feeling my eyes upon her, she turned and her welcoming smile brightened up an already fabulous day. She lifted a hand in a casual wave. I waved back and resumed my trek toward her, stepping carefully around the shoveled square that had brought back to the surface the foundation of what had once been the cabin.

Quickly joining her on the dock, I slipped an arm around her waist and leaned into her body as I, too, looked across the frozen expanse of the lake, watching as the ducks finally found a patch of melted ice in which to land. "Beautiful day," I murmured quietly, unwilling to break the peaceful silence with too much idle chatter.

"Mm."

We stood there in companionable silence, enjoying each other and the day, for quite awhile before my attention was captured by a young boy and his dog who were coming toward us from the right. The boy threw a stick, and the dog, with a volley of barks that echoed across the lake, ran to retrieve it.

His attention was diverted, apparently, by the ducks which, alarmed by his barks, rose to take flight, and he headed out after them, his paws slipping on the ice.

"King!" the boy shouted, running after his fleeing dog, "Come back!" His feet slipped on the slick surface and he fell, hitting his head a good one against the ice, but he was quickly back up and running again.

Suddenly, I heard a loud crack and the ice opened up to swallow the scrambling dog, which yelped and tried desperately to get back up out of the water.

Seeing what had happened, the boy tried to stop, but the ice's slickness, combined with his forward momentum, caused him to follow his friend into the water's icy depths.

Ice was out of my arms and running before I even thought to blink. "Ice! No!" Like the dog's yelps, and the boy's screams, my words echoed over the lake, damning me repeatedly with their sheer impotence.

Her feet were slipping and sliding in the worn boots she'd donned, but she managed to keep her footing and continue forward, ignoring my cry. "Get help!" she shouted, not even looking at me as she headed for the hole in the ice that had claimed two victims in a moment's short time.

I couldn't move. Couldn't respond to her tersely voiced order. My body condemned me to stand and watch as the boy's head disappeared beneath the ice and my lover, not hesitating for even a second, gathered up her strength and dove into the water.

"Ice!"

My rebellious body moved quickly then, though still not in the direction my partner had ordered. I was out on the ice before my feet even realized it, which caused me to fall after a single step. My head hit hard against the edge of the dock, causing stars to float tantalizingly before my eyes, as I lay dazed for a moment, staring up into the sky and wondering what my name was.

It came back to me in a flash, though, and I tried to regain my footing, only to fall once again. "Damnit! Ice!"

A strong hand hauled me back to my feet and pulled me easily onto the dock. I spun to take in the heavily bearded face of a large man who was looking at me with wide eyes. "What happened?"

Shaking my head, I tried to jerk from his grasp, my need to get out on that lake paramount. But he held me easily in his grip, shaking me as one would a rag doll. "What happened?" he asked again.

"A dog...a boy...chased the dog into the water! My friend went to help. Let me go!!"

"No! It's too dangerous. You can't go out there."

"Like *hell* I can't!" Raising my leg, I stamped down hard on his foot, wrenching away at the same time. I would have toppled back onto the ice for a second time if he hadn't reached out and grabbed me, pulling me to him once again.

"Listen to me. People are coming to help. People who are used to this kind of thing. You need to stay here. You'll only get in the way. Do you understand?" He spoke to me as if speaking to an infant, his words slow and clearly enunciated.

"*You* don't understand! That's my friend out there! She needs help!"

"And that's exactly what she's gonna get. Now just stay here and let us do our jobs, alright?"

After a moment, I relaxed and nodded, convinced by the sincerity in both his voice and eyes.

He smiled. "Good."

Releasing me, he turned his head, and I followed his gaze to where a group of men were hurrying down the small hill and onto the ice, armed with hooks and nylon ropes, looking for all the world like an army of industrious ants after a discarded candy wrapper.

"Where'd they all come from so quickly?" I asked, not aware I was speaking aloud until the man turned his smile back on me.

"Well, you hear a dog yelp, a boy scream, and a woman yell 'ice', and you get the picture pretty quick, ma'am."

The mention of my lover's name, though not intended, caused my attention to snap back to the lake and its unfolding drama. I could just see Ice's dark head bobbing above the tilted sheets of ice which had fractured even more with the struggling of three living beings trapped within its confines. I could also see, and hear, the crazed struggling of the dog, but of the boy, there was nothing.

Ice took in a deep breath, and then she too disappeared into the black and hungry water.

Everything went silent then. Or at least it seemed that way to me. I found myself holding my breath in empathy with Ice until spots swirling before my eyes threatened to merge together into unconsciousness.

Gasping, I took in a fresh breath of air, then blinked.

Only the dog could be seen, paddling in useless circles in the ever widening pool, obviously too cold and too tired to even try to get a purchase on the ice surrounding him.

It's been too long. Too long. Too long.

My mind replayed this endless litany like a mantra that, instead of soothing, forced adrenaline and hopelessness through my body in equal measures.

I had just made up my mind to bolt off the dock yet again when Ice resurfaced, the small boy clenched tightly against her chest. Gasping for air, she flung her head back and opened her mouth to the sky, her hair slinging rainbow sheets into the warm, moist air. Her choking gasps were the only sounds I could hear above the joyful beating of my heart at the sight of her, alive and whole.

With a mighty heave worthy of a Titan, she threw the boy onto the firmer section of the ice. He slid several feet before stopping, a rag doll at Nature's cruel mercy. His skin was marbled purple and pasty white, his lips and the flesh around them a sullen blue, and I imagined, were I to touch him, that he would feel the way he looked, a marble statue tossed aside by a forsaken god.

Beneath his drenched parka, his chest was still and lifeless.

The group of men crept forward on tentative legs, one reaching out with a large grappling hook and snaring his jacket, tugging the lifeless boy slowly, carefully, back toward the shore.

Another splash. Another body hitting the ice.

This time it was the dog that'd started the entire chain reaction, and of the three victims the water had captured in its gaping maw, only he looked none the worse for wear. Scrambling to his feet, he shook the water briskly from his fur, and after a moment of stumbling, trotted back toward the shoreline, seemingly without a care in the world. Another rescuer grabbed the dog and bundled him in a warm blanket.

All that was left in the middle of the half-frozen lake was my lover.

The sounds of sirens in the distance were unimportant things to me as I watched Ice try for purchase on the twisted blocks surrounding her. I could see her steady herself and take a few deep breaths for strength. My entire body clenched, a coiled spring, as I willed my strength to her from across the lake, my jaw clenched so hard I swore I could feel pieces of my teeth chipping away.

With a last, deep breath, she straightened her arms, her

powerful strength managing to drag her body half out of the water and onto the ice. Her legs still dangled in the murky depths, kicking hard to give her the momentum needed to pull out fully.

The force was apparently too much for the still weakening ice to bear, and it split once again, sending a wide fissure almost to the shore and dumping my partner back into the freezing water.

When her body disappeared completely beneath the water, my paralysis broke and, without thinking, I ran out onto the ice, using my arms the way a tight-rope walker would, keeping my balance only by the strength of my will.

And where Ice was concerned, my will was pure steel.

Unfortunately, will doesn't count for much when you're tackled from behind by a bearded behemoth who's twice as strong as you'll ever dream of being.

I hit the ground hard enough to force the air from my lungs in a coughing bark, and the stars that had faded from my last meeting with the dock's splintered edge came back with a vengeance, swirling around me like multicolored fireflies.

I was hooked under the arms and unceremoniously dragged back toward the shore, my jacket and shirt rucking up around my shoulders, the ice burning my bare flesh as it slid beneath me.

The shouts of the men combined with the swiftly approaching sirens, both sounds helping to clear my head. I struggled to sit up, turning my head just in time to see a yellow nylon rope, a large loop knotted at one end, sail toward the hole where Ice had fallen.

The second fall through the ice had profoundly affected my lover, as I could tell by the slow, almost clumsy movements of her arms as she tried to reach out and grab the rope so close to her.

"Slip it over your head and under your arms!" one of the men yelled as another tied the other end off around a stout tree that hung out over the water like a flightless vulture.

I could see her dark head nod as she tried to follow her rescuer's instructions, fumbling several times with the rope before finally getting it under her arms.

"Hold on! We're gonna pull you out!"

She nodded again, trying to get a firm grip on the narrow rope with hands, I was sure, that were numb past the point of feeling anything but pain, if even that.

"One! Two! Three!" Several men stood on the ice, the rope firmly clenched in their gloved hands. On the final count, they pulled, snapping the rope taut and slowly dragging Ice up out of the water, their grunts combining with the ice's moaning protests at having to give up its feast and filling the air in a primal symphony.

Something happened, and to this day I don't know what, but she suddenly stopped helping and fell limp against the ice, her body half in, half out of the water. The men, still pulling, dragged her a few scant inches before her arms slipped upwards and the rope pulled away completely, leaving her stranded once again; this time totally unable to help free herself from the icy prison trapping her.

"Ice!" I screamed, trying desperately to get some reaction from her. My heart shattered into splintered fragments as the ice beneath her moaned threateningly and her body teetered on the edge of oblivion.

She lay there, limp and unheeding. My mind flashed back to another time, another place. Kneeling over her, holding her life in my hands as her blood pumped between my fingers in a red river. Begging anyone who would listen to help her, to save her.

No. Not again. Please, not again. Please. I can't go through this again.

Realizing what had happened, one of the men, throwing all caution to the wind, grabbed a long hook and ran out onto the ice with surefooted grace, straddling the fissure that was threatening to become wider as he ran.

My sigh of relief came out in a wail as he managed to hook the back of her sodden jacket and carefully pulled her away from the immediate danger. He pulled her to him, then dropped the hook and grabbed her under the arms, much as my own rescuer had grabbed me, and carefully pulled her to the safety of the shore.

I was by her side in a heartbeat, tears liberally mixing with the melting snow my knees were pressed into. "Ice?" I asked, brushing the wet hair back from her brow. "Ice? Can you hear me?"

There was no reaction, though I could tell that she was still alive by the faint movement of her chest against my free hand. I clenched the fabric of her shirt in that hand and shook her, angry at her utter stillness. "Damnit, Ice! Wake up! I didn't come this far with you for you to give up now, so you'd just better damn well wake the hell up or I swear I'll hunt you down and kill you myself!"

After a moment, her eyes fluttered open, and I've never, not even after an entire month of rainy days, been so glad to see the color blue in my life. Her gaze was dazed and glassy and, though she was looking right at me, I could tell she wasn't seeing me. But that didn't matter. Not really.

She was alive, and that was all that mattered.

And she'd stay that way if I had anything to do with it.

And, by any god ever worshipped on this planet or any other, I would have *everything* to do with it.

The skin of her face, the only exposed surface I could see, was pasty white. Water droplets clung there like clear, fat leeches sucking away her vitality. Her lips were the deep purple of ripe berries, and so swollen that I wondered if they weren't just going to split, right there, to expose the ice water that had replaced the blood in her veins.

Two men joined the third and bundled Ice into warm quilts they'd brought with them. They wore the rough cloth garb of Ice's rescuers and not the uniforms I was expecting. I looked up, a question in my eyes. As if in response to my silent query, a tall, bespectacled, sandy-haired man squatted down beside me, an apologetic look on his face. "The little boy your friend saved is alive, but barely. The paramedics didn't want to wait to see if she was gonna make it out of there too. There just wasn't enough time. Unfortunately, there's only the one ambulance, so it's going to take a while before they can make it back here."

I swallowed hard at the news, then nodded, wiping my eyes with the back of my hand. Aware or not, Ice needed my strength, not my tears. "Is there anything we can do while we wait?"

Reaching down, I grasped her hand, taking it into my own. God, it was like touching a corpse. Or at least what I thought touching a corpse would feel like, not having had the actual experience myself. Her flesh was chilled, damp, and stiff beneath my hand and I shuddered, half in revulsion, half in fear.

"Getting her someplace warm would be a good start. Where do you live?"

"With me," came Ruby's voice off to my right. The crowd parted like the Red Sea, bearing forth my diminutive neighbor in all her headmistress glory. Taking charge in her typical style, she pointed to two of the biggest men standing with us; bearded giants, both of them. "You and you, bring her up to the house. Carefully. I'll go draw a bath."

I looked on in awe as the men, without hesitation, simply did as she ordered, lifting Ice's limp body in their massive arms. A chill ran through me that had nothing to do with the snow I was kneeling in.

Never had I seen my lover looking so small, so helpless, so utterly defenseless.

It was a scene that, if I should live to five times the age I am now, I wish to never view again. At the time, I was sure the scene would haunt my dreams. And, true to my word, it has.

"No, no baths," the man squatting next to me interceded. "Just light a fire and warm some blankets. We'll need to warm her up slowly or the shock could kill her." Standing, he reached down and helped me to my feet. "I'm Steve, by the way. The town calls me 'Doc', so I guess that's what I am." His smile was charming and I found myself warming up to him.

"I'm Tyler. This is Morgan."

"Well, Tyler, you have a very brave friend. Let's see what we can do about keeping her that way, ok?"

I nodded, the words stolen from me as I watched the men haul Ice's body back towards Ruby's house.

"Let's go, then."

Chapter 4

The house was overly warm as I entered, shedding my jacket like a snake's second skin and walking over to the fireplace to be at Ice's side as she was gently laid on the hearth rug. As the men stepped away, I took their place, grasping her hand once again and looking into eyes that seemed to be staring into eternity. "Stay with me, Morgan. You're gonna be ok. Just stay with me."

The fire blazed high and hot within its stone confines, sending out a heat which caused beads of sweat to form on my forehead, dripping and stinging my wide, staring eyes. I wiped them away without thought, looking to the doctor who came to kneel beside me as one might a Savior, with bright hope and a subtle sense of doom lurking in the shadows of my heart.

He unbuttoned her jacket quickly, then disposed of her shirt by renting it from hem to collar with one savage tug, and exposing belly and breasts that were as pasty white and marbled as the flesh of her immobile face.

I felt a moment's discomfort at the action, remembering her dispassionate tale of men who had stripped her and posed her for their own pleasures. Suddenly, I felt the almost overwhelming need to cover her, to preserve a dignity, which she had never thought overmuch of, given the rude circumstances of her benumbed youth.

A plush towel dropped into my hands, and I used it as much to dry her as to cover her from eyes, which, I felt, had no right to look upon such vulnerability.

As I was drying her upper body, the doctor reached for the button of her jeans. I immediately dropped my hands, easily displacing his on the soaked fabric. "Let me," I said in a voice which brooked no argument.

He looked at me and I swore there was understanding in his eyes before he grabbed my towel and resumed my forgotten task as I worked to undo the frozen zipper.

Within moments, it was done and she was covered with quilts heated by the fire, as warm and dry as we could possibly make her. The doctor withdrew his hand from beneath the quilts, bearing a thermometer which he looked at, brows drawn in a pensive frown, before shaking it down and placing it back in his case.

She lay still as death beneath her vestments of cloth and down, too deep within her own mind to even react to the intimate touches she was receiving from a stranger. My heart hurt looking at her. My guts twisted and roiled inside me as I stared on, helpless.

"Why isn't she shivering?" I managed to finally get out from between lips that seemed to forget how to form words.

"Her body can't waste the energy that would take. Everything's going to keeping her vital organs alive. She was in that water a long time." He turned to meet my gaze. "When she warms up, she'll start shivering."

When. Not if.

I smiled a little, bolstered by his confidence.

He returned my smile, then turned away, reaching into his medical bag and pulling out an object wrapped in plastic. Opening the wrapping, he removed a long, flexible tube that was closed on one end, open on the other. "What's that?"

"We need to warm up her on the inside, too, but she's too weak to be able to take anything in by mouth right now, so I'm going to slip this tube into her stomach through her nose and introduce some water that Ruby's got heating up on the stove. That should help bring her core body temperature up."

The warming up the inside part sounded good. The sticking a garden hose down the nose, however, didn't. "Will it hurt her?"

The doctor smiled slightly as he lubed up one end of the tube from a foil packet he'd ripped open. "Well, most people gag when it's going down, but I don't think we have to worry about that in this case. She's pretty out of it. It shouldn't hurt, no."

I looked at him doubtfully, but as he seemed pretty certain of his words, I didn't argue.

I should have.

After he measured from her nose, to her ear, and down to

the tip of her sternum, he tilted her head back and deftly pushed the tube into her right nostril, feeding it through a little at a time.

Ice reacted the way I half expected her to, the way I imagined a wildcat would when trapped in a hunter's snare; snarling, twisting her face away from the offending object, and lashing out blindly with both arms.

In her unthinking rage, she managed to crack one muscled forearm hard against the doctor's cheek and send him flying back toward the fireplace, where only the upraised stone hearth kept him from being pitched headfirst into the flames.

I immediately dove into the fray, trying with all my strength to pin Ice's arms down to her sides while laying my body atop hers to somehow stop her insane struggling.

She threw me off her body as if I were a child, and a small one at that, but I scrambled back on top of her, forgoing the useless attempt to hold her arms down and instead using my hands to gently cradle her face. "Ice, it's me. It's Angel. You need to relax. You're safe here. No one's going to hurt you. Please. You need to relax."

My soothing tones seemed to be penetrating the thick fog of her mind, because gradually she began to slow her struggles, her tense body softening beneath my own. Her eyes opened once again, and though her gaze was still dazed, I could see the faintest glimmer of the woman I loved looking back at me.

I smiled with probably more relief than I've ever known, before or since. "Welcome back, my love," I whispered, tears sparkling in my eyes once again.

Her arm moved up slowly, but before I could stop her, she ripped the NG tube out of her nose and flung it away, gagging. She turned her head just in time as her chest heaved and a great glut of lake water spilled out onto the towel next to her head.

I clambered off of her and stroked her brow as she continued to retch weakly, gagging until nothing more was left to expel. Then she started to shiver, violently, her tremors so strong that she almost seemed to be having some sort of seizure.

I looked up, alarmed, at the doctor who was just now getting back to his feet and wiping the bleeding cut Ice had given his cheek. "She packs a mean punch," he muttered, shaking his head and coming to kneel beside us both.

Even in her misery, Ice managed to turn her head in his direction and narrow her eyes in a murderous glare before turning back to me, an eternity's worth of questions in her eyes.

"His name is Steve. He's a doctor, and he's here to help." My smile became wider as I gently caressed a cheek which was already becoming warmer. "So don't go turning him into dog meat just yet, huh?"

She shot him another glare, but remained calm, if still wracked with violent spasms, beneath my hands.

At my nod, Steve came closer, bringing his head into Ice's field of vision. "I'd ask how you're feeling, but it's pretty obvious what the answer's gonna be, so I think we'll just skip that one. You're suffering from severe hypothermia. Your shivering is a good sign, but your body temperature wouldn't even register on my thermometer, so I'm gonna have to put that tube back down into your stomach so we can warm you up, ok?"

The good doctor had obviously learned a painful lesson on how to respect his patients, if his calm, coherent, and logical explanation to my partner was any indication. I couldn't help an internal smirk. Ice had a way of teaching people things they'd never dreamed of learning. And not always in ways they'd expect to be taught, either.

By some superhuman strength of will, she managed to unclench her jaw and force words out from a raw throat. "N-no t-t-tube."

He smiled then. That patently false "And just where did you get *your* medical degree" doctor smile that's issued, I believe, with the diploma and Hippocratic oath upon graduation from Medical School. Hippocrates himself probably practiced that expression while looking into still pools and waiting for his latest crop of peasants with foot rot to arrive.

I laid a quick hand on his arm, hoping to forestall the storm I could see brewing in Ice's eyes. Eyes which were becoming more clear and more aware, and yes, more icy as the seconds passed. "Look. It's probably better if you just...."

He raised his eyes to mine. "If there were any other way, I'd use it. But she's shivering too hard to be able to drink. The tube goes back in."

Then his face paled as an incredibly strong hand clamped down on his wrist. He tried to pull away, but to no avail.

"No. Tube." She didn't even look at him. Just continued to clamp down on his arm while the rest of her continued to shiver violently.

Oh boy.

I looked from one to the other, surprised that I wasn't more surprised that a woman who was dying moments ago could be more than holding her own against a strong and apparently healthy man.

After all, the woman in question *was* Ice.

"Ok!" I said brightly. "It seems we're in a bit of a standoff here." And I was the resident expert on standoffs, having endured several during my time in prison. Of course, expertise didn't help when I felt my head nearly being seared off by two sets of scorching glances sent my way.

I smiled. Broadly. Then chose the pair of eyes to look into that didn't stand the best chance of incinerating me where I knelt.

"She doesn't want a tube shoved down her nose. You don't want your arm broken. I think we've got a little common ground to work with here, don't you?"

After a long, tense moment, he nodded. I think he was in too much pain to speak. I know I would have been.

"Good. Then here's my idea. You go into the kitchen and ask Ruby to change the water she's warming into a weak tea. Then we'll see if she can drink it. But if she chokes, or even sputters just once," and here I took a chance and looked down at Ice, "the tube goes back in. Deal?"

When Ice closed her eyes in resignation, I knew the war was won. Almost as an afterthought, I turned my attention back to the doctor, who was looking at me with a mixture of pain and amazement in his eyes. "Deal?"

When he finally nodded, I reached down and gently grasped my lover's hand, carefully prying her fingers loose from the doctor's wrist. "C'mon, Ice," I murmured, my lips close to the frozen shell of her ear. "You need to let go so he can get your tea, ok?"

After several long seconds, I had her grip loosened enough so that Steve could remove his arm, which he promptly did, rubbing it and looking at both of us as if he'd never seen us before. Smiling up at him, I gestured with my eyes. his path to the kitchen, and when he got the hint and left us alone, I lowered my head the rest of the way and pressed a kiss to my lover's lips, hoping to warm them with my own. "Thank you," I whispered, smiling into her eyes.

She blinked once, in acknowledgement I thought, then rolled away from me and toward the fire, curled up into a fetal ball of shivering misery.

Unable to stand seeing her that way, I lifted up the covers and joined her beneath them, pressing my front against her back and slipping one arm around her waist, melding, as best I could, our bodies together.

The chill of her bare flesh was intense against the inadequate shielding of my T-shirt, and the violence of her shivering caused my own teeth to chatter.

It was like trying to hold onto an avalanche.

But hold on I did, as the voice of an old science teacher I'd had once filtered through my mind, telling me that skin on skin contact was one way to combat the ravages of hypothermia. Pulling away slightly, I yanked my T-shirt up and over my head then cuddled back down, wincing as my warm flesh came into contact with her icy skin. I resisted the urge to pull away, instead forcing myself to move closer, wrapping my arm once again around her waist and hanging on for dear life as the tremors of her body went through both of us.

Placing my head against the back of her neck, I hummed something nonsensical and off-key, doing my best to let her know that I was there and wasn't going anywhere any time soon. At least not without her.

It seemed to work, or maybe my mind was just telling me something my heart needed to hear, truth or not, but her spastic tremors seemed to calm somewhat the longer she lay in my arms. Was her flesh just the slightest bit warmer, or was it my body that was so numb that it only felt that way to me?

Either way, I held on, prepared to do so for an eternity if that's what it took.

Ruby came out into the den, followed by the doctor. Both were holding two mugs in their hands and bearing identical, concerned expressions on their faces. Ruby's eyes narrowed as she took in my position beneath the blankets with Ice, and I swore I could see the little computer in her mind clacking away and filing this new bit of information for further use.

At any other time, I might have felt some concern over this, but as things were then, I just couldn't give a rat's hindquarters what she thought, as long as she helped Ice recover. There'd be time enough for tap dancing around the issue later.

Much later.

"How's she doing?" Steve asked, coming to stand beside us.

"I don't know. I think she might be a little warmer, but I'm not sure."

He squatted down. "Well, I kept my part of the bargain, for all the good it'll do. Here's the tea. How do you suggest we get her to drink it?"

To be perfectly honest, I hadn't thought that far ahead, but I sure as hell wasn't going to tell him that. Especially not with the slight sheen of condescension I could see shining in his eyes.

Well, Mister small town, know it all, got my license to practice medicine from K-Mart, I've stood up against a whole ocean of fish bigger than you.

Biting the inside of my lip for a second, I hit upon an idea that I hoped would work and rolled up to a sitting position, keeping a firm grip on Ice's waist as I did so. For being a woman without an ounce of fat on her, Ice was very heavy, especially now, trembling and dead weight as she was in my arms. Still, wanting to rub someone's face in their own mess makes for good motivation and with a strength I didn't know I possessed, I managed to bring her up to a semi-reclining position against my chest.

Even if someone had offered me, right then, a million dollars, I couldn't have kept the smirk off my face at the expression on the doctor's.

Take that, you little two-bit know it all.

Of course, the hard part was still ahead. Ice was still shivering so violently that the clacking of her teeth was easily heard over the roaring of the fire. Just how she was supposed to drink tea with a jaw that was vibrating like an overused car engine I hadn't the first clue.

So I smiled, effectively putting the ball back into the doctor's court once again.

He caught my look and scowled, but to his credit, did the best he could. Which, unfortunately, wasn't very good at all.

With tentative hands, he lifted one of the mugs after setting the other down near the hearth. I wasn't sure who was shaking more, doctor or patient, but the end result was that Ice was receiving a very impromptu, and by her expression very unwelcome, tea bath. After a few more fumbling attempts, he pulled the mug away, his eyes beseeching me to give in just this once.

Ruby chose that moment to step in, moving him out of the way and kneeling in his place. "Let me take care of this," she said in a voice just a hair short of disgusted. "Make yourself useful and go get some more blankets to warm by the fire. They're in the closet right down the hallway there."

I was sure I could detect his sigh of relief as he rose to his feet and hurried off to do Ruby's bidding.

"Men," she muttered to herself while wiping the tea off of Ice's skin. "Worse than a pack of half-blind sled dogs, they are."

Right then, she sounded so much like Corinne I couldn't help but laugh, even given the gravity of the situation I was in. She looked at me and winked before applying herself back to the task at hand.

Finished with her mopping job, Ruby lay down the towel and used her left hand to firmly grasp Ice's quaking jaw. She raised the mug to my lover's lips with a steady hand. Tilting the mug just slightly, she poured the liquid in in tiny bits so that, before I knew it, Ice had finished half a mug without choking or sputtering even once. The second half went even quicker as the tepid tea began to work its magic on her insides, warming them slightly and allowing blood to spread to the rest of her body.

A quarter of the way through the second mug, Ice had had enough and turned her head away from the offering. "No more," she whispered.

To my surprise, Ruby didn't push, just wiped Ice's lips and handed the mugs back to Steve, who'd come in sometime between the first cup and the second, and was staring at us dumbly, hands on hips. "I think she's earned a bit of a rest, don't you?" she asked no one in particular.

I looked up at Steve, who half-smiled, half-shrugged, the way a pet dog might who's trying hard to get back into your good graces, yet not knowing quite what to do to get there. "I...um...should check her temperature again."

"Ok," I replied, drawing the word out as I wondered why he was looking so hesitant.

He winced. "She's...um...still shivering too hard to take it by mouth."

I winced in empathy as his little problem became clear as crystal. The man had suffered a black eye from sticking a tube down Ice's nose. Where he needed to place the thermometer would probably rate emasculation. "Oh. I...see your point." I smiled weakly. "She feels a lot warmer. Does that count?"

"Not really, no."

"Just get on with it already," Ice's rough voice chimed in.

Spurred into action as if struck by a whip, the doctor literally jumped to his bag, removed his thermometer, and most likely took the fastest temperature in the history of humankind.

Silently closing the door to Ice's room, I padded back down the hallway and descended the stairs, a curious mixture of relief and dread coursing through me.

As evening claimed the day, Ice began to recover, slowly becoming warmer as my arms continued to enfold her, pressing her close to my body. Steve and Ruby had talked quietly, their words unheard over the fireplace's cheery crackles, and I felt my lover slowly begin to relax in my arms, finally falling into a deep, and I hoped restful, sleep.

The stresses of the day caught up to me, and I gave in to the insidious craving for sleep that seemed to envelop me like the blankets laying over both of us, only to be awakened what seemed to be a second later by a gentle touch to my shoulder.

After taking another temperature and proclaiming her safely

in the land of the living once again, Steve helped me take Ice up the stairs and into her bedroom, escorting her to the bed and piling her high with blankets to ward off whatever residual chill that might have been lingering unseen by the two of us, waiting to take hold of her body once our backs were turned.

After handing me a bottle of antibiotic pills for the pneumonia he was sure would follow Ice's icy swim, he smiled, still slightly embarrassed, and took his leave, gently shutting the door behind him, bathing the room in a gentle darkness.

I sat on the side of the bed for long moments, stroking Ice's hair and trying desperately not to allow my mind to replay the events of the day. I needed to shut down, to tune out, to forget, even for a moment, how close I came to losing her.

Again.

Will it always be like this for us? Are we destined to forever stand at the precipice, gazing down into its gaping maw and praying for a gentle wind?

Shaking my head at my sudden attack of the blues, I placed a kiss on Ice's forehead, then stood and smoothed clothes, taking in a deep breath and mentally preparing myself to face the music, which this time came in the form of a diminutive woman named Ruby.

What is it with me and my penchant for attracting, and having to answer to, elderly matrons, anyway?

Too deeply asleep to hear my silent question, Ice had no answers to give on this particular subject, though no doubt her advice would have been wryly humorous, had she deigned to give any at all.

I snorted softly. "Probably the same as yours for attracting blondes, psychotic or otherwise."

I, of course, did not count myself among that particular genus, blonde though I am, though I'm sure some, maybe even some of you reading this right now, would beg to differ with my rather glowing self-assessment.

Alright, Angel. Enough stalling.

If there was one thing I'd learned during my time behind bars, it was to do today what otherwise would get you killed tomorrow. Bravery had taken its sweet time in coming, but it had finally arrived and changed my way of thinking, and doing, for good.

"Wish me luck," I whispered to the silent figure on the bed before letting myself out of the room and into the line of fire, such that it was.

I came to the foot of the stairs like a condemned inmate—and given my experiences, that analogy isn't exactly foreign to me, let me remind you—and walked into the den, which was lit only by the still blazing fire. Ruby was sitting on one of the couches, a cup of coffee in her hand. Her eyes met mine immediately as I stepped into the room, as if she'd been expecting my entrance all along, which, in truth, she probably had.

I summoned up a smile from somewhere and continued my advance, detouring over to the fire and holding my hands out to warm them, though they were already quite warm. Sweating, in fact.

"Everything's quiet, I trust?"

Her voice was flat, uninflected, and therefore difficult to read.

I stood, still turned away from her, and nodded, staring into the flames, my muscles almost as tense as they'd ever been during my time in the Bog, when my life, and not just my pride, was at stake.

"Would you like some coffee? I just made a fresh pot." Her voice was warmer this time.

Damning my cowardice, I continued to stare into the flames, shaking my head slowly in the negative.

"What's wrong, Angel?"

I stiffened further, then turned, sure my face was an open-mouthed mask of shock. "How did you...?"

"She called you that. When you were both sleeping." Ruby's smile deepened, her eyes bright with understanding. "It fits you, somehow."

"Ruby, I...."

She held up one hand. "No need to explain, Tyler. I might be old and gray, but I know love when it's staring me in the face." Her smile warmed the craggy plains of her face. "And you love her very much, don't you?" It wasn't a question.

Beyond stunned, I could only let my heart answer. "Yes."

Nodding sagely, she took another sip of her coffee, her eyes never leaving mine. "She's a very lucky woman."

Somehow, I knew she wasn't talking about Ice's escape from what seemed to be certain death.

"You're wrong," I countered, feeling the sting of fresh tears as they pricked at my eyes. "I'm the lucky one."

"Perhaps you both are."

And, just like that, I managed to find acceptance, and even love, in the one place I most needed for it to be, in the eyes of my childhood confidant. Noticing my tears, she held open her arms and I rushed into them, burying my face and body in the abundant and fragrant warmth of her, allowing myself the emotional catharsis I so desperately needed.

My tears fell in a cleansing rain, dampening the front of her housecoat. She just held me and rocked me, humming like she used to do when I was young and had been put off by my parents.

And so, a day that had started off wonderfully and gone steadily, horribly downhill from there, ended on a note much sweeter than I had any right to request.

And for that, I was very thankful.

The events of the next two weeks would have tried the patience of a Saint and, since I'm not about to be canonized anytime in the foreseeable future, let's just say that every day brought to me new and inventive definitions for the word "frustration" and leave it at that.

True to the good doctor's word, pneumonia did indeed decide to pay a little visit to my beleaguered partner. To say that Ice was a poor patient would be somewhat akin to observing that Mother Theresa is a nice woman; technically true, but an understatement of extreme proportions.

That's not that she was the whiney type, because she wasn't. Whiney I could have dealt with easily, having had more than my share of exposure to it while still a young girl living under the roof of two parents who elevated that particular sickbed response to somewhat of an art form.

No, Ice was more the "don't tell me I'm sick, because I'm not" type. The "you're the one who needs to see a doctor, because I feel just fine" type. The ...well, you get the picture.

It took all my not inconsiderable powers of persuasion to convince her that fevers rising above one hundred three degrees, coughing until blue in the face after such strenuous activities as sitting up or yawning, and vomiting up one's toenails at the mere mention of food was not normal in the course of human events.

Of course, my lover also suffered from selective hearing loss, and there were times where I was sure my voice was the perfect decibel level to activate that particular condition, much to my extreme vexation.

She showed enough presence of mind, however, to take the antibiotics I nearly shoved down her throat and, just prior to my appropriating some rope from Ruby and earning a question and answer session on our bedroom habits, the illness began to lose its interest in my partner and the light at the end of the tunnel stopped being an oncoming train.

Spring began to show her colors during my week of enforced isolation, and by the time Ice was again ready to step outside and wash the jailhouse pallor from her face, the snow had melted completely, revealing a verdant carpet underneath.

One morning, I decided that a walk into town was in order and, probably because she'd grown somewhat used to my more dominant position during her illness and convalescence, Ice followed without much comment.

I knew that situation would change, and soon, but I was determined to enjoy it for as long as I could.

We walked slowly through a forest coming alive with spring's bright blessing. Birds, animals, and insects were everywhere and flowers bloomed in a riot of color. The tree-fractured sun was warm on my shoulders and the smile on my face was as wide as they came.

The sky was May soft and stitched with clouds which cast friendly shadows over the ground as they strolled their slow lover's promenade across the vast expanse of warming blue.

The last row of trees gave way and the town opened up beyond the woods. The initial sight of it made me stop and stare, astounded by how much of a difference three weeks could make.

Gone was the gray of a desolate community dying by slow inches. In its place stood something fresh, vibrant, new. Even the church, always the first building you passed no matter which way you came into town, looked inviting instead of imposing with its new coat of whitewash and its open, beckoning doors.

The *Silver Pine* looked as if the tornado of Oz had spun it away and replaced it with Glenda's house. Big men on tall ladders washed windows and painted shutters. Some were even hanging honest-to-God bunting from the eaves, as if the Queen were expected to pop by for a visit sometime in the very near future.

From the corner of my eye, I caught something very large and very yellow sail around the corner of the Inn, leaving a high falsetto voice and mumbled orders that caused the working men to redouble their efforts. I wondered about that for a moment, suspecting I had at last seen the much-maligned (by Ruby, at least) proprietress of the place, but before I had a chance to step forward and indulge my always rampant curiosity, Ice stiffened beside me and I looked up, catching the scowling expression on her face.

Following her gaze, I took in the scene presented me. A large, beefy, and florid-faced man wearing a brown suit which screamed "discount department store" was standing beside the driver's door of a battered silver Volvo with Indiana tags and screaming into the impassive face of a man who'd been ancient when I was a young girl; Mr. Willamette, the owner of the town's only gas station.

When the large man pulled back his fist and made as if to punch kindly Mr. Willamette, Ice stepped into action, getting there just in time to save the old man from eating dinner through a straw for the rest of his life.

I slid to a stop before the group just as Mr. Fist turned to stare disbelievingly at my partner, his rubbery lips parted to reveal crooked, nicotine-stained teeth and the flesh of his hand blanched white where Ice's fingers were gripping it.

She gave him that smile that makes you wonder if she's contemplating adding *homo idiotus* to her list of dietary delicacies.

"What seems to be the problem?" I asked brightly, more to keep Ice from turning the man into a human stew than because I really wanted to know.

As I'd learned from long and painful years of experience, asking the obvious question is sometimes the way to go in situations like these. While the bully in question is straining his somewhat less than vast mental resources to come up with a witty comeback, you usually have more than enough time to get your lips out of the way of his fist.

"Car's broke," came the voice of Mr. Willamette from my right.

"Brilliant deduction, Mr. Fixit," the stranger replied, pulling his hand loose from Ice, who was willing to let it go. "*My* question is: what are you gonna do about it?"

"Can't do anything about it. Like I told you, my mechanic's laid up till fall, at least."

Temple vein throbbing, the man lunged forward again, only to be caught by his lapels by Ice, who shoved him back against the car and stared deep into his eyes, that little smirk still curving her lips.

"Who are you? The old goat's bodyguard?"

Ice's smile widened. "Nah. Just someone who likes to see how many limbs she can rip off before her victim starts screaming." She made a show of looking the man up and down. "I think one will do just fine here."

Wanting to stop this before the stranger stained his trousers, I stepped up to Ice and laid a hand against her lower back. "Maybe we could hear his side of the story?"

When she turned to look at me, her eyes were filled with mirth, and I relaxed slightly and looked around her broad back and into the face of the man who I was sure was going to be dashing off a very nasty note to the Volvo people at his first available opportunity. Assuming he managed to get through this with all parts intact, of course. Which, at this point, looked to be a toss-up.

Releasing the man's lapels and brushing them flat against his natty suit jacket, Ice stepped back a pace and crossed her muscled arms over her chest, her raised-eyebrow expression leaving no doubt in the man's mind that if he were even to start *thinking* about acting stupid again, she'd take great pleasure in pulling his spine up through his throat and beating him to death with it.

His mouth opened. Then closed. Opened. Closed.

Then hung open like a trap door and stayed that way.

"Okay," I said, breaking the silence and drawing the word out when it became obvious the man didn't have the presence of mind to say anything at the moment. (And having your bowels turned to water by six feet of muscled beauty will do that to you every time, believe me.) I turned to Mr. Willamette. "What are his options?"

"Well, like I told him, there's a phone in the station that he's welcome to use to call a tow that'll take him up the road to the next town over. They got a mechanic works full-time there. Have him fixed up quick." He shrugged. "Believe me, I could use the money, but I ain't no mechanic so it'd be useless to keep the car here. It'd only gather dust."

I turned back to the stranger. "Sounds pretty reasonable to me."

"It's *not* reasonable. I can't afford to wait around this two bit little town while some toothless old geezer decides to dust off his '23 pickup and jaunt down here to tow my car to another two bit town. I have a meeting that I'm already," he looked at his watch, "three hours late for." He looked back up. "I want my car fixed and I want it fixed now, damnit!"

"And I already told you that I can't fix it, Mister. Now or ever. I don't know what part of that ain't getting through, but the mechanic fairy ain't gonna crap on my head just because you're whinin' about it like some kid that lost his mommy, eh?"

Stepping forward before Ice could carry out her unvoiced threat, I pushed the man back against his car myself when it looked like he was going to damn the torpedoes and push foolishly ahead. "Look. We're all human beings here, right? Now, if you just relax and act like the gentleman I know is down there somewhere, I just might be able to help you out here, alright?"

The stranger looked at Ice over the top of my head, and whatever he saw there made him blanch several shades of white. Still, the maggot inside him wouldn't let go completely. "And what would *you* know about anything, blondie? You probably don't even know which part's the engine."

Resisting the urge to backhand him myself, I settled for a conciliatory smile. "Maybe not, but I might know someone who does. And if you play nice, I just might be persuaded to ask for help."

His eyes narrowed. "Yeah? From who?"

I jerked my head to the left. "From her."

His eyes widened back up. "Her? That..."

"Now, now, now. Do you want your car fixed or do you want to spend the rest of your life as a stain on the road here?" Releasing him, I stepped away, standing next to Ice and crossing my arms. "Your choice."

He looked at the three of us individually before settling his gaze back on me once again. "I...um...I..." His eyes examined the ground at his feet. "I guess I could use the help."

In the silence, I was sure I could hear the sound of the male ego deflating.

It was glorious.

When no one answered, he looked back up at us, his eyebrows raised. "What?"

"Aren't you forgetting something?" I asked.

"What?!"

"Well, the polite thing to do would be to ask for help, don't you think?"

His jaw dropped again. "But...you said..." He sighed. "Alright." He looked to Ice. "Can you fix my car?" He hesitated a moment, then looked at his watch. "Please?"

Ice looked at him, assessing, then turned to Mr. Willamette. "You have tools?"

"Mechanic left 'em here when he got hurt. Welcome to use 'em. The garage, too."

She nodded, then turned back to gaze impassively at the stranger. "Alright."

The resulting smile transformed his face into something almost resembling handsome. If you squinted real hard and threw in a healthy dose of cosmetic surgery for good measure. "Great! I'll just go use the telephone to let my clients know I haven't dropped off the face of the earth."

As he started forward, he was stopped yet again, this time by a strong hand gripping the arm of his jacket. The smile disappeared. "What now?!"

Ice narrowed her eyes at his tone. "Unless Volvo has made some drastic changes in the last five years, I don't think that car of yours is just gonna drive itself into the garage, do you?"

"But my clients!"

"You either help me put this car in the garage where I can

take a look at it, or you start walking. Maybe you'll get lucky and some trucker who hasn't seen his wife in six months will give you a lift." Her smile wasn't a pleasant one, but by the stranger's expression, it seemed to get the point across quite nicely.

With shoulders slumped in bitter-tasting defeat, the man walked back over to his car, opened the door and began to push it in the direction of the waiting garage.

A short time later, shorter than I expected, actually, the car was back out under the mid-spring sky, motor humming complacently. The stranger, one George Roger Grayson by name, was just putting his wallet back into his coat pocket after having considered, I could tell, pitching yet another fit over the cost Mr. Willamette had quoted him. In the end, though, he paid and we watched as he pulled away in a cloud of dust.

"Good riddance to bad rubbish," the shop owner observed, pulling his ball-cap back onto his head. "This is yours, I believe." He handed the somewhat sizable stack of bills to Ice, who just looked at the offering, not accepting. "C'mon now. You did all the work. All I did was supply the place."

"And the tools."

Wetting his thumb, he peeled back a couple bills, stuffed them into his pocket, and again held out the money to Ice who, with reluctance, finally accepted it.

"There's work for you if you want it. Not now, maybe, but come summer, I'll be up to my eyeballs in broken down cars. Could use a pair of hands like yours around here. You're some skilled."

The corner of Ice's lip curled. "I'm not exactly the employee type."

"Never said you had to be. I get a car, I call you. If you're around, you can come help. If not," he shrugged, "only costs a dime to get a tow. Good money in it. Cash on the barrelhead." His eyes glinted with the light of a man who enjoyed getting one over on the government. "Deal?"

After thinking on it a moment, Ice finally nodded. "Deal."

They shook to seal it.

"Name's Willamette, by the way. But most folks call me Pop."

"Morgan. This is...."

"The Moore girl. Tyler, right? I remember you when you were some smaller comin' up here with your folks in summer.

Place burned down a few years back. You thinkin' to rebuild?"

I smiled. "We're hoping to, yes."

He nodded sagely. "Be good to have the place back up again." He turned to look at Ice again. "I heard what you done for the Halloran boy. The whole town's been buzzin' about it for weeks. Like a bunch of hornets, they are. Bet no one's thought to thank you yet, so let me be the first. Most strangers wouldn't have thought to do what you did, puttin' themselves in danger and all. So thanks."

Ice looked a little taken aback by what passed for effusive praise from the normally reticent man and brushed off his praise with a shrug. "Did what I had to do."

"More 'n most people would have. It'll be good havin' you here. You, too, Tyler." He tipped his cap in a courtly gesture. "Best be getting back to work now, such as it is. Be seein' you."

As he walked back to his shop, I shook my head and laughed. Ice turned to look at me. "What?"

"Only you, Ice."

A raised eyebrow asked me to continue.

"Only you could break up a fight and wind up with a job."

If she were the blushing type, I probably would have gotten one out of her for that, but since she wasn't, all I received was a scowl and a half muttered comment that was probably better unheard. I laughed again. "Can I treat you to a cup of coffee, Ms. Mechanic? Maybe we'll get better service this time out."

Without bothering to reply, Ice started off toward the café, leaving me to trail behind, a growing smile covering my face.

The next several weeks saw our lives settle into a comfortable routine, which was very welcome, given the adventures we'd had since we met. Ice had been called into the shop several times by Pop and, true to his word, been paid quite handsomely for her work. Her reputation as an excellent mechanic was beginning to spread, and I could imagine, given the look she sometimes wore, that she wondered why this gift hadn't befallen her several years back, when she had tried to make a go of the very same career, only to be rebuffed at every turn. Which, of course, led her straight into the arms of the Mob and the events that led to our meeting in the Bog.

Jealously, I was glad that events turned out the way they had, if only because if she hadn't come into prison when she did, we would never have met. That's a horrible way to feel, to actually be glad of someone's murdering past, but I've never been anything but honest with myself, and those feelings *were* there, even if I'd rather have had my toenails pulled out than to mention them to her, even in passing.

Over Ruby's staunch objections, Ice began to use some of her earnings to buy food and sundries for our hostess, brushing each complaint off as if she hadn't heard the woman practically screaming in her ear. She showed remarkable patience with Ruby who could, I'll freely admit, be a bit trying at times. I don't know what happened to cause them to come to a sort of mutual understanding, but whatever it was, I was grateful for it.

We'd spend many evenings in front of the fire, where yet another of Ice's multitude of talents was revealed: drawing. She would tell me to close my eyes and describe the house I'd known and, with a pencil and sketchpad that she'd bought at the general store, she brought to life the visions that were inside my head. The detail was so exact that I couldn't help but be astounded, as well as a little nonplused. Perhaps the woman *could* read minds, after all.

The only real drawback to this idyllic time was the fact that we still slept in separate rooms. Not by Ruby's doing, either. No, she had even gone so far as to offer us the use of her own room, the only one large enough to fit more than a single bed into. Rather, it was my stubbornness—pure cussedness my mother called it when I was getting on her last nerve—that kept us apart. We hadn't made love since that time in the hunter's shack, and my hormones were complaining daily, to the point where I seriously considered booking a weekend at *The Silver Pine* just to have her in my arms again. But still, I refused.

That my actions were paralleling Ice's in refusing an offered gift crossed my mind not at all. At least not then.

And so when the evening was over and we went to our single beds, closing the doors behind us, I was, in a sense, returning to my prison cell all over again. Only this time, it was a prison of my own making.

And then the nightmares started.

During the light of day, Ice's fugitive status, and therefore my own, stayed deep down inside of me, aided, no doubt, by my continuing bliss in my freedom. But in the silence of the night, when the past comes out of its gloomy shadows, my dreams made me see what I refused to awake.

I'd often wake in a cold sweat, clutching a damp sheet to my chest and breathing as if I'd run a marathon. Every creak in the old house became an ominous sign. I'd lay awake, my heart rabbiting in my chest, waiting for the sound of sirens, or the pounding on the door announcing the arrival of the police. I tried to force the thoughts away, but they wouldn't go. They'd stay and taunt me with their vividness, their plausibility, their ultimate truth.

But many times, on nights that were the worst, when the scream I so badly needed to utter stayed locked behind my lips in a prison of its own, I'd hear my door softly open and then she'd be there, coming to me and taking me into her arms, stroking my hair and soothing my demons. It was only on those nights when I could slip away into a dreamless sleep, comforted by the solid, living reality of her in my arms.

We never spoke about those nights and haven't to this day. Somehow she knew, and continues to know, exactly when I need to be comforted the most, and offers herself completely and without reservation.

I suspect she knows exactly what demons haunt my sweat-drenched nights. I suspect they haunt hers, too. And perhaps, if we confront them, unspoken but together, they will remain specters in the night and never leave their cave to stand in the daylight.

Perhaps.

Chapter
5

On a particular Saturday morning in late spring, I awoke with a knot of happy anticipation curling in my stomach. After several intense discussions, a heated argument or two, and a final pooling of our less than vast monetary resources, this would be the day we would finally break ground on the cabin.

After a thorough inspection of the foundation already laid, Ice declared it unfit for a new home, the snow and water damage having crumbled and weakened it in some parts. She had spent the past several days, when not working, using a pickaxe to break up the pieces of concrete and move them out of the way so that the ground would be fresh for the new foundation to be laid on the ashes of the old.

A smile on my lips, I jumped from my bed and quickly showered and completed my morning routine, throwing on an old pair of shorts I'd somehow managed to save and my grungiest T-shirt. As I stepped from the bathroom, I wasn't all that surprised to see Ice standing in the hallway, a slight smile curving her lips.

She looked fantastic in a pair of cut-off shorts and a tight, black tank top that displayed her body to its best advantage. Many days of hard labor had further defined her already chiseled body and my eyes devoured what they were seeing like a starving man might when presented with the banquet of his delirious dreams.

Closing the distance between us, she took me into her arms and lowered her head, capturing my lips effortlessly in a kiss of slowly burning passion. I grabbed her waist and pulled her closer, my entire being reacting to the feelings she was sparking within.

God, it felt so good to have her love me.

After several moments, she pulled away, holding me at arms' length and smiling down on me, her eyes gone silver in the dim lighting of the hallway. "Ready?"

My head spun. "Oh yeah."

Grabbing her hand, I tried to tug her into my own bedroom, not caring at that moment if the Pope himself was sleeping in the next room, such was my need for her. My forward progress was quickly halted by a swift tug on my hand, and I spun back to face her, my disappointment, I was sure, showing clearly on my face.

Her silvered eyes glinted in fond amusement. "I was referring to the cabin."

"Oh. That." I sighed, then stepped closer, noticing a thick vein which trailed over her bicep; a vein which practically begged me to run my tongue over it just so I could feel her pulse bounding. "Right now?"

"Right now," she confirmed, ducking her head down to kiss me senseless once more.

"But—"

"The faster we get this cabin built, the faster we get to finish what we've started here, my Angel."

Sexual bribery provided me the impetus to set a new record in the "down the hall, through the house and out the door" dash.

A record which, I believe, stands to this day.

My fingers drummed a riff on the hood of the bastardized truck Ice had brought with her from work one day. "It followed me home," she said, that half cocky grin lighting her eyes.

A mongrel it was, too, and an ugly one at that, with parts scavenged from half a dozen other cars and trucks which sat on the grounds around Pop's station collecting rust. He'd let her tinker with the engine and, when it was up and running, she bartered it for a couple of days' free labor. No fool, Pop, he snatched that offer before it had time to fully leave her lungs.

At least that's how Ice tells it. I never quite got up the nerve to ask the deal maker himself.

"C'mon, Ice. Christmas'll be here before you know it." I didn't have to raise my voice. I knew she'd hear me easily.

A moment later and she sauntered out of the house, twirling the keys on her finger and sporting a definite cat-ate-the-canary grin. At any other time, I might have called her on it, but I was much too anxious to get this particular show on the road. I'd waited too long and too hard for this day to let the smugness of my partner ruin it for me.

Much, anyway.

I settled for throwing her my best scowl as she purposely brushed against me while reaching around to open the passenger's side door. As I was about to sound off with a particularly, I believed, witty retort, she froze in place, head cocked. I could almost see her ears twitch to hone in on whatever sound she'd caught.

I knew that look, having seen it more times than I'd care to count. "What?"

She brushed by me again, only this time walking toward the small hill that separated Ruby's property from our own. More than a little curious, I followed behind.

I almost ran into her back as she stopped at the crest of the small rise and, looking around her long body, I stopped too, my jaw dropping open. "I...think I'm seeing things." I rubbed my eyes, hard, then blinked.

The scene before me didn't change. Not one iota.

"If you are, then so am I," Ice replied, her voice flat.

The sound of our voices attracted some attention, and a man turned around, a broad grin on his face. It was Pop, dressed in a pair of heavy-duty overalls and a thick sweatshirt. "Mornin', eh? 'Bout time you two got up. Thought we was gonna have to start without ya."

As I groped dumbly around for something to say, his grin broadened. "Cat got your tongue?"

"What's...going on here?"

"Never seen a barn raising before?" he asked.

More silence.

"Is he speaking English?" I asked Ice out of the corner of my mouth.

"No."

I started a bit at that, then realized she wasn't replying to me.

Shaking his head, Pop pulled off his ball-cap and trotted up the small hill, coming to a stop before the both of us. "Sorry about springing it on you like this. I tried to tell 'em to wait and ask you first, but..." He shrugged. "That's not the way things work around here, mostly. They get a bee in their bonnet and it's full speed ahead, damn the consequences, if you'll pardon my French."

I pinched myself. It hurt. Dreaming was out, then. Alien abduction, however, was still in the running.

I looked from Pop to Ice the way a neophyte might who is trying to divine the truth of the meaning of life from an important yogi. When nothing was forthcoming, I cleared my throat and watched as two pairs of eyes lit upon mine. "Would either of you mind terribly filling me in here?"

After a moment, Pop nodded and flung out his hand, gesturing to the mob who stood below us, all trying to pretend they weren't doing their level best to eavesdrop, and failing miserably. I looked from the group back to Pop, eyebrows raised. "Folks around here ain't much on thank-you's," he explained. "Not with words, anyway. So, this is their way of sayin' it without really sayin' it. Understand?"

Unfortunately, the answer to that one was still a resounding "no." My expression told him as much.

He sighed, then tried again. "They wanna help break ground on your cabin. As a way to pay ya back for savin' the boy's life."

Success!

"We don't need any thanks," Ice said, her tone still expressionless. She looked angry, and for once, I could understand why, even if the townspeople hadn't meant to hurt us with their gesture, which I'm sure they didn't. I knew how much she'd been looking forward to building that cabin, pitting herself against wood and steel and bending them to her will, forming something out of nothing with her own hands.

To tell the truth, I had been looking forward to it, too.

"I tried to tell 'em that. Tried to tell 'em it'd be best if they asked first." He shook his head. "They're good people, though, if stubborner than a pack of mules sometimes." He gestured to the crowd again. "That Clayton Dodd, he's a right fair carpenter; been buildin' here for years, him and his dad both. And Mary Lynch is the best electrician in these parts, bar none. The Drew boys own their own plumbing company and service most of the towns around here." He looked back at Ice, his gaze beseeching. "They won't take nothin' away from ya. Follow your orders to the letter, they will. Work like dogs when you want 'em to, stop when ya don't. Just got to give the word, either way, and we'll follow it." He put his cap back on, straightening the brim with a brief tug. "I understand what it's like ta want ta build something with your own sweat. Did my own house that way. But ...sometimes a little help is a good thing, too. And it ain't charity, so don't go thinkin' it is. It's just a thank-you said in the only way these folks know how, that's all."

After a long, silent moment, Ice abruptly spun on her heel and strode back toward Ruby's house, never once looking behind her.

Pop sighed, removed his cap again, and twisted it in his hands. "Knew I should'a made 'em ask first."

"Ice...isn't very comfortable accepting surprise gifts," I replied, stating the obvious just for something to say. "She's a pretty private person."

"I know." He shrugged. "It was worth a shot, anyway. Thanks for at least listenin', Tyler. I'll get the folks and leave you two alone. Sorry for the intrusion. Won't happen again."

"Wait," I said, looking toward the house and seeing a shadow pass against the open door. Ice reappeared, something in her hand. When she got even with us, she shoved it at me, then breezed by us both.

"Let's get on with it, shall we?"

Stunned, I looked down. Her sketchpad, filled with all the drawings of our future home sat in my hands. I looked at Pop. He looked back. Then we both turned and watched as she was swallowed up by the grinning crowd of eager helpers.

"Well, whadda ya know," Pop half-whispered.

Indeed.

It was the first week in July before the lake was warm enough to swim in. For me, anyway. Our neighbors had been sampling the "refreshing" water since May, but that didn't surprise me, since I was convinced a common Canadian ancestor had once mated with a Polar Bear somewhere along the line anyway.

As for Ice, she'd taken to washing off her sweat in the lake since early June, which in and of itself posed somewhat of a problem, since she regularly shucked down to her civvies in full view of the working crew before diving in. Doc Brown, the town's dentist, had to take a week off after bashing his thumb a good one with his hammer, and one of the Drew boys almost met an unfortunate end when his brother let go of the ladder he was holding in order to take in the splendor that was my lover.

I nearly burst my spleen trying to hold back my laughter over that one and, finally, for the health of the men and women, as well as our cabin, had to inform my partner exactly what havoc her mid-day swims were causing in the crew, asking her nicely to please wait until work was done for the day before showing off what the good lord and years of hard work have given her.

She accepted, somewhat graciously I thought, though our helpers threatened to stage a revolt over the sudden halt to their daily entertainment.

The cabin's building was going better than I expected, though the work had started to ease off some, given that the tourist season was beginning and most of our helpers were up to their eyebrows in paying tasks that had priority over this, as it should be.

Though the Fourth of July was, obviously, an American holiday, it marked the beginning of the tourist season in this part of the land, and the town was soon filled to overcrowding with a great many Americans anxious to spend their hard-earned dollars on a bit of rest and relaxation.

That sounded good to me as well. At least, the R & R part did. So when Ice suggested a day's break from our building labors, in celebration of the holiday, I jumped at the chance with all the grace of a wounded gazelle trying to escape the jaws of a hungry lion.

Enthusiastically, to say the least.

I grinned evilly to myself as I slipped on the bottom half of my secretly purchased bikini. Of course, *half* wasn't the best word for what I was now wearing. "Pitifully thin strip of clingy material barely covering one's more delicate parts" would have been a more apt, if a bit long-winded, description.

Still, as I wasn't planning on a vigorous game of water polo, the positive effects of wearing little more than dental floss and a smile far outweighed the negatives, in my opinion. The biggest positive, of course, being the look that was sure to appear on Ice's face when she saw me in it. The second biggest being what she might want to do to, for, and with me after seeing me in it for several hours.

Ah, yes, this particular Angel had fallen. Hard.

Grabbing a towel, I ran out of the house, blithely ignoring the scandalized looks thrown my by the members of Ruby's bridge party as I passed through. I got partway down the long hill that separated the house from the private beach before realizing my error in neglecting to don footwear for the trek. Dried pine needles pricked at my feet in retaliation for thoughtlessly crushing them. I hopped around trying to brush them off, but the sticky resin coating the needles made the effort a lost cause.

Hearing laughter and splashing from the direction of the water, I resolved to grin and bear it, and resumed my quick trot down to the beach where my lover waited.

She sat on our dock, one leg tucked under her, the other playing idly through the water as she watched the colorful parade of sailboats glide around the lake. The sun was continuing to bestow its blessings upon her, tanning her skin to a rich mahogany brown that blended nicely with the black racing suit she was wearing. Her hair was wet from a no-doubt recent swim and brushed back from her face in a shining mass of inky black, bringing her features, even in profile, into sharp relief.

So intent on watching her, I impaled my big toe on a rather large pinecone lying in wait for my tender foot. Cursing a blue streak, I hopped around on one foot while disentangling myself from my spiny intruder. Task completed, I looked up to see Ice watching me, amusement sparkling in her eyes.

Not quite the entrance I'd imagined.

Gathering up the last tattered shreds of my dignity, I pulled myself together and settled for my most sultry walk instead, hoping to make up lost ground.

Sultry isn't easy to do when you're limping.

I was about to chuck the whole thing and settle for some good old fashioned groveling when the look in her eyes stopped me dead in my tracks, my sore toe completely, utterly forgotten.

It was a look that could have incinerated an iceberg, had any been laying handily about. My entire body pulsed with the intensity of it and my knees hit the oatmeal stage. The temperature, already pleasantly warm, shot up another twenty degrees in a split second.

Then she stood and the sight of her long, lean body, all oiled skin and rippling muscles, dried up every single bit of moisture my body had ever thought to produce.

The upper half, anyway.

"Very nice," she purred, still raking my body with her searing gaze. "Very nice indeed, little Angel."

Oh, for the gift of words. I'd have given a kingdom, had one been mine to give. Lacking that, I settled for trying to remain standing as she stalked over to me, the most sensual smile I'd ever seen curving her full lips. When the tiniest sliver of her tongue darted out to wet them, I was sure that the sand and I were destined to become one.

From somewhere, I heard a whimper and, from the darkening of her eyes, I realized it had come from me.

Then her hands were hot on my shoulders, scorching through me and branding my soul. She slowly—*God* so slowly—lowered her lips to mine and merged us together by the passion of our kiss.

I didn't care that we were doing this in full view of everyone on the lake. Didn't care that there might well be repercussions later. I wanted her, *needed* her in a way that surprised even me.

To be truthful, kissing Ice this way in public was a bit of a turn-on for me, as if it were even possible for me to be more turned-on than I already was. The irony of my feelings didn't escape me, either. With very few, and therefore all the more precious, exceptions, making love in prison meant doing it in full view of whoever happened to wander by. And during those times, when it was possible for me to think at all, I wished for privacy. Now, with the possibility of a private rendezvous just a closed and locked door away (when we actually obtained doors and their attendant locks, that is) I found myself reveling in a more public display.

Then she deepened the kiss, melding our bodies together, and I stopped thinking of anything at all.

When she finally broke away, the only thing keeping me upright were her firm grip on my shoulders. Shaking my head to clear it—a lost cause—I cleared my throat instead, tasted my lips, and opened my eyes to see her smiling down at me. "You know you're killing me, right?"

Her only answer was a smirk.

"I'm about one second away from chucking this whole 'day off' thing and getting back to building the cabin. There's only so much of this extended foreplay I can stand here, and I'm just about at my limit."

When will I ever get it through this thick head of mine that statements like that only served to incite the woman who lived for a challenge? She closed in and kissed me again, so deeply that the only sound I could hear was the rapid and thundering beat of my heart in my ears.

This time, it was *my* turn to pull away, which I did, but not without great reluctance, and, shrugging out of her grip, made an abrupt right turn and threw myself into the lake. The chilly water did nothing to dampen my ardor, but it did wonders for my spinning head. I came up after a long moment and wiped the hair back from my eyes, treading water and looking toward shore. Ice was standing there, hands on hips, shaking her head at me.

"Better now?"

"Not really, no."

She grinned, obviously quite pleased with herself.

"Care to join me?" I asked, wondering if it was possible to get the jump on her in the water and give her the dunking of her life for putting me through such wonderful torture. Barring that, I was more than willing to see just how long I could hold my breath underwater by returning her torture a thousand-fold. A flock of goose bumps broke over my wet skin at the image flashing behind my eyes.

"I have a better idea, if you're interested." She cocked her head to the left and, looking in that direction, I noticed for the first time the colorful sails of a small boat floating complacently in the small cove next to the dock. I recognized it immediately as being a 16' Hobie Cat, a sailboat that I'd always loved as a child.

"Where in the world did you get that?" I asked. Hobie Cats weren't cheap. My father told me as much every time I would beg him to trade in our old Sunfish for one. And certainly not on *our* shoestring budget.

"I was informed by a certain irritating old woman that you loved to sail and if I had the sense God gave a rooster, I'd go into the garage, dig this old fossil out, and take you out on it."

"You're kidding."

"Nope."

"You know how to sail?"

"Yup."

"Why doesn't that surprise me?"

One broad shoulder lifted in a careless shrug. "Dunno."

I grinned. "That's one of the things I love most about you, Ice. Your utter verbosity."

She shot me a mock scowl. "You wanna go sailing or not?"

"Aye, aye, Cap'n!" I tipped off a jaunty salute just for the irritation factor.

Oh. I was *so* dead.

Wow!

Painfully inadequate as far as descriptions of joy went, but about the only word I could come up with as the water's spray needled into my grinning face. Balanced precariously on one of the pontoons and leaning back to avoid toppling head first into the glistening water below, I watched the lake race by beneath the boat, my eyes wide as silver dollars and the grin threatening to permanently etch itself into the lines of my face.

To my left, Ice's long body lay almost full out in the racing sling, keeping the boat balanced on one pontoon while using the rigging to keep us going in the right direction, all at an incredible and mind-numbing (for me, at least) speeds.

I felt the true power of nature there, as if the rushing wind, beaming sun and spraying water were all conspiring to give me a high that was near to being untouchable in my experience. The only thing close would be making love, but this was a great, if somewhat distant, second.

Ice followed the gentle curve of the lake's central island, a tiny, tree covered affair, and bled the boat's speed until it was resting on both pontoons once again.

"Why are we stopping?" I asked, not a little disappointed.

"Your turn."

"My... But I don't know how to sail."

She turned her head slowly to pin me with her gaze, one eyebrow raised high on her forehead.

I looked back, feeling a little defensive. "Well, I don't! I begged my father to teach me, but he said that sailing was for men. Women just had to learn how to look pretty while sitting in the boat."

My partner snorted. "What a crock of shit."

I shrugged. "Yeah, but he was my father. There wasn't anyone around who wanted to cross him, on that point anyway, so I just got used to sitting in the boat and looking pretty." I looked down at my feet, unaccountably embarrassed over the revelation.

A warm hand under my chin urged my head back up. I looked into eyes the color of the summer sky and swallowed hard. "There are few things in my life I have to be grateful for, Angel, but right now I'd have to say that not having the dubious pleasure of meeting your father ranks near the top of that short list." She dropped her hand and her smile became bittersweet. "I sometimes wonder how you came to be the person you are with the upbringing you had. And at the same time, I can't help but think that my own parents are rolling in their graves over what I've become." She turned her head and looked toward the sun, her face once again a stone mask.

Moved beyond words over the precious glimpse into her heart, I could only reach out my hand and gently lay it on her arm in a woefully inadequate gesture of support and thanks.

A moment later, she turned back toward me, the pain in her eyes pushed back into whatever place she kept it. She shot that endearing half-grin at me. "C'mon. Let's teach you how to sail."

I sat on the sofa, legs curled beneath me, reading the same passage for the seventh time (or was it the tenth?) and trying desperately not to look at the clock that was ticking impudently at me from its place on the mantle. *She'll be back. We've fought before. She just needs some time to cool off. She'll be back.*

Maybe if I thought it hard enough,. I could even make myself believe it.

After all, it wasn't as if we hadn't ever had words before.

There were times in the Bog, more often than I'd like to admit, when we seemed to be avoiding one another more often than we sought one another out. As partnerships went, we had more than our share of bones of contention hanging in skeleton filled closets. A fight wasn't anything new, or particularly unexpected. Even now.

So why was I so worried? Why were my guts a tangled knot somewhere in the vicinity of my larynx? Why was that damn clock moving so damn slow?

I had awoken that morning with a vague feeling of unease, which had begun to plague me during the preceding week. A nebulous feeling of anxiety, perhaps mixed with a touch of depression, it left me feeling out-of-sorts. It wasn't something I could articulate, even to Ice, who'd noticed my mood quickly and had asked what was going on with me.

With Ruby off visiting friends and Ice again working at the garage, I was left alone with my thoughts, there being little else to do on a rainy July day but think.

And then it hit me.

I wasn't anxious or depressed. At least, not primarily.

What I was feeling was useless.

Leaning my head back against the rough fabric of the couch, I mulled the revelation over, not liking the bitter taste it left on my tongue, but forced to admit the truth of it nonetheless.

It stirred within me feelings, emotions I'd thought long buried beneath the weight of time and experience.

As a teen, I'd railed against my father's indictment that a woman didn't need a job to find happiness. Happiness was a pregnant belly, a hearth and home, and a husband to care for. Peter carried on that corollary, and except for the pregnant part, fulfilled my father's dreams for me to absolute perfection.

The irony of finding freedom in a prison never escaped me. It was there that I was nurtured and given the freedom to grow into the woman I believe I was meant to be.

And now, I was forced to face the fact that once outside those confining and, yes, comforting walls, I'd fallen back into old habits and perhaps an old view of myself, much too quickly.

And this time, I had no one to blame but myself.

Leaving the matter of blame behind for a moment, I tried to think of ways to rectify the situation. Unfortunately, however, all the alleys I went down led to dead ends. After all, I wasn't in Canada legally. I wasn't a national. I wasn't even a landed immigrant. I had snuck over the boarder like a draft dodger, aiding and abetting the escape of a fugitive from justice, no less. Not something likely employers were apt to turn a blind eye towards.

Ice was lucky, in that Pop didn't give a horse's behind who or what she was, as long as she was good at what she did, which she undeniably was, and still is. Problem was, however, that there most likely wasn't more than one "Pop" in a town this size. Without immigrant papers, without even so much as a passport, I was dead in the water, so to speak.

My mood went from bad to worse and, when the rain stopped, I went outside and took my frustrations out on the cabin, pounding nails until my hands were blistered and raw.

And when Ice came over the breast of the hill, a jaunty step to her walk and a wad of cash in her hand for a night on the town, I'm afraid I did a butcher's job of ripping her head off.

Figuratively, of course.

And in that nanosecond of eternity between the words "oh" and "shit" when I realized just what I had done and whom I had done it to, my anger was gone, replaced with a recrimination so deep, I could have drowned in it, if it would have let me.

If Ice had decided to return the favor, I most likely wouldn't be writing this today.

Instead, with a patience rarely shown to anyone but me, she offered a strong shoulder and a listening ear, if I would just reach out and take them.

And I repaid her kindness with words that shame me to this day, proving that my anger hadn't left entirely, coward that it was. Only waited for another chance to ambush her in a fit of jealousy so green the world seemed bathed in it, a bloody wound for which there is no salvation.

Her face set in stony lines, she turned away from me, dropping the money she'd hoped to spend on a nice evening for both of us at my feet, then walked away without saying another word.

And so it was that I found myself sitting alone on a couch in Ruby's house, staring at words in a book I had no desire to read, listening to soft orchestral music from the kitchen that I had no desire to hear, and watching a clock giving up minutes as sparingly as a miser extends loans.

So deep within the well of my thoughts was I that I didn't hear the knocking on the door, and nearly jumped from my perch on the couch when Ruby's graying head poked itself from the door to the kitchen, a slight smile creasing her lips. "There's someone here to see you, Tyler."

I was halfway across the room, my apology ready to birth itself from my throat before I was stopped by the vision, not of Ice, but of a young woman walking into the room, a clutch of books clasped awkwardly to her chest.

Stopping in my tracks, I gaped at her, my mind changing gears with the swiftness of a semi lumbering uphill. From somewhere unknown, my manners managed to reassert themselves, and a smile, which was most likely, totally false bloomed on my face. " ...hello..."

The young woman returned my smile, though hers was notably more genuine. "Hello, Ms. Moore," she said with a shyness known only to pretty young woman of her age.

"Do I...know you from somewhere?" Oh yes, the old eighteen wheeler was still chugging uphill alright. In first gear.

The girl blushed. "Um, yes, ma'am. We met in the café a few months ago. I'm afraid I wasn't very polite to you."

Then it clicked. The young woman looking at me through half-lowered eyelids was the same waitress I'd taken for twice her age when we first came into town. *Amazing how slathering makeup on with a trowel ages a person*, my still-laboring mind supplied cheerily. *Someone should tell her that this looks much better than the "rode hard, put away wet" one she seems to favor.*

Silence made its presence felt in the suddenly-too-hot room.

Oh. She's waiting for some kind of response. "Um...nice to see you again." *Ok, that didn't come out very well. Shall we try again?* "Is...there something I can help you with?"

The woman blushed again. "I...um...heard you were a teacher?"

From who? Then I remembered telling Ruby a severely edited tale of the teaching I'd done prior to making the move up to Canada. She didn't need to know that my students were hardened criminals, after all. Our gracious, if nosy, host probably passed that information on during one of her weekly gossip exchange sessions that masqueraded as bridge tournaments. "I've done some teaching," I allowed, curious as to where this particular conversation was going, since I didn't have the faintest clue.

The girl's face lit up. "Cool!"

The silence stretched out once again.

"Was there something you needed?" I asked, finally, imagining I could feel moss start to grow on the north side of my body.

"Oh! Yeah. Um...I need some help. I...kinda...dropped out of school last year. I got bored with it, I guess." She shrugged. "Wasn't learning that much anyway. Figured I'd be better off taking the waitress job full time and having some money in my pocket."

I nodded. "And now you think you made a mistake."

She snorted. "A big one. I don't wanna be a waitress all my life, but without a diploma, no one will look twice at me, so I'm kinda stuck."

"Why don't you just go back to school, then?"

"It's not that easy. See, I raised kind of a big stink about leaving. I'd be too embarrassed to go back now."

I nodded again, then waited for her to state whatever case she was interested in bringing to the bar.

She took in a deep breath, then let it out slowly. "So ...when I heard that you were a teacher, I wondered if maybe you could help me out. See, there's a way I can get my diploma without having to go back to school. There's a test I can take, and if I pass it, I get my diploma. And I really only need help with two classes. English and World History." She showed me the textbooks she still held close to her body. "I borrowed these from my brother. He was smart and stayed in school." She took in another breath. "So, if you're interested or anything, I was hoping you might be able to help me out. You know, like tutor me? I'd pay for your help. My parents even offered to put up some money," she hastened to add, her face as earnest as her plea to me. "I'll come every day after work, if you want. Stay as long as you need me to. Anything."

I thought about it for a long moment, staring into her eyes and watching as she fought hard not to fidget beneath the weight of my gaze. I realized that the answers to some of my problems was standing before me and refused to look a gift equine in the cuspids. "Sure. Why not? We can start tomorrow, if you want." Another thought struck me. "Ruby?"

The graying head popped out, too quickly, from the kitchen beyond. "My house is yours, Tyler. You know that. You're welcome to use the study."

I resisted shooting my most menacing glare at my snooping hostess. Instead, I tried my most gracious smile on for size. It was almost a perfect fit. "Thanks!" I turned back to the girl. "Looks like we have a deal then...um...I don't know your name."

"Oh! I'm sorry. It's Kelly." She stuck out her hand and promptly dropped her books.

We knocked heads reaching down to pick them up.

Then burst out laughing.

If only making things up to Ice could be so simple.

After Kelly had left, thanking me profusely and apologizing yet again about the rapidly swelling knot on my head, I poked my head into the kitchen and smiled down at Ruby who was studiously working on a crossword puzzle and drinking coffee. "Thanks."

She looked up, her eyes magnified behind the reading glasses she wore for close work. "For letting you use the study? You're welcome, but you really didn't need to ask."

"Well, for that, too. But really, thanks for spreading the word that I was a teacher. I was worried about not having a job, and you helped me get one."

"Wish I could take the credit for that one, Tyler, but I really haven't told anybody anything about you or Morgan. It's up to you to share whatever you want with them. It's none of their business, otherwise."

"But if you didn't..."

But even as I asked, I knew. Knew it with every fiber of my being. Knew there was only one person who would go to such lengths to assure my happiness.

Ice.

If my lover ever made it home that fateful evening, I don't know. We've never spoken of it, even to this day when so much water has gone over, under, and around the bridge that spans our life together.

All I know for sure is that she hadn't returned when at last my eyes rebelled against my edict to stay open *or else*, leading me down into a fitful sleep filled with night terrors. If she came to my bed to soothe my dreams, I never woke to feel it, and when I awoke the next morning, she was gone from the house as if she'd never been. Even Ruby didn't know; or if she did, she wasn't talking.

The only thing that stilled my fears, if only by the tiniest of measures, was that her room was exactly as she'd left it, all her possessions stored away with the almost military precision so characteristic of her. How I resisted the almost overwhelming impulse to bury my face in the lone T-shirt that lay at the bottom of her hamper, I'll never know, but with a firm resolution I thought near lost, I turned from the room, determined to track her down and settle the lingering business between us.

I should have known that trying to hunt down a woman who was, in her former life, a Mafia assassin was a fruitless task at best, but with a stubbornness that would have done my father proud, I searched almost every square inch of the town in the hopes of finding my deliberately missing lover.

And came back empty-handed and heavy-hearted to the place where it all started; the half-built cabin by the lake.

She sat near the cornerstone, her back pressed flat against the foundation, one leg cocked, the other resting flat against the ground. A pine needle twirled and whirled between long fingers as she looked down over the path that led to a lake which was whipping up whitecaps in response to the wind's intermittent gusts.

Thunderheads stacked, a child's block castle, one atop the other far across the water, but I sensed that the tempest brewing beneath the gathering clouds could well give the encroaching storm quite a run for its money.

I stared at her for long moments, running opening gambits through my mind as I tried to ignore the fact that she was ignoring my presence. The coward in me wanted to run and hide, but the woman my lover had helped develop stood her ground, wanting nothing more than to breach the walls my own words had erected around her heart.

An apology, no matter how heartfelt and brimming with tearful promises, seemed much too shallow a thing to give.

Finally, the wind whipping the forest around us into a frenzy, I stepped forward, breaking the palpable distance between us. "Thanks," I said simply, too soft to be heard over the wind's howling cry, yet knowing she would hear it anyway.

She turned to me then, and the look in her eyes, one of absolute resignation, tore at my heart more than any angry recrimination ever could. "For what?"

Swallowing against the feelings her expression was engendering in me, I took a step closer, then stopped once again. "For sending Kelly my way. That was an incredibly wonderful thing to do, especially for someone who treated you the way I did."

Lifting her shoulder in a half-hearted shrug, she nimbly leapt to her feet and pushed off of the foundation. "Glad it helped."

She closed the distance between us and moved to brush by me. In a sudden fit of what I can only describe as insanity, I reached out and grabbed her forearm to keep her from passing. She stopped, turned, then looked down at my hand on her arm. She looked into my eyes, her own flashing a message that even the most slow-witted among us could easily divine.

Snatching my hand quickly away, I opened my mouth to say something, anything, when the strangest sensation came over me. The wind, which up until then had been changing directions as if trying to make up its mind which way it wanted to blow, stopped suddenly. Every hair on my body then lifted and a curious, and not very pleasant, tingle erupted along my nerve endings.

The next thing I knew, I was being borne to the ground, covered by a living blanket of protection as something fast and bright and loud and stinking of burned wiring exploded all around me, deafening me to anything else.

Then something, I didn't know what, collapsed down on top of us, driving the breath from my lungs, and when my head impacted with the cement foundation behind me, everything went black and silent once again.

When I awoke, it was to the sound of a heavy rain rattling off of the plastic tarp that covered the partially finished roof of the cabin.

At least, that's where I thought I was. With a head that felt like day six of a five day bender and a chest that wondered if it had been used as a Chicago Bears tackling dummy some time in the recent past, I could have been trapped within a plastic bag and not known the difference. Or cared much, really.

After a moment, it occurred to me that opening my eyes might be a good idea, and so I did. Then closed them quickly when four of everything stared back at me through a blurry mist.

Something brushed against my head and I jumped, then immediately regretted it as the world around me spun threateningly out of control for a long moment. My stomach instantly rebelled, but thankfully, there wasn't anything in it, and so after a moment, it grudgingly settled back down.

When I was quite sure that everything that was in my body was going to stay there—and for a moment there, it looked like my brains were lobbying hard for an exit through my ears—I chanced opening my eyes again. When the blurriness cleared, I saw Ice looking down at me, concern etched clearly in every line of her face. I smiled weakly. "Hey."

"You alright?" she asked, the look in her eyes belying the gruffness of her voice.

"As soon as you give me the license plate number of the truck that hit me, yeah." When she didn't rise to the bait—and poor as it was, I didn't blame her—I sighed, shifting a little. "I'm fine. Really."

The touch to my head came again, and this time I recognized it for what it was, Ice's hand stroking through my hair. I then realized that the hard surface my head was pillowed upon was, in fact, her thigh. I resisted the urge to snuggle, not knowing how things were between us, even given the relative intimacy of my current position. "What happened?"

"Lightning strike. It hit the big pine next to the house and one of the limbs came down on us." She shifted a little, and I caught a carefully controlled, and almost hidden, look of pain cross her face for the briefest of moments.

"You're hurt."

"I'm fine."

"But..." I struggled to sit up, a truly hopeless task as her free hand rested itself on my chest, anchoring my body to the floor.

"I'm. Fine."

If the tone of her voice hadn't gotten through, the look in her eyes certainly finished the job, and so I obediently settled back down on her thigh. After a moment, her hand began to stroke my hair again, softly, doing more for my pounding headache than an entire mountain of painkillers. Chancing things, I reached up and covered the large hand, which rested on my chest, giving it the briefest of squeezes. "Thank you for saving my life. Again."

That got the reaction I was looking for, a small, wry smile that even reached the blue of her eyes. "Comes with the job."

I could feel my eyebrows raise behind the fringe of my hair. "Job?"

Her smile deepened minutely. "Someone's gotta look after you. Might as well be me."

I returned her smile with a rueful one of my own. "Hard job, sometimes. The working conditions aren't always the best. And the salary sucks." I swallowed hard against the tears closing my throat as the conversation suddenly took on a deeper meaning.

Her hand left my hair, and I felt her knuckles as they gently grazed against the skin of my cheek. "Maybe. But the experience it's given me is something I wouldn't trade for all the money in the world."

The tears came then, rolling hot and heavy down my cheeks and dampening the hand which continued to gently stroke my skin. "I'm so sorry, Morgan. I...I don't know what came over me yesterday. I didn't mean those words I said. Not one of them. God...I'm...I'm sorry." When had words suddenly become so inadequate? How could they cut to the bone one minute and become anemic the next?

Giving in to my misery, I shifted to my side, curling up in a fetal ball and pressing my heated face up against her lower abdomen, sobbing my heart out like a small child.

She said nothing, just continued to stroke my hair, letting me get out everything trapped inside, her very presence telling me more about her love for me than any words spoken ever could.

Finally emptied of the poison inside, I rolled back onto my back and looked up at her through tear-swollen eyes. "Can you ever forgive me?"

Reaching down, she brushed her finger tenderly against my lips. "Yes," she whispered.

The relief that ran through me was nothing short of dizzying. "Thank you."

She smiled at me, then gathered me close, and we waited out the storm in comfortable silence.

Chapter 6

Summer was rapidly drawing to a close and, with it, our time under Ruby's generous, if sometimes intrusive, hospitality. The cabin was almost complete, needing only a few finishing touches to make it into the home I had dreamed of for so long.

On a certain summer's morning, I made my way into town on an errand for Ice, to retrieve a particular tool she had left back at Pop's garage. Walking down the main street, my curiosity was caught, as it often was, by the open door of *The Silver Pine*. Ruby had filled my head with stories of the new owner's many eccentricities, and so I decided that a quick detour to assuage my curiosity would be just the ticket for my somewhat mischievous mood.

Arriving at the front door, I was just about to poke my head in for a quick look around when a large chartreuse mountain collided with me, sending me back into the courtyard, my arms flailing to keep my balance.

"Are you alright, dear?" the mountain asked in a thick Bronx accent. "I wasn't expecting any visitors this time of the day. Do I know you from somewhere? You seem terribly familiar to me. The Hamptons, perhaps?"

Completely taken aback, I could only stare dumbly at the woman as she peppered me with her rapid-fire inquisition. Not even in prison had I ever seen a woman quite so large. She easily topped even Ice's six foot-plus frame and was perhaps three or four times as wide. All done up, from head to toe, in blinding pink made her a true sight to behold, and behold it I did, my jaw slack with amazement.

Her body was literally dripping with jewels—faux or real I couldn't tell—and gaudy ones at that. Rings adorned every finger and hideous broaches attached themselves, like leeches, to her massive chest. A heavy cloud of perfume wafted from her, trapping me in its none-too-fragrant net. I rubbed my nose against the urge to sneeze.

Underneath one massive arm peeped the head of a tiny dog of indeterminate ancestry, though I guessed, by its white fluffiness, that poodle was buried somewhere deep within the mix. Just how deep, I couldn't tell. Its brown beady eyes bulged at me and I was treated to the sight of needle-sharp teeth and a curled tongue, leading me to believe, in my fuzzy-headed way, that perhaps a rat was also among this creature's less-than-noble forbearers.

Returning my stare look for look, the woman tilted her head, her eyes wide with a compassion that is only seen in the truly snobbish. "Oh, I'm so sorry, dear. Are you deaf as well?" she asked at a decibel level, which could have broken window glass several miles away. "Forgive me for my mistake. You just look so *normal.*"

Resisting the urge to toss out a snappish retort, I instead gave her a gracious smile. "I can hear. I was just...startled."

She brought her free hand up to her chest, her many bracelets tinkling discordantly with her exaggerated movements. "Oh, isn't *that* a relief! And here I thought we'd have absolutely no way of communicating."

I just smiled. And nodded. A lot.

"Where *are* my manners?" she asked after another uncomfortable pause. Sticking out a hand, she engulfed one of my own, pumping vigorously. It was like shaking hands with cold, wet bread dough. And that would be insulting to the dough. "My name is Millicent Harding Post. Hard on the 'T', dear, as in 'titillating.'" She chirped a bird-like laughter through ruby red lips.

Disengaging my hand, I resisted the urge to wipe it off on my shorts. "It's a pleasure to meet you, Ms. Post," I replied, making sure to stress the "T."

"Oh please, dearie. We're all friends here, aren't we? Millicent will do just fine. And you are?"

"Tyler Moore."

Her eyes, magnified behind half-glasses, widened comically. "Oh you poor, poor dear. What *were* your parents thinking?"

Probably the same thing your parents were when they decided to name you "Millicent," you pompous old windbag.

Not that I said that aloud, of course. Though, to be perfectly honest, there was a moment there where I was sorely tempted. I smiled in wry acknowledgement of her false pity and steered the conversation into another, and hopefully safer, direction. "Are you the new owner of *The Silver Pine*?"

Millicent turned to look over one meaty shoulder at the building in question, then turned back to me. "Unfortunately, yes. It's been my cross to bear since Mother Carmody passed on."

"I'm sorry for your loss."

She flapped a hand at me. "Don't be, dear. Why, I didn't even know I had an aunt until some lawyer in a monkey suit and California tan darkened my doorstep one morning and told me the old bat had kicked off, leaving me saddled with this useless pile of wood." She shook her head, a true martyr to the cause, then fondly patted her dog's head, engulfing the poor thing entirely with the size of her hand. I briefly wondered if she was giving it a concussion. "I was sorely tempted to just sell the thing and be done with it, but Puddles here told me that she'd like a chance to see how the other half lives, and so off we came. Isn't that right, Puddles? Of course it is. You're mama's little sweetums, aren't you?"

Just when it appeared that "mama's little sweetums" was going to add some additional breathing holes to mama's little nose in retaliation for squeezing its innards out of its ears, Millicent pulled away and grinned at me, her capped white teeth bloody with smeared lipstick. "Isn't she just the sweetest little thing you've ever seen in your life?"

I took in the bulging eyes, the pointy teeth, the curled tongue, and the muzzle now smeared red by Millicent's kisses. "Oh, yes. Very sweet." I surreptitiously checked my own nose just to see if it had grown.

She tilted her head once again. "Are you sure we haven't met before? I never forget a face, and yours is *very* familiar to me."

"Well, I come into town quite often...?"

Flapping her hand at me again, she shook her head. "No, not *here*, dearie. Unless they're paying customers, I never notice anyone *here*. You're one of us, yes?"

"Excuse me?"

"One of us, dear. An American. Not one of those... *Canadians.* I thought I detected a bit of a Midwestern drawl to your speech."

The way she looked at me, I knew I'd just been called a hick, though in the most polite of ways. "I was born in the

United States," I allowed.

She nodded triumphantly. "She was right then."

I looked hard at her, trying to process the non-sequitor. "Who was right?"

"Why, Puddles, of course. She told me I'd meet a charming young American today, and what do you know? I have!"

I spared a brief moment wondering if perhaps her perfume contained some mind-altering chemical, because the conversation was taking on a decidedly strange bent.

"So...would you like to see what I've done with the place? You simply wouldn't *believe* what I had to work with."

"Um, actually, I would," I replied. "I used to come here every summer with my family. I loved the *Silver Pine*."

Turning back to me, Millicent eyed me the way I would imagine one would stare at a particularly revolting display of rat droppings arranged on one's kitchen table. "Of course you did, dear."

Then, after another moment, she smiled. "But you were a child then. I'm sure, as an adult, your tastes have changed *drastically*, no? Just come in for a quick look. I promise, you won't be disappointed."

"Well, there *is* something I really have to..."

"Nonsense, dear. There can't possibly be anything so important that you can't spare just a *moment* to ease a fellow American's mind."

"Actually, there..."

She flung an arm heavy as a lead weight over my shoulders, the cloying scent of her perfume causing my eyes to tear and my head to spin. "It's settled then. You simply won't believe what a little time, effort, and *taste* will do to a facility. Even one such as this, in the middle of absolutely nowhere."

Now most probably, I could have gotten away from her had I tried hard enough, but to tell the truth, she could have taken me to the Dante's Seventh Circle and I would have gone, such was the state of my mind at the time.

She led me into the lobby, then slipped away, no doubt to give me the necessary room to stand and stare in wide-eyed wonder at the changes she had wrought.

Being the accommodating sort, I did just that, though a decidedly queasy sensation quickly replaced the wonder I was expected to feel upon viewing the work of her interior designer, a person whom I was quite sure read Harlequin Romances for inspiration.

Gone were the comfortable weathered wood and nautical trappings that had so delighted me as a child. In their place were heavy red velvet and gold brocade tapestries, antique furniture, and intricate rugs more common to a French house of ill repute than a simple lakeside Bed and Breakfast. So perfect was the illusion that I half-expected to see scantily dressed whores waiting perched upon the heavily embroidered couches for the next customer to saunter by. In one corner, Puddles was living up to her name, christening a Persian rug. I wondered if it was expensive.

I couldn't help grinning at that, but hid it quickly.

Millicent smiled at her pet fondly before turning to me, her huge arms outspread to encompass the entire lobby. "Well, what do you think?"

"It's...it's..." *Ok, Angel, think. She's a whole foot taller and about three hundred pounds heavier than you, so whatever you come up with, it better be good.* "Well, it's...different."

She smiled as if I had just told her I was the lead photographer for *House Beautiful.* "I just *knew* you'd love it, dear. I could tell you were a woman of exquisite taste the moment I laid eyes on you."

Smiling and nodding, I scratched the back of my neck as further words failed me.

Taking a step closer, she made as if to engulf me once again. "Come, let me give you the grand tour. Each guest room has a different theme. You'll love them, I'm sure."

Deftly stepping out of the way of her oncoming arm, I held up my hands in a warding-off gesture I hoped she'd read. "Much as I'd love to do just that, I promised a friend I'd do something for her, and I really need to do it. She's counting on me." I gave her my most winning smile, one that had worked on women you wouldn't want to meet in a dark alley. "Another time perhaps?"

The pout she gave me made her eyes disappear into the vast folds of her cheeks, but when she saw it wasn't working on me, she relaxed the expression into a smile instead. "Of course, dear. I wouldn't want to keep you away from anything *important.* Come, let me walk you back outside. After all, it's the least I can do in return for your aid."

Repressing a small shudder, I allowed her to place her arm around my shoulders once again as she guided me back the way we'd come. I felt a decided sense of relief when the fresh air of the outside world claimed me once again, clearing my mind as well as my sinuses.

Squinting my eyes against the brightness of the day, I noticed a very familiar form casually sauntering down the street toward Pop's garage. *Shit. She probably thinks I forgot about her.*

Which I hadn't, of course. Not even for a second.

I felt Millicent stiffen beside me and, looking up, I saw her following Ice's easy movements with her eyes, an expression reminiscent of one biting into the most sour of lemons stamped on her florid features for all to see.

"Is something wrong?" I asked, wondering if she was seeing something I wasn't.

"Typical. Just typical."

"Excuse me?"

A large, bejeweled hand flung out in the direction of my partner. "Her, dear. So common. So...manly."

My eyebrows raised. "Manly?" I took a closer look, something I enjoyed in the extreme, my eyes running over her lean form with great pleasure. "I think she's beautiful." Which was, of course, the truth, though I'm sure my tone of voice did little to hide my true feelings.

She turned to me, that sour-lemon look still on her face. "If you like that type, I suppose. Genetic beauty is fine for commoners. *True* beauty takes style, poise, *breeding*. It's quite obvious she has none of those things." She clucked her tongue. "Why, I'll wager that that woman wouldn't know a Chippendale if she tripped over one."

Somehow, and I don't know how, I resisted the urge to tell the overblown windbag that not only did Ice have more style, poise, and breeding in the smallest of her fingers than she had in her entire abundant body, but also that she could, and did, read Kafka and Solzhenitzyn in the language of their birth, and could sing Elena's aria from *La donna del lago* so beautifully that statues would weep with the joy of hearing it.

I didn't say any of those things, though. What would have been the point? Closed minds took time to pry open. Time I didn't wish to spare with the likes of her.

I dredged up a smile from somewhere and turned it on her. "Well, if you'll excuse me, I really do need to get going. Thanks for the tour and the conversation. It was nice to have met you."

"Same to you, dear. Come back around anytime. Just make sure to stay away from women like her. Believe me, they're nothing but trouble."

More than you know, lady. More than you know.

My eyes adjusting to the darkness of the garage, I walked over to where Ice was rummaging through one of the tall tool chests scattered throughout the large, open structure. "Sorry about that. I got snared in by the proprietress of the Silver Pine. She wouldn't take 'no' for an answer."

Looking up, Ice favored me with a half-grin. "Figured as much. No big deal. I needed another tool anyway."

I moved closer to give her a kiss when a cleared throat interrupted my action. Turning, I spied Pop standing just inside the garage, his hat off as he ran a hand through his hair. "Afternoon, Tyler, Morgan."

"Hi, Pop!" Blinking, I took another look at the man. Something didn't seem right with him, somehow. Curious, I walked over to him, noticing as he ducked his head shyly away from me. "What happened to you?" I asked, taking in the starburst of brilliant color over his swollen right eye as well as the jagged cut down one grizzled cheek. "Who did this?"

"Ain't no big deal," he replied, taking a step away from me.

"What happened?" Ice's commanding voice floated to us from the depths of the shadowed garage.

"Buncha young toughs from the bar up the road got their peckers up, pardon the language. Should'a known better than ta go up there, my age bein' what it is, but I had a taste for a cold one and I never could turn that down." He shrugged his narrow shoulders. "Do my drinkin' at home from now on. Like I said, ain't no big deal."

"It's a big deal to me," I countered. "No one has the right to beat up someone else. It's stupid and just plain rude."

He grinned at me. "They ain't known for their brains or their manners, Tyler. Don't get all upset about 'em anyway. Ain't worth it. I learned my lesson."

Though I couldn't see Ice in the dark, I thought I caught a short nod directed at me, which made me feel much better about the whole situation. Enough to let it drop, with Pop at least. "Well, you make sure you put some ice on that eye to keep it from swelling any more than it already has."

"Got me a pound of raw hamburger waitin' to do just that, Tyler." He shrugged again. "'s what my wife used to use on me, anyway. Figure it'll do the same now as it did back then."

He turned his head toward Ice. "Speakin' of which, my wife's sister took ill up-country. Ain't seen her in years, but I promised my Maggie that I'd look after her kin after she'd passed on, so I reckon that's what I'll do. Was wonderin', Morgan, if you wouldn't mind lookin' after the place for me. I'll close 'er up good and tight when I leave, but I like my things to stay where I left 'em, and you never can be too sure these days, even in a town like this one. If it'll set ya back, say so. I'll find someone else."

"No need to shut it down," Ice replied. "I don't mind filling in for a few days."

"Couldn't ask that of ya..."

"Then don't. Just consider it done."

Now, Pop might have been old, but he was also smart. He knew when he'd been beaten and had no bones about saying so. Nodding, he put his cap back on his head and straightened the oil-stained brim. "I'll give you my thanks and leave ya to 'er then. I'm leavin' first thing tomorrow, so whenever ya get here is when you'll be open."

"Fine."

"Alright then. Got a trip to get ready for. Be seein' ya." And with that, he turned and left the cool garage, heading back toward the station proper and his tidy little house beyond.

Ice, too, left the shadows, coming to stand beside me, her arms laden with tools. Grabbing one, I turned to her, and smiled. "That was really sweet of you."

She snorted. "I don't do 'sweet.'"

"Suuuuuure ya don't." I know she doesn't like being teased, but sometimes I just can't help myself. She just makes it so darned easy.

She scowled, but kept her peace, fiddling with the oversized wrench in her hand. "C'mon. I got a cabin to finish."

As I broke into a jog to keep some sort of pace with my lover's long strides, the corner of my eye caught a bright flash of pink from the direction of the *Silver Pine*. Turning my head, I saw Millicent eyeing me, that pinched look still on her face; only now, it was directed at me as well as my partner.

Unable to resist that little voice in my head, I trotted forward a couple steps and snared my arm around Ice's lean waist, hugging her close so that our hips bumped as we walked.

"What was that for?"

"Oh," I smirked, glancing over my shoulder at Millicent's frowning reaction, "nothing."

Heh. Heh. Heh.

After puttering around the cabin with Ice for a few hours, I left to shower and freshen up for my afternoon job. Like Ice's before me, my own reputation had spread beyond Ruby's study. Before I knew it, offers for tutoring jobs came in more quickly than I could handle them, from young and old alike.

However, since I had to help build my home, there just weren't enough hours in the day to help all who asked, so I learned to be selective, something that didn't come easily to me, especially when it came down to deciding who to teach and who to regretfully decline. After all, an education is one of the most important things in the world and something everyone deserves a chance to receive.

The student that I was helping that particular late summer's day was a wonderful, mentally challenged seven-year-old boy named Nikki who had left school the year before because of the teasing he'd received from his classmates. I'd shunned monetary offers from his parents, but when they pointed out that I was treating their son as a special case by doing so, and that was something they most definitely did *not* want to have happen, I gave in to their undeniable logic and accepted both money and son into my care. Something I've never regretted.

My lessons finished for the day, I found myself at Ruby's kitchen table, regaling her with my rendition of my first meeting with the incomparable Millicent Harding Post. Tears were rolling down my face as she told a few tales of her own about the woman and her many strange habits, treating Puddles as if the dog were human the very least among them.

Ice had come in shortly before, grimy from her labors, and had run upstairs to shower and change before going back into town with me in search of some dinner.

Night was quickly drawing down when the phone rang. Getting up from her place at the table, Ruby answered it, then cradled it to her chest as she yelled up the stairs. "Morgan, it's for you."

After a muffled "Got it" floated down from upstairs, the room fell silent save for the ticking of the clock above the stove.

Time passed in its slow, quiet way as the conversation between Ruby and I ground down to dust. I heard the door to Ice's room open, then quietly close, followed again by stillness. Ruby and I looked at one another. She smiled. "You might as well go on up. I know it's killing you, not knowing."

I blushed a little, but stood anyway, knowing I was well and truly caught. "I'm sure it's nothing. Probably some last minute instructions from Pop about not lighting a match around the gas pumps or something." Still, I couldn't quite push away the feeling of dread that seemed to come from nowhere as the moments ticked away.

Shaking my head at my foolishness, I smiled my thanks to Ruby, then pushed away from the table and strode to the stairs, taking them two at a time until I was practically running. I stopped in front of Ice's door, knocked, then entered her room without waiting for a response. A rude thing for me to do, I'll agree, but manners were the last thing on my mind at that moment. I couldn't explain why my body was giving me the messages it was, only that it was. And after living in prison for so many years, that was enough for me.

She was standing by the window, with its view that faced the forest beyond, her profile bathed in moonlight. One hand gripped the narrow sill, and even in the darkness in which I was standing, I could see the tendons in that hand stand out in bold relief against the moon-bleached pallor of her skin.

Closing the door behind me, I crossed the room without even being aware that I had done so. "Is something wrong?" I whispered my question, too afraid to make it real by voicing it too loudly.

She didn't answer. Just kept staring out at the gently swaying pines that laid a canopy over the road meandering behind the house.

I laid a hand on her forearm, feeling the iron tension in the muscles slumbering there. "Please talk to me, Ice. My guts are churning here. Whatever it is, I need to know. Maybe I can help."

She turned, at last, from the window, a sad smile on her face. "You can't help with this one, Angel." Above her smile, her eyes were clear, colorless pools from which her pain radiated.

Trailing my hand down her strong arm, I grasped her hand and gently pulled it loose from its hold on the window sill, placing it against my rapidly beating heart. "Please, Ice. Talk to me. Anything, even the worst news, is better than this not knowing."

I could easily see the thoughts whirling behind those strangely colorless eyes, and held my breath when they announced their final decision.

"Cavallo's out."

Whatever news I had expected in my panic, it surely wasn't this. "What?"

"He's out. His lawyer got the judge to throw out the conviction on appeal."

I looked at her, struck dumb with confusion. "But...," I got out finally, "I thought he was dead. The news reports..."

"Lied, apparently. Or else they weren't given the truth by those higher up. Cavallo *was* gunned down by Salvatore's men. He just wasn't killed."

"Then why...?"

"Cover-up of the century for them, I'd imagine. Figured they could make a deal with him after pulling his ass out of the fire. He must have reneged at some point, though, because they wound up trying and convicting him."

"Then what happened?" I asked, still trying to wrap my mind around her bombshell. Of all the things I'd considered in the deepest part of the night, when Ice's fugitive status came right up and sat on my chest, this possibility wasn't one of them. *Not only the police, but the Mob, too? Jesus Christ.*

"The papers I planted in his car. Apparently, they were the major block on which the prosecution built its case. On appeal, they got thrown out in an 'illegal search and seizure' ruling. Without that evidence, the case pretty much fell apart. And since I'm the one who planted them there in the first place..." She shrugged. "Shitty deal, all the way around."

"God *damn* it! How did you find this out?"

"Andre. He's been keeping an ear out for me. Called me as soon as he heard."

As I gazed up at her, I had the distinct sense that the story wasn't over. "There's more, isn't there?"

After a long moment, she finally nodded, her tongue darting out to moisten dry lips. "Cavallo put the word out. He wants his pound of flesh. From me. And nothing's gonna stop him until he gets it. Andre also told me that Cavallo's sniffing around up this way. Somehow, he managed to blunder onto at least part of my trail, though I don't think he's quite got the brains to think I went over the border. Yet." Pulling her hand from mine, she turned away from me again, her clenched fist rattling the window as it came down hard on the sill. "I *knew* I shoulda killed that bastard when I had the chance." Reaching up, she dragged her hand through her thick hair, snorting in self-derision. "I must be crazy."

"You're not crazy, Ice. You did the right thing."

She spun back toward me, her eyes narrowed and filled with fire. "For *who*? Who, Angel? You? Me?"

"Us!" I shouted, then quickly lowered my voice, very much conscious of the fact that we weren't really alone. "Your dreams. Remember?"

"Those dreams are dead. I should have never listened to them in the first place."

I gasped, then stepped away, stung beyond belief by her thoughtless words. "Do you really mean that?"

Her eyes softened, as did her voice. "Angel, I'm a killer. That's who I am. What I am. It's how I've managed to stay alive all these years; by being worse than the worst they could throw at me. And the one time I go against who I am, this is what happens." She smiled again, that sad smile that broke my heart into tiny fragments. "I was never meant to live this life,

Angel. Peace isn't something I deserve. *Love* isn't something I deserve." She paused, as if weighing the weight of her words. "It was foolish of me to ever believe that I could be the person you see when you look at me. Foolish *and* dangerous."

She looked away again, out through the window and into the night beyond. "And now I've dragged you down with me. I've done the one thing I promised myself I'd never do." Her even breaths gently fogged the window, turning the view beyond white with a surreal mist. Her jaw set in granite determination, an expression I knew only too well. My stomach did a slow, lazy flip deep inside.

Her voice, when it came, was soft as death. "He wants to play games? Fine. We'll play."

"What...are you going to do?"

Ice snorted softly. "Find him before he finds me."

"And then?"

In slow motion, her dark head turned in my direction, her eyes alight with a glee I imagined a crocodile might have when a fat young deer waded a touch too far into his favorite watering hole.

"I'm gonna kill him."

"Ice...no."

"Yes, Angel. This isn't some game Cavallo's playing for kicks. This is real. And I'm not about to let that bastard get me a second time. Not while I'm alive enough to do something about it."

"But..."

"Look. We both knew something like this was gonna happen sooner or later. It just happens to be sooner. I don't like it, but the choice has been taken out of my hands." She looked at me intently, bathing me in the blue of her eyes. "Angel, you know how much I love you. Nothing can ever take that away from me. But this ...this is something I gotta do."

She sighed, then looked down at her hands, which were clenched into tight fists. "You'll be safe here, Angel. I'll make sure of it. You have friends here, people who love you. They'll help you finish the cabin so you can finally have your dream."

I laughed; a cold, disgusted sound that surprised even me. "My dream? My *dream*?! That cabin out there isn't my dream, Ice. It hasn't been for five years now. If I had to, I'd take a match and turn it into the biggest bonfire this town's seen since the last time it burned down."

She eyed me strangely, her head cocked at a slight angle.

"You just don't get it, do you?"

She shook her head slowly.

"This place, that cabin, those people, they're not my dream. I'd give them all up without a second's pause *or* regret. And do you know why?"

Again, a shake of negation.

"Because *you*, Morgan Steele, are my dream. None of the rest of this means a goddamn thing unless you're here to share it with me."

"Your home..."

"It's *not* my home! *You're* my home! Why can't you ever believe that? Why do you insist on continuing to see me as some naïve little child who has no clue about what she wants or needs?" I wasn't, obviously, giving her any time to answer my questions, but I didn't care at that moment. This blow-up had been a long time in coming, and I wasn't going to stop until I purged myself of the poison inside. "Why do you insist on treating me like some fragile, priceless object that you have to store away in some display case somewhere so no dust gets on it?"

"You *are* priceless, Angel," she managed to interject.

"But I'm not an object, Ice! I'm a person! A grown *woman*, quite capable of deciding how to live my life and who to live it with." My voice softened as I stared at her with as much emotion as I could force into my eyes. "Why is it so hard for you to believe that the person I choose to live it with is you?"

For a moment, just a moment, I knew what it was like to look into the eyes of a Morgan who had just lost her parents; a young girl heartsick with the pain of loss and too innocent to know how to cover that up with layers of concrete so thick no human could ever get inside those walls again.

But that moment passed in an instant, and I was shown just how vast a gulf the agony of years had created between that Morgan and this. The pain in her eyes vanished as if it had never been, to be replaced with the Morgan Steele the outside world knew; tough, unfeeling, uncaring. A robot incapable of experiencing even the most banal of emotions.

"I can't afford to let myself believe that, Angel."

"Why?"

"Because if I do, I lose a very important part of myself. A part I need to stay one step away from everyone who wants a shot at me; the cops, the Mob, and God knows who else. If I let my guard down even for an instant, things happen. People die, Angel. *You* could die. And if I'd thought about that when I had my gun to Cavallo's head, I would have done the right thing for me, and there'd be one less thing to worry about right now." Her eyes warmed just slightly; a drop of rain upon a frozen wasteland. "Instead, I thought about a dream I could never really have and let the lure of it prod me into a decision that I never should have made."

"And after you kill him, assuming he doesn't get you first, what then?" I really couldn't believe I was actually talking about this in a rational manner, but there I was, speaking as if we were discussing the weather over afternoon tea.

She shrugged. "Come back over the border. Go up further north, winter in one of Bull's cabins, I suppose."

I nodded. "Alright then. I'll be sure to pack some warm clothes."

"Angel..."

"Don't 'Angel' me, Ice. If you're so bound and determined to go through with this, then you'd better get used to the fact that I'm gonna be there right along with you."

Her eyes narrowed.

I smiled.

"You think you can stop me, Ice? How? Tie me up? I'll get loose." I looked deliberately down at her still-clenched fists. "Beat me up? Break my legs? I'll heal. And then I'll search for you. And I'll keep searching until I find you." I could hear my voice rising, but I didn't care. "If you insist on martyring yourself for me, Morgan, then by damn, I'll be your cross. I'll be an albatross around your neck. And one day, maybe, you'll finally get it through your thick head that where you go, I go. Period."

Then I gave her my own dangerous grin, one I'd learned well at the feet of the Master. "Because unlike you, Ice, I don't give up that easy."

The look she returned me would have turned the bowels of even the most hearty of men to water. I forced myself to remain, outwardly at least, unaffected. "What are you talking about?"

I flung my hands out. "Isn't it obvious? It is to me. You let an idiot like Cavallo scare you away from a dream I *know* you have." Barking a laugh, I shook my head. "You forget who you're dealing with here, Ice. I *know* you. Better than you think I do. I see that look on your face when you think no one's looking. Like some kid on Christmas morning waiting for someone to tell her that Santa Claus really doesn't exist and that all the presents she thought were hers actually belong to the kids down the street."

I took a step closer to her, pleased when she didn't try to back away. "You've been waiting for this excuse all along, haven't you? You've been waiting for the perfect reason to bolt. Because the longer you stay here, the longer you live among people who respect the person you are instead of the dangerous murderer you *think* you are, the more you're forced to believe that there's actually a person inside you worthy of such respect. And adoration. And love."

Reaching out, I laid a hand on her arm. She flinched, but didn't pull away, so I applied pressure to her wrist, holding it in a firm clasp. "We both knew what we were getting into when we started this journey, Ice. But my fears, my concerns are, I think, easier for me to deal with than yours are for you. Because mine are easily seen. I know that all this stands a very good chance at coming to an end, and perhaps a violent one, someday. I know that and continue the journey anyway, because to me, to *me,* Ice, being with you is much more important than being without you."

I took that final step, brushing my body against hers. I thought I could feel her tremble faintly, but it was probably my imagination. "And I know you share those fears. But they're easy ones for you, because you've had the same things to deal with most of your life. Life and death decisions are easy for you to make. But *feeling*...that's hard. *Believing* is hard. And allowing yourself to love and be loved is probably the hardest thing of all."

"Everything I love dies," she whispered, her voice raspy with tears she wouldn't, couldn't shed.

I wrapped her in an embrace so tight I don't think a mote of dust could pass between us, and wished with all my strength that I was taller so I could rest her head against my chest as she had done for me so many times as to be uncountable. "I know," I whispered, my own tears rolling down my cheeks, tears I shed for the both of us. "I know."

Those deaths passed between us then, in some sort of metaphysical osmosis that filled the room like a pall. Her mother. Her father. Her best friend. Josephine. Other friends. Perhaps other lovers, ones we hadn't spoken of. Her innocence. Her belief in the power of love.

After a moment, she pulled away from me, angrily swiping at a tear that had managed to escape the imprisonment of her eyes. She turned toward the window again, and I could feel the distance between us begin to grow. Oddly, though, it didn't seem to be a distance of hurt, but rather of healing. A distance that told me she had heard my words and needed a minute alone to process them and their implications for her life.

Smiling slightly, I stepped back away from her. "I'll support you in whatever decision you make, Morgan. Just, please, don't let him win, ok?"

Her nod was the last thing I saw before I turned and left the room.

The next morning dawned clear and hot. I was up before the sun, though that had a great deal to do with the fact that I hadn't really slept at all during the night. Much as it shames me to admit, I spent morning's moon-shadowed hours with both ears peeled for the slightest sound of Ice's footfall in the hallway outside my door.

Not that that would have helped any, of course, should Ice have been so inclined as to desire an escape in the middle of the night. The woman was more silent than fog and twice as stealthy.

Still, keeping my eyes open had a sort of talismanic feel to it, and so, as a promise against an uncertain future, I sacrificed a few hours of sleep to stand guard against the possibility of my darkest nightmare coming true.

My morning routine completed, I stepped out into the still-dark hallway and tried desperately not to look as if I was checking up on my lover, which, of course, I was. The corridor was empty and quiet. Giving in to my need to know, I walked softly to Ice's room and grasped the doorknob.

Just a quick peek, I promised myself. *Just to be sure.*

Before I could think to do more, the knob turned from the inside, pulling me inward when the door opened and landing me in Ice's surprised arms.

"Hello," I said, blushing. "Fancy meeting you here."

A raised eyebrow was the reply.

"I was ...checking to see if you were awake yet?"

The eyebrow raised higher.

I sighed, knowing only the truth would be enough to satisfy her. "I wanted to make sure you hadn't decided to leave."

"Don't trust me, huh."

"I do trust you, Ice. You didn't...exactly tell me what your decision was going to be."

"Probably because I haven't made one yet."

"Well, you're still here. That's something, at least."

A corner of her mouth lifted briefly. "It's somethin', alright."

Coming to the tips of my toes, I placed a small kiss on that upturned corner, then stood normally again, pleased at the small victory which had kept her home, at least for the moment. "Could I interest you in some breakfast?"

"Nah. I'm just gonna head over to the garage and get started."

"Mind some company?"

She looked down at me, an amused smirk in her eyes.

I scowled. "Alright, so I've never owned a car. I think I have the mechanics of pumping gas down straight, though." I gave her my best mischievous grin. "You just put the nozzle in that little pipe that comes out of the back of the car underneath, right?"

Rolling her eyes, she let me go and gave me a push back into the hallway, following me out and closing the door behind her. "Let's go."

It was still rather dark as we made our meandering way through the heavily shadowed forest on our way into town. In deference to the almost cathedral-like atmosphere of the newly awakening day, we kept our silence, leaving only the sound of our footfalls upon the heavily carpeted ground as signs to mark our passing.

When the trees gave up their hold on the land and we stepped into the town's border, I noticed a small crowd gathering in the distance, near Pop's garage. Something about the scene struck me as odd, and after staring at it for a moment, I noticed that the gentle breeze was rustling the blinds which covered the large plate-glass windows of the gas station, from the *inside*.

"Ice?" I asked, puzzled, to a partner who had moved off during my musings and was rapidly gaining momentum, walking with a determined stride toward the slowly gathering crowd. "Shit," I muttered, moving after her at a sprint.

Slipping my way through the group, one of which was a shining purple object wearing Millicent's face, I came to a stop next to Ice, who was kneeling on the ground, glass shards scattered around her like trumpery diamonds. Laying next to my partner, crumpled in a tattered and bloody heap, was Pop, his left cheek zippered open and spilling a river of blood. His nose was squashed almost flat against his face, and his eye, which had only been faintly puffy the day before, had almost exploded with swelling. One arm bent at an odd angle above the elbow, obviously broken in at least one place.

I watched as Ice's long fingers gently probed an area in his neck, obviously searching for a pulse. "Is he...?"

She looked up at me, eyes simmering with anger. "He's alive. Just badly beaten." Shifting her gaze from me, her eyes lanced through the gathered crowd. "Who did this?"

The men and women looked at one another, their feet shuffling uncomfortably against the dusty ground.

She came slowly, gracefully to her feet, a giant among dwarfs, filling the area with her intense presence. "I won't ask again."

From the back of the crowd, a young man stepped forward, his hands stuffed deep into his pockets. "Three or four guys, I think. I only heard 'em when the glass started breaking. By the time I got here, they were driving off on their bikes. He was like that when I got here." The young man shrugged, face flushed pink with what I guessed was embarrassment.

"Anyone else see anything?" Ice asked, her face set in lines of anger.

No one came forward.

Pop moaned and Ice squatted quickly back down again, offering what comfort she could, which was, in truth, not very much.

A thought came into my head. "Did anyone call an ambulance?"

Again, an embarrassed silence.

I turned to Millicent, the only face I knew. "Would you...?"

She held her dog in front of her as, perhaps, a shield, though against what, I didn't know. "Oh, I couldn't possibly..."

Ice looked up from her position at Pop's side. "Call an ambulance. Now."

"I'll do it," I said, stepping forward to head this particular argument off at the pass.

"No. I need you to stay here." She looked back up at Millicent. "Do it."

"*I'll* do it," the young man who'd made his sheepish report interjected, moving off toward Pop's destroyed office before anyone had a chance to stop him; no doubt interested in redeeming himself in the eyes of his neighbors.

Giving a short nod, Ice again rose to her feet, giving one last menacing glare to Millicent before turning away and stepping out of the circle of bystanders. "Stay with him," she said to me.

"Where are you going?"

"To take care of some business."

"Then I'm going with you."

She rounded on me, then, eyes hard as diamonds that glittered with both anger and anticipation. I stood my ground, arms crossed tight over my chest, not giving an inch. "There are more than enough people to look after Pop until the ambulance comes," I reminded her. "And I want to get to the bottom of this as much as you do."

That got a slight smile out of her. "Even if it means cracking a few skulls?"

"That wouldn't be my first choice, no." I cleared my throat. "But if a few hormonally challenged idiots want to prove how macho they are by beating up an old man, then they deserve whatever's coming to them." And, boy, were they in for a rude awakening when they found exactly who, and what, *was* coming to them.

"Let's go then. I've got some asses to kick."

As she began to walk away again, I stopped her with a hand to her arm. "Ice?"

She turned. "What now?"

"Um...where are we going, exactly?"

Her eyes twinkled with a mad sort of mischief. "You'll see."

"That's what I thought."

Goody.

We arrived at our destination with alacrity, if not in style, riding as we were in another one of Pop's old junkers, which had seen better days several decades ago, and new a decade or so before that. Another classic, Ice had said. A classic *what*, she didn't exactly reveal, but a classic nonetheless.

Who was I to doubt her?

I stepped out of the car after pulling on the rusted door handle for several frustrating seconds, wiping dust and other accumulated, and thankfully unknown, debris from my shirt and pants as I did so. We had pulled in front of a run-down old shanty, which, by the sign above the door, also doubled as a tavern.

"The *Rusted Nut*. Charming." A misnomer if ever there was one, of course, since the establishment, from the outside at least, was anything *but* charming. I had my doubts that the view from the inside would be any more so.

On the weed and glass strewn lot in front of the building stood four motorcycles of the type my father used to call "hogs." I laid my hand on the gas-tank of the one closest to me. "Still warm." I looked over at Ice, who was assessing the building with expert eyes. "How did you know?"

I received no reply as my partner stepped silently onto the rotten, sagging porch that ran the length of the bar. Prudently, I stayed where I was as she crossed to the door and eased her hand around the thick knob that jutted out from the weathered wood. After a moment, she stepped away, giving the building another assessing glance.

Then, without word or warning, she drew back her leg and launched a truly spectacular kick, literally blowing the door inward in a squealing shower of wood splinters and rust. She followed the door into the building, and I came in right behind her, attaching myself to her left shoulder.

Four young men and one older bartender looked up, comical astonishment frozen on their faces and upraised beers frozen in their fists.

"Hello, boys," Ice rumbled, her voice low and sensual. "Worked up a pretty big thirst, have you?"

"We're closed, lady," the bartender said, a bar rag in one ham-sized fist. "Get the hell outta here before I call the cops."

Perching one hip on the corner of a more or less solid table, Ice fiddled with the thick silver bracelet on her left arm, a gift from me several months back, and one she hadn't taken off since the giving. "Oh, don't let me stop you," she replied, eyes seemingly absorbed in her task and not bothering to look up at the no-doubt dangerous men sharing space with her. "I'm sure the police would be very interested in hearing why your young friends here seemed to have worked up such a sweat so early in the day, hmm?" The smirk on her lips was quite knowing, and I'm sure I saw at least one of the men pale at the implication.

The other three, however, clearly weren't as observant. The largest of the trio, a stout tree with bendable appendages, stood, slamming his mug of beer down on the table and managing to douse his pants with the sudsy liquid. "What the fuck are you talkin' about, bitch?"

Since I couldn't resist, I didn't. "She's talking about the trip you made into town this morning." I met the man's angry stare dead on, hands on my hips. "I'm sure it took a lot out of you, beating the crap out of a defenseless old man like that."

"You die, bitch!" The behemoth tossed aside the table in front of him as if it were made of balsa.

Ice stepped in front of me, and I whirled around, grabbing the first weapon that came to hand, which happened to be an old and splintered pool cue keeping lonely watch on a rack just inside the now useless door.

I didn't have time to be scared, didn't have time to wonder what would happen if the bartender followed through on his threat to call the authorities. Adrenaline rushed through me like a speeding train, spurred on by the memory of Pop's crumpled and bleeding body lying amidst the shattered ruins of his shop.

The man lumbered forward, his fists clenched and his face beet red, even beneath his short, red-blonde crew cut. His advance was stopped cold, however, by a solid right to his jaw which sent him stumbling back toward his compatriots, arms pinwheeling for balance and failing in their task.

The other men seemed too stunned to move and, when he crashed through their ranks, they let him fall backward, turning another table into kindling. Jumping back to his feet, he pushed his useless buddies out of the way, swiping at the blood trickling from his mouth with the back of his hand and examining it closely. His muddy hazel eyes rose slowly to meet Ice's. "Ya know," he said in a conversational tone, "you and your little friend there are mighty fine pieces of ass. I wouldn't have minded fucking you both senseless after I taught you your lessons. But now...." His voice trailed off as he reached for an empty beer bottle standing on one of the few remaining tables. Hefting the bottle by the neck, he smashed it against the edge of the table, leaving a deadly, if crude, weapon in his hand. "Now, I think I'll just see how many other holes I can poke in you before you die. *Then* I'll fuck ya." He grinned, lips bloody and twisted. "How's that sound to you, bitch?"

"Like you don't go out on very many dates, maggot." She smirked. "At least, not outside the morgue."

Bellowing in rage, the man rushed my partner, swing the broken bottle wildly as he did so. At the very last second, Ice side-stepped his charge, allowing his momentum to carry him into the lone pool table and double over on top of it, though not before he had managed to use his weapon to slice her above her left elbow.

Her smile was glacier cold as she rubbed the blood between two long fingers. "That wasn't very nice," she purred to the man who managed to straighten up and turn once again to face her.

His eyes sparkled with glee as he noticed the damage he'd done. "There's more where that came from, bitch."

"Let's see whatcha got then, handsome." She beckoned him with her hands, waggling her fingers enticingly.

Before he could get more than two steps away from the pool table, the man suddenly found himself quite weaponless as a booted foot snapped his wrist and sent the jagged bottleneck flying across the room to shatter completely against the front of the bar. He dropped like a head-shot deer, grabbing his wrist and howling in agony.

That, apparently, was the impetus needed to finally kick the brains, minute though they were, of his companions into gear. As a unit, they turned toward the both of us, expressions of anger stamped heavy on their faces. One reached into the pocket of his tattered jeans and pulled out a butterfly knife, which he opened with a series of fancy moves that would have been truly impressive, had he not almost cut his own leg off while performing them.

They started forward, all attention completely on the dangerous menace that was Ice and ignoring me completely.

Which was just the way I liked it, though not for the reasons you're probably thinking.

My own safety wasn't something that interested me right then. Helping my lover *was.*

Like a lion culling the weakest antelope from the herd, I stepped in, cue in hand, and turned one of the onrushing thug's attention to me. He grinned a little, shrugged, and obliged me by balling up one huge, freckled fist and launching it in the direction of my face.

Dodging my head to one side, I allowed his fist to rustle the air past my ear, then used my ersatz staff to deliver a hard, stinging blow to his forearm. As he yelped in pain, I swung the thicker end of the cue up and across, cracking it against the side of his head and using just enough strength behind the blow to stun him. I'd learned my lesson well with Peter and had no intention of traveling back down that particular pathway to Hell ever again.

His eyes went glassy and he staggered as his hand slapped against the rapidly forming welt I'd raised on his scalp. Weapon still to hand, I ushered him backward until the edge of the pool table smacked against his behind, then pressed hard until he was half standing, half laying across the table on his back. Then I placed the butt of the cue between his nipples and pushed.

Hard.

"Stay down."

He didn't respond, but by the look on his face, I knew he was considering doing something stupid. A quick jab to the sternum, however, seemed to change his mind, and he relaxed back against the table, settling for what I imagine he thought was an intimidating scowl.

Which, of course, it wasn't. Not by a long shot. To me, anyway.

Now, I realize that turning my back to the action was not the brightest of things to do. But if experience taught me anything, it was that Ice was more than capable of protecting my back, and her own as well, without any help from me.

When the butterfly knife wielded so inexpertly by one of the men came skittering to a stop next to my right foot, I grinned, knowing my trust in my partner was indeed well-placed. So, instead of turning back around to view the action, I continued to keep watch on my "prisoner" and played a game with myself, imagining the actions that went with the sounds I was hearing.

Two grunting exhales meant twin blows to overfed bellies. The distinctive sound of fist against flesh, followed by the sound of yet another table being splintered to firewood could only be an uppercut to the jaw, launching the unfortunate up and away. A high-pitched squeal just had to be a knee to the privates.

Even *I* winced at that one, then bestowed a sweet grin upon my suddenly sweating captive. "Bet that hurt, huh?" I couldn't resist rubbing in.

The sound of bone hitting bone, followed by twin thuds, meant that Ice had finished Act Four of her martial ballet by slamming her two friends' skulls together, as promised, and allowing them to drop, undoubtedly unconscious, to the floor.

The space beside me was suddenly filled with her warm, energy-filled presence, and I took a step away as a tanned hand reached down and grabbed the idiot I had dealt with by his ragged collar, introducing him to the far wall in a way that was all her own.

She held him there easily against the splintered wood, his toes barely in contact with the floor beneath his feet. She smiled a slow, dark one that was full of vengeful promise. "Since you're the only one awake at the moment," she began, thrusting him harder against the wall for emphasis, "I'm gonna explain a few things to you, alright?"

Staring wide-eyed at my lover, the man could do little but nod. Emphatically.

Ice's smile broadened. "Good. Looks like you're the brains of the outfit." Her expression then became deadly serious. "First thing. If you ever so much as *think* about touching one of my friends again...." Her voice trailed off as she leaned in close. "I'll kill ya. Understand?"

The man nodded again, fat beads of sweat dripping down from his wrinkled forehead.

"Second thing. If I ever see you or any of your buddies in my town again, I'll kill ya. Am I making myself real clear, maggot?"

"Y-yes," the man squeaked.

"Alright then. As long as we understand one another." She set him on his feet again, then brushed his wrinkled shirt smooth with the palms of her hands. She made as if to turn away as a huge sigh of relief gusted from the man's lungs, then turned back again, the smile once more on her face. "Oh yeah. Here's the third thing." Pulling her arm back, she cocked her fist and drove it into the man's nose, flattening it in a nauseating crunch of shattered cartilage. "Pop says hello."

Eyes rolled back in his head so only the whites showed through, the man slumped peacefully to the ground, out for the count.

Shaking her head in disgust, Ice stepped over the fallen body and walked toward the shattered door. Then she looked up at the bartender, who was still standing behind his bar, frozen to the floor as if he'd been lacquered there, bar rag dangling from one useless hand. "If you're thinking of calling the cops over this little disagreement, I suggest you think again. I have twenty witnesses back in town who saw what your friends did to Pop and his shop." She quirked a grin at him. "And I'm sure I can dig up twenty more who will swear on bibles that my partner and I were rescuing babies from wells around about the time we were supposed to be making a mess of your fine ... establishment." A shrug of broad shoulders. "So be smart and put paid to this, alright?"

The bartender didn't respond, just continued to stand there, frozen, staring at us both through glazed eyes.

Snorting and shaking her head, Ice stepped over, around, and through the debris she'd made and out into the sunshine once again.

The ride back into town was quiet, as I'd known it would be. Not the most loquacious of women even in the best of circumstances, I'd learned the hard way that Ice *really* shut down after a fight. It was her way, I suppose, of taming the beast she'd unleashed lest it turn on her and seek its bloody sport among those undeserving of its vengeful wrath.

My only remark, a question about the cut in her arm, was answered in a monosyllabic grunt that I had no trouble translating.

Besides, it had already stopped bleeding.

Our arrival in the town went unheralded, as the crowd from earlier had dispersed, most going back to their day jobs, no doubt. The only one who remained was the young man who'd witnessed the attack. He had appropriated a janitor's broom from somewhere and was sweeping the glass from the ground in long, if somewhat morose, strokes.

Tom Drew, one of the plumbers, was putting the finishing touches on the plywood he'd put up in lieu of a window, and turned around to greet us with a smile as we stepped out of the car. Wiping his hands off on his ever-present red handkerchief, he walked toward us, his eyebrow furrowed as he took in the cut on my partner's arm, as well as our state of general dishevelment.

"Out grizzly huntin'?"

Ice smiled slightly. "Nah. Just took out some trash."

After a moment, he nodded sagely, stuffing the handkerchief back into one pocket of his overalls. "Would have tended to it myself if I hadn't been standing hip deep in old Mrs. Symmond's waste water at the time." He shook his head in disgust. "Damn pipes picked one hell of a time to burst."

My partner shrugged. "I took care of it."

"Did Pop get off ok?" I piped up from my place beside Ice.

Tom nodded. "Yeah. I got here just as the ambulance pulled up. He was awake and grousing, like he always does. I'm sure he'll be fine after a sleeping pill or two."

"That's good to hear," I replied, relieved. I looked at him more closely then, sensing that he knew more than he was telling us. "Is there something else?"

He looked at both of us, then over where the young man, whose name, I later learned, was Richard, continued his sweeping duties, before returning his gaze to us again. "Want to go inside the station for a cold drink? I know I could use one."

I looked to Ice, who nodded her acquiescence, and together we followed Tom into the shadowed confines of Pop's office. Reaching into the cold case, he pulled out three cans of Coke, handing us our drinks before leaning back against the counter and pressing the cold can against his sweaty forehead and sighing with relief.

Ice left her soda unopened until Tom popped the top of his can and guzzled the cold liquid down in one healthy gulp, then let out a healthy belch. "Ahh. Hits the spot." He tossed the empty can into the wastebasket, then looked over at Ice, wiping his mouth with the back of his hand. "Those idiots you took care of today are a little bit more than your average, run-of-the-mill thug. Or, at least, they like to think they are."

"What are they, then?" I asked, my curiosity piqued.

"They like to think of themselves as some great extortionist clique." He laughed lightly. "Problem is, they're not very good at it. They came down here a few times and tried to get 'protection' money from some of the businesses around here." He laughed again, shaking his head. "In a backwater town like this. Protection money. Protection from what?"

"Them," Ice replied with the wisdom of one who knew exactly what she was talking about. "You give them money, they don't beat the crap outta you. I take it Pop didn't accept their kind offer?"

Tom snorted. "None of us did. I ran 'em out myself a few months back. Haven't seen hide nor hair of 'em since. Till now."

"So what happened?" I asked.

"Pop's pretty stubborn. The Rusted Root's their hangout, and I warned him not to go back there." He blushed to the roots of his hair. "I guess I should have been harder on him. I knew he wouldn't listen." He sighed, looking down at his hands. "It almost got him killed."

"You can't blame yourself, Tom." Reaching out, I laid a hand on his arm. "Pop's a grown man. He knew what the consequences could be. He chose to take the risk anyway. That's not your fault." Turning to Ice, I smiled ruefully. "I've been known to do the same thing myself, on occasion."

She tipped her head in acknowledgement before turning back to Tom. "My guess is they'll be a little too busy licking their wounds to make a return visit just yet. When they do come back, we'll just have to make sure we're ready for them."

"Sounds like a plan." He rubbed his large, callused hands together, grinning. "I'd like a chance at 'em myself."

"Let's not tempt the Fates, alright?"

He blushed again, giving Ice a "caught in the cookie jar" grin. "Yes'm."

Nodding, Ice finished off her own drink, then crushed the can and tossed it into the waste-bin. "Alright, then. Seems I've got a station to run for longer than I intended. Best get to it."

"My brother and I will help as much as we can." He gestured out the open door. "Would you let Richard stay and help? He feels pretty bad about not being there to stop what happened."

"He wouldn't have been able to do anything," I protested.

"Yeah, I know that, but he doesn't. He's just a kid, still, you know? Kid in a man's body. He wants to make up for things somehow. This would probably be the best thing for him."

After a moment, Ice tilted her head in acquiescence. "Fine. Let's go, then."

And so we did.

Chapter
7

It was done. Finally.

After what seemed like eons of working, planning, sweating, and dreaming, our home was finally completed and waiting for us to move in.

The last of the details had fallen into place the night before, and I had spent the evening in happy anticipation, only to have my hopes dashed the next morning when Ice met me in the hallway, brushed a gentle kiss upon my waiting lips, and told me she'd be back later in the evening after finishing up her work at Pop's garage, before continuing on her way.

"But...I thought..."

She turned, long hair fanning over one shoulder like a matador's cape. "What?" Her expression showed polite interest, but nothing more.

I sighed, then looked down at my feet. "Nothing," I mumbled.

The sound of her approach was strangely muted in the long, dim hallway, and I only looked up when a gentle hand beneath my chin urged my head to tilt in that direction. "What is it, Angel?"

I sighed, realizing how juvenile my request would likely sound, even to my own ears. I'm sure I was blushing, but with the intense heat Ice always radiated bathing and burning through me, it was difficult to be positive on it. "I...um...thought," I cleared my throat to ease the sudden "Stevie Nicks" quality in my voice, "since the house is ready and all, we could start moving our things in?"

I didn't mean for it to come out as a question, but there it was, my timidity laid bare for the world to see, as it were.

My lover smiled; that soft, loving one she gifted me with on occasion; the one that turned my insides into warm mush. "Why don't you go on ahead? I'll move my stuff in when I get back."

I shook my head. "I kinda wanted us to do this together, as incredibly sappy as that sounds."

Her smile deepened, reaching all the way up to her eyes. "It doesn't sound sappy."

I threw one of her own hiked eyebrows right back at her, something I'd become rather proficient at, if I do say so myself.

She chuckled, a low, deep rumbling in her chest. "Alright, it's pretty sappy." She gathered me close and hugged me gently in her strong arms, before pulling away again and pinning me with her gaze. "Tell ya what. I promised Pop I'd help him out with a few things he's working on. If I promise to make an early day of it, will you wait for me? We'll move our stuff in as soon as I come back."

As compromises went, it was a fair one, but that didn't stop me from seriously considering petulance as my next course of action. Only the realization that it would have exactly the opposite reaction from Ice as the one I'd hoped to achieve stayed my hand. "Alright," I said, pretending a long-suffering attitude that had more than a grain of truth in it. "I suppose I can do that. Just know that it'll be killing me."

She shook her head, then kissed me once again, then left me dazzled in the hallway thanking God that the walls holding me up in lieu of my suddenly turned-to-jelly legs were solid.

So there I sat, in my bedroom, on my bed, staring out the window at the very top of the roof of our home. I felt like a child on Christmas morning, up before the dawn and staring at a pile of presents she can't touch until her parents wake up. Each minute took its own sweet time strolling by, smirking at me as it passed. Even the sun seemed to partake in the conspiracy, deciding for the first time in its long life to take a much-needed siesta before continuing on its westward journey.

As a way to pass the time, I thought back over the last few weeks, when everything seemed to fall into place and we were finally able to turn four walls and a roof into a home fit for living.

The house was almost fully furnished, and while not, perhaps, with objects we would have chosen had we been independently wealthy, the items in question were well made, sturdy, and, to me at least, aesthetically pleasing.

Since money *was* an object, I had to fall back on a skill I'd learned when becoming the "get it" girl in the Bog. Barter. And it was pretty pleasing to see that I hadn't lost my touch in the intervening months.

The couch, chairs, tables, and rugs were actually the easiest to obtain in this manner, especially since I wasn't really bartering for them at all. Pop, a man who it was said could squeeze a penny until it begged for mercy, had come by the furniture quite honestly, relieving as he did the burden of the unfortunate soul who'd been bullied into removing it from Millicent's sight during her gargantuan—not to mention tasteless—redecoration phase. The items were stored in the large shed attached to his home, keeping company with various and sundry other objects, prosaic and non, which had struck his fancy over the years.

I didn't know that, however, when I approached him on the day he returned home from the hospital after a two night stay with his arm in a cast and his facial topographic map from the beating he'd received. I had only come to offer my help in performing the basic domestic duties which his injuries would make difficult for him to do on his own.

Being the person he was, Pop wouldn't take no for an answer until he had me swear a practical blood oath that I'd take the furniture in question off his hands at a very reasonable price.

In other words, for free.

Like its predecessor, this cabin had a huge expanse of windows that needed covering of some form or other. Mrs. Symmonds, she of the broken plumbing, was an outstanding seamstress, even though legally blind. As payment for wonderfully rendered curtains, as well as a truly spectacular quilt which lies atop our bed to this day, I agreed to read to her during her daily labors. Unfortunately for me, her reading tastes equaled my mother's. Which is to say, she enjoyed torrid romance novels of the type that can be found in the cashier's rack of any discount department chain around the world.

Several times during the reading of such novels, if they can truly be called such, I was sure I was just a degree or two away from setting off the heat detector with my blushing as I articulated such phrases as "towering manhood" and "gates of Venus" and "pleasure pearl."

Still, a little emotional discomfort was a small price to pay for such beautiful work, and so I set about my appointed task with determination, though not much relish, to be sure.

Pots, pans, and assorted other kitchen objects came at the cost of two week's labor as a waitress in the café while one of the others took a well-deserved vacation.

And so it went, slowly, until the cabin came to be filled with objects we were both pleased to own.

The sudden closing of the downstairs door roused me from my musings and fluttered my heart in happy anticipation. The soft sound of conversation muted by my own closed door, and then I was able to track Ice's progress through the house by the distinctive, if rather soft, sound of her tread.

A moment later, and another door closed, followed close behind by the sound of the shower being turned on full blast. Scarcely three minutes later—so timed by the clock on my bed-side table—the shower was silent once again and I pictured my lover wiping down that glorious body of hers.

A body which, by night's end, I would know in intimate detail once again.

That thought sent an ocean of blood speeding for parts south and I rode the wave, feeling a happy grin stretch the muscles of my face. I was ready.

Oh *boy,* was I ready.

A few moments later, and I was treated to the sight of a freshly bathed Ice, her still damp hair glistening in the after-noon's slowly waning light and her cheeks still flushed from the heat of the water she'd bathed in.

Did I mention I was ready?

She smirked at me. "You all packed?"

I smirked right back. "Only since this morning. After all, what else did I have to do with my time while you were lollygag-ging around doing God knows what with yours?"

Rolling her eyes, she shook her head and held out her hand, helping me to my feet. "Let's get this show on the road, then, shall we?"

"You won't hear any complaints from me!"

After a quick stop in Ice's room to pick up her box of metic-ulously packed belongings, and a slightly longer pause to thank Ruby for her kindness yet again, we finally made it outside before the early Autumn sun had sunk completely behind the lake.

I felt a sense of déjà vu rush through me as I heard, faintly, the sounds of voices at the bottom of the small hill where our cabin stood. Unlike last time, however, Ice seemed at her ease, content to walk along side me without displaying even one iota of curiosity over the sounds I well knew she could hear even bet-ter than I.

Which, of course, made me even *more* nervous.

Several more steps and we were at the breast of the hill and looking down at what seemed fully half the town gathered around our newly built home. A garish purple ribbon was tied up in a neat bow and strung across the doorway of the cabin, apparently waiting to be cut by the both of us, as if we were some famous figures and our simple cabin was a brand new office building or hotel or something equally as grandiose.

Several portable grills had been hauled onto our property and the smells of slowly cooking meat and vegetables caused my mouth to water and my stomach to announce its sudden need to be part of the action.

A large bonfire blazed merrily in a carefully cleared space to the west of the house, and the silver beer-kegs stored somewhat nearby winked in its flickering light.

Pop, his long cast reduced now to one that ended below the elbow, gave us both a cheery, and I'm sure half drunk, grin, beckoning us wildly with his good arm.

The party had, apparently, been going on for some time, if the somewhat slurred greetings we received were any indication. Plastic cups of foaming beer were raised, and spilled, in salute to us as we stood at the top of the hill, taking in the scene below.

"You knew about this, didn't you," I muttered to my oh-so-smug partner, chancing a soft elbow to her muscled side.

"Only when I came back to the house."

"And you didn't think to mention it?"

The smirk deepened. "I was sworn to secrecy."

"I'll just bet you were." Still, I couldn't help but laugh. I'd always enjoyed parties as a young girl, and something told me I wouldn't mind them so much as an adult either. "Shall we join them, seeing as we're the guests of honor?"

A long arm pointed the way down the hill with an open hand. "After you."

The party lasted a good long time and though I've never had much of a taste for liquor of any sort, I must admit that, after a few cups of Pop's special beer, I had a hard time remembering just why it was that I didn't like the stuff.

Of course, after a few more cups, I would have had trouble remembering my own name, so I chose, for me, the wisest course of action, which was to abstain after just two.

Or maybe it was three.

As I've said, Pop's brew was a potent concoction.

The man in question finally came forth near the end of the evening, handing me a pair of scissors and Ice a set of door keys. Cheering loudly, the crowd urged us over to the beribboned door for the final act in the night's play.

Taking the scissors to hand, I made some insipid speech

which, mercifully, escapes my mind to this day (I told you about Pop's beer, remember) and, with a silly grin, cut the ribbon, making clear the path to the door.

With her usual no-nonsense style, Ice simply walked up to the door, inserted the key into the lock, turned, and opened it wide.

The crowd cheered, then fell quiet as the scent of cedar and fresh paint wafted out to greet me, elevating my already giddy mood even more. After a moment, I became aware of the silence behind me, and slowly turned to see the crowd eyeing us somewhat expectantly. With a brain not quite operating on all cylinders, I stared out at the gathered group of my neighbors, wondering if someone would be kind enough to tell me what came next, since it was obviously something of no small import.

With no answers immediately forthcoming, I turned back to the door where my partner stood, the question plain, I'm sure, in my eyes.

The world spun then, and not from the alcohol, as I was lifted like a new bride into the strong arms of my intended and carried cross the threshold in the most wonderful of ways.

That seemed to be the action the crowd was waiting for, because they erupted into a spontaneous cheer that I was sure could be easily heard across the lake, and perhaps even further than that. The cheering muted somewhat as Ice closed the door with her heel then set me down gently on the varnished boards of our floor, steadying me with one hand to my shoulder.

You couldn't have wiped the grin off of my face with a jackhammer and some TNT.

I snuggled into the length of her lean body, resting my head against her shoulder as we watched the crowd cheerfully disperse through the small window by the side of the door.

"That was really sweet of them," I said finally as the last of the grills and half-empty kegs were loaded aboard several pickup trucks, which littered our driveway.

"It wasn't bad."

A tanned hand came into my field of vision and gently closed the blinds, shutting us off, for the moment, from the outside world. That same hand then flipped the switch near the door and the small alcove we were standing in became bathed in a soft, white light.

Breaking away from Ice, I turned and took in the fresh, gleaming beauty that was our home. "I can't believe it," I whispered, as much to myself as to my lover. "After all this time, it's finally here. Finally."

I just wanted to stand there for long hours and take it all in, which was impossible from where I was standing, but even that small alcove was the most precious thing I'd ever seen, unless one counted as I did the quiet presence standing beside me.

"How about if I build a fire?" Ice asked. "It's gonna get chilly tonight."

I nodded a bit absently, too wrapped up in this blanket of warmth I'd pulled over myself to notice much of anything at that moment. I knew when she left me though, the absence of her warm body allowing the faint chill in the house to seep in, raising goose bumps on my skin.

The chill gave me the impetus needed to stop playing statue and move away from the door, which, though labeled as the "front" door, was really in the rear of the house. It, as I've already written, opened into a small alcove, which in turned opened into a huge glassed in porch of sorts that ran along the back and one side of the house in an "L" shape. To the left of the door, as I faced away from it, were the usual porch accoutrements, a swinging lounger and some wooden chairs Pop had pressed upon me as well as two small glass-topped tables and a small reading lamp. To the right, and along the same wall as the alcove, was another door which led to the stand-alone kitchen which, though bearing little more than a stove, refrigerator, some pots and pans and a few dishes and glasses, was a room I was looking forward to getting to know a little more.

Staying with Ruby, I'd discovered a joy in cooking which I'd never had before. I suppose it was the teacher I had. Ruby was much more patient than my own mother, who, after watching me for a few scant seconds, would invariably throw up her hands in maternal disgust and insist on doing things herself.

With the pressure off, I discovered that not only did I enjoy the art of cooking, I found that I was pretty good at it as well, if I do say so myself.

Standing in the kitchen and looking outward, the short arm of the "L" came into view, an area totally empty at the time, but would be used as a storage area of sorts more commonly called a "mud room," where the washer and dryer would be hooked up, as soon as we had enough money to buy them.

Directly opposite the alcove, which bore the "front" door, was yet another door, and it was this door which led into the house proper.

Taking in a deep, happy breath and filling my lungs with the smell of *newness*, I stepped through that door and into the main body of my new home. This part of the cabin was, basically, one gigantic open area, with the dining, living, and reading rooms separated only by the differing types of furniture in each.

Along the back wall, the one which fronted the glassed in area where I had just been, was a long line of exquisitely made cabinetry which was broken in the middle by a huge—and I do mean *huge*—fireplace. Large enough for Ice to stand in without stooping over and wide enough for her to hold both arms out to their fullest extension without touching either side, the fireplace had been the center of many a family gathering in my youth, and I very much hoped for it to be that way again.

Turning away from the wall that housed the fireplace, the first thing that came to my vision was the view of the moonlight playing on the lake; a view made possible by an entire wall made up of windows, windows which looked out not only upon the pristine blue of the lake, but also upon the screened porch which ran the entire length of the front of the house.

The dining room, with its large and solid oak table, was to my right. In front of me, opposite the fireplace, were the couches, tables and chairs that made up the living room. To the left of that was the cozy library with its recessed bookcases taking up space on two walls, its comfortable chairs, and the small lamps which rested on corner tables.

Another recessed alcove stood next to the fireplace, and in that alcove was the bathroom and what had been, in the cabin's first incarnation, the master bedroom. It was now assigned visitor's duties because of the one change I'd made to the original specs of the cabin.

A set of stairs shared space with the library to the extreme left of the house, steps which led up to a loft which, like the porch below it, ran the entire length of the cabin. When I'd stayed there as a young girl, the loft had been broken up into four separate bedrooms, each with its own walls and door. Now, however, there were no walls and no doors, just one gigantic open space that made up the master bedroom.

The loft was bordered on one side by a huge window, and on the other by a wooden railing styled to look like a weathered split-rail fence, which allowed one to look down into the rest of the cabin when standing before it. It didn't, of course, allow much in the way of privacy, but the open, airy feel, plus the immense size of the newly converted room more than made up for that, in my opinion.

Sighing in pure, unadulterated bliss, I turned to see my lover watching me, an expression of amused fondness on her face. I walked over to her, enjoying the heat of the now roaring fire on my skin as I did so, and wrapped myself against her body like a limpet, soaking up every precious second of this time.

I took in her scent, the scent of the house, and the scent of burning logs and committed it all to memory; a memory I'd pull out again and again to savor when the days were long and the nights, longer.

"Thank you," I whispered against the fabric covering her chest. "It's everything I dreamed of and so much more. You made my dream come true."

"You made your own dream come true, my Angel," she rumbled, pressing her cheek against the top of my head. "I just helped out a little, that's all."

In no mood for arguing, I simply wrapped myself more tightly around her, closing my eyes and feeling on top of the world.

And when Ice's close presence, the warmth of the fire at my back, the excitement of the day, and two—or was it three?—glasses of Pop's brew combined to make me yawn for the third time in as many minutes, Ice pulled gently away from me, grated the fire, and, grasping my hand gently, led me toward the steps that led to the bedroom.

Our bedroom.

That thought caused the sleepiness to vanish as if it never were and each step up the stairs caused me to be come more awake, more aware, and definitely more excited.

Coming to the top of the stairs, Ice released my hand and allowed me to precede her into the loft, which I gladly did, taking in everything around me with wondering, and appreciative, eyes.

Then I stopped when something struck me as odd about the bed we had both chosen, a huge king-sized wonder that made a very large dent in whatever savings we'd heretofore managed to accumulate.

It wasn't the bed per se, but rather the headboard that seemed ...different.

Walking to the foot of the bed and looking at the headboard straight on in the light of the fire flickering below, the difference struck me and the breath left my lungs at about the same time the blood left my brain, causing me to feel just the slightest bit faint.

"Oh my God," I whispered, awestruck.

Where a simple cherry headboard had stood before, a massive walnut one stood in its stead. In the center was a meticulously carved oval, and within that oval, carved in bas relief, was the most gorgeous rendering of a bonsai tree that I'd ever seen, and believe me when I tell you that I've become quite an expert on all things bonsai over the years, being Ice's partner as I am.

Dumbstruck, I turned to look at Ice. "Where did you get this?"

The faintest of blushes highlighted her features, nearly hidden by the flickering firelight. "I made it," she said simply.

"You made...you *made* this?!"

The blush deepened as she nodded slowly, her expression telling me she was unsure how I was taking her magnificent gift.

Tears trebled my vision as I held a hand out, silently asking her to join me by the bed. When she came, I wrapped her in a hug so tight that an atom would have been hard-pressed to get between us. "If I live to be a thousand, I don't think I'll ever see anything more beautiful," I whispered, my voice muffled by tears as well as by Ice's chest where my lips rested.

After a moment, she pulled away and wiped my tears with gentle fingers. "Please don't cry, Angel."

"I can't help it. Every time I think I couldn't possibly be any more loved, you go and do something like this." I smiled a watery smile. "You touch my soul, Morgan. That's where the tears come from."

She smiled at me, rested her fingers tenderly against my cheek for a moment, then gathered me back into the wonderful nest of her arms, placing a gentle kiss on the crown of my head. "You *are* loved, my sweet Angel. More than you will ever know."

Her poetic words, all the more beautiful for being so rare, only caused my tears to fall that much harder. As I rested my head against her chest, I looked again at the magnificent carving that appeared to live and breathe and dance as the light from the fire played over it. "Does it have a name?" I asked finally, well remembering my lover's penchant for naming her trees.

"The Freedom of Desire," she whispered, her lips just brushing against the exquisitely sensitive shell of my ear.

My body erupted into flames to rival the hottest fire nature had to offer, and when her tongue grazed along the path her lips had made, followed by the soft nip of her sharp teeth, I was well and truly lost to the searing heat of our joined passion.

Strong arms lifted me up and placed me in our bed with a tenderness reserved for priceless objects while lips and tongue and teeth moved slowly down to continue their assault, this time on the flesh of my neck; flesh that was flushed rosy with the heat that Ice was generating within me.

A shift of the mattress and suddenly I was covered with a living blanket, enveloped in the intoxicating scents of primal musk and exotic spice, the fire within burning ever hotter when full, wet lips searched out and found my own, setting my body to writhing beneath the heavier weight of my lover.

The kiss deepened and I tasted the deep moan that rumbled

from her chest. Tasted it, savored it, and returned it with one of my own as her fingers threaded themselves through the shortened locks of my hair. Her lips parted and I took her tongue into me, worshiping it with my own as our bodies danced in tandem atop the bed sheets.

After long moments of bliss, her lips left mine and I felt the scrape of her teeth along my jugular as her hands slipped from their hold on my hair, trailing down my body in an electrical current of passion. A strong thigh parted my trembling legs while her hands worked the fly of my jeans, tugging it down forcefully as she grunted her need into the hollow of my throat.

A teasing hand slipped past the barrier of my briefs, fingers bathing themselves in the slickness found there as a wicked grin curved the corners of her gorgeous mouth and a darting tongue teased out to wet lips ripe for kissing.

Withdrawing her hand, she rolled up to her knees, yanking my jeans and underwear off in one fluid move and tossing them on the floor beside the bed. The faint chill of the air against my heated skin provided a pleasure all its own.

A pleasure that was quickly surpassed when she then straddled my naked hips and slowly removed her T-shirt, baring her magnificent breasts to me. Unable to stop myself, I reached up and covered them with my hands, feeling them tighten and grow full beneath the tender flesh of my palms. Backlit by the fire, she was my dark goddess, all primal heat and intoxicating beauty.

Her eyes glittered silver beneath long lashes and her hips took up a slow rocking, and I could feel the molten heat of her even through the thick denim of her jeans as they rode against my own heat in a rhythm that had my hips pumping against her, begging for more contact.

"Harder," she growled, and I squeezed her breasts more firmly, then took her straining nipples between my fingers and squeezed hard enough to cause the whites of her eyes to show as her thrusts against me became stronger, causing my own arousal to double until it was all that I could do not to just surrender to the edge that danced at the periphery of my vision.

She leaned down closer then, her fragrant hair falling in a curtain around my head, and rested the weight of her upper body onto clenched fists on either side of my shoulders. Her hips slipped down and in between my splayed legs as her thrusts continued, accompanied by guttural grunts with each forward motion of her body.

"Harder," she growled again and I could do nothing but obey as stiff fabric of her jeans slid against me again and again without pause or mercy. My legs lifted of their own accord, my ankles locking behind her bent knees, lending strength to her thrusts.

Her long, graceful neck arched backward, exposing her throat as a long, low moan erupted, filling the air with its primal sound.

"Oh God," I whispered as I watched her climax run through her, darkening and heating her skin with a rosy flush. "Dear, *sweet* God."

White teeth gleamed and jaw muscles bulged as she rode out the last of her orgasm with a few more thrusts against me. Then she slumped down full on top of me, panting into the skin of my neck as her hot lips nuzzled against my flesh, gently suckling as she regained her breath.

Her lips became more insistent as she began to regain her strength, sucking at my pulse-point as if to take the beating of my heart down deep into her. Her hands unclenched and began to re-map the terrain of my body, skimming firmly over the hills and valleys they found there, exciting me still more with the fierce passion in her touch. Finally they came to rest at the collar of my T-shirt and, with a great rending tear, exposed the rest of my body to the heady heat of the night.

She was relentless, ravenous in her tasting of my breasts, lapping up the sweat bathing them as a cat to cream, leaving no square inch of tingling flesh untouched. Her hands continued their own relentless trek, her palms, callused from her long labors, teasing and taunting me as I writhed beneath her merciless attentions, never staying in one place long enough to give me even the briefest hint of relief.

But it was there, oh yes. I could see it, feel it, taste it, and smell it with every teasing nip of her teeth, with every heated caress. It was there, painted on the insides of my eyelids, humming in my ears, promising freedom.

Promising salvation.

And then, when she had wound me up so tightly that it felt as if every atom of my body was being bathed and stroked and wonderfully loved, her hot, wet mouth cupped over me, moaning into my greedy flesh, and with the first touch of her wondrous tongue, the salvation I had so desperately sought was mine and I flew higher and harder than I ever had before.

My body convulsed in joyous release as my fingers threaded through the midnight black of her hair, using it as an anchor to keep from flying completely away and becoming lost within the bliss I had become.

And when the summit was reached and I found myself tumbling heedless down the other side, she filled me full, curling her fingers and stroking me within and without, mixing slowness with quickness, gentleness with ferocity, feeding me, lifting me until the scream of my release echoed loud in my ears.

And then she gentled me as a trainer calms a skittish colt, her fingers curled tight and nestling gently against my womb, her lips bestowing tender kisses designed not to arouse but to calm, and I came back into myself in the sweetest of ways, to find her head resting on my thigh, her chin tilted up to look at me, a joyous, happy light shining from the blue of her eyes.

"God, I love you," was all I had breath to say as I stroked the sweaty hair from her brow, my body bathed in the love of her eyes.

The smile she gave me stopped my heart, its sheer brilliance telling me more than words ever could.

After a moment, she gently withdrew and slid up beside me, molding our bodies together and stroking my back soothingly. I reached up to kiss her, and the taste of myself on her lips sent renewed energy from somewhere racing through my body. But she pulled away, her thumb running along my lips, and she slowly shook her head. "Rest now, sweet Angel. We have all night."

Too sated to be much disappointed, I gave into my languid body's stronger craving and felt myself fall asleep within the warm, tender strength of her arms, safe in the knowing that she would keep watch over whatever demons might think to invade my dreams.

And with her standing guard, they didn't dare.

Late the next morning, I awoke to the pleasant weight of Ice's head resting on my lower abdomen. Her sleep-tousled hair partially hid her face from me. Tendrils of it stirred gently with each long, slow exhale, tickling against me and raising goose bumps across my flesh.

Her breath was cool on the skin of my slowly awakening body and I resisted the urge to squirm, realizing yet again what a wonderful rejuvenator sleep really is. As if sensing my predicament, she stirred, just slightly, tightening her hold around my thigh and rubbing her cheek against the skin of my belly in an unconscious gesture full of trust and love.

I held my breath against the possibility of her awakening too soon, wanting nothing more at the moment than to cherish the rare chance to watch her in sleep, then relaxed as her own breathing once again deepened in slumber.

The autumn sun streaming in through the window cast her in burnished bronze, a living sculpture made by the finest of craftsmen in the image of a goddess called to earth. I watched as the swaying trees outside the window moved interesting shadows over her naked skin, highlighting, then obscuring, the thick muscles of her back.

As I looked on, I tried to think back to a time I had been more at peace and couldn't. Even the ever-present specter of justice failed to hold sway over me that morning.

I was loved. I was safe.

I was home.

Lifting my hand, I gently stroked her hair, allowing my mind to drift aimlessly over everything and nothing, content in the tranquility of an early fall morning.

She stirred again, likely under the effects of my languid petting, and nuzzled my belly once more before placing a kiss on the inside of my right thigh, and then my left. Then, her body bed warm and sleep soft, she rose up beside me, drawing me into her arms and capturing my lips in her own in a kiss which left my senses reeling.

"Morning," I said, my voice suspiciously husky, when she finally pulled away.

"Mmmm," she rumbled, smacking her lips, "that it is."

"Sleep well?"

"Very."

"Good." And with a grin full of devilment and a heart full of lust, I slid down her body and took a patiently waiting nipple into my mouth, humming with delight when it grew firm beneath the suckling strokes of my tongue.

Ice's gentle murmurings and her guiding hand to the back of my head encouraged me to give full vent to my morning passions. Her body responded instantly to my increasingly bold touches and I felt her breathing go labored as my hand trekked southward, skimming the flat, muscled plane of her belly and feeling it contract beneath my fingers.

And when I delved deep into her wet heat and felt her clenching, welcoming grip on my fingers, the low, responsive moans in my ear let me know that heaven, far from being unattainable, was a simple bed in a simple cabin in a backwater town miles away from anywhere.

And that's *exactly* where I wanted it to be.

Time is a funny thing. Sometimes it's in the hands of a greedy miser doling out seconds like moth-eaten dollars. And sometimes it's in the hands of a downhill skier, rushing by so quickly that you can only stop and wonder where the days have gone when you look in the mirror and spot your first gray hair. Not that I've found any yet, mind you, but I'm sure you get my point.

To say that our first few weeks of co-habitation in our new home were filled with carnal and spiritual bliss would be overstating things by a good margin. Well, perhaps not the "carnal" part. That was most definitely bliss of the highest order, and, if I'm to be totally truthful, still is.

But there were bumps along the road which, I suppose, happen to any couple setting up housekeeping for the first time. The roadblocks were a great deal smaller than when I had spent time doing the very same thing with Peter years ago, but they were there nonetheless and, given the love I have for Ice, were far more jarring to me than similar problems with my deceased husband ever were.

One of the first things I discovered was that my love of open spaces might well have put a nail into a coffin not even built yet.

If there is any one thing that Ice guards more zealously than her privacy, I haven't found it yet. Even in the Bog, the very antithesis of a secluded retreat (even in solitary, you're watched more closely than a hawk choosing his dinner menu), she managed to make it quite clear to all and sundry that if she was in her cell and her door was closed, God help the woman, guard or inmate, who attempted to intrude without a written invitation.

But in a cabin with few rooms and even fewer doors, a private space for either of us was something sorely lacking, and something I wished at the time I had had the foresight to think of before the place was finished. Particularly when I moved my "classroom" from Ruby's study to our house and young people seemed always to be underfoot. Paying gig or not, it began to get a bit much, even for so gregarious a soul as myself.

However, since spilled milk only gets sour when you shed tears over it, the only real choice we had was to just go ahead and make the best of the situation.

One of the first changes I made was to turn the back porch into a classroom of sorts. It was comfortable, brightly lit, and glassed in to protect us from the elements. It also kept curious eyes out of the main part of the house, unless the bathroom needed to be utilized and, when that happened, they went accompanied by me.

That way, when Ice came home, all she needed to do was go into the main cabin and close the door behind her, giving her all the privacy she needed after a long day working with people. At least until "school" was out and I came inside to join her.

She always seemed more than ready to see me by then.

As for myself, well, I've never really needed all that much private time. And when I do crave it, a long, luxurious, solitary bath complete with sweet smelling bubbles, candles, and a good book fills the bill quite nicely.

As autumn's chilly hold on the weather deepened, I also began to notice signs of restlessness in my partner. Ice has always been, and I believe always will be at heart, a woman of action. The building of our home combined with the hard work Pop gave her to do kept her mind and body busy during the long spring and summer months.

But now, with the cabin built and the work slowing down with the ending of the summer tourist season, there really didn't look to be that much for her to do besides chopping logs for our ravenous fireplace, a task which she took to with a relish usually reserved for a blind person gaining sight.

And so, the restiveness began to assert its hold. It showed itself in small ways. Like when she began to leave the warm nest of our shared bed at ungodly hours of the morning to strap on running shoes and go charging through the forest at break-neck speeds, perhaps chasing her demons, perhaps running from them. There was also the meticulously stitched canvas bag filled with God knows what suddenly hanging from the eaves in the corner of the house. Sounds of her beating it into quivering submission became a nightly occurrence around the ol' homestead. Though, to be honest, I've done my share of damage to that bag in the time we've been here. Self-defense skills, once learned, need to be kept up, as silver needs to be polished to avoid tarnish.

Besides, it was fun to have a crack at something that didn't hit back. Much, anyway.

But, since the winter's snows weren't far in the future, I knew that even these activities would soon be but a memory. And if she couldn't keep her body busy, I needed to find some way of keeping her brilliant mind that way.

And then an idea came to me and I kicked myself for not having thought of it sooner.

As I got to know him better, I developed a sort of kindred-spirit relationship with Pop. Like I had been in the Bog, he was the man to see if you needed something you couldn't otherwise get your hands on. He had his fingers in a great number of pies, and if he liked you, he wasn't at all averse to sharing the spoils. For a price of course. Though in my case, the price was so low as to be negligible.

And so I went to him on a certain fall day with several requests, and, with a knowing glint in his eye, he accepted the challenge and agreed to do his best to get me what I needed. With Pop on the case, I knew my merchandise was as good as in my hands.

Sure enough, not more than a week went by when I received a call asking me to come and retrieve my packages. And for the price of one home-cooked meal, I took home some things that I hoped would help get Ice through the long winter ahead.

She came home that night, sweaty and disheveled from a day cutting wood, not only for our own fireplace but, by the amount of moisture gluing her shirt to her body, for half the town as well. She had also been helping some of the townspeople replace the roof on Mrs. Symmonds' house before the snows set in.

After letting her shower, sharing dinner with her and talking about nothing important, I handed her a slim square box wrapped up in pretty paper.

I was treated to a raised eyebrow before she looked at the box in her hands, turning it over in the light.

"Well?" I asked, impatient as always. "Aren't you gonna open it?"

"I dunno. Will it bite me?" Her grin was one of pure devilment.

"No. But *I* might if you don't open the damn thing."

"Oooo. Now *there's* a frightening thought." Her eyes positively radiated amusement.

I gave her back my best scowl and considered throwing in a pout for good measure. I was pretty sure I could even manufacture tears if it would get her to open the box faster.

With a truly pious look of beleaguered long-suffering, she set to opening the gift I'd given her, ripping the paper down to the box below, setting it aside, then opening the box itself. Her gaze, when it finally met mine, held within it an interesting mixture of curiosity and fondness. "Brings back some memories," she said, smiling.

I returned her grin. "Yeah. Mostly stupid ones, for me. Still, if you hadn't asked, I never would have met you, so my naïveté aside, they're pretty good ones."

Walking over to me, box in hand, she gave me a gentle kiss on the lips. "Thanks."

"You're welcome. It...um...it's part of a larger gift. If

you'll follow me?"

After a moment, she nodded and followed me to the door beneath the stairs, which led to the front porch, whose screens were covered with glass windows in anticipation of winter, and therefore made a perfect home for my gifts.

Turning on the recessed lights we had installed, I stepped back and allowed her to precede me onto the porch. I stood in the shadows, waiting and hoping against hope that she'd be pleased with my gift.

The expression on her face when she turned to look at me left no doubt in my mind that she was.

"I...um...know you were never able to get the ones you left behind, so I figured that you could just replicate them here." I shrugged, the tiniest bit embarrassed. "Or do whatever with them."

I wanted to say more, to perhaps explain myself better, but found myself suddenly engulfed in an embrace I never wanted to leave.

Ya done good, Angel, I heard Corinne's voice say in my mind. *Ya done real good.*

And with a shift of her strong body, I felt myself borne aloft and carried with the utmost grace and gentleness out of the porch and up to our bed.

To be thanked, properly, for the four bonsai trees spending their first night on a long table on the porch of our home.

Chapter 8

If March is said to sometimes go out like a lion, October went out like a sunning rattler who'd just had his tail stepped on by an annoying tourist trying to get that "perfect" shot of the wife and kids in front of the Grand Canyon.

Which is to say, a very nasty mood indeed.

The rains moved in, apparently liked what they saw, and decided to stay around a good long while, loitering like a guest who wouldn't know a hint if it hit him between the eyes.

Everything in town came to a halt and our neighbors began to make nervous jokes about arks when the lake began to overrun its boundaries and started to encroach on the surrounding properties, most of which were year-round housing for the town's residents. Ice and I kept pretty busy helping our friends and neighbors weatherproof their homes and prepare for winter's long siege.

One afternoon saw the sky dark and dangerous. Just a degree or so below freezing, the storm unleashed its fury, sending sheets of sleet pounding against our windows as if trying desperately to get inside. Outside, the world looked like a fairyland, the trees hooded in cloaks of shimmering ice.

I sat on the couch in front of a roaring, toasty fire, wrapped comfortably in my warmest robe and listening as Ice idly hummed along to an aria playing on our sound system as she leafed through some magazine or other. The paper sat on my lap unread as I took in the beautiful sounds of her voice, allowing the music to flow over and through me, warming spots even the fire couldn't touch.

Leaning my head against the back of the couch, I closed my eyes and smiled, pleasantly sleepy and very much content with my lot in life at that particular moment. While Mother Nature spewed out her worst, I was warm, and dry, and loved.

Ah yes, and well loved at that. We'd spent most of the morning and part of the afternoon in a loving tangle of insatiable passion, relishing the opportunity to do so whenever our desires took us without fear of prying eyes or ears.

I let those thoughts flow through my mind and body, smiling wider at the tightening in my groin from the sensations they produced. Then I opened my eyes and shook my head, chiding myself for my foolishness. Picking up the paper and shaking it out, I lazily flipped through the pages of newsprint, looking for something to spark my interest.

A subscription to the *New York Times* had been a housewarming gift from Ruby, whose newspaper I had always pilfered while staying under her roof, depriving her of her much beloved crosswords. While I didn't miss living in the U.S. per se, it was still nice to keep up on what was going on over there occasionally and so the paper was a welcome gift.

Turning to the world news section, I idly scanned the headlines, looking for anything of interest, when something caught my eye. I stopped, blinked, and read again. And then again. When I finally looked up, it was to find Ice watching me intently.

"You alright?"

"I...don't know. I think so. I'm just...not really sure, I guess."

Laying her book down on the table, she rose gracefully to her feet and came to stand behind the couch. "What's up?"

I handed the paper to her. "Would you mind reading this over and telling me if I'm seeing what I think I'm seeing?"

After a moment, the paper was handed back down to me again. "Yup."

I looked back over the printed text, trying to wrap my mind around what it was telling me.

PITTSBURGH, PENNSYLVANIA (AP) - America's oldest female inmate will soon enjoy her first taste of freedom in 45 years.

Corinne Weaver, 71, is set to leave Rainwater Women's Correctional Facility near Pittsburgh on Thursday. Weaver, serving a three consecutive life sentence term for the poisoning deaths of her four husbands, was granted a pardon last month by Governor George Green.

Weaver's case was taken up by human rights activists after she recently suffered a series of strokes that left her confined to a wheelchair.

"It's inhumane to keep an elderly woman locked up in her final years in her condition," said Al Merman, president of Human Rights Now!

After numerous letter writing campaigns and many protests staged outside the governor's mansion, Gov. Green relented. "I've reviewed Mrs. Weaver's case," the Governor said at a press conference on Monday, "and I find she is no longer a threat to society. The right thing to do is to let her have her freedom."

Green's main opponent in next month's elections, Sam Jones, was quick to support Weaver's case. "It's a shame the governor had to be hounded into this decision," he said. "It's obvious this woman will only suffer more by staying in a system in sore need of serious reform."

Weaver's lawyer, Donita Bonnsuer, a known Human Rights activist, was unavailable for comment.

"Did you know about this?" I asked, trying to keep the accusatory tone from my voice. I knew that Ice had, from the time she left prison for the first time, always kept tabs on Corinne, keeping her safe from predatory inmates who thought beating up little old librarians was the height of fun and games. To think that Ice would keep the news of Corinne's failing health, let alone her pending release, from me was making me very angry indeed.

"Not about the strokes, no." She came to sit down beside me, not touching, but close. "I knew about the protests, and Donita told me that there was a good chance she'd get her parole granted, but she asked me to cut off all contact with Corinne. For the same reason I left you alone when I escaped."

"So you couldn't be linked to her."

"Exactly."

"But why didn't you tell me?"

Ice sighed. "Because I didn't want to get your hopes up." She turned her head to look at me. "Look. I know how much Corinne means to you. She means a great deal to me, too. I just wanted to be sure before telling you anything, one way or another. If that was a mistake on my part, then I'm sorry."

I sighed as well. "I appreciate why you think you had to keep this to yourself, Ice, but I'd really rather be treated as an adult by you. I'm not a child, Morgan. I *can* deal with disappointments, you know."

Ice looked down at her hands resting in her lap. "I know,"

she replied softly. "I just don't like to see you have to. Especially if I can help it."

Touched by the sweetness of her gesture, even if I didn't agree with it, I pulled her over into a heartfelt hug, happy when she finally lifted her arms to return it. To let her off the hook, I changed the subject, slightly. "What's going to happen to her?"

"Donita will help her out, I'm sure. Just like she was willing to help you. Corinne's got a lot of money stashed away. She'll be just fine."

I breathed heavily into her shirt. "I miss her."

She rubbed my back soothingly. "I know, Angel. I do, too. Corinne's a good person."

I pulled away slightly. "I hate to think of her all alone down there. Sick. Not able to walk. Surrounded by strangers. Even in prison, she had her books, her job, her friends. Now what does she have?" I looked down at my own hands. "All the money in the world won't get those things for her now."

"She has Donita," Ice replied gently, chafing my hands in her own. "And Donita has a great number of contacts, Angel. People who will be happy to befriend Corinne without a thought to how rich she is. She'll be well looked after, believe me." Her eyes blazed into my own. "I wouldn't say it if it wasn't true."

I nodded, then looked down at our joined hands. "I know. I believe you, Ice. It's just..." I sighed again. "I want to help her. She's done so much for me and I just want to give something back to her." After a moment, I looked up at her again. "After she's released, do you think there's any way I could contact her? Even for just a second? To convince myself she's alright? I'll understand if you think it isn't safe. I just need to be sure, that's all."

After a moment, Ice smiled at me and squeezed my hands. "I'll see what I can do."

And *that* I believed.

The days stretched slowly into weeks and, finally, the winter snows came to lay claim on the land. The holiday season was quickly approaching and a winter-gloomy town seemed to brighten just slightly at the prospect. Trees and wreaths started appearing through windows and doors and the people all seemed to be a bit friendlier—not that they weren't friendly already—greeting everyone they passed with a cheery "Happy Holidays!"

Ice wasn't home much during this early part of winter. Though the work at Pop's station might have dried up for the moment, there was still plenty of other work to be had if one only knew where to look and was willing to sweat for it.

And Ice, of course, knew how to do both. In spades.

For myself, I kept busy with my students, their number growing ever larger as children from other towns began to pay me weekly visits for tutoring sessions. I also spent a good deal of time with Ruby, talking about nothing in particular, just enjoying her company and her delicious coffee.

Though I resolved not to, I found myself asking Ice quite a few times about Corinne. Her answer was always the same. "I'm doing my best, Angel."

To keep my mind off upsetting her too much with my incessant questioning, I turned my thoughts to other things. Namely what to get my absolutely impossible to buy for lover for Christmas. The book signed by Solzhenitzyn was one of the few things to survive her escape from the Bog intact, and the four bonsai trees I'd purchased were doing incredibly well under her talented hands. A new set of mechanic's tools, while practical, seemed hardly the romantic, or meaningful, gift I wanted to give her on our first Christmas as free women.

It had to be something special. Something rare. Something perfect.

And then I had it. An absolutely perfect—to my mind, at least—gift. There were only two problems. One was to see if such a gift even existed. The other would be going about finding it if it did indeed exist.

So, of course, I went to Pop with both problems. And with his usual knowing grin, he resolved to help in any way he could.

I returned home well satisfied.

Thanksgiving came and went and, for it being my first one as a hostess, it went off pretty well, if I do say so myself. Ruby and Pop joined us at our table and, with Ice's patient help, dinner went without a hitch, the freshly butchered turkey golden brown, succulent, and as good as I'd ever remembered my mother's tasting.

And after dinner and dessert were consumed, the conversation finished for the night, and our guests seen safely to their homes, we spent the rest of the evening giving thanks in a much more intimate and pleasurable way.

It was, I do believe, the best part of the day.

Christmas, then, was fast approaching and, after several tension-filled weeks, Pop finally came through on his promise and my gift was stored safely away at the bottom of my closet, a place Ice never looked, her own need for a private space prohibiting her from even thinking of looking into mine, even if I had minded, which I most certainly didn't.

On one evening, a week or so before the holiday, I was sitting alone, reading a book and waiting for the sound of Ice's footfall outside the cabin. She'd been away since before dawn, helping the Drew brothers repair some pipes which had frozen, then burst with the winter's deep freeze. She'd called me once to let me know she'd be late and not to wait dinner on her, and so I didn't, eating my own and keeping her portion warm inside the oven.

Then I smiled as I heard the crunch of the truck's tires on the neatly salted and cindered driveway. Getting up, I threw another log on the fire, bringing the heat up so Ice could warm herself after working in the cold for an entire day. Then I lit some candles for ambience and patiently waited for her to come into the house, fiddling a little with the Christmas decorations I'd put up that afternoon as a way to pass time waiting for her to return home.

A knock on the door chased the pleasant thoughts from my mind and my heart rate accelerated. No one visited this late at night. The only reason someone would have to knock would be to deliver bad news.

Stop thinking crazy, Angel. Ice probably misplaced her key or something. But that thought, in and of itself, was crazy. Ice never misplaced *anything.*

Ok, then maybe her hands are full and she needs help getting the door open.

Yeah, right. Since when has that ever happened?

It could.

When hell freezes over.

Shut up! Just shut up.

Biting the inside of my lip, I startled as the knock sounded again, more urgently this time. Feeling my breathing pick up its pace, I crossed the living room and opened the door that led onto the back porch, my eyes detecting nothing through the frost-glazed windows.

With a trembling hand, I tried to open the door, but the knob obstinately refused to turn. Once I realized it was locked, I quickly thumbed the release and tried again. It turned easily in my hand and I slowly pulled open the door, resisting the urge to close my eyes to whatever sight awaited me.

And what awaited me was something I would never have believed if I hadn't been standing there looking at it with my own two eyes.

The blood rushed straight down from my brain, leaving me breathless and faint, as I stared out at a person who *could not* be standing there. Could not. Yet there she was.

Corinne, her face wreathed in a breathtaking smile, stood before the threshold waiting to be let in.

"Oh. My. God."

Her grin broadened. "Not quite. Will I do in a pinch?"

Her outline became hazy through the film of my tears and I blindly reached out to her, engulfing her in a hug almost as tight as any I'd given Ice, forgetting for a moment her advanced age and frail health.

"Corinne!" I blubbered in her ear, taking in the scent of her with a great, heaving gasp. "Where did you...? How did you...?"

After squeezing me back just as hard, Corinne pulled away, her own eyes suspiciously bright beneath the glare of her glasses. "Wouldn't you know? There I was, just minding my own business when out of nowhere comes this big gorgeous lunk of a woman who kidnaps me, throws me in some godawful truck not fit for man nor beast, and drives hell bent for leather through miles and miles of backwoods roads with me hanging on for dear life. The next thing I know, here I am."

Her eyes twinkled merrily as she leaned in close once again to whisper in my ear. "I think I'm supposed to be your Christmas present. If I were you, I'd ask for a refund."

Pulling away from me again, she stepped aside, treating me to a view of Ice, who stood beside the truck, her hands stuffed deep in her pockets, a half-embarrassed expression on her face.

I almost knocked Corinne over into the snow as I ran outside the door and leapt into Ice's arms, arms which caught me and held me easily as I covered her face with grateful kisses. "Thank you," I whispered, too overcome to say anything else.

"You're welcome, sweet Angel," she murmured into my hair. "Merry Christmas."

I laughed and cried and squeezed her so tightly that I think if she had been anyone other than who she was, I might have broken a rib or two.

A prudently cleared throat pulled me back to reality and I turned my head to see Corinne smirking at us both. "Touching as this reunion is, my dears, I don't think my future includes turning into a rather decrepit looking ice sculpture. So, if you wouldn't mind too terribly much...."

Blushing in embarrassment, I loosened my hold around Ice at the same time she released me, placing me gently back on the ground. "God, I'm so sorry, Corinne! Come on. Let me show you inside. Do you have any bags?"

"No worries," she said airily, flapping her hand behind her. "The charming valet will get them for me."

I laughed at the low growl emanating from the chest of said valet and grasped Corinne's hand, leading her into the house. Then I stopped. "Wait a minute. Aren't you supposed to be in a wheelchair?"

Her eyes widened into the picture of perfect innocence. "That old thing?" Then she grinned. Evilly. "The doctor says I've gotten *much* better. Must be all that free air I've been taking in."

I looked at her. "Corinne. You didn't."

"Didn't what?" The woman was positively unrepentant.

"You know damn well what I'm talking about. You didn't fake your disability just to get out of prison, did you?"

"And what if I had?" Her look was one of defiant challenge.

She had a point. Still... "Did you?"

After a moment, she backed down. "No. Unfortunately, my disability, as you so politely call it, is quite real. I had a series of small strokes which did indeed manage to leave me confined to a wheelchair for a good little while. But you know how the press likes to blow things out of proportion, Angel. 'Confined' is a bit too strong a word. I still use it on occasion if I'm expected to walk a great distance or I've been on my feet too long, but otherwise, it just sits in a corner gathering dust."

"Did you bring it with you?"

"Of course. Wouldn't leave home without it."

Another cleared throat interrupted me, and when I looked over my shoulder this time, I saw Ice carrying the aforementioned wheelchair, together with several huge and no-doubt heavy bags and looking more like a pack mule than my lover, and waiting none-too-patiently for us to move out of the doorway.

Laughing, I went back outside to divest Ice of some of her burden, groaning when I slung a couple of the bags over my shoulder, almost toppling into the snow with the weight of them. "Dear God, Corinne! What do you have in here? Rocks?"

She pinned me with her patented withering stare. "Never you mind, missy. A woman has to have *some* secrets, after all."

Laughing and shaking my head, I tottered back into the house, my back groaning under the weight of Corinne's bags. Ice followed me in, finally out of the cold, and together we walked into the guest bedroom, depositing the luggage onto the bed and stretching abused muscles. Corinne joined us there and looked around the room appreciatively. "Not bad, ladies. Not bad at all. A body could get used to a place like this."

I grinned happily, pleased with her stamp of approval. "Well, it's yours for as long as you want it." Then I paused as a thought struck me and scratched at the back of my neck. "Speaking of which, how long *are* you staying with us?"

Corinne looked at me, over to Ice, then back to me again. She frowned a little. "Um...perhaps you and your partner there might want to have a little talk. I'll just stay here and ...freshen up a bit."

I looked to Ice, who gave a short nod and gestured the way out with a brief sweep of her arm. After a second's pause, I left the room, followed by Ice, who closed the door gently behind her.

I rounded on her, hands on my hips. "Ok. What's going on?" Though I'm sure I sounded angry, I really wasn't. Consciously, I softened my tone. "Is something wrong?"

"No. Nothing's wrong." She spread her hands wide. "It's just that the invitation's pretty open-ended."

I could feel my eyes narrowing. "What does that mean, exactly?" For a woman who turned "blunt" into an art form, she could be quite ambiguous when she wanted to be.

Her eyes narrowed right back at me. "It means just what I said, Angel. As far as I'm concerned, she's welcome to stay as long as she likes. I didn't put a specific time limit on it."

Nodding slowly, I crossed my arms over my chest. "Something tells me this could turn in to more than just a visit."

She smiled. "Only if that's what we all want it to be, Angel. I'm only speaking for myself here. You were worried about how she'd get on after prison. In truth, so was I, though I know Donita and I know she'd take the best care of Corinne she could." Turning away, she walked over to one of the chairs in the library and sat down, her hands clasped and hanging loosely between her knees. When she looked up at me, her face was as sincere as I'd ever seen it. "Your life isn't the only one Corinne has saved, Angel. And I think maybe I want to give something back to her, too."

Her head bowed and, unable to help myself even if I had wanted to, I walked over to the chair and perched carefully on one arm, sliding an arm around her shoulders and hugging her to me. It seemed quite obvious to me that something more than the current conversation was bothering her. "You wanna talk about it?"

After a moment, her head lifted and she quirked a small smile at me. "Maybe later."

Which meant, of course, that the subject was as closed as it could possibly get. For now.

I smiled to lighten the load. "Alright. You know where I live."

She butted me playfully with her head. "I know alright."

"So, shall we pay the piper for making her wait so long in that bedroom?"

Ice snorted. "Wait, my ass. She's heard every word we've been saying."

The door eased open and Corinne's perfectly coifed head poked out, her smile broad and knowing. "Was there ever any doubt?"

Laughing, I jumped up from the arm of Ice's chair and escorted our guest over to the couch. "You're incorrigible, Corinne."

"Mmm. So a lover or two has said in their time, yes."

Damnit! She did it again! Even after so long apart, that blasted woman still had the power to make me blush harder and more deeply than anyone save Ice. A change of subject was definitely in order. "Would you like some tea? Food? Anything?"

"No food, thank you. Ms. Tall, Dark, and Mute over there somehow managed to dig up her manners from whatever grave she'd buried them in and got some 'food on the hoof' on the way in. Though I think I'm still picking gristle from what few remain of my real teeth."

I looked over at Ice, who simply rolled her eyes and went back to the book she'd been reading the night before; something by Elliot, I believe, though she went through them so quickly it was difficult to be sure from one hour to the next.

"How about some tea, then?" I asked Corinne.

"That would be lovely."

"I'll get it," Ice said, coming to her feet and laying the book down on one of the tables. "You two just ...catch up or something."

Laying a hand on her arm as she passed by, I pulled her to a stop. "I've got your dinner in the oven if you're still hungry."

She smiled and kissed my hair. "Great. Be back in a bit."

And with that, she was gone, leaving us both to stare after her.

"You have done that woman a world of good, Angel," Corinne remarked finally, softly.

"Freedom did that, Corinne. I just helped it along a little, that's all."

Smiling at me with infinite fondness, she tugged my hand, getting me to sit beside her and engulfing me in a wonderful hug.

"Nonsense, sweetheart. You tended a soul that was sickly and dying. You made it strong and full of life again. No one and nothing else can take credit for that, Angel. That woman in there is the way she is now because of you. Never sell yourself short on that. It doesn't become you."

Sometimes prayers you didn't even know you had are answered with such sweet simplicity that your heart swells in your chest and fills you with a warmth that even the sunniest spring day could never rival.

For me, this was one of those times. I allowed myself the comfort of an embrace I'd missed far more than I'd even admitted to myself, letting her love and kindness flow over me, soothing insecurities that I didn't realize I possessed.

Then I straightened up, drying my tears with the back of my hand and gave Corinne a watery smile. "So," I began after clearing my throat, "tell me how you *really* got here."

Laughing, she leaned her head against the back of the couch and grasped one of my hands, pulling it into her lap and holding it closely between both of her own. "That, my dear Angel, is a story and a half." Behind the thick lenses of her glasses, her gaze turned inward. "The Bog changed a great deal after you left it, Angel. The warden who'd replaced that idiot, Morrison, was forced to step down after some scandal or other, and the next one was hand-chosen by the governor himself, it being close to elections and all, don't you know."

She laughed, but it was a bitter sound. "He's a good man, as far as wardens go, I suppose. What is it they used to say? 'Strict, but fair.' He fired most of the guards, though. Said their attitudes 'weren't in keeping with the welfare of the prisoners' or some such blather." She waved a hand. "I didn't bother keeping up with the rest of his reformer's lingo after that."

"What about Sandra?" I asked in a hesitant voice. The head guard had been a very special person in my life during those long, cold, and sometimes bitter years in prison.

"He showed some smarts by keeping her on. If nothing else, she has the respect of the inmates and he can't afford to be without that link to the animals in his cages." She shifted slightly on the couch, adjusting the glasses as they rested on her nose. "In any event, not all the changes were visible ones. I suppose you could say that the Bog lost its spirit."

And here, she turned to me, her smile sad, but loving. "One it never knew it had."

I was tempted to throw in some offhand comment, but her previous gentle rebuke against selling myself short made me hold my tongue, though in no way have I ever felt that I gave that place any type of spirit at all.

Smiling slightly, she continued. "I'd seemed to have misplaced my own sense of spirit somewhere along the line as well. When I first began to feel unwell, I chalked it up to a healthy dose of convict's depression and let it go at that." She shrugged. "Didn't seem much point in doing otherwise."

I could feel the tears, hot and wet, as they rolled down my face, blurring my vision of her as she recited her tale with all the dispassion of a woman reading a faintly interesting newspaper article.

"Don't cry, Angel," she said, using much the same tone Ice did when making that same request. "The story *does* have a happy ending, after all."

"I know," I said, sniffling—something I hated to do, by the way. "I just wish I could have been there with you. For you."

"I'm just as glad that you weren't," she replied, gripping my arm with a strong hand. "I would have never wanted you to see me like that, Angel. Never."

"But..."

"No. Do *not* blame yourself. Those strokes would have come whether you'd been there or not."

"But, maybe..."

"Stop." She laid a gentle finger across my lips, halting my words, her eyes stern. "No more."

After a moment, I nodded and she removed her finger. "Good. Now, where was I?" Then she smiled. "Ahh. Finally. I thought perhaps you'd gone to China to fetch the leaves yourself."

Slightly startled, I looked up to see Ice standing next to me, two mugs of tea in her hands and a concerned expression on her face. Coming to my feet, I took the mugs from her hands, put them on the table, and hugged her to me to allay whatever fears her expression was revealing. The arms that encircled me in return were hesitant at first, but when I simply squeezed harder, their grip around me tightened and I smiled, the last of my tears drying on the fabric of her shirt. "I'm alright."

She pulled away, staring at me with intent. "You sure?"

Smiling more broadly, I nodded. "Yeah. It just hit me hard for a minute there. I'm ok now."

After looking at both of us for a very long moment, Ice finally released me completely and walked over to the library, sitting down and picking up her book once again.

Reclaiming my spot on the couch, I picked up my mug, handed Corinne hers, and together we sipped our tea in silence, listening to the crackle of the fire's flames.

After several quiet moments had passed, Corinne resumed her tale. "One morning, I awoke to discover I couldn't move much on the left side of my body. I tried to call for help, but found I couldn't speak well, either." Then she laughed. "I suppose it was one of the first times in my life that I was actually happy I was in prison. Once I'd missed headcount, the guards came looking for me, and the next thing I knew, I was taking a nice ambulance ride to the county hospital."

She took another sip of tea, then continued. "The doctors couldn't do much for me. Apparently I'd had several strokes in quick succession over the past several days, the last one being the biggest. They gave me some medication they said might help and arranged for me to be transferred to a Rehabilitation Hospital to learn how to walk, talk, and care for myself again."

Her face became stony. "The warden forbade it. He demanded they discharge me and send me back to prison without therapy. To their credit, the doctors put up a good fight, but in the end, the warden won out. They put me in a wheelchair and off I went, back to the Bog."

"Jesus," I breathed, beyond incensed at the insensitivity of the warden. "I thought you said he was fair!"

"He *is* fair, Angel. I'm a murderer, remember? The Black Widow. He didn't want to have the taxpayers up in arms over my rehabilitation." She shrugged. "Just the way of the world."

I sat up straight on the couch, seeing red. "It shouldn't be, damnit! Everyone deserves the right to be treated like a human being!"

Throwing back her head, Corinne laughed. "There's that fire I've been waiting for!"

"It's not funny, Corinne," I replied indignantly.

"Of course it is, Angel! It's wonderful! Do you know how long I've waited to hear your blazing tones of righteous indignation? I swear, that's what kept me going through all this."

Still angry, I crossed my arms, flinching away as she reached up to pinch my cheek, something she *knew* I detested with a passion, and so, of course, did at every available opportunity.

I couldn't stay angry with her for long, though, and with a final scowl, I relaxed back against the couch once again, grabbing my mug and downing the rest of my tea as I waited for her to continue, resolving not to give her still more fodder by losing my temper again.

"In any event," she finally relented, "I found myself back in the Bog much worse for the wear. I only thank the goddess that I'm right handed and could still do some things for myself, else I likely would have thought up a way to get myself killed just to end the indignities." She smiled to take the sting from her words. "Critter was a great deal of help to me, as were Pony and Sonny and some of the others. They spent long hours trying to encourage me, in their own special ways, to follow the exercise plan the doctors had managed to slip into my bag when I left the hospital, but I'm afraid I was quite cross with them all. Like I said before, there didn't seem to be much point in it."

"So what happened?" I asked, looking at a woman who was as far from a crippled invalid as I could possibly imagine.

She grinned. "Ah, at last, an easy question. One day, while I was in the library feeling quite sorry for myself, Pony came in and without so much as a 'how-do-you-do', promptly wheeled me into the common room, one of the few places to escape the wrath of the warden's redecoration scheme. She parked me in front of the television and turned the volume up full-bore, as if I'd gone deaf as well as paralyzed."

"Well?" I asked when she paused. I looked over at Ice who, though she appeared engrossed in her reading, I could tell was listening as intently as I was.

"It was the local news and a reporter was standing in front of the governor's mansion. In back of her were all these people shouting and waving banners. Most of the banners said 'Free Corinne' or 'Prisoners are Humans Too' and other slogans of that nature. I was quite stunned, as I'm sure you'd suppose."

I just nodded, keeping to myself the fact that, were I in her position, I'd most probably be a good deal more than "stunned" to see people protesting on my behalf no matter *what* the reasons.

"When the view switched back to the reporter," Corinne continued, "I saw a very familiar face standing next to her."

"Who?"

"A certain lawyer we all know and love."

"Donita?" I was shocked, and yet I wasn't. Somewhere deep inside, I knew Donita had an important part to play.

"The very same."

"I didn't know she was your lawyer."

"Neither did I." This was said with a significant glance in Ice's direction, who, prudently, I thought, chose to keep her nose buried in her book.

When she saw that my partner wasn't going to rise to the bait, she turned her attention back on me. "She played the part of the virtuous well, standing on her soapbox and explaining my condition in the bleakest terms possible, describing how I'd been denied, in her terms, even the most basic of health care; how I sat paralyzed in my wheelchair, unable to tend to even the most basic of my needs, at the mercy of uncaring guards and prisoners. She was so good that even I found myself feeling some small sympathy for this woman behind bars; a woman, I thought, not very much like me at all."

She stretched a bit, then settled back against the couch once again, draining the last dregs of her tea from the mug and setting it down on the end table. I kept silent, rapt with attention in her tale. "She also put forth more salient, less emotional, points. Like how I was the oldest female inmate in the nation. How I had already served almost twice the prison time that the average male offender with an equal or greater sentence served before release. How, with my current disability, I would be unable to speak for myself when the time for my next parole hearing came." Corinne smiled fondly. "She put her points forth so well that I think that, if a petition for my immediate release had been there right then, even the reporter would have dropped her microphone to sign it."

"I don't doubt that for a minute. Donita's very...passionate...about her work."

"And about other things as well, if memory serves," Corinne shot back, eyeing Ice yet again.

This time, the collected works of Elliot lowered and blue eyes glittered with a look that would have fused metal. I think even my fillings felt the assault.

Unrepentant, Corinne simply stared right back over the tops of her glasses, her lips curved in a smile that was evil incarnate. Though the heat in the room seemed to rise several degrees, I shivered, as if a goose had toddled across my grave and decided to build a nest there.

"Can we get back to the story please?" I finally interjected to stop the battle of wills that was quickly escalating into a full-scale war, even without a word being said on either side.

"Fine," Corinne finally replied, turning to me and folding her hands primly on her lap.

I breathed a silent sigh of relief.

"When the spot was over and the news moved on to more worthy issues, the television was turned off and I was wheeled back into the library by three Amazons with passions of their own. Once there, I was locked into place, and then told in no uncertain terms that if so many total strangers were willing to fight for me, I'd damn well better start fighting for myself. Or else. The 'else' part of the equation, of course, wasn't spelled out, but I was led to believe that the consequences of my refusal would be very dire indeed."

"So you told them to go to hell."

She grinned again. "Perhaps a bit more garbled than that, but essentially, yes. Even gave them directions if they were so inclined to take my suggestion."

Shaking my head, I couldn't help but laugh. The strokes might have weakened Corinne's body, but it was glaringly evident that her mind, as well as her spirit, was still very much intact. "Obviously you must have listened at some point, though," I observed, looking at her apparently intact body.

She shrugged. "There may be no fool like an old fool, but I do manage to come to my senses eventually."

T.S. Eliot snorted. Or at least his book did.

"That's quite enough out of you, missy," Corinne said in the general direction of Ice, her nose lifted to quite a regal angle. "Don't think that your lover here knows so much about you that she wouldn't be surprised by some of the more sordid tales of you I have stored away."

Casting Corinne her most droll look, Ice closed her book, placed it back on the bookshelf, and stood, slowly stretching the kinks out of her body caused by a hard day's work. I felt my mouth go dry at the sight, as it almost always did, even after so many years together.

Walking over to us, she placed a kiss on my forehead and one on Corinne's proffered cheek, then threaded long fingers through her hair and shook it out before bidding us both a quiet goodnight.

After her long, lithe body disappeared up the stairs, Corinne and I let out twin sighs, as if we were a couple of school-girls who'd just seen the high school quarterback stroll by on campus.

I turned to look at her, swallowing against the dryness in my throat. "Tea?" I croaked.

"Tea," she returned.

We talked well into the night. Corinne continued her tale, picking it up from where she left the Bog for the first time in forty-five years.

"I was quite overwhelmed. You'll remember that I was incarcerated sometime after the war. Things were different then. Simpler. Smaller. When I left prison, it didn't only feel like I was entering a new country. It felt as if I was entering a new world. For a minute there, just a minute, I wanted to just forget everything and go back inside to a place I knew."

I found myself nodding in empathy, knowing exactly what

she had gone through, having had the same reaction myself, though not on so grand a scale, to be sure. If five years had changed the outside world so much, how much more could nine times that many?

She then went on to explain where she'd gone once out of prison. Donita had offered to put her up. Her lover, a singer of some small renown, was out on tour and the house was more than large enough to accommodate them both for as long as Corinne felt the need to stay.

"I took her up on the offer. Though I made it clear that the arrangement wasn't by far a permanent one. As temporary lodgings went, however, it was quite fine. I was up and walking by then, and the grounds were quite large and secluded as well, so I built up my strength by taking long, solitary walks, still marveling in the freedom to do as I wished, when I wished."

I nodded in commiseration with that as well, remembering well my own first forays into a world without bars, without fences; a world whose only constrictions were the ones I myself placed upon it.

"Then one evening, shortly after my release, a quite delicious young man appeared quite unexpectedly on the doorstep." She grinned, touching her hair. "And me, without my makeup."

Laughing, I gently slapped her arm, then shifted to a more comfortable position on the couch, various parts of my anatomy beginning to voice their displeasure over remaining dormant for such a long stretch of time.

As if taking a hint I wasn't aware I was projecting, she sped up her story, quickly telling me that, though she initially had reservations about the handsome—and she made it a point to state that word quite a few times, as if I'd missed it the first time, and the second, and third—stranger, they were soon laid to rest by Donita's apparently complete acceptance of the man.

And any doubts, which might have been left to linger in her mind, were irrevocably erased when he handed her an item he said came from a friend. Reaching into her purse, she then handed me the same item and I sat staring at it, stunned.

It was the picture of Ice and her family.

The only one she had.

"Who gave you this?" I asked, trailing a gentle finger over the forever-frozen figure of Ice as a child.

"He said his name was Andre."

My guess confirmed, I nodded, still looking at the picture in my hand. The very fact that it made it back to me safely showed me how much trust Ice had placed in both Andre and Corinne. I spared a second to wonder briefly just who Andre was to Ice, beyond a friend and contact. They had seemed comfortable with each other the one time I'd seen them together. Was he, like Donita, another lover? Ice had never mentioned a liking for what my father called "outdoor plumbing," but then again, I'd never really asked, so I couldn't be sure one way or the other.

That thought bothered me more than I wanted to admit.

Showing once again her disquieting propensity to read my thoughts, Corinne clamped a gentle hand around my wrist. "Worry not, sweet Angel. Andre is a friend to Ice, nothing more."

Flushing at having been read so easily, I looked up at her. "How do you know?" It wasn't asked in defense, but rather with curiosity.

She laughed lightly, squeezing my wrist. "Well, aside from the fact that he's as gay as my old dad's hatband, don't you think Ice would have mentioned if anything more had gone on between them? After all, she was quite up front about her former relationship with your lawyer."

I smiled with more relief than perhaps I should have shown, but the revelation *did* make me feel better. I said as much to Corinne, who returned my smile knowingly. Then she returned to other matters.

"Donita excused herself, and I led Andre to the living-room, where we sat and shared tea as he talked, in a roundabout way, about my 'getting away from it all' and how nice certain parts of Canada were this time of year." She snorted. "For Eskimos, perhaps, but I didn't debate the point with him. He had piqued my interest in a most pleasant way, and it wasn't just the body he was hiding under those rugged clothes either."

She looked at me again, her eyes filled with sadness. "You see, I didn't know where you had gone, Angel. For the first time in my life in the Bog, all my questions were met with silence. Andre was Ice's contact with Donita, but under strict orders from the tall, dark, and deadly one, he was forbidden to reveal any locations whatsoever. And that included yours."

"To keep her from knowing too much, right?" I guessed, well knowing how Ice's mind worked in such instances. "Don't ask, don't tell?"

"Exactly. Even with lawyer-client privilege, Ice didn't want to put Donita in a position untenable to her. I didn't even know if she'd managed to find you after you'd been released, though I imagined she did. She loved you much too much to let you go so easily." She smiled sadly. "It was the fantasy of the two of you, striding off into the proverbial sunset together, that got me through many a depression-filled night in the Bog, Angel."

Turning my wrist, I grasped her hand in mine, gently stroking the smooth skin with the tips of my fingers. "I'm sorry you had to go through that, Corinne." Tears, those damnable emotional weathervanes, came to my eyes once again, and this time, I let them fall. "I thought about you all the time. Wondered how you were doing, what you were thinking, and how you were coping. I missed you so much."

"The feeling is very mutual, Angel. There wasn't a day that went by in that hell-bound place that I didn't think of you and pray that you'd found your happiness." Lifting her free hand, she gently brushed away my tears, then cupped my cheek. Drawing her face to mine, she tenderly kissed my lips, then pulled away, a loving smile on her face. "You taught an old woman how to love again, Angel. And for that, you'll always be in my heart."

Smiling back at her, I covered her hand with my own, nuzzling into her palm and enjoying the closeness, too long absent, between us.

After a moment, she pulled her hand away, laughing slightly. "Enough of this mutual admiration society, Angel, lest your lover find us kissing in the living-room like a couple of school-girls and decide my head would look best as a bookend."

I laughed. "Oh yeah. I can see *that* happening."

"You never know. It could. And I'd best not stick around to find out." She stretched. "I believe the rest of this story is best left for another day. It's late and that wonderful bed is calling me."

"Don't you dare, Corinne! You have to finish the story! You can't leave me hanging like this!"

She threw that evil grin at me. "You must have me confused with someone else, Angel. I would *never* leave you hanging, my dear."

Ah, what wealth I would give to have a face that knew how to hide a blush. Since I didn't, however, I resolved to bear her teasing by ignoring it. Verbally, at least.

Corinne laughed, charmed. "Not to worry, Angel. The story will still be here in the morning. I'm not going anywhere. Unless you tell me to, of course."

I pretended to think about that for a moment. Then grinned, standing and helping her to her feet. "Nah. I think we'll keep you around for awhile." Wrapping her in a heartfelt hug, I kissed her cheek. "Goodnight, Corinne. Thanks for the story. And thanks for being here. You're one of the best Christmas presents I've ever had."

She wrapped me in her living and precious warmth for a

long moment, then pulled away, a crooked smile on her face belying the suspicious brightness of her eyes. "Enough of this now, or the next thing you know the Hallmark people will be pounding on our door and suing for copyright infringement."

"A fate worse than death," I agreed, kissing her once more on the cheek before she batted me away. "Goodnight, my friend."

"And a good night to you as well, sweetheart." Then she winked. "Don't do anything I wouldn't."

I felt my own evil grin surface. "Oh, Corinne, I do things you've never even dreamed."

For one of the first times since I'd known her, I caught the great wordsmith speechless.

I basked in the moment.

Which, of course, ended fifty-nine seconds too soon.

She eyed me brazenly from head to toe, her gaze roaming intently over every inch of my body. A slow smile broke out over her face. "Oh, I don't know about that, Angel. My dreams can be *quite* inventive."

Then like a general who leaves the battlefield after the last shot has been fired, assured of his easy victory, Corinne walked away, waving casually over her shoulder.

I couldn't help but laugh.

It was good to have her home.

Chapter 9

After placing the mugs in the kitchen to be dealt with later and conducting my nighttime ritual, I ascended the steps to the bedroom, stopping at the top to take in the picture of Ice, her body sculpted in fractured moonlight. She lay on her back, her hands clasped behind her head, and I could tell by the even rise and fall of her gloriously naked breasts that she wasn't asleep.

Stripping off my own clothing quickly and quietly, I joined her on our bed, propping myself up on one elbow and gently stroking the bangs from her forehead. "Can't sleep?"

"Just thinking," she burred in a low tone.

"'bout what?"

I didn't really expect an answer, and so wasn't surprised when I didn't get one. Continuing to gently stroke her brow, I watched her eyes dart from one shadow to another on the ceiling, seeming to read them as a Turkish fortune-teller reads coffee grounds.

"Corinne alright?" she asked after a long moment.

I laughed softly. "Yup. All tucked away and dreaming whatever dreams her evil mind conjures up when it's not busy thinking up ways to poke holes in someone with her rapier wit."

Intense blue eyes drilled into mine. "Did she hurt you?"

I snorted. "Me? Nah. I can handle the likes of her." Still chuckling, I ruffled her disheveled bangs. "After all, I've had a lot of practice over the years."

Her eyes turned back to their study of the ceiling again and the silence stretched out between us, its weight palpable. Though seemingly relaxed, I could feel the coiled tension in the body lying next to me. Something was bothering her; that much was obvious. But what, among the dozens, if not hundreds, of possibilities could it be?

Not one, usually, for beating around low, hedge-like growths, I simply asked the first question that came to mind. "Are you worried that Corinne might have been followed?"

"Andre's very good at his job."

While that didn't answer my question exactly, it *did* serve to bring up another. "Who *is* Andre, by the way? I've been meaning to ask you that for awhile now."

"A restaurateur," she replied after a moment, not moving her gaze from its study of the ceiling.

"Ah," I nodded, as if that explained everything. "And that gives him the skills to make sure Corinne wasn't followed, how?" I laughed. "Good at hiding from angry customers when the steak's slightly overcooked, is he?"

And that, not surprisingly, rated me another non-answer. Despite our time together and the level of trust that had developed between us, there are still very large parts of Ice's life which are walled off to me, even to this day.

I'd be lying if I said that that doesn't bother me a little. Well, more than a little. But if patience is a virtue, then after living with Ice for as long as I have, I'm the most virtuous woman alive.

Well seeing the bright neon roadblock preventing me from merging onto that particular lane of conversation, I decided a slight detour was in order. I paused for a second, ordering the question precisely in my mind, knowing that if I didn't word it correctly, I'd be flush up against yet another logjam.

Taking a deep breath, I dove in with both feet. "When you told me earlier that my life wasn't the only one Corinne had saved, were you talking about yourself?"

After a long moment, I could feel the brief nod of her head under my hand. Encouraged, I decided to take things just a bit further, drowning in curiosity as I was. "Could you ...tell me a little bit about what you meant?" I asked finally, treading very carefully. "I don't know very much about your first time in prison, beyond what little Corinne told me, and I'd kinda like to know how it was for you then. If it's not too hard for you to talk about," I added, giving her an out if she needed it.

"There really isn't that much to talk about," she said finally, after a very long span of silence. "I went in, did my time, and got released. Nothing very remarkable."

I could have let it go at that, and perhaps I should have. Her body was sending me very distinct signals relating to the prudence of allowing slumbering canines to rest undisturbed. Still, for all those signals, I couldn't let it go. She knew so much about my life while I knew so little about hers. And though I knew there'd probably never be a time when those two states would equal out, I wasn't about to withdraw my foot from a door partly opened.

"Share?" I asked simply, softly as I could. "Please?"

Her breasts rose, then fell beneath the weight of an exhaled sigh. "I was very young and very tired. The trial had taken what little strength I still had left, and by the time that prison door closed behind me," she raised a hand briefly, then let it fall on the blanket, "there wasn't anything."

I let the silence draw out for a moment before resuming my gentle, and careful, prodding. "Corinne said you just wanted to do your time quietly."

Her eyes tracked to mine briefly before slipping away once again. "Did she? I don't remember telling her that." She shook her head. "What I do remember is being ...numb. Everything just sorta came down on me and I couldn't feel anything." She shrugged. "And I really didn't care if I never felt anything again."

"How did she save your life?" I asked, still finding it hard to wrap my mind around that thought. Even at her weakest, my mind still insisted on picturing Ice as a woman of uncommon strength and will, never needing someone else to do what she was supremely qualified to do for herself; save her own life.

"As I said," she resumed after a small pause, "I didn't care about anything anymore. And when the predators came, I didn't bother fighting them. Just let them do what they wanted to me." She laughed bitterly, a choked sound caught in her throat.

I couldn't muffle the gasp that came from my own throat, much as I wanted to. Suddenly, I was *very* sorry I had pushed her into telling this particular tale. I wanted to tell her, beg her, to stop, but like a motorist drawn to the sight of a grisly car wreck, I couldn't.

She turned again to look at me, sensing my distress. She smiled slightly, softly, though there was still that touch of old anger in her eyes. "Don't be upset, Angel. After all, it wasn't anything different than what I'd had people pay me to do before. Better in some ways, really. As long as I cooperated, I was pretty much left alone when they were through taking their pleasures from me."

In many ways, her dispassionate tone made things just that much worse, as if her heart and soul were so cold and dead that even the tale of her savage raping at the hands of strangers was of little more consequence to her than a dog passing by on the sidewalk.

But still, the tense, coiled energy of her body belied the casually spoken words, and I knew beyond the slightest shadow of a doubt that this poison within her had been too-long festering and needed to come out before it again released its toxins on a soul not fully mended.

I lay still and near, close enough to touch, but keeping my hands, and my words, to myself, knowing that if I interrupted this self-revelation with even so much as the slightest breath of a whisper, the story would be ended then and there, buried so deep it would never see the light of day again.

"One day, the leader of one of the other gangs caught sight of me and decided she wanted a sample of what I was offering to the others. She dragged me from my cell just as a member of the first gang was coming in to grab an afternoon snack." The bitter smile flashed briefly again. "There was a bit of a tussle over exactly whose 'bitch' I was, and after it was over, I became the new trophy of the leader of the rival gang."

"Why didn't you fight!?" I demanded, my anger spilling over, not caring if I never heard the ending to the sordid tale. "Why didn't you stand up for yourself? Why did you just let them do that to you? Didn't you even care?" It wasn't just simple anger I was feeling. It was rage. Clear and uncomplicated and utter rage. I could feel my teeth grinding against one another with the power of it.

"No."

One word.

Simple. Stark. Brutal.

Heartbreaking.

"Why?" I whispered through my anguished, and angry, tears.

"Why not? They were only getting a body, after all." She turned her head so it faced away from me. "My soul was already dead."

My anger vanished as if it had never been, leaving only a bone deep ache behind. "And Corinne?" I whispered because I had to know.

"I'd met her briefly when I was first locked up. She tried to convince me to fight them. Tried to tell me that I was worth more than being someone's whore." She laughed. "I didn't listen, though. Being a whore was something I knew, and if it gave me the oblivion I wanted, it didn't seem a bad tradeoff. So I basically told her where she could stick her advice. Even offered to put it there for her."

The laugh came again, though this time it held more awe than bitterness. "She told me to go right on ahead and do it. At least it would show her that I still had some spirit left in me."

"You didn't listen to her though, did you?" I asked, already knowing the answer.

"Nope. At the time, I was too wrapped up in my own misery to recognize the hand she was holding out to me. So I left her standing there and went back to the life I'd chosen to live."

"What happened?"

"The gang leader who'd won me decided to put on a show for her friends, so she dragged me into the laundry room where she could have her audience. She'd just ripped my uniform off and was getting down to business when Corinne walked in, a broom in her hand. She told me that if I was too stupid to fight for myself, then she'd do the fighting for me."

She shook her head in amazement over the memories. "She was a tough old broad even back then. Took out nearly half the watchers before someone got in a lucky shot and stole her weapon from her. She didn't give an inch though. Not one single inch. They jumped her, punching and kicking her, and she just stared at me, daring me to just lie there while they beat her bloody."

She looked up at the ceiling again, running a hand over her face. "God, her eyes. I can still remember them, burning into me, never showing any of the pain I knew she was feeling. She didn't blink, not once. Not even when one of them kicked her in the gut and made her lose her lunch. And when I heard her ribs break, something in me snapped. Something raw. Dark. Angry. Something I thought I'd lost when I woke up in the hospital after the shootings."

I could see the tears sparkle in her eyes, but there was a savage joy in there as well. And pride. For Corinne. For herself. "I threw those idiots off of me and got up, half naked and all angry. I walked up to the biggest one and punched her so hard that I thought my hand had broken. And I kept on punching, and kicking, and gouging, until the only person left standing was Corinne. I grabbed her and hightailed us both out of there as fast as we could go." She shook her head again, black hair fanning over her face, partially obscuring it from my view. "It didn't help any, of course. We both got solitary for a month. It was the shortest month I'd ever done, before or since."

Brushing her hair from her face, she turned to face me once again. "So you see, Angel, Corinne did save my life, in a manner of speaking. She gave me a reason to fight. She gave me a reason to live." She grasped my hand tightly and held it to her chest, letting me feel the passion in the mighty heart which beat there. "And if giving up a little privacy enables her to live out the rest of her life in comfort and love, then that's a very small price to pay for giving me my soul back. I'll be forever in her debt."

She wound down then, like a toy soldier whose spring had given out. She lay there looking at me, her eyes asking me to hear her words, to understand the message they imparted to me, and to simply accept without judging the path she'd chosen to travel so long ago.

And because I knew she needed to be strong, perhaps more at that moment than at any other, I laid myself down beside her, resting my head on her shoulder and wrapping one arm around her waist, showing my love and support without smothering her in it.

And when her arms finally came around me, one gently cupping the back of my head, I knew that somehow, God had blessed me with the ability to do the right thing, even if just this once.

I prayed, as fervently as I knew how, never to be without that ability again.

I nearly shocked the starch out of Corinne when I saw her the next morning, giving her a hug that would have popped her eyeballs had they not been so firmly attached to her skull. The bemused look on her face as she pulled away said it all, but all she got in return was another hug and a laugh from me.

Let her chew on that *for awhile,* I thought, leaving her to stare dumbfounded after me as I made my way toward the kitchen and some much needed coffee.

Ice was long gone by the time we sat down to a breakfast of eggs, coffee, and toast in the dining room, and over an after-breakfast mug of tea, Corinne told me the rest of her tale.

It seems that to throw off any suspicion there might have been, Andre decided to take Corinne a wee bit south of Canada.

Mexico, to be exact.

To hear Corinne tell it, they spent two weeks of fun in the sun, ogling half-naked, tanned bodies as they paraded their wares up and down the beaches; she, the women; Andre, the men. Then, after doing whatever checks men like Andre do to make sure the coast is clear, they hopped aboard another plane, bypassed the United States entirely, and landed in Canada. She entered the country legally, requesting and being granted, a tourist visa with the possible option of applying for landed immigrant status sometime in the future.

I was surprised at that. As far as I knew, Canada was pretty much like any other country when it came to immigration laws. If you were young, able-bodied, willing to work, and didn't have anything in your background which made it likely that you would plant bombs on school buses or office buildings, you stood a chance of being welcomed.

Corinne, however, was elderly, frail, of an age where advancing medical costs would eat up a very large budget very quickly, and had a prison record that would make any immigration official worth his salt sit up and whistle—before he personally escorted her to the first plane headed for points south.

When I expressed my disbelief, she responded with a wicked grin and pushed over a document that contained her financial statement in all its multi-zeroed glory.

The coffee in my mouth sprayed halfway across the room.

"Seven *million* dollars?"

"And change, yes," she replied, wearing the mask of the eternally smug and loving every minute of it.

"*Seven* million *dollars*?"

Clicking her tongue at me, she reached up and placed a hand on my forehead, the way you would do if you were testing a child for fever. "Poor dear," her eyes alight with wicked compassion, "are you coming down with something? Perhaps a trip to the doctor is in order this morning?"

Scowling, I batted her hands away the dollar amount still repeating itself in my head like a jukebox record that had developed an unfortunate scratch.

"Relax, Angel. It's not as if I'm taking afternoon tea with the Rockefellers, you know." Then she grinned. "Besides, you should be happy. It's all yours when I finally shuffle off this mortal coil."

I looked up at her. "I can't accept this, Corinne."

Her smile became hard. "Whyever not, Angel? Afraid to sully your hands with a little ill-gotten gain?" Her teeth flashed. "Blood money not good enough for you?"

"That's enough, Corinne," I snapped, rising to my feet. "I don't deserve that from you."

After a long moment of intense silence, she finally backed down, the smile slipping from her face. "You're right. You don't. I'm sorry." A plea then came to both eyes and voice. "Won't you please sit back down, Angel? Forgive an old woman her foolishness?" She paused for just a heartbeat, then whispered, "Please?"

A moment later, my anger receding but not yet gone, I sat

back down, placing my hands flat on the table. I looked at her expectantly, using a raised-eyebrow expression that I'd only recently begun to truly master.

Reaching into her purse, she pulled out another document, which she carefully unfolded and slid across the table to me. I looked down at it, tracing the dollar amount displayed with my finger. It made the amount on the original statement look almost like pocket-change. Another document was then laid atop the first and I scanned it quickly, then read more carefully as the contents finally wove their way into my brain.

The paper I was reading was a receipt of sorts, which detailed the final disposition of the vast fortune on the document beneath. One half was used to set up a fund to help surviving family members whose loved ones had been killed in a violent crime. A quarter, and I smiled when I read this, went into a fund that helped feed, clothe, house and educate teens living on the streets. And the last quarter went into what was termed the "Fallen Angels" fund, to provide free legal counsel and representation for women who, like I, had been tried and/or convicted of killing their husbands as a result of domestic abuse.

I looked up at her, my eyes wide. "What...?"

"That's the money I made from killing my husbands. Every last cent of it."

"But you said..."

"I know what I said, Angel," she interrupted, tossing my argument away with a careless flick of her hand. "But things change. And sometimes, if they're lucky, people do as well." She smiled a little; one that was loving, a touch shy, and totally endearing. "In any event, sitting paralyzed in a wheelchair does give one quite a bit of time for quiet reflection. And while any remorse I might have had over the killing of my husbands had long ago turned to dust, the thought of living high on the money left behind somehow lost the allure it had previously given me." Snorting, she shook her head. "Never grow old, Angel. It makes you soft in all the wrong places."

Though the door was wide open and an entire army of people pled with me to step through it, I wisely refrained from any comment I might have made to her observation. The sparkle in her eye praised my restraint, though I was sure she had already thought up at least one hundred witty and cutting retorts.

Reaching out almost primly, she plucked the document that had started this whole conversation and held it up to the light. "This is what became of the sock money I'd earned working at the few menial jobs I'd managed to find before and in between husbands. When I knew the arrest was coming, I gave it, along with the other money, to an accountant friend of mine. And as you can plainly see, she had quite a way with numbers." Her eyes sparkled again with wicked wit. "Among other things."

I just grinned and rolled my eyes. God, I'd missed her.

"And it *is* yours, Angel. Yours and Ice's, of course. To do with as you wish. You could use it to line the fireplace, for all I care. You just need to accept it." She smiled. "After all, I'm not going to be around forever and I'd like to know that I had some small part in making your lives, if not easier, at least a bit more interesting."

I winced. "If I agree to think about it, can we get off the topic of death? It's not something I really want to talk about right now."

"Death happens to us all, Angel."

"I know that, Corinne," I replied, a bit more sternly than I had intended, the images of my lover too near death raising their heads in Technicolor glory. "I'd just like to stop having it threaten to visit quite so often."

She nodded at me, eyes bright with compassion. Then she turned to look out the large window. "Very well, sweet Angel. It's a beautiful day, even for winter. Let's let death take care of itself while we embrace life, hmm?"

I couldn't help grinning. "You're on."

After the breakfast dishes were dried and put away, and we had showered and dressed, we decided—or rather Corinne decided; I was just along for the ride at this point—that a little sightseeing was in order.

Though the temperature outside was beyond bitter, the sun was out and the walks clear of ice and slush. Feeling just a touch of cabin fever myself, even so early in the season, I found myself not really minding the prospect of losing the feeling in my fingers and toes.

After donning layers of winter gear (and in this, Corinne came supremely prepared) we headed out into the cold and toward our first stop of the day, which was, of course, Ruby's house.

I'd called her prior, asking if she was available to meet a friend of mine who was visiting for the holidays, and she invited us over happily, seemingly excited at the prospect of meeting someone new. I found myself smiling at her excitement, picturing a wonderful meeting between two women I held dear; two women who, because they were of an age, would have a great deal in common and just might become the best of friends.

I couldn't have been more wrong.

The beaming smile Ruby bestowed on us when she opened the door faded just a touch when her eyes took in the swaddled figure standing beside me. I could feel Corinne stiffen as Ruby backed away, inviting us in.

What the hell is going on here?

After setting our coats to warm and dry near the fire, we ventured into the kitchen, where Ruby bade us sit while she fixed coffee and a plate of fresh-made cookies that smelled heavenly and tasted even better.

After setting the mugs and plate down, she stood next to her chair, eyeing me expectantly, if a bit strangely. After a moment, I caught on and gave her my brightest grin. "Ruby, I'd like you to meet a dear friend of mine, Corinne..." And there I trailed off, blindsided by my first major hurdle of the day.

Ruby, if you'll remember, read the same paper I did. Introducing Corinne by her full name was inviting trouble I wasn't prepared to deal with. My neighbor was still in the dark as to the true circumstances of my coming to Canada. And more than anything else, I wanted her to remain that way for as long as possible. It wasn't that I didn't trust Ruby; far from it. It was just that the less information she had, the less, or so I hoped, she would be hurt in the long run.

Not that I was inviting that sort of trouble, mind you. But, in the words of the immortal Boy Scouts, it's always best to be prepared.

I only wished I'd remembered that particular motto prior to setting out for Ruby's house that morning.

Corinne, however, master politician that she was, covered my slight stumble as smooth as oil over lard, grasping Ruby's outstretched hand and giving it a firm shake, her smile genuine as it could be. For those who didn't know her as well as I did.

"Corinne LaPointe, at your service."

Ruby returned the handshake and the smile. "Welcome to my home, Corinne. It is alright if I call you Corinne, isn't it?"

"Only if you allow me the same pleasure."

I could see Ruby visibly relax as she released Corinne's hand and sat down at the table with us. "Corinne it is, then," she said, toasting her with a mug of coffee. Her eyes gained a speculative look. "Tyler tells me you've known one another a good long while."

Damn. I'd forgotten that Ruby knew me as Tyler. I found myself sitting very still, not daring to turn my head even the slightest inch, lest I detect whatever expression was on Corinne's face. An expression which I was sure would not be even one iota to my liking.

And, of course, I was right on that count.

My friend's voice oozed charm and hidden laughter. "A good long while indeed, Ruby. Why, when I first saw her, I thought 'Now there's a girl who can turn the world on with her smile.'"

Dead silence.

Then an isolated chuckle, sounding much like the lone backfire of a car with a bad muffler.

Then another chuckle, followed by another, until both of my so-called friends were just about fainting with laughter at my expense.

I felt my head turn slowly to my right, my eyebrows contracting as I shot my nearly convulsive friend my darkest of looks. Corinne returned my look with a twinkling, mischievous one of her own and subtly mouthed "sorry," before she turned back to Ruby and started the laughter train rolling down the tracks all over again.

But with that single gesture, I felt what anger I'd had drain away, realizing Corinne's joke for what it was, a successful attempt to lighten the tense atmosphere and set a suspicious Ruby at ease. So I gave a few calculated grumbles for show, and patiently waited until the last of their laughter died out, leaving a much more comfortable silence in its wake.

Oh yes, Corrine was good. She was *very* good.

Then she proceeded to prove just how good she really was by continuing with a story she was weaving out of whole cloth as she went along. "Yes, Tyler and I have known one another for quite awhile, as she's told you. I was a teacher in the school where she'd come after earning her degree. In fact, she took over my class as I was set to retire. The children fell in love with her the moment they saw her." She smiled again, this one most definitely genuine. "We all did. She was an Angel come to earth. A very needed brightness in an otherwise dark and sad world."

Ruby smiled slightly at that. "Ahh. So that's where she got her charming nickname."

"Indeed it was. One of my students came up to us after I'd introduced her—you know how charming first-graders can be—and asked her if she was an angel." She grinned. "And from that moment on, she was known as Ms. Angel to everyone."

It was one of the few times in my life when I was actually glad of my ability to blush. Corinne was depending on my reactions to prove the veracity of her story, and I didn't let her down, blushing for all I was worth.

Apparently charmed, Ruby smiled and visibly relaxed her ramrod straight posture, actually allowing her shoulders to touch the back of the chair upon which she was sitting.

Inwardly sighing with relief, I relaxed as well, letting myself become completely absorbed within the web Corinne was spinning. If I had held any lingering doubts about exactly what the woman's capacity was for getting people to believe exactly what she wanted them to, they vanished into the mist on that sunny winter's day.

Though that realization probably should have given me pause, and might have had I been any younger or more innocent in the ways of my friend, but instead it gave me a sort of guilty thrill, like the thrill a young child gets when she does something she knows she's not supposed to, and gets away with it.

The rest of the afternoon passed quickly by, and at the end of it, goodbyes were made with more warmth than the hellos had been.

Still, for Corinne's undeniable charm and Ruby's gentle warmth, there seemed to be a barrier between them that didn't show any signs of coming down. Puzzled by that, I mentioned it to Ice after Corinne was tucked safely away, dreaming whatever naughty little dreams that steel trap of a mind conjured up.

Ice had laughed and enfolded me in her warm embrace. "Sounds simple enough to me."

Pulling away slightly, I fixed her with a stare. "It does, huh? Care to share, oh Wise One?" Then I laughed and lowered my chin down until it rested in the sweet valley between her breasts. "Or shall I beat you senseless with my fists of steel."

Her eyes widened in mock horror before ruffling my hair and settling me more comfortably atop her. "They're jealous."

"Jealous?! Of what?!"

"Each other. They're playing a little game of tug-o-war and you just happen to be the rope."

I looked at her, disbelieving. "You wanna tell me how you came up with that one?"

Her lips pursed slightly as she shrugged. "Easy. They're two women who fulfill much the same role in your life. Mother figure. Confidant. Comfort-giver. And they both know it." She shrugged again. "And if I had to guess, I'd say each one is afraid you're going to become too close with the other and leave the remaining one out of your life altogether."

"That's ridiculous!"

"Maybe. Doesn't make it any less true for them, though."

I thought about that for a moment, quite unsettled. Then I looked up again. "There's a flaw in your theory."

Her eyebrow raised. "Oh?"

I grinned. "Yup."

"And that might be...."

"You." Rolling off of her warm, strong body, I adopted my best "scholarly" pose. "You see, my dear Ice, if one were to follow your theory through to its logical conclusion, whatever little jealousy they might have between themselves would be vastly overshadowed by the jealousy they would have for you. You are, after all, number one in my heart, among other places."

"Perhaps," she admitted, "though there's a flaw in *your* theory."

I could feel my eyebrow rumple. "Yeah? What's that?"

Her smile was slow and sexy. "I'm not exactly the mothering type."

Laughing, I rolled back on top of her, slipping a leg between her slightly spread thighs, pleased by her immediate and wonderful response. "Thank God for that," I said in a voice which was suspiciously husky. "I can't imagine doing what we've been doing for the last two hours with my mother."

Chuckling softly, she melded our bodies together and proceeded to spend the *next* two hours reinforcing that idea.

And in *that* theory, there were no flaws at all.

If Corinne and Ruby rubbed against one another like two dogs going after the same bone—and I'd finally come to the realization that Ice was right on that score—Corinne and Pop, when they first met, gave the impression of age-old friends reuniting after just a few moments apart.

I stood by and watched in open-mouthed awe as the normally reticent Pop actually spoke in complete sentences to Corinne, playing the part of the perfect gentleman and escorting her into his station for some coffee, which was always warming on the hotplate near the cash register.

"You're gonna catch flies if you're not careful," Ice said, materializing beside me and wiping her greasy hands off on an oil stained rag.

"I just can't believe it," I replied, leaning easily into her warmth. "It's like...it's like...I don't know *what* it's like. I mean, I'd hoped they'd hit it off, but...*wow.*"

She grunted as she leaned against me, peering with narrowed eyes into the interior of the station. "He does seem quite taken with her."

"I'll say. I don't think I've seen him talk that long to anyone."

Tossing the rag back into the garage, Ice blew on her hands to warm them, then stuffed them deep into the pockets of her jacket. "Yeah, well don't go planning the wedding just yet, Angel. Corinne's still a little too taken with the ladies, and I don't think Pop's the type who likes to share." She turned to look at me, her eyes twinkling with mischief. "And I really don't wanna have to hide the arsenic."

"Ice!"

The grin in her eyes made it to her lips, and she reached out to ruffle my hair. "Relax, Angel. It's okay to joke about these things sometimes."

"I know, but...Jesus! I swear, I don't know what gets into you sometimes."

She responded by taking in a deep breath, then letting it out gustily. "Fresh air and sunshine, sweet Angel. Fresh air and sunshine."

And with that, she walked back into the garage, leaving me to stare after her, bemused and grinning all at the same time.

Chapter 10

And then it was Christmas Eve.

Cold enough to freeze a crone's anatomy in her brass brassiere, the night sky shown bright with stars hanging so low it was almost as if I could reach up and grab one to keep.

Leaving Corinne to take over the kitchen (and it should be noted that the aforementioned was a demand of hers and not a request of ours) Ice and I set off in search of a Christmas tree.

Simply walking into town and purchasing one of the many which stood, like wooden soldiers, on vacant lots was out of the question, of course. No, we actually had to search for and find our very own tree, one grown especially for us, willing to give up its life to make our holiday more festive.

I suppose I shouldn't sound so sarcastic about it, since it *was* my suggestion, after all.

Borrowing an old, but sturdy, nine-foot toboggan and a saw from Ruby, we walked into a section of the woods which had suffered, several years before, a lightning-spawned forest fire which had burned away much of the old growth and left room for new life to flourish.

After a great deal of critical fault-finding by me and a greater deal of eye rolling by Ice, we finally found the perfect tree; one that was lush, bursting with that wonderful evergreen color and scent, and large enough without being too large. Framing it from afar with my hands like some psychotic photographer trying for the perfect shot, I pictured it standing next to the fireplace, bedecked with garland and trinkets, with a plethora of gaily wrapped presents underneath, and promptly announced my approval.

"You're sure," Ice replied, lifting the saw yet again and

brandishing it in a way which let me know that if I wasn't, I stood a good chance of being a good two feet shorter than I already was in the very near future.

"Positive," I announced with a nod of finality.

Something sounding suspiciously like "It's about goddamn time" came floating back to me as Ice turned away and began to clear the snowpack from around the base of the tree I'd selected.

"Wait!" I interrupted just as she had put blade to bark.

"What now?"

Saw blade and white teeth glittered in the light of a half moon, but I did my best to ignore them both as I walked one more time around the tree, viewing it from all possible angles save, of course, from above. "Just making sure."

More words, intelligible but quite unrepeatable, floated up from the base of the tree as I completed my appraisal. "Alright. Go for it. Just make sure you cut off those branches near the bottom there. They look like they're dying."

"Are you sure you wouldn't like to do this your self, my dear?" came a silken purr. "After all, I wouldn't want to ruin your perfect tree with my ineffective bumbling."

"Oh no," I replied airily, waving off her sarcasm-laced concern. "You can do it. I know how much you love working up a sweat."

Before I could even think to move, I was lifted in strong arms and tossed a good distance to land in a deep pile of snow. Laughing and sputtering and trying to dig mounds of the cold, wet stuff out of places it had no business being, I watched as the tree I'd picked finally surrendered to the might of my lover's sharp saw and strong muscles. By the time I'd regained my footing, both saw and tree were safely stored aboard the toboggan and Ice was looking down at me, an incurably smug expression on her face.

Did I mention something about paybacks?

The gathering we'd arranged was in full swing by the time we arrived back at the cabin, tree in tow. Laughter and the muted tones of Christmas carols could be heard just outside the door. The porch windows were fogged from the warmth within and I could see surreal shapes seemingly float in and out of the mist on the other side of the glass.

Then the door opened and John Drew, Tom's brother, came out to greet us, bedecked in a festive, if rather pornographic, holiday sweater. After enduring good-natured teasing over my need to assess "every damn tree in the whole damn country," we finally went inside, the three of us carrying the tree over the threshold and into the living room, where Ice had built a stand for it.

After the tree was up and suitably "ooh-ed" and "ahh-ed" over, we began to decorate it with the popcorn and cranberries Corinne had supplied.

Or, should I say, we *tried* to decorate it. Attempting to thread a tiny needle through a tinier cranberry while under the influence of a couple of cups of Corinne's one-hundred-eighty proof eggnog became an exercise in futility rather quickly.

Ruby, whose blood-pressure medication forbade more than one cup of the stuff, primly took over threading duty while the rest of us, save Ice who's never been much for imbibing, became progressively giddier.

Then Corinne set out a feast fit for royalty and we all followed our noses and grumbling bellies to the table like children after a day of hard play. Ice sat at one end of the table, Corinne at the other, and our guests—Pop, Ruby, the Drew brothers and their wives, and a smattering of others who we'd become friendly with—interspersed in between. It wouldn't be stretching the truth any to say that that Christmas Eve dinner was the best I've ever eaten, before or since. Corinne is an outstanding cook, and forty-five years in prison hadn't diminished her talent one bit, for which we were all profoundly grateful.

Pleasantly stuffed and more than half-drunk, we finished decorating the tree while Ice and Corinne, over my staunch, if slightly slurred, objections, set about cleaning the mound of dirty dishes we'd left behind.

The evening passed slowly, as wonderful evenings sometimes will, in a warm and friendly haze that I'd often dreamed about as a child when Christmas Eve seemed to be nothing more than simply another day in my life.

As it drew to a close, Ice appointed herself the task of making sure all of our guests found their way safely home. Corinne and I stayed behind to tidy up what little mess there was, and then she went off to the comfort of her own bed while I stayed awake, awaiting my lover's return.

I was feeling many things during that short wait, but pain definitely wasn't one of them. Corinne's eggnog could have loosened the limbs of a marble statue.

Ice returned quietly as I was staring into the flames of the fire, fascinated, in my gently drunken way, by the myriad of colors displayed. I wobbled over to greet her and she held me tightly, then kissed me in front of the tree it had taken so long for us to find.

And then, to put a perfect cap to a perfect evening, we made long, slow love on the thick rug in front of the blazing fire and I fell into a blissful sleep in the arms of the woman I loved more than anyone or anything in the world.

And as Christmas Eve gradually gave way to Christmas Day, yet another dream had come true.

Christmas morning dawned cold and blustery with more than a hint of snow in the air.

I awoke to a throbbing head and a stomach that was most definitely protesting my overindulgence of the night before. Rolling to my side, I pulled the covers up over my shoulder before realizing that where I had awoken was not the place I'd fallen asleep the night before.

Reaching out with my free hand while my eyes were still closed, I wasn't surprised to find Ice already up and about, though the sheets were still warm from her body, so I guessed that she hadn't been gone for very long.

Pulling her pillow toward me blindly, I burrowed my head into it, happily inhaling her scent as my sleepy body began to lose its hold on consciousness once again.

I had just begun to drift back off when the sound of Ice's footfall on the top of the steps caused me to come fully awake. This time, my eyes deigned to open and I took in her sleep-tousled beauty, my hangover seeming to recede as a flush of welcoming warmth quickly took its place. She stood there in a loosely belted robe with nothing else beneath, the V in the robe providing a tantalizing glimpse of the creamy flesh it covered. A tray was easily held in her large hands, bearing what I hoped was some strong black coffee and an entire bottle of aspirin.

"Hello there, gorgeous. You lookin' for me?" I asked in what I hoped was a sultry tone, but which was probably, in reality, a pale imitation, given the conflicting messages my abused body was giving me.

It got a smile out of her, though, and she crossed to the bed, setting the tray down on the bedside table next to the clock. "How're ya feelin'?" she asked, laying a cool hand on my fevered brow, sending my body into yet another bout of sensory overload.

"A minute ago? Like an entire family of cats had used me for a litter box. Now?" I grinned goofily. "Juuuuust fine."

Smiling crookedly and shaking her head, she climbed back

into bed and sat with her back against the headboard, gathering me into her arms and resting me against her chest. Then, reaching one long arm out, she grabbed the coffee and held the steaming mug to my lips. "Drink this. It should make you feel better."

And so I did, contentedly sipping the strong coffee and swallowing the handful of aspirin Ice gave me. Then I relaxed back against her, absorbing the warmth of her body into mine, her very presence a better hangover remedy than all the coffee and aspirin in the world ever had a hope of being. When her hand came up to gently stroke my hair, my headache vanished as if it had never been.

"Can I ask you a question?"

"Sure." Her deep, melodious voice rumbled up from her chest, against which my ear was pressed.

"How'd I wind up here? The last thing I remember, I fell asleep downstairs in front of the fire."

Her chuckle burred pleasantly into my ear. "Well, it was either carry you up here or risk Corinne waking up and wanting to join in on the festivities. I figured the first course of action was the wisest."

"Mmmm," I agreed, nuzzling my cheek against the smooth skin of her chest while one hand toyed idly with the belt on her robe. Then a thought struck me and I smiled. "Did Santa come?"

"Yup. And from the looks of things, his reindeer were much happier when they took off again."

I felt myself tensing just a little. "I thought we agreed not to go overboard this year."

Ice continued to stroke my hair, unconcerned. "Apparently, someone forgot to fill Ms. Moneybags in on the rules."

"She didn't."

"Oh, she did, alright."

"Great."

At that moment, Corinne's slightly off-key humming floated up to us from the living room, along with the gentle tinkle of silverware and porcelain. "Oh my, look at all these presents. Since no one else seems to be around, they must all be for me. How lucky!"

Smothering my laugh against Ice's chest, I hugged her tight to me before releasing her and pushing myself up to sit on my own. "Sounds like our cue."

Ice rolled off the bed, coming to her feet and gently helping me climb out as well. Then she twirled my robe over my shoulders and belted it securely across my belly, straightening out the edges so they lay flat against my skin. "Ready?"

"Almost." Reaching out, I opened her belt, resettled her robe so that it completely covered all pertinent parts, then belted it securely. "There."

An eyebrow was raised at me.

"Hey! She's already had a stroke. Do you want to give her a heart attack, too?"

"I hardly think I have anything she hasn't seen before, Angel."

"Maybe not," I agreed, "but it's the way what you have is put together. One look, and she'd be in intensive care for sure."

Rolling her eyes, Ice grabbed my hand and, together, we walked down the stairs to see what Santa, in the guise of a little old librarian from Pittsburgh, had left for us.

Corinne outdid herself with the breakfast she served as we sat on the floor like children opening piles of gaily wrapped presents. And she further outdid herself with both the quantity and quality of the gifts she'd purchased for us. I felt a moment's discomfort over this, but a quick look from her convinced me to gracefully accept them as an expression of her love and caring.

Mounds of much needed clothing turned quickly into mountains. Sheets, blankets, and comforters guaranteed we'd never sleep on the same set twice. We received enough cookware to stock the finest restaurant, enough cleaning supplies to sanitize an entire hotel and enough books to fill the shelves of a good-sized library.

There were other, more ...private ...gifts as well, but if it's all the same to you, I'll keep the identity of those to myself, thank you. Suffice it to say that my face, when I viewed these gifts in all their glory, would have far surpassed Rudolph's red nose in brightness.

After giving Corinne her presents from us, Ice and I exchanged our own gifts. Because money was still very much an object—we were determined that we would repay every cent of the material charges that went toward the building of our home—we'd agreed to keep Christmas simple that year.

So we exchanged the few practical gifts we'd bought for one another, and then Ice handed me a small box wrapped in simple gold foil. The look on her face, almost shy, told me this was a special gift.

I took it into my hands, testing its weight. It was quite heavy for its small size and I hadn't the faintest glimmer of a clue what lay inside. I looked up, questioningly, but her expression betrayed nothing.

Slowly, I opened the wrapping to reveal a plain white box

about the length and breadth of my hand. Prying the cover off, I gently nudged away the tissue paper covering the object, then stared inside, my breath temporarily taken away.

Inside laid a beautifully carved wooden horse.

Now, in order for you to appreciate the enormity of this seemingly simple gift, I find the need to backtrack just a little.

Well, more like a lot. Back to my childhood, to be exact.

When I was growing up, I had an aunt, Rose, whom I worshipped. There was a strong bond between us and though I didn't see her often, she was always in my thoughts and in my heart. She was married to an Army Captain and moved from place to place very frequently. Most of those places were overseas. Every time they were stationed somewhere new, she would send me a little gift what was unique to the country they were living in.

In hardly any time at all, my room was full to bursting with gifts from all over the world; dolls, carved animals, clocks, books, and all manner of assorted trinkets.

One year, when they were stationed more or less permanently in Germany, a year that had been a very hard one for me in terms of my steadily souring relationship with my parents, she sent me a beautifully carved wooden horse, his saddle and bridle brightly painted in the style of the Bavarian artisans.

Inside was a little note, penned in her hand, which I have to this day.

Tyler:

I know things have been hard with your parents. I wish I were there to help see you through the rough times. Know always that you're in my thoughts and prayers.

Since I can't be there in person, I'm sending you Alwin. My friends here call him a "dreaming spirit" and he's a good friend to have around.

When things in your life aren't going so good, just hold him close, close your eyes, and dream of faraway lands where all your troubles are gone. Let him take you there and he'll always protect you.

One day, I know, those dreams will become a reality for you and you'll find a place where you are cherished and loved as much as I cherish and love you.

Until then, please accept Alwin as a token of my love and keep him close to your heart as you are in mine.

Yours,
Rose

From that day forward, Alwin never left my sight. He was with me when I woke up in the morning, when I went to school (my schoolmates took to calling me "Linus" briefly), when I played, and when I went to bed at night.

Rose was right. He *was* a good friend. He was never angry with me. He never talked down to me. He never ignored me. He listened to my troubles, and to my joys, without ever once belittling me.

He might not have licked my face or wagged his tail, but then I didn't have to clean up after him or feed him, so that was a pretty even trade, as far as I was concerned.

And then one day, in a fit of rage over a transgression I can no longer remember, my father took a hammer to that horse, making me watch as he pounded it into splinters, and then into dust, taking my dreams with it as he did so.

I was heartbroken as only a young girl who has lost her best friend can possibly be and retreated from the room in tears, refusing to speak to my father, or to my mother who'd watched the incident without once trying to stop him, for an entire month.

It was the one thing I've never forgiven him for, not even to this day when his body is nothing more than dust in the ground and forgiveness means no more than the letters it's formed from.

And I'm not sure I ever will.

I'd mentioned Alwin briefly in passing to Ice when I saw a similar horse in a store window we were passing one day, though I never told her what happened to him, nor exactly what he meant to me as a young girl.

Yet she must have picked up something from my wistful tone of voice, because before me that Christmas morning lay an exact replica of that long destroyed wooden horse, right down to the brightly painted saddle and bridle and the inquisitive look on his face.

With slightly trembling fingers, I plucked the horse out of its nest of tissue paper and held it up for closer inspection. It was absolutely perfect in every single detail.

"Where did you get this?" I breathed, Pop and his ability to find just about anything for anybody immediately coming to mind.

"Actually, I carved it," she replied, her face slightly flushed with the admission.

"But how...?"

"I thought there was a little more to the story then you were letting on, so I spoke to Ruby about it one day. She was more than happy to fill me in on the details. She's got a damn good memory." She chuckled. "Anyway, after she filled me in on all the pertinent details, I went to work." She peered at the horse for a moment, then at me, a question in her eyes. "Was I close?"

"Close?! My *God*, Ice, it's perfect! There isn't one single difference between this and the one I had as a child!" Looking over the horse yet again, I realized that my words were completely true. It *was* perfect.

She smiled, a relaxed, genuine, beautiful one that reached into her eyes and beyond. "I'm glad. Ruby told me how much that horse had meant to you. And how your father destroyed it." The smile slipped from her face. "Again, I'm just glad that bastard's dead, because I'd take great pleasure in killing him for what he put you through."

"Ice..."

Waving off my concern, she continued. "In any event, I just wanted to give something back to you that had been taken from you." The smile returned. "You're not a little girl anymore, but you can always use another friend."

Grinning right back at her, tears shining in my eyes, I reached over and hugged her tightly to me, realizing that the words my aunt had written so long ago had finally come true. My dreams *did* become reality, and with them, I found a place where I was cherished and loved.

Thank you, Rose.

After a long moment, I pulled away and reached under the tree, retrieving the gift I'd placed there the night before while Ice was escorting our guests back to their homes. "Here. This is for you."

She looked at me questioningly for a moment as she accepted the gift, its size and shape immediately giving away its contents. Unwrapping the paper I'd put on for festivities' sake, she pulled out my gift, a record in a jacket that was devoid of any artistry, as I had requested from Pop.

I smiled. "Go ahead. Put it on."

Rising gracefully to her feet, she walked over to the sound system and removed the dust cover from the turntable, carefully removing the album from its protective jacket and placing it on the spindle. Turning the system on, she carefully moved the arm over and set the needle down in the first groove, then stepped back, head cocked intently.

When the first strands of music swelled out into the room, I saw her body stiffen to statue-like rigidity. Her face paled, and I wondered if I had just made a horrible mistake.

Then a voice, more beautiful than any nightingale's joined with the music and I saw her chest hitch once, convulsively, before it settled down again. Her eyes, a brilliant blue, slipped closed as the music continued to swell from the speakers.

"Dear God," Corinne whispered beside me, her hand coming up to her chest. "Is that Ecaterina DuPrie? I absolutely adore her work!"

Living with Ice for as long as I had, I knew my opera singers. I smiled, not taking my eyes off my raptly listening partner. "I didn't know you were such a connoisseur, Corinne. That's exactly who it is."

Corinne laughed softly. "Figures you'd know. What a wonderful gift! To have anything by Ms. DuPrie is a treasure indeed. It must have taken you ages to find."

"It wasn't as hard as you might think," I whispered back, still watching Ice.

The first stanza of the aria had ended, and when the second stanza began, I saw her chest hitch again, but this time, when the Prima Donna's voice sounded clear and beautiful, Ice lifted her own voice to the heavens, matching the singer note for note.

I felt a chill go down my spine.

Apparently, I wasn't the only one. "My God in heaven, that is absolutely uncanny! I never knew she could sing so beautifully!"

I led my proud smile say it all.

"It's like hearing a voice from beyond the grave," Corinne murmured, almost reverently. "Ice sounds exactly like her!"

"She should."

"Why?"

"Ecaterina DuPrie is her mother."

Corinne's brief slump against my side finally took my gaze from my partner. "Are you alright?"

"Never tease an old woman, Angel," she growled. "Our hearts can't take it."

"I'm not teasing, Corinne. I thought you knew."

She looked at me, eyes wide. "Knew? How in the world could I know something like that?" She peered more closely at Ice, as if truly seeing her for the first time. "Though perhaps I should have guessed. They do bear some striking similarities."

Before I could reply, the aria ended and one of those similarities—from what Ice had told me—made its appearance felt when my lover opened her eyes. Her expression seemed rather dazed, as if she'd been dealt a hard blow and was only now beginning to shake it off. Her hand moved in a dream-like fashion toward the sound system, removing the needle from the record before another song could begin.

Then her expression cleared and her eyes drilled into mine.

Unable to keep from obeying the unvoiced command, I

found myself rising to my feet, my gaze trapped helplessly within the surreal magnetism of hers.

After a long moment that seemed to span an eternity in which entire galaxies were born, lived out their lives, and died in brilliant blazes of glory, I felt, as much as saw, her step toward me, and saw, as much as felt, her body crush itself against mine, the entire length of her trembling. Her face, flushed and hot, pressed itself against the curve of my neck and I felt the gentle rain of tears scald a sweet brand upon my skin.

"Thank you," she whispered once, and then again, and then again, until it became a mantra, a prayer, and a benediction.

Holding her tight to me, I reached up one hand to stoke her hair and her back, awed and humbled beyond measure at the gift Ice was giving me at that moment; that one unguarded moment where all barriers were down and only one thing was left standing.

Her soul.

Only the sound of Corinne moving away to give us our privacy broke the timeless lock of our embrace. Ice pulled away, but instead of hiding her tears, she seemed to bear them proudly, her carriage erect and her gaze unswerving. "It's alright, Corinne," she said in a voice that was still husky. "You don't have to leave."

Smiling slightly as Corinne took an uncertain step forward, she held open her arms and welcomed our friend into her embrace, enfolding her tenderly and placing a kiss upon her cheek.

When the gentle hug ended, Ice turned back to me. "How?" she asked simply.

I grinned. "You can thank Pop for the legwork. I gave him my request and he ran with it."

She took in a deep breath, then let it out slowly. "I will." She then shook her head in amazement. "I haven't heard that voice in fifteen years. I didn't realize how much I missed it. Until now." The look in her eyes was incredibly tender and I fought hard against my own tears resurfacing.

Then a thought struck me, and I sobered. "The...um...last two tracks on the other side are from *Werther*."

She nodded in understanding. "I might wait awhile to listen to them."

I realized immediately what she meant and I knew that I wouldn't be hearing those particular songs for a good long while, if ever. Ice would need to be alone to deal with the feelings dredged up by that music and it was a privacy I would willingly grant her. I nodded, smiling.

"Thank you," she said again, her voice soft.

"You're welcome." And then I intentionally echoed her words. "I just wanted to give something back to you that had been taken from you." And unspoken but still heard between us: *the sound of your mother's voice.*

It was a Christmas I would always remember.

Chapter 11

Winter took its own sweet time stepping aside for spring, but it finally did and seemingly before I knew it, a year had passed since we first set foot upon Canadian soil. So many things had happened in my life since then. A year seemed much too short a time span for them all to have taken place.

And yet, there I was, standing on my own porch, looking out of my own window, down across my own land, watching sailboats promenade across a vast expanse of deep blue lake.

I pinched myself, just once, and when it hurt, I was convinced that what I was seeing was truly real and not the fevered dreams of a sad young girl or a prison inmate desperate for freedom.

I was totally alone in the house, but the solitude was welcome and comforting after the bustle of the holiday season and the long, gray winter that followed. Ice had left sometime before sunrise, intending to get in a nice long run over grass newly sprung from the once frozen earth. Corinne, for her part, had announced her cabin fever quite loudly to one and all, both of which were me, and had left an hour before to do some exploring. She departed with the look I imagine a fox gets when he's contemplating the chicken coop across the barnyard, and I spared a moment of pity for whomever her explorations pitted her against that day.

I suddenly felt the urge to get outside myself, and after donning a light jacket—yet another gift from Corinne—I stepped out into the warmth and sunshine of the newly born spring, taking in a deep breath of fresh air and smiling for all I was worth.

Walking down the small hill that separated the house from the lake, I stepped out onto the tiny green dock which I'd painted the day before, continuing to watch the sailboats as they fought both gravity and wind to remain upright in the water.

I spared a moment for wistful longing before remembering that I too knew how to sail.

My decision quickly made, I stepped back onto the shore and walked to the small cove where Ice and I had placed the Hobie after making it once again ready for sailing that past weekend. After readying the rigging, unfurling and hoisting the sails, and attaching the sling, I gently pushed the boat out into the shallows, then stepped aboard, my boot momentarily sinking into the icy water and causing my whole body to tense up in chilled reaction.

Still, I'd made up my mind and wasn't about to let a little cold water dampen my enthusiasm, and so, with a healthy shove that chilled my body even more, I managed to catch the wind and started off toward the center of the lake, icy spray piercing my face with its needled drops.

The freedom I felt was incredible as I carved out a line and stuck to it, battling the wind and the water for my right to fly.

And fly I did, over the glassy blue lake, like a colorful bird just skimming over the water with one eye open for breakfast, controlling nature with a flick of my hand or a twist of my body, my smile, I'm sure, fierce and proud and wild and free.

When my soaked clothes and icy skin began to get the better of my endorphins, I turned for home. As I drew closer, I noticed that someone had taken up residence on the green dock. Still closer, I noted that "someone" as Corinne, who'd appropriated a deck chair and her dark shawl, and was sitting quite comfortably, watching me as I approached, a grin on her face.

I resisted—only just—cutting sharply to the left and spraying her with a nice fan of icy water. Instead, I behaved myself and brought the Hobie in for a gentle landing against the sandy shore, then hopped from the boat and tugged it partly onto the beach, lowering the sails so it wouldn't decide to take off again, preferring the water to a land-bound existence.

As I turned toward my friend, I suddenly found myself with a face full of towel. Grabbing it before it fell to the sand, I vigorously rubbed my chilled cheeks and icy hair, restoring circulation as best I could while I walked toward the dock. "Thanks."

"More than welcome, my dear. You're quite the sailor. I'm impressed."

"Thanks," I said again, stepping on to the dock and draping the towel over one of the posts to dry in the warm spring sun.

"Just another little something I picked up from Ice. She's a great teacher."

"Indeed she is. But the best teacher in the world can't help someone who doesn't have at least a bit of natural ability. You, Angel, looked as if you'd been sailing all your life."

Feeling another blush coming on, I hid it by turning back toward the lake, watching the sailboats as they continued to make their way around the lake in endless circles.

Corinne chuckled, then reached under her chair, and came up with a thermos, from which she poured a steaming cup of tea and handed it to me. Taking the warm drink gratefully, I inhaled the wonderful scent and took a bracing sip, feeling the heat warm my insides in a most pleasant way. "God, that's good." I took another sip, then turned back to look at her. "So, did you have fun 'exploring?'"

Her teeth flashed white in a predator's grin. "Oh, yes. A great deal of fun. It's amazing what sorts of rocks one can turn over when one has the right tools for the job."

Snorting, I finished the rest of my tea and handed the cup back to her. "It's good to know you love your work."

She laughed. " Oh, I do indeed. Small towns like this have such juicy little secrets. The people hold to them so tightly, as if in giving them up, they'd somehow lose an important part of themselves." Her delighted laughter sounded again. "I do *so* enjoy poking holes in balloons of contention."

Shaking my head, I lowered myself to the sun-warmed wood of the dock, enjoying the feel of the gentle breeze against my slowly drying body. "So," I said after a moment, "what balloons did you manage to pop today?"

Corinne's eyes went wide in mock surprise. "Am I hearing correctly? My little Angel actually *wants* to hear gossip? And here I thought that was beneath you."

I scowled at her, then closed my eyes and tipped my face toward the sun. "Fine. If you don't want to tell me..."

Never one to resist a challenge, even if it was being made at her expense, Corinne remained silent for two whole seconds before beginning to tell her tale. "Were you aware that there's a bit of a feud between a certain rather rotund and fashion-challenged innkeeper and a gentleman of your acquaintance who just happens to own the business establishment across the street?"

My head lowered, my eyes opened, and I found myself suddenly very much interested in her words. "What kind of feud?"

Her expression was one of a fisherman when he knows that his prey has been caught, hook, line, and sinker. "Well," she said after a moment, "it seems that your friend Millicent..."

"She's hardly my friend, Corinne."

"In *any* event," she said, her tone telling me exactly what she thought of my untimely interruption, "it seems that Millicent filed suit against Pop for having what she called an 'unzoned eyesore'. She demanded that the old cars be removed post haste and the lot tidied up so that her guests would not have to be forced to look at lumps of rusted metal every time they peered out of their windows."

"And Pop refused, right?"

"Correct. He told her in no uncertain terms that both he and his eyesore—which *is* correctly zoned, by the way—were here to stay, and if she didn't like that fact, she was free to...well, I'm sure you can get the appropriate picture without my having to paint it for you, no?"

"Good for him! What did the courts say?"

"What could they say? He has a permit and the ability to do with the land what he wishes, short of putting up a waste treatment plant or a topless bar, of course. She lost. And so, of course, she simply filed again."

"Damn. She obviously doesn't know the meaning of the phrase 'graceful loser.' How long has this been going on?"

"Ever since she first took over the *Silver Pine* from her deceased aunt, I believe."

"Wow. I wonder why he never told us about it." I looked up at her. "How did you manage to pry it out of him?"

She contrived to look pious. "A lady never boasts about her sexual prowess, my dear."

I almost choked on my own saliva. "Yeah. Right."

She laughed. "Actually, that little tidbit didn't come from Pop. Doreen Symmonds gave it up quite easily after I stopped by and was conned into reading a few chapters of those torridly awful romance novels that warm her house with their tawdry splendor."

The mental picture of Corinne reading such stories to a raptly listening, and no doubt intently sewing, Mrs. Symmonds almost dumped me into the lake as I collapsed against the floor of the dock in laughter. She waited out my small storm with tolerant amusement, and when my gales of laughter finally wound down to isolated chuckles, she continued. "Doreen has a great deal of interesting knowledge—dirt, I believe it's called these days. She's lived here far longer than anyone else, and because of her blindness, I think people believe her deaf as well."

Serious again, I sat back upright, resting my arms atop my crossed legs. "Did she have anything else interesting to say?"

"More than can be told in one sitting, to be sure. She's a

veritable fountain of information just waiting for a coin to be tossed her way."

"Anything else on Millicent and Pop?"

"Well, it appears that Millicent's hatred of Pop doesn't extend to owners of gas stations, and their attendant eyesores, in general. From what I've heard, she's been seen courting a rather repulsive gentleman by the name of Conrad who just happens to own the station in the next town to the north."

I could feel my face drawing up in a grimace. "Yeah. I've seen him a few times. He's been trying his damnedest to get Ice away from Pop and work for him. Ice has come very close to rearranging his face for him more than once. Not that you'd be able to tell if she did, though. That man looks like a truck ran over him, stopped, backed up, and ran over him again for good measure. Millicent's probably the only woman on this planet who'd look at him twice."

"I hear he's as rich as sin."

"That'd do it."

"Trying to take Ice away would make sense," Corinne mused. "He managed to sway Pop's original mechanic into his fold. I imagine he feels that if he lured Ice away as well, especially as good and popular as she is, Pop would be forced to shut down and Millicent's problems would be solved."

"That's not gonna happen," I replied with some heat. "That bitch is gonna have to try a whole lot harder than that." I could feel my muscles tense as my clenched fists beat a tattoo on my thighs. "God damn her! What gives her the right to act like such an ass?"

Corinne laughed. "Since when did someone need a right to act like an malicious fool, Angel? Dear God, woman, you've been dealing with people of her ilk for five full years! Did you just think them confined to prison?"

"Of course not, Corinne. It's just that..." I sighed, then looked up at her again. "Pop is my friend. And I don't like to see my friends screwed with. Especially not by the likes of her." I came to my feet. "I think that woman needs to be knocked down a few pegs."

Corinne held out an arm. "Relax, Angel. Act in haste, repent in leisure, and all that. The best way to teach someone like dear Millicent a lesson is to use her own tactics against her."

Stopping as Corinne's sage advice reached my ears, I resolutely let go my anger, knowing she was right on that count. I turned back to her. "Fine. As long as I get a part in whatever play you're putting on."

She smiled enigmatically. "Oh, I think I might be able to

come up with a role for you, sweet Angel."

As someone has been known to say however, the best laid plans of mice and men...

Late that very same night, I was awakened from a deep, dreamless sleep by the incongruous sound of a bell ringing. Immediately thinking of midnight phone calls and the bad omens they portended, I shot straight up in bed, looking around wildly. "Ice?"

"Right here," came a voice to my left. Turning my head in that direction, I saw her shadowed form bent over at the waist and apparently tugging her pants on.

"What's going on? What's that ringing?"

"Fire bell," she bit off as she stood once again to her full height and dragged a T-shirt over her head, settling her hair outside of the collar.

That got me up and moving. The town didn't have a fire station. In fact, the nearest one was almost forty miles away. So when the fire bell sounded, *everyone* ran to pitch in. It was either that or sit back and watch the entire town and half the surrounding forest go up in a puff of smoke.

"Hang on a minute, I just need to find my...ah, there they are." I stepped over to the railing to retrieve jeans that had been flung there in the heat of the moment. My shirt, thankfully whole though a bit worse for wear, lay on the floor nearby and I pulled it on quickly, running my fingers through my hair. I slipped my feet into my ratty sneakers and turned to face my waiting lover. "Ready."

"Let's go, then."

After pausing briefly to reassure a concerned Corinne, we stepped outside into the chilly spring night. The thick scent of smoke was heavy in the still air. I sniffed. "Smells like burning rubber."

"It's Pop's place," Ice retorted, pointing over the treeline toward the town. A thick plume of oily black smoke could be seen rising above it, alive and malicious in the light of a waxing moon.

My body came alive with tension. "Shit! The gas pumps!"

"I know. Let's get moving."

We jumped into the truck, and Ice floored it, leaving me to hang on for dear life as we flew down the cracked and pitted street that connected our small neighborhood to the town itself. The stench of burning rubber became thicker and more cloying the closer we got, and as the truck came around the last bend, the sight of hungry flames licking upwards filled the windshield.

It seemed that almost half the town was already in attendance, with more arriving every minute. Several bucket brigades had already been formed, and men and women were busily spraying water from hoses attached to the businesses to the left and right of Pop's garage.

Thankfully, the fire appeared, for the moment, to be contained to the junkyard, which was perhaps fifty yards away from the islands that held the gas pumps.

"Promise me something, Ice," I said as we jumped from the truck and ran to join the helpers.

"What's that?"

"No running into burning buildings to save a litter of kittens, alright? I've already been through that once with you. I don't think I could bear going through it again."

Her teeth flashed in the light of the fire. "No promises, Angel, but I'll try my best."

She moved off into the line of fire, as it were, while I stepped up to Mary Lynch, who was directing the helpers to keep everyone organized and focused on their tasks. Mary pointed me in the direction of another rapidly forming bucket brigade and I gladly pitched in, grabbing and passing on each water-filled bucket that came my way.

As I became engrossed in the rather mindless work, I spared a moment to look around at the beehive of frantic, yet controlled, activity, feeling a surge of pride for a town which had, over the course of a year, become mine. There was no arguing or jostling or trying for glory. Everyone did their jobs without fuss or complaint, their entire focus on one goal and one goal only. To help out a friend in need.

After five years in jail, it felt good to be part of something like that.

Millicent, however, was conspicuous by her absence.

Turning my head, I looked at the darkened inn across the street, swearing that I could see a curtain flutter in one of the upper rooms. The anger that had left me hours before returned in full force. *I'll bet my last dollar that bitch has something to do with this.*

Still watching the inn, I noticed something out of the corner of my eye and shifted my gaze downward toward the row of hedges which bordered her property. My eyes were past the point of burning tears from the smoke, but as I continued to watch, I saw again what had attracted my attention.

The bushes moved.

Then they moved again.

"Son of a bitch. Here, hold this." Blindly thrusting the bucket I was holding into the hands of the next person in line, I broke free from the bucket brigade and started off across the street.

Whoever was watching the fire obviously saw me and tried to bolt. The bushes moved violently again, and I broke into a sprint. "Oh no ya don't!"

Running as fast as I could, I launched myself in a flying tackle, managing to wrap my arms around the ankles of the person trying to flee, and bring us both hard to the unforgiving ground. Getting quickly to my knees, I rolled the person I'd tackled over and saw the snarling face of a young man—no more than a boy, really—hot-spots of adolescent acne clear on his face.

Gritting his teeth, he began to struggle, but I held him rather easily, straddling his heaving chest and placing my knees squarely on his biceps, effectively pinning him. "Get offa me!" he yelled in a high, cracked voice.

"Not until you tell me what you were doing in those bushes."

"What the hell do ya think, I was doin', lady? Jerkin' off? I was watchin' the fire!" He renewed his struggle to escape, becoming more red-faced with the effort. "Come on, lady! Get offa me. I wasn't doin' nothin' wrong!"

"I think you're lying," I replied, staring down at him and adjusting to the frantic movements of his body beneath me. I inhaled deeply and tried not to choke on the smoke which filled the air. "You smell like gasoline. I think you started that fire."

"I didn't start nothin', bitch." Seeing his struggles were fruitless, he opted for staring sullenly at me. "Maybe *you* started it and are lookin' for someone ta blame."

I smiled coolly. "I think we both know that's not the truth." Then I tried another tactic. "If you didn't start the fire, maybe you saw who did? After all, you had a front row seat over there, didn't you?"

"I didn't see nothin'." His face was closed, walled off. That expression wasn't exactly something I was unfamiliar with.

I sighed. "Fine." Then I moved off of him, coming to my feet and offering him a hand.

Swatting it away, he jumped to his own feet, smirking at me. "Bitch."

I allowed him to turn, and as he did so, I grabbed his wrist and wrenched it up high and hard behind his back. He came to his toes immediately, squeaking in pain. "What the fuck are ya doin'?"

"You're a witness to a crime. You didn't think I was just gonna let you go, did you?"

"I told ya, bitch, I didn't see nothin'!"

"Yeah, I know. You didn't see anything, you didn't hear anything, you didn't do anything. A regular Casper Milquetoast, you are."

"Huh?"

"Never mind. Just move."

And move we did, right back toward the still burning fire, with my reluctant captive struggling every step of the way. Though he was a good five inches taller and fifty or so pounds heavier than I was, I had little trouble marching him back the way we'd come. After all, it was a move I'd practiced on Ice more times than I cared to count, and if I could do it with her, I had no doubt that I could immobilize Mr. Universe if I had to.

For a second, anyway.

We passed the first line of helpers, most of whom gave us curious glances as we walked through the area of controlled chaos. They returned quickly to their tasks, though, and we moved forward pretty much unmolested.

When the smoke became too thick for breathing, I stopped, eyes darting around, trying to find my partner through the haze of oily smoke. Which was, of course, trying to find a needle in a mountain of haystacks.

"Ice!" I shouted, trying mightily to be heard over the din of the fire and the shouts of the helpers. When there was no answer, I tried again. "Ice! I need to see you for a second, please!"

After a long moment, the smoke seemed to coalesce and take on human form. Then my lover stepped through the fumes, her hair drenched with sweat, her face black with soot from which two icy sapphire chips sparkled, her clothes dirty and pasted to her body, and a large axe gripped surely in one hand.

If a Hollywood casting director had been there looking for someone to play a demon from hell, he would have hired her on the spot, no questions asked.

The young man standing in front of me stiffened, and I could feel his pulse-rate double beneath my hand. He renewed his efforts to break free, but I held him easily, watching as my partner approached, a no-nonsense look on what could be seen of her face. "What's going on?" she asked, still holding the axe, her voice harsh from the smoke she'd inhaled.

"I found my friend here hiding in the bushes across the street," I replied, noticing out of the corner of my eye that Pop, almost equally soot-covered and sweating, moved out of the smoke to join us. "He seems to have been affected with a sudden case of stupidity, so I figured I'd bring him over here and let you wise him up."

Reaching out with her free hand, Ice grabbed the young man by the front of his T-shirt and jerked him forward until their faces were scarcely an inch apart. I quickly let his arm go, fearing that the sudden pressure would tear it free from its socket.

"Did you start this fire?" Ice growled, the harshness of her voice only magnifying the malevolent effect.

Stepping to one side, I looked up, noticing that the surly youngster's eyes were now wide as saucers while his face paled to the color of curdled cream, unfortunate acne standing out in spots of high color on his cheeks, forehead and chin.

"Answer me!" Ice growled again, shaking him as a terrier might shake a chew toy.

I knew he was past the point of forming coherent words, and was just about to step in when Pop, apparently having the same idea, put a blackened hand on Ice's arm and stepped closer to the pair, peering up into the face of the unfortunate boy. "You're Duke Johnson's boy from up-country, ain't ya? I seen you around a few times when I've been up that way."

As if desperate to ingratiate himself to one who wasn't about to rip his head off and chop up what was left into tiny pieces, the boy nodded frantically, his Adam's apple bobbing as he gulped past the pressure Ice was putting on his throat.

Pop nodded. "Thought so. What you doin' so far from home, boy? Ain't you got school in the mornin'?"

He nodded again, which, of course, didn't come close to answering either question.

"Ease up on him a little, Morgan. Boy looks like he's gonna pass out and piss himself all at the same time. Let's see what he's got ta say."

Ice relaxed her grip just slightly, allowing the boy to stand comfortably on both feet once again, but didn't release him entirely, in case he thought about doing something stupid. Like running, for instance.

The way she was staring at him, I thought breathing might be another example in the "doing something stupid" department, unless she got the answers she was looking for.

Pop's eyes were compassionate. "Who put you up to this, boy? Just gimme a name, and you're free to go."

"I didn't *do* nothin'!" Instead of surliness, the young man's tone had changed to one of petulance, with a dose of good, old-fashioned fright thrown in for good measure.

"I know your father, boy. He's a good man. Don't think he's got it in him to raise stupid sons. Just tell me who set you up for this and he won't have ta visit you in the jail."

At the mention of jail, the boy's lip trembled slightly, but he remained stubbornly silent.

Pop took off his cap, slapping it against his thigh. "God *damn* it, boy! Don't you realize just what a shitpile you got yourself into? If I hadn't been nearby when you threw your damn cocktail in there, you wouldn't just be lookin' at arson. You'd be lookin' at murder, a dozen times over."

"What are you talkin' about?"

"I was wrong. Your old man *did* manage ta raise a stupid kid. Can't you see how close you came to explodin' my gas tanks?! This whole town coulda gone up, and most of the people too! Yourself included, ya shit-fer-brains idiot!"

The boy's legs buckled at that, and the only thing that kept him on his feet was Ice's firm grip to his shirt. Pop brought his face up close, much as Ice had done the moment prior. "Who done this, boy? Who put you up to it? A name's all I need. You gimme that and you're free to go."

There was a long moment of silence, punctuated only by the shouts of the people still fighting the slowly diminishing fire. Then the boy looked up, his eyes bright with tears I knew weren't caused by the smoke. "I didn't do nothin'. I didn't see nothin'. I told ya that already. Can I please go home now?"

Pop sighed, then placed his cap back on his head. "Let 'im go, Morgan." He nodded at her look to him. "It's alright. Let 'im go. I think he's learned his lesson for the night. Ain't that right, boy."

The boy nodded, then turned to leave as Ice released her grip on his shirt. Pop stopped him with one hand on his arm. "One more thing, son. If, when yer walkin' home, yer good sense does return to ya, I'd suggest going up to the coward who put ya up to this and tellin' him next time not ta send a boy to do a man's work. Tell him next time he wants ta fight, do it himself. Got that?"

"Yeah. I got it."

"Good. Now get yer ass outta here before I change my mind and let my big friend with the axe here chop ya up fer firewood."

As if shot from a cannon, he took off, not pausing even once to look back, and disappeared quickly into the woods, leaving only the stench of his fear behind.

Snorting in disgust, Ice hefted her axe and, without a word to either of us, went back to fighting the fire.

"Why'd you let him go like that?" I asked Pop, disbelief

plain in the tone of my voice.

"Wasn't worth the hassle of keepin' him around, Angel. He's just a little fish in an even littler pond."

"Yeah, but that little fish almost destroyed this entire town."

"And he knows it, too." He turned to me, his eyes wise even beyond their advanced years. "He had the fear o' God scared into him tonight, Angel. Somethin' a whole lifetime in prison wouldn't do. And when he comes ta realize just how close he came ta endin' it all, he'll go right up to the idiot that set him up and give him my message. Killin' two birds with one stone, and all that."

"Screw the two birds, Pop. You know who set him up as much as I do," I replied, gritting my teeth in anger.

His eyes went wide for a second, then narrowed. "So, ya heard about that, huh?"

"Yeah. I heard. And I'm not gonna let her get away with it."

"Don't go doin' nothin' rash, Tyler. Don't wanna go visitin' you in the pen any more than I wanted ta put that boy in there."

"Oh, I'm not planning on doing anything rash. Unless you count ripping her fat little head off and shoving it up her ass as being rash."

He laughed. "Morgan's rubbin' off on ya, I see."

"No. I come by this naturally, Pop." I crossed my arms over my chest. "I'm mad as hell at that witch for what she's doing to you. Why do I seem to be the only one?"

He smiled, the tender expression at odds with the definite blaze of anger in his eyes. "You're not the only one, sweetheart, though I gotta say you win the prize for originality."

"Then why don't you do something about her? Why just let her get off scot-free? Does someone have to die before justice is served here?"

"Naw. No one's gonna die, Tyler. She'll get what's comin' to her alright. We all just gotta wait a little." His eyes glittered. "Ya know what they say about revenge, right?"

I sighed. "Yeah. It likes to be refrigerated."

He grinned. "Somethin' like that, yeah." Then he threw a companionable arm around my shoulders. "C'mon, then. Let's get back to fightin' this fire before Morgan there gets all the glory fer puttin' it out single-handed, eh?"

Sighing again for effect, I caved in to his gentle entreaty. There wasn't much else I could do about it, after all. But as I walked back toward the fire, I entertained myself with visions of my fingers wrapping around Millicent's bejeweled and fleshy neck as her beady brown eyes popped out like a couple of overripe grapes.

Oh yes, revenge might be a dish best served cold, but even the best ice cream in the world didn't have so sweet a taste.

Dawn began to lighten the sky to the east when the last of the fire was finally laid to rest. Only those overcome by the heat and smoke had left. The rest stayed and fought side by side until finally the battle was won.

Beyond exhausted, I gratefully dropped the last water-filled bucket to the ground at my feet, wiping sweaty, blistered and raw hands uselessly against an equally sweaty, not to mention black with soot, shirt. I took in a deep breath before realizing my mistake, then almost collapsed when spasms of coughing shook my already weakened body. Spots flashed before my eyes and I fought to regain my breathing before I passed out on the muddy ground.

Feeling a cool hand to the back of my sweat-sticky neck, I looked up into the concerned eyes of Corinne. Coughing a few more times, then gratefully feeling my lungs begin to accept the gift of fresh air, I slowly straightened, every muscle in my body tight and aching. Smiling, she handed me a tall glass, which was filled to the brim with her special sweet tea that I adored.

I held the glass up to my brow for a moment, relishing the chill against my flesh. Then I gulped down the entire offering, almost moaning in pleasure as it hit my belly and cooled me instantly. "You're a goddess, Corinne. Thanks."

Rescuing the glass from my hand, she poured another tall drink from her thermos and handed it back to me. "Think nothing of it, Angel. Drink up, now. You're about to fall right over."

"You don't know the half of it," I replied, gulping down the second drink as quickly as I had the first and feeling the icy needles of too much cold too quickly spiking into my brain. "Owww."

Laughing gently, Corinne took back her glass as I rubbed at my forehead, willing the sharp pain to recede.

It calmed gradually, disappearing completely just as a warm, and very welcome presence made itself known at my side. Feeling a grin surface, I looked up at a soot-covered partner who looked nearly as exhausted as I felt, her eyes red rimmed and puffy. "Hey, stranger," I said, bumping her thigh with my hip.

"Hey." She cocked a questioning eyebrow at me. "You alright?"

"Nothing a year's worth of sleep won't cure. You?"

She shrugged. "I'm fine."

I looked at her, assessing the truth of her words. She bore several fresh scrapes to the left side of her face, and peeking beneath the ruins of a once pristine T-shirt, an ugly red burn stood out angrily on the smooth skin of her muscled belly. "What happened?"

She looked down as if noticing the burn for the first time. "Got a little too close to the fire, I guess. Doesn't hurt."

"It will."

"Maybe."

Corinne pressed the glass of tea into her hand and she quaffed it quickly, then handed the glass back and lifted the half-filled bucket laying at my feet and dumping its contents over her head. Groaning, she shook her head, spraying us all with the droplets that flew out from her hair.

As my skin greedily took in the precious moisture offered, I turned to look at the charred remains of Pop's automobile graveyard. There wasn't much left. "At least we kept the tanks from going up."

"True enough," Ice replied, gliding an arm around my shoulders and hugging me into her side.

Tearing my gaze away from the carnage, I looked toward the inn. Once again, I could swear I saw the curtains twitch just a little, as if released by a hidden hand. I turned back to Ice. "She did this, you know. She might not have been the one to start the fire, but she's just as guilty."

Ice nodded. "I know."

"Well, if you know, and I know, and Pop knows, and everybody in this whole damn town knows, why isn't anybody doing anything about it?"

She squeezed me tighter for a minute. "You know why, Angel. This is Pop's show. And as much as I want to rearrange the bitch's arms and legs for her, we need to let Pop take the lead on this one."

"But for how much longer? Damnit, Ice, he's already been beaten to a bloody pulp, had his shop trashed, and now this! I know he's an adult and this is his life, but when is it going to end? When is that bitch going to stop getting away with it?"

She looked down at me, her eyes steel-gray in the light of a new dawn. "Pop or no Pop, Angel, she *will* not get away with this. That I promise you."

After a moment, I let go my anger and relaxed against her. After all, who knew better than I that when Morgan Steele made a promise, you went to the bank with it.

Released from the false energy of both my anger and Corinne's caffeine-and-sugar laden tea, I slumped wearily against Ice's side. "Can we go home now? I think I can hear the bed calling from here, and if I don't get there quick, I'll just fall asleep in this nice juicy mud-puddle instead."

She hugged me tight. "Sure. This mess will still be around to clean up later. Let's go."

Saying our goodbyes to Pop and the other firefighters, we then collected Corinne, squeezed into the truck, and headed for home, weary to the bone.

And after three successive showers finally managed to clean the soot and smoke from my body, I climbed into my big, soft, clean and oh so wonderful bed and fell asleep before my head hit the pillow, leaving my angers and my worries to wait for another day, when I was more equipped, not to mention awake, to deal with them.

Chapter 12

The next several days passed quietly, though not without activity. The fire had left behind huge clumps of twisted, charred metal only vaguely resembling the cars they once were. Shattered bits of safety glass lay glittering under the mid-day sun like a tiny galaxy being viewed from above by an omnipotent god. Charred upholstery, tires, and hundreds of other items rendered unidentifiable by the conflagration were waiting patiently to be cleared away.

I lobbied hard against such a clean up, reasoning—quite logically, I thought—that it would be just desserts of the highest order to have Millicent and her guests be forced to look down upon the true eyesore her efforts had wrought.

Pop, however, was a better person than I that day and lobbied just as hard to clean the mess up. His reasoning that other people would have to look at it, too, couldn't be argued with, and finally I put away my snit for the day and pitched in, though not without a few half-muttered curses that even had Corinne looking at me with newfound respect.

Then one morning, while coming downstairs after changing the sheets on our bed, I spied Corinne standing before the mirror on the back of the bathroom door, putting the finishing touches on the outfit she'd chosen for the day.

And a fine outfit it was. A simple black dress and matching shoes were complimented by tasteful—and obviously expensive—jewelry. Her hair and makeup were done to perfection, and when she turned to face me, I suddenly saw just what it was that attracted so many to her, both in the days of her youth, and now, when that youth was a far away thing, never to be seen again.

She was, in a word, beautiful.

"Wow!" I commented, giving her my best wolf whistle. "Don't *you* clean up nice."

"One does one's best with what one has," she replied, her twinkling eyes and smug grin belying the false modesty of her words.

"Who's the lucky guy?" I grinned. "Or girl."

"Getting a bit nosey are we?"

"What can I say? I learned from the best," I replied, reaching out to straighten her collar.

"Well, if you *must* know, I'm about to pay Millicent a visit."

I could feel my nose wrinkling. "I thought your standards were higher than that, Corinne."

She laughed. "Oh, you can be sure that they most definitely are. I'm considering this a little fact-finding mission. That stubborn mule of a gas station owner won't let even the tiniest hair springing from Millicent's moles be harmed. He wants irrefutable proof that she was behind the attacks against him. I intend to give him that proof."

"Ahh," I said, nodding. "Would you like some company?"

She looked at me critically. "I don't know if that's wise, Angel. Millicent doesn't seem predisposed toward having warm feelings for you, especially given recent events and the part you've played in them."

"True. But I hardly think that's an obstacle the great Corinne Weaver can't overcome." Playing to her ego was a surefire way to get myself a seat of honor at the main event. Besides, it was only the truth, and we both knew it.

Her eyes softened and she acknowledged my tactic with a slight tilt of her head, causing me to display my triumph with a toothy grin. Still, she couldn't help putting a touch of the martyr in her voice. "Oh, very well. If you feel you *must* come along, hurry up and change. I'm not getting any younger, you know."

"But you're aging beautifully," I said, dodging in and giving her a teasing kiss before darting away and running up the stairs to change into something more presentable. From the floor below, I heard her muttering something about impertinent brats and their need of a good strapping, and I couldn't help but laugh.

After changing into a pair of clean, pressed shorts and a simple green top, I slipped a pair of sandals on and walked back downstairs to join Corinne, bearing her scrutiny stoically.

"The innocent little girl look. I like it." Her dark eyes twinkled. "I like it a great deal, in fact."

"Down, Fido," I joked. "Let's just get this show on the

road, ok?"

"Spoilsport."

"Chicken-hawk."

Her laugh sounded its music behind me as I made for the door.

God I had missed her!

Twenty minutes later, we found ourselves standing outside the open door to the *Silver Pine*. The bustle of workers busily readying the inn for its upcoming season filled the space around us. Looking around, I wasn't surprised to find many of the same people who had fought the fire were there, sprucing up the arsonist's business establishment.

Though it looked to all the world like Millicent had gotten off without a hitch, in reality, she was being watched like a hawk by those working for her. With so many townspeople in and around her home, she couldn't blow her nose without it becoming town gossip within seconds.

The men and women up on ladders, or raking the grounds, or bearing buckets and scrub brushes gave me little grins or covert winks as our gazes met, as if to assure me that they were on the job and ready for action.

Millicent came to the door then, wearing a dress the exact shade, not to mention size, of a huge wad of bubblegum in a teenaged girl's mouth. Her lipstick, a frosted pink that had last been popular during the disco era, tried its best to match, but failed miserably. Even the ribbons entangled in poor Puddles' fur couldn't come close to the true atrocity that was Millicent's dress. Her feet were adorned with dainty slippers more suited to the ballet, and which were straining at the seams from being forced to carry a weight far heavier than their maker no-doubt intended. And, of course, the jewels were out in full bloom, covering what seemed to be every inch of exposed skin.

Since I was closest to the door, she spied me first and her face took on that sour lemon look I'd come to associate with her. I gave her my best smile, then stepped aside as the great Corinne moved forward to take center stage in the play she was directing.

Her lips hinted at a somewhat regal half-smile as she assessed Millicent from head to toe, looking at her as if she might just be a rival for a cherished mate's affections. "Ms. Harding-Post, I presume?"

Millicent reacted immediately, her carriage becoming more erect, as befitting one meeting a social peer for the first time and not wanting it to get back to the powers that be that one was slacking off in one's duties. "Yes. And you are?"

"Corinne LaPointe. Of the LaPointes of North Hampton. Perhaps you recognize the name?"

Like the biggest large-mouth ever landed, Millicent took the bait, her face breaking into a beaming smile. "Indeed I do, Mrs. LaPointe. Indeed I do! It's so wonderful to meet a fellow Islander. Won't you please come in?"

"I'd be delighted. My wonderful niece has told me so much about you, Ms. Harding-Post. It was all I could do just to wait the respectable amount of time before coming to pay you a visit."

Millicent tittered coyly, her broad face dimpling. "Oh please, Mrs. LaPointe. Millicent, if you don't mind. Such formality is for those beneath one's station, don't you agree?"

"Oh, I do indeed, Millicent. Perhaps you'll return the favor and call me Corinne, yes?"

"It would be a great honor, Corinne. Won't you please come in?"

"Your invitation is most welcome, Millicent. Thank you."

One of my father's many down-home sayings chose that moment to pop into my mind. *When a shit storm's blowin' your way, Tyler, best thing you can do is get out of the way and plug up your nose.*

And so I did, stepping aside so that Corinne could pass in front of me. Though this time, instead of plugging my nose, I held tight to the laughter that was threatening to erupt as I watched the genius that was my friend.

Following close behind, I couldn't help but watch as Corinne took in the interior of the Bed and Breakfast with what seemed to be wide-eyed and appreciative wonder.

"What a beautiful home you have, Millicent! You simply *must* give me the name of your designer."

Millicent's eyes narrowed just a touch. "Why? Are you thinking of opening up a business here?"

"Me?" Corinne's hand came up to her chest and she laughed. "Oh no, my dear. My dabbling days are long over, I'm afraid. I'll leave the fine art of business to those much younger and more beautiful than I."

If I hadn't seen it with my own eyes, I would have found it impossible to believe that Millicent Harding-Post could become even larger than she already was, yet there it was, plain as day, her body seeming to puff up with the praise she'd received, much as a peacock's will when spreading his plumage.

I wondered if asking for quick directions to the bathroom

was out.

Millicent uttered that queer tittering laugh again, flapping her hand at Corinne. "Nonsense, dear. You're absolutely *charming*, and I mean that in only the *best* of ways!"

"How kind of you to say, Millicent."

"I only speak the truth, Corinne." Bustling us into the lobby, she indicated a rather uncomfortable looking couch which sat catty-corner to the overdone fireplace monopolizing one wall. "Won't you please sit down? I'd offer you the grand tour, but I'm afraid the horrid winter has done just dreadful things to the rooms upstairs. They won't be fit for man nor beast for a month, at least!"

Corinne nodded in commiseration. "I understand perfectly, Millicent. Your hospitality is a gift beyond measure." She sat down on the couch, the very essence of regality. I stood next to her, wondering if it was proper to sit next to such royalty, or if it was more proper that I kneel by her side, a footman bearing scepter and crown. She looked at me, the faintest hint of amusement in her eyes. "Please sit, Tyler. You're offending our hostess."

Even though said in jest, the mock rebuke stung and, true to my childhood programming, I sat down quickly, eyes cast to the floor. "Yes, ma'am."

"There's a good girl," she replied, patting my hand.

I looked up, first at Corrine, then at Millicent.

Oh, how I ached to wipe that look of smug condescension from her face.

With an axe.

Not that anyone would notice the difference if I did.

Corinne must have caught my tension, because she squeezed my hand briefly before releasing it and clasping her hands primly in her lap.

"Would you like some tea?" Millicent asked.

"Only if it isn't too much trouble, dear."

"Oh, no trouble at all. I was just about to fix myself a cup when you came calling. Be back in a flash."

I maintained my silence for all of a second after she left, taking her stench and her oh-so-refined air with her. Then I did a slow head turn until Corinne was fully in my sights. "Is it permissible to vomit in the potted palm, my Lady?"

Corinne laughed, her whole body shaking with mirth. "Patience, dear Angel. In order to grow a proper garden, one needs to visit the cow pasture first."

"Yeah, but I'm only wearing sandals."

"Just relax and follow my lead."

I sighed. "I'll try. It's not gonna be easy, though."

She smiled. "I have all the faith in the world in you, Angel."

Though it should have, her statement didn't make me feel any better.

Millicent returned after a short time, rolling in a silver tea-cart upon which various tea accouterments were tinkling when they jostled together as the wheels rolled along from rug to hideous rug.

Stopping the cart nearby, she then proceeded to pour out the tea and hand us delicate china cups brimming with the dark, steaming brew.

Corinne sipped hers, smiling in appreciation. On cue, I sipped my own tea, not really tasting it for the bile still in my throat.

Apparently satisfied with Corinne's tacit approval, Millicent poured her own tea, then sat down in the armchair on the other side of the fireplace. Puddles promptly jumped into her somewhat more than generous lap and helped herself to a long drink, her entire body shuddering in what looked to be the throes of ecstasy.

"So," Millicent said after rescuing her tea from Puddles and drinking down the rest of it without a thought to how it must look, "what brings you here, Corinne? Surely it isn't the scenery. Or the populace." She said the last with a visible shudder.

"My niece," Corinne answered succinctly.

Millicent's eyebrows raised. Mine almost went up as well. "Oh?"

"Yes. Tyler is very much loved by her family, but I'm afraid she's become a bit much, even for them lately." She leaned closer to Millicent, as if imparting a dark secret. "Left her poor fiancée at the altar. My brother is heartbroken about it. Simply heartbroken."

"Oh, how truly sad," Millicent replied, shaking her head in sympathy and looking at me as if I'd suddenly grown Vampire teeth and might bite. "However is he coping?"

"Not very well, I'm afraid. Her mother took ill, as one might expect, and it's all he can to just to coax the poor dear out of bed in the morning. They had such high hopes for this marriage. It was the perfect match. Hand picked, you know."

"Is there any other kind?"

"Not for us, no." She turned to me and smiled. "Tyler's always been a bit headstrong. Many children are these days, no matter how much love and guidance their parents give them."

"I think it's in the water," Millicent pronounced with God-like authority.

"It may well be at that. She announced, bold as you please, that she wanted to see a bit of the world first before settling down and becoming the proper wife to a prosperous young man. Being young once myself, I could empathize with her passions. Little did I know, however, just what sort of passions they were."

Looking in my direction once again, Millicent's face screwed up in that sour expression I so detested.

Corinne smiled. "I see you've met her."

"Not to talk to, certainly," Millicent said in a haughty tone. "But in passing, yes. Utterly base and without any hint of a redeeming quality whatsoever."

"Yes, but with a sort of magnetism that a young woman like Tyler can't help but be attracted to. Even I felt myself drawn, if only for a moment."

Millicent's eyes went round. "You did?"

"Oh yes. She has a power. Demon-given, I'm sure, but a power nonetheless. And without the benefit of experience which you and I have in spades, poor Tyler was powerless against her attentions. It happens to the best of us, sometimes."

"They recruit, you know," Millicent said, her voice once again full of authority. Then she looked at me once more, scanning me intently from head to toe. "And your niece is exactly the type they like to prey on. Young. Innocent. Mildly attractive."

Corinne's quick hand on my wrist was the only thing that stopped me from ripping the woman's tongue out and feeding it to her.

"Really? I find her quite attractive. She reminds me a little of myself when I was younger."

"Oh, no offense meant, Corinne," Millicent said hastily, to cover her faux pas, no doubt. "The family resemblance is quite striking, if I may say so. Quite striking. Why, in the right light, you look as if you could almost be sisters."

I resisted the urge to look around for the cow I just knew had to be hiding somewhere.

Corinne smiled as if the compliment was nothing but the utter truth as she saw things. "You're very kind to say so, Millicent." She sighed. "One of the unfortunate truths of life is that age does catch up with a body. I try my best to stave off its effects for as long as possible."

"And you're doing a magnificent job of it, Corinne. Simply magnificent. Why, I'm surprised you don't have suitors surrounding you like birds to a fountain. Even in this corner of God's hell."

"Oh, there's been some interest, to be sure. But honestly, I hardly see myself as pairing up with an elderly gas-station attendant, do you?"

Bulls-eye!

"Oh, not *him*. He's a perfectly dreadful little man. And a bit of a pervert as well, if you don't mind such base language. I simply can't think of a better way to describe him."

"I don't mind at all." Which wasn't, of course, near to being the truth. Though she didn't show it outwardly, I could feel Corinne's temper click up a notch based on the sudden, if imperceptible to anyone but me, stiffness in her body. "Has he made improper advances toward you, Millicent?"

"No. Well, not exactly. But every time I see him, it's as if he's undressing me with his eyes." She shuddered.

I almost swallowed my tongue at the mental image.

I could tell by the silent tremor next to me that Corinne was trying desperately to hold back a laugh. It was a very close call.

"How simply dreadful for you, poor dear," she said finally in a voice which was not quite her own. Then, because she was about a millisecond away from losing her composure, she turned her head to look out of the window, a broad grin cracking the staid plains of her face as she did so.

I almost hated her for a moment, jealous of her ability to take such a needed escape while I had to sit still and proper, playing the part of a lost little girl who's finally seen the light. A quick vision of Pop's face as he surveyed the damage Millicent had caused sobered me quickly and sent a warm, welcome flush of anger through limbs made stiff with inactivity. I kept my eyes glued to the teacup, studying the dainty pattern of trailing roses so as not to betray my emotions.

After a long moment, Corinne finally turned back, her face fully settled once again. "Unfortunate view," she commented, not bothering to point out the picture of Pop's burned out junkyard that stared in through the large window. "Does it affect your business any?"

Millicent's lips thinned and a very real anger sparked in her eyes. "You don't know the half of it. Why, when I first learned this place had befallen me, I had such high hopes. An entire society of wealthy friends has a taste for slumming, provided the proper accommodations are available, of course. Why, my volunteer circle alone could feed and house this entire backwater hellhole for years! Not to mention my friends at the country club. My only thoughts were to do right by this place, backward though it is. To show its people a touch of class, to help the needy, to be a good neighbor." Fat, crocodile tears beaded in the corners of her eyes, their very presence turning my stomach. "And what was I given in return? Hatred. Suspicion. Cruelty."

Pulling out a lace handkerchief as large as a tablecloth, she dabbed her eyes as her gelatinous body quivered with imagined grief.

It was one of the hardest things I've ever done, not giving into the almost insane urge to rip that handkerchief out of her hands and knot it around her neck like a noose. The tea sat sour and curdled in my belly and I had to swallow a few times just to make sure the joking threat I'd made to Corinne about baptizing a houseplant didn't become a reality.

For her part, Corinne sat still and quiet as a church mouse, a smile frozen on her face as she watched Millicent play out the part of well-meaning but horribly mistreated philanthropist.

It might not have been so bad, even for all that, had Millicent not kept peeking up at Corinne, a flat sheen of cool calculation in eyes filled with false tears, to judge the effect her mournful display was having.

After a few more heartbroken sobs were manufactured for good measure, she wiped her face, then replaced the handkerchief in a hidden pocket somewhere on her person. I mourned the loss of so fine a weapon.

"So you can see that this hasn't been an easy road to travel. Out here, all alone, without one friend to call my own." She affected a deep sigh, swelling her already huge bosom to truly astounding proportions. "But, as always, I shall persevere, despite whatever these cretins try to throw at me."

"Have you tried to fight back?" Corinne asked in as compassionate a tone as she could manage under the circumstances.

"Indeed I have. I filed suits, I called in the police, I did everything I could think of. Nothing. No help for the inconvenienced." She laughed bitterly. "Justice, they say. Ha! They wouldn't know justice if they tripped over it."

"I can't say I'm a bit surprised," Corinne replied. "These Canadians have a way of protecting their own when it comes to outsiders. You simply wouldn't believe all the hoops I was forced to jump through just to rescue my beloved niece." She smiled; one that was hard with knowing. "Sometimes, I've found that it's best just to take matters into one's own hands."

Millicent's face then took on a cast of a young girl with a very deep secret and I knew the moment was at hand. I felt myself lean forward as adrenaline rushed its way through my body, speeding my heart. "Do you?" she asked in a very small voice.

"I do indeed. Sad as it is to say, gone are the days when

one's station in life guaranteed one good service, Millicent. Now it's every person for himself. There are no free rides anymore."

I could almost feel the internal debate that was raging inside Millicent. Her eyes seemed far away as she nervously chewed on her bottom lip. Then she looked up, her eyes filled with something I'd never seen in them before: trepidation. "Have you ever done something like that?" she asked finally.

Corinne grinned. "I'm here, aren't I?"

Millicent's entire body relaxed with the statement and a huge smile of relief came over her face, making her look, for just a second, mildly attractive. Still, she didn't spill the beans, and so Corinne decided to nudge the boat just a little. "Surely there is someone in this tiny little town who detests the man as much as you do. There simply must be. Towns this size have entire graveyards of skeletons hanging in closets and a veritable mountain of rocks waiting to be turned over."

"Oh no, not here. Believe me, I've looked." Then she stopped, aware that she'd just given much too much away. She looked at me, then over to Corinne.

"Don't worry about Tyler, Millicent. She's learned her lessons well. Haven't you, Tyler."

I contrived to look the part of the successfully reprogrammed. "Yes, ma'am," I replied, twisting my hands a little and lowering my eyes for good measure.

Millicent seemed satisfied with the gesture. "I *have* been speaking with a few good gentlemen outside of this town, however. Men with some bones to pick with a certain Mr. Willamette. Large bones. Old bones."

"And are they willing to help you with your problem?"

Millicent's answering smile was coy. "Oh, they already have. Accidents have a way of happening, you know. Quite without warning. His place is a deathtrap anyway."

Corinne nodded sagely. "And has this helped any?"

"It's much too soon to tell, of course. I'm confident that it will, eventually. I want this badly, and I always get what I want. Always."

"I can see that you are a person who does, yes."

Then, like a message from Providence, the phone rang, and Millicent heaved herself up to her feet to answer it.

A long, meaningful look passed between Corinne and I. We'd come for answers, and we'd gotten them. In spades.

Neither of us was sad to see the conversation come to an end when Millicent rushed back into the room, her face flushed with some unidentifiable emotion, and tell us that an emergency had occurred and she needed to be elsewhere.

We excused ourselves gracefully and left, filled with a knowledge neither of us particularly wanted to have.

It made for an interesting walk home.

"You wanted proof? Now you've got it. Question is, what are you going to do with it?" Corinne sat back in her chair, fingers running relentlessly over the polished wood of the dining room table, and pinning Pop to his seat with her eyes.

He seemed to shrink a little before coming back into himself and mirroring her position in his own chair. "Don't know yet. Didn't expect you to come up with it quite so fast."

She smiled. "That's just because you don't know me well enough. You're not the only person in this little town who can get what he wants, when he wants it."

"S'ppose you're right." He lapsed into silence once again.

"Well?"

"Corinne..." I interjected softly, reaching across the table to lay a hand on her constantly moving wrist.

Turning her head, she shot me the same look she was using on Pop, but when I didn't shrink from it, she gradually relaxed and huffed out a dramatic sigh. "Fine. If he doesn't want to act on the information, there's not much more I can do, is there?"

"Didn't say I wasn't gonna act on it, Corinne. Only that ya didn't give me any time to think on it."

She turned back to him. "Time? Dear God, man! You've had time to think about this since Millicent sent over those thugs to beat you within an inch of your life!"

"Now don't go sayin' that, Corinne. No one knows for sure she was behind what happened there. Them guys are scum, pure and simple. No needin' to think any harder on that."

Corinne slowly shook her head, disbelief plain as day on her face. "For a man who supposedly knows it all, you're painfully naïve at times, Willamette."

Pop narrowed his eyes at her. "What're you sayin', woman?"

"Just what it sounds like. I find it hard to believe that you don't know that that pump jockey Millicent's been seen around just happens to be the brother-in-law of the owner of the *Rusted Nut*. From what I've heard, those two men are thick as thieves."

"I knew that."

"You knew that and...what? You put two and two together and came up with seventeen? Twenty? What?"

I tried again, alarmed at the plum cast that was taking over Corinne's face. "Corinne, please calm down, ok? This isn't getting us anywhere."

She looked from me, to Pop, and back again. Then she pushed herself up from the table. "I need some air."

And with that, she left.

I began to stand up to follow her, when a slow shake of Ice's head sat me right back down again. Sighing myself, I looked around the table. Pop, Ice and I weren't the only ones who had been treated to Corinne's somewhat uncharacteristic outburst. Tom Drew and Mary Lynch had both come calling, curious as to what had gone on behind Millicent's closed doors earlier in the afternoon. Because they were both on the front lines, so to speak, by virtue of their professions and the work they were doing on the Inn, they'd both been invited to the impromptu strategy session.

"Why don't we just call the police?" Mary said, logically. I couldn't help my heart rate as it sped up at the mention of that particular word. I looked over at Ice, who returned my look steadily. "I mean, if we spelled it out for them, with Corinne telling what she knew, wouldn't they at least investigate?"

Pop shook his head. "No. No cops. I've had my fair share of dealin's with them in the past and I don't want 'em in here, investigatin' all over everything. Cause more trouble than it's worth, getting them involved."

"But...."

"No cops. I ain't gonna say it again."

Tom Drew spoke up next. "Well, if you won't let us beat her up or burn her down, why don't we just squeeze her out? She won't be able to run that inn without us there, fixing what breaks."

"Sure she will," Pop said. "She'll just call fer help up-country, like she been doin' all along. Then we'll have even more strangers tied up in this mess."

"But..."

"He's right," Ice commented softly, speaking for the first time since the meeting started. "If you try to shut her down by withholding needed services, she'll only go somewhere else for them and you'll lose the only excuse you have to keep an eye on her from up close."

"Then what *do* we do?" Mary asked her.

The entire table looked at Ice. Myself included. Even without knowing anything of her past, all you had to do was stand in her presence for more than a second to know, with absolute certainty, that this was a woman who got things done. A woman who had the answers, even if you didn't want to hear them. Even if you didn't know what the question was to begin with.

She met each of our gazes in turn, long fingers trailing over the tabletop. After a long moment, she spoke. "If it were up to me, I'd teach Millicent Harding-Post exactly what it means to mess with one of my friends." Her voice got that dark and dangerous edge that never failed to raise the hairs on the back of my neck. I could see the same reaction in my friends around the table as well. "But it isn't up to me. It's up to Pop. And until he can't speak for himself anymore, I, for one, am gonna abide by what he says." Then she met Pop's gaze squarely, her expression unmistakable. "For now."

Nodding his understanding, Pop turned to look at the rest of us. "Look. I didn't say I was rulin' out any one of your ideas. Just need some time ta think on 'em is all. Things ain't the way they used ta be when I was some younger." He paused for a very long stretch of time, then continued, his gaze fixed on the table. "I killed a man once. I killed men in the War, yeah, but this was the first one I did just 'cause I was angry. The first one I looked in the eyes when I done it." He shook his head, his eyes long ago and far away.

"He was thinkin' ta force his attentions on Maggie, my wife. And when he wouldn't take 'no' for an answer, he said he'd show 'er." He laughed. "Well, I showed him. I showed 'im just what it means to a man ta see his wife in danger. Bout damn near ripped his head off his shoulders. I meant ta kill him, and that's just what I did."

When he looked up again, his eyes were ancient seers of a distant past. "Learned a lot about myself between then and now. And one of the things I learned is that I c'n take a lot more when it's comin' at me than when it's comin' at someone I care about. So all I can ask of ya is ta let me do some thinkin'. She ain't goin' nowhere, an' neither am I. Deal?"

Nods around the table.

He nodded right back. "Alright then. Guess it's about time we busted up this little shindig. Tomorrow's chores ain't gonna wait for us."

And that ended the meeting. Chairs scraped against the wooden floor as seats were pushed out and people rose to their feet, stretching out weary bodies. There was very little talk as our guests excused themselves and walked out into the cool darkness of the late spring night. As I waved to them, I searched the darkness for a glimpse of Corinne, but she was nowhere within my sight.

Ice came up behind me and laid a hand on my shoulder. "Go

ahead and hunt her down. She's probably by the water. I'll stay here and clean up."

"Are you sure? I could..."

"Nah. G'wan down. I think she needs someone to talk to, and you're better at that than I am."

Grinning, I squeezed the hand that still lay on my shoulder. "I dunno. You seem to be softening up just a little in your advancing years." Then winced as the hand became a vice on my flesh, fingers digging in just enough to give me a glimpse of the somewhat astounding physical strength I knew was there but didn't always see. "Uncle!" I cried, though she wasn't hurting me.

The grip relaxed, but didn't release, and the next thing I knew, I was being spun around, held firmly, and kissed so soundly that the room around me also began to spin.

And then I was alone as my lover retreated back within the depths of the cabin.

Ice soft?

Never in a million years.

Corinne was exactly where Ice had said she would be. Sitting on the dock, her back propped against one of the tall wooden supports, staring out over the night-dark water. It was still a little too early in the season for the frogs to be singing chorus, and the only sounds were the gentle lapping of waves against the wood of the dock and the gentle, but somehow mournful, wind as it blew through the pines and sent ropes hitting against aluminum boat masts.

What little moon there was highlighted the silver in her hair. She turned slightly as she heard me coming and gave me a wan little smile, suddenly looking far older than her stated age. My heart squeezed a little at that. It hurt to see her looking frail, this strong woman I so loved.

"Did Ice send you out to find me?"

Smiling, I walked out onto the dock and lowered myself to sit cross-legged next to her. "Nah. She just gave me a likely starting point. I came here on my own." I laid a hand on her arm. "Did the fresh air help?"

"Not as much as you might think."

"I'm sorry, Corinne."

"Nothing to be sorry for, Angel. I don't normally lose my temper like that, as you well know." She turned her head to look over the water again. "I was incarcerated for so long that I think

I forgot what it was like to fight for justice on the outside." Her voice was soft, and a touch sad. "In prison, meting out justice was a simple thing. Do unto others. And if that doing got you some time in solitary, well, that was only the accepted manner of things. Out here," she held out an arm, encompassing everything, "things aren't so simply undertaken. Meetings by committee. Democracy. Strategy sessions." She laughed, softly. "Sometimes I wonder whether I wasn't happier in the Bog."

She must have felt my reaction to that statement, because she turned to me and held my face in her hands. "I didn't mean that the way it sounded, Angel. I love you. I love Ice. And I love the life you're allowing me to share with the two of you." She smiled. "Don't be bothered by the crazed ramblings of an old woman. We're not known for making sense in the best of times."

Returning her gentle smile, I caressed the backs of her hands with my own. "I love you, Corinne. We both do. You've made such a difference in our lives and I don't know what either one of us would have done without you. So please don't put yourself down or call yourself old and crazy. To me, you'll always be one of the most wonderful women I've ever known. Bad temper and all."

Leaning in, she kissed me softly on the lips, then pulled away, smiling. "If Ice didn't already have your heart, Angel..."

Not letting her get away with it, I pulled her into a tight hug and kissed a still-smooth cheek. Then, releasing her, I stood up. "You gonna come back to the house?"

"In a bit. It's a nice night out. I think I'll watch the water and do some thinking."

"Alright. Goodnight, Corinne."

"Goodnight, sweet Angel. Sleep well."

"You, too."

On my way back to the cabin, I could hear the soft, soothing strains of music as it filtered through the speakers Ice had set up outside the house. Which was at definite odds with the sounds of flesh hitting canvas and a chain squealing out its anger over the abuse.

Rounding the corner, I took in the sight of Ice working off the day's frustrations on the heavy-bag that hung from beneath the roof. She had on a pair of gray shorts which clung to her body like a snake's second skin and a matching sweatshirt cut off at the midriff and shoulders, displaying her sculpted body wonderfully to my appreciative eyes.

Her movements were tight, precise, controlled, yet also had an almost balletic, wild and free air to them, somewhat akin to a big cat's stealthy stalking of a potential meal.

A quick double-kick, first low, then almost impossibly high, was immediately followed by a fist, and then an elbow to the middle of the canvas bag, rocking it wildly on its chain anchor.

A spinning kick, a flurry of punches too quick and too numerous to count, and a final thundering kick that almost blew the cabin off its foundation, and she came to absolute stillness, her body covered with a fine sheen of sweat, but her lungs heaving not at all.

Opening her eyes, she saw me and smiled, then reached down and grabbed a towel that was lying on the ground beyond my sight, wiping her face and neck with it. "Corinne alright?"

"Yeah," I replied, coming closer and feeling the charged energy still flowing through her. "She's still a little upset and, maybe, a little confused, but she's calmed down a lot from earlier. She's gonna be fine."

"Good to hear." Putting the towel back down, she lowered herself to the ground and leaned back against the house, closing her eyes again and tilting her head, allowing the gentle breeze to dry the sweat from her body.

I sat down next to her, close, so that our shoulders were just touching and enjoyed the quiet spring evening.

"Ice?"

"Mm?"

"Can I ask you a question?"

"Sure."

"Are you happy?"

Blue eyes opened and she turned her head toward me, surprise written clearly on her features. "What brought that on?"

"I don't know, really. I've been meaning to ask you for a while now, but things just keep coming up and it gets shuffled back behind other stuff. But I want to know. Are you?" I swallowed. "Happy, I mean?"

Turning away and once again resting her head against the foundation, she was silent for a long moment before she finally spoke. "For a very long time, Angel, I would have told you that I didn't even know what the meaning of that word was."

"Not even when you were young? With your parents?"

"When I was young, yes, I remember being happy. But those memories are faded; almost as if that happiness belonged to another person entirely and I was simply hearing their story. And then, after the killings and my incarceration, I didn't feel anything at all."

"And after prison? When you had a family again?"

"The Briacci's were very good to me. They treated me as a member of their own family; it's true. But by then, given everything that had happened before, any thoughts of happiness had already been pretty much burned out of me. Oh, I could still feel. Satisfaction, mostly. Pride in my work and my abilities. Anger. Rage."

"How about with your lovers?" I couldn't help smiling, though I know she couldn't see me. "You said you had a few."

She laughed softly. "Oh, I had more than a few, Angel. But I wasn't with them for happiness. Physical release, yes. Not happiness."

"Not even with Donita?"

"No. Though she lasted the longest of any of them. We were much too different, and the life I lived with her was based on a lie. She never knew, until the end, exactly what I did for a living. And when she found out, she was very hurt."

"But she still cared enough for you to want to defend you in court."

Ice nodded slowly, her eyes still closed. "Yes. And I cared enough for her not to let her."

Which meant that Ice cared for her a great deal indeed. My estimation of the beautiful lawyer, already impossibly high, went up another few notches.

"And after?" I asked, surprised at how small my voice sounded.

She smiled then, a grudging one that battled hard for its right to take its place on her lips. "I met you," she said simply. "And everything changed."

"How did it change?" I asked, honestly curious. We had never really spoken of this. I knew Ice's feelings, her love for me, ran very deep. But how they came to be, I had really no idea. At least, not one that could be confirmed. Or denied.

"It's hard to put into words," she replied after a moment. She still had her eyes closed, her face turned partially away, and so was even harder to read than normal. "It was as if, in looking at you, I was given a window through which to see something I didn't think I needed anymore. Goodness. Innocence. A kind of strength that comes from giving and not taking. I felt myself attracted to it even though, deep inside myself, I didn't want to be. Overcoming that part of myself, the one that wanted to keep things as they were, was one of the hardest things I've ever done." She sighed. "I still struggle with it. Every day. But I do know this."

Opening her eyes, she turned once again to face me, her eyes penetrating, intense, looking through the person I was and laying claim to the soul beneath. "Now that I've found these feelings, found you, I know that I never want to be without them again. I want to grow old with you, Angel. I want the feel of you in my arms, the taste of you on my lips, to be what I take with me when I die. And if that's what happiness means, Angel, then yes, I'm happy. I'm very, *very* happy."

And then I found myself wrapped in a hug that smelled of clean sweat and exotic spices, and let it carry me away in that one perfect moment into the place from which all good things come.

Chapter 13

Several weeks went by without much action on any front. The opening of tourist season for another year came and went with the usual fanfare and (mostly) goodwill. With so many more strangers coming into and leaving town, it was difficult to keep track of Millicent and her minions, but it appeared, for the moment at least, that our efficient bush telegraph was in fine working order.

One day, about mid-season or so, Ice came home for lunch, which was, in and of itself, unusual for her. Normally, she would skip lunch altogether, too wrapped up in helping Pop to grab more than a quick drink at the station. I harped on her about that a time or ten, but she always answered the same way, with a mock scowl and a shooing motion, and I finally accepted the fact that on this, I would never change her.

Not that I really minded. Of all the things we could be at loggerheads over, given our differences, lunch was a pretty insignificant thing in the grand scheme of it all.

Didn't stop me from shoving the massive sandwich I'd made for myself into her hands as she stepped through the door though, along with a kiss to seal the deal. She accepted both gracefully, though she tore the sandwich in half and presented it back to me with another kiss.

The kiss, of course, kept me from grumping.

It also kept me from thinking for a couple seconds, but that's neither here nor there.

"So," I began once I was again fully capable of speech, "to what do I owe the honor of this unexpected, but wonderful, visit?"

Before answering, she finished her meal, wiped her mouth

with the extra napkin I'd brought, and pegged the used tissue in the wastebasket near the door. "Pop's sister-in-law died."

"Oh, God, I'm sorry to hear that. Is he alright?"

"Yeah, he's doing ok. It was the one who got sick when those punks came around and beat the crap outta him. She got better, but her death wasn't exactly unexpected. At least, not to him." She turned fully to face me. "He's asked me to go with him to the funeral."

I grew somewhat alarmed. "Is something the matter?"

Sensing my fear, she put a warm hand on my arm. "No, nothing like that. It's just that he's been having some trouble with his arm since it's been broken, and he doesn't feel comfortable driving for six or eight hours straight."

I breathed out a sigh of relief. "I'm glad it wasn't something else."

"Nope. That's it."

"How long will you be gone?"

Ice shrugged. "Four days. Maybe a week, tops. If I decide to go."

I could feel my eyebrows raise. "*If* you decide to go? Why wouldn't you?"

"Once word gets out that Pop's gonna be out of the way for a while, I wouldn't put it past Millicent to do something stupid."

"Stupid*er* you mean, right?"

She chuckled. "Yeah. So I don't know if it's wise that I leave as well. I'm sure we can find someone else who won't mind driving."

I looked up at her. "Ice, Pop asked you to do this for a reason. He likes you and he trusts you. You know this. The town can take care of itself for a while. And besides," I couldn't help grinning, "I don't think I make a half-bad Ice stand-in." Then I flexed my muscles like some steroid-hyped bodybuilder. "Strong like a bull."

And looked up to find six feet of lust incarnate staring back at me, her eyes dark and hooded, her nostrils flaring just slightly.

Everything inside my skin simultaneously tightened and turned to water. You may know the feeling I'm talking about if you've ever had someone look at you like they're the desert and you're the rain. "Ice?"

She smiled, slow and dark. Her voice echoed her smile; deep, sexy, smoky. "If I didn't need to get back and tell Pop it's a go, I'd take you right here on the dining room table, Angel."

"Oh... Jesus." I tried to swallow, but my mouth had turned to dust. "D-do you think you could just tell him over the phone?"

"And spare us both the anticipation of waiting?" Her smile grew. "Oh, no. I don't think so, Angel."

"I ...don't need to remind you that we waited more than six months, do I?"

That damnable eyebrow again, poised and ready to fire. "At whose insistence?"

I looked down. "Mine," I whispered.

"Exactly." Stepping closer, she trailed one long finger just barely against my jaw. "Goodbye, Angel."

After a long moment, I broke free of my sudden paralysis. "Ice! Wait! You can't...!"

The closing of the screen door told me just how much she *could.*

It was going to be a long, *long* day.

That night I knelt up on the bed, my body pressed half against the headboard as I looked out the window and watched the full, heavy moon lay a brilliant stripe across the lake. In the distance, I could see the tiny, bobbing headlights of fishing boats as they trolled across the gently rippling water.

The wood of the headboard felt smooth and warm against the simple white slip I'd chosen to wear. There wasn't anything X-rated about it, nor even particularly daring, but when I'd seen it shopping one day, I knew it was something I wanted, even though I knew it probably wouldn't stay on very long, given the reason I'd would be wearing it in the first place.

Corinne had come in about an hour or so after Ice had left. Something must have been lingering in the air, because she took one look at me, grinned wickedly, disappeared into her bedroom, and came back out, an overnight bag clasped securely in one hand. "I can see there's a bit of a private party planned for this evening," she'd said. "I think I'll spend the night with Pop. Too bad we won't be having as much fun as you will."

And then she'd disappeared, leaving me alone once again with my thoughts. And my hormones.

I smiled a little as I heard the truck pull up and Ice let herself into the house. Closing my eyes for a moment, I pictured her movements through the cabin, stopping first at the dining-room table to deposit her keys and wallet, then crossing through the living room with sure, quiet strides and making a turn into the bathroom. I listened as the door closed softly behind her and the shower came on. Never one for lengthy showers, the water was off almost immediately and I pictured her slowly drying her dripping body and brushing her long, shining, wet hair.

Then there was a long silence, during which my body reacted to pictures my mind insisted sending.

To avoid driving myself completely crazy with building want, I opened my eyes again and concentrated on the spectacular view presented to me through the large window, getting lost in the gentle movement of the water and the way the moon sparkled against it.

So lost, in fact, that I didn't even hear her come up the stairs. Nor did I hear, or feel, her climb up on the bed.

But when her hot hands came gently down on my shoulders and her lips pressed against the sensitive skin of the back of my neck, I came into myself so quickly, I almost passed out in sheer shock.

My body reacted instantly to her touch, though, and a moan forced its way up from somewhere very deep inside me.

"You're very beautiful tonight, Angel," she said in the same deep, smoky tone she'd used earlier in the day. Her palms slid the delicate straps down off my shoulders slowly. "Soft. Innocent. Pure."

Each word was punctuated by a soft, lingering kiss to the flesh she'd bared, and then I felt the heated wetness of her tongue as she drew a path from one shoulder to the other, then back again.

I couldn't help shuddering, and my breathing quickened as my teeth bit down hard on my bottom lip to keep from crying out.

"A virgin, waiting to be taken."

Her hands ran down my arms, across my belly, then up my sides until they cupped my breasts. My body arched up forcefully into her palms, my nipples becoming so tight that they were almost painful.

She caressed me briefly as her tongue worked magic on the muscles of my neck. Then her long fingers hooked themselves into the bodice of my slip and pulled the yielding fabric down and away, exposing me to the mid-summer's night as it peeked in through the window.

Her hands came up quickly again, the very tips of her fingers drawing teasing circles around my nipples, before lifting my breasts as if in homage, allowing the light of the moon to bathe them in its brilliance.

"Do you know how much I love to make love to you, my sweet Angel?"

Strong thumbs brushed against my nipples, bringing them even further erect.

"Do you know how much I love to feel your body react to my touch?"

Leaving my breasts for the moment, she gently urged the fabric of my slip downwards, kissing and running her tongue along my back in intricate, fanciful designs.

"To feel you move against me?" she breathed into the skin of my back.

It was all I could do not to try and squeeze my thighs together in an attempt to quench, if even minutely, the flame she was rousing within me.

That deep chuckle came again as my body betrayed my thoughts. Her hands left the silk of my slip and slid along the tops of my thighs, burning with an intense heat that was so much a part of her. Her fingers skimmed the insides of my thighs then, barely touching flesh which humped up, as if trying its best to draw her in.

"To taste you on my lips?"

Up and down, up and down, until my body was swaying to her caress as a serpent to its handler and my legs spread of their own accord, as she no doubt intended.

"To hear your cry my name out into the night?"

Reaching between my legs, she cupped me and pulled me backward against her hard, heated body, her soft, full breasts molding themselves to the plane of my back as our bodies melded together, back to front. Her muscled thighs rested beneath my own, her calves brushing against mine as she settled us together.

"Rock yourself against me, Angel."

Unable to disobey even if I'd wanted to, I worked my hips back and forth against the slightly callused skin of her palm, my movements becoming smoother as her hand became bathed in the slick moisture my body was so eagerly providing.

I could feel her thighs as they flexed and released beneath me, bringing her own body into motion and aiding me in my gentle thrusts against her hand. And when her fingers, long and sure, slipped inside of me, my head lolled back against one broad shoulder as I cried out my pleasure into the night.

"Yes, Angel," she purred, lips nipping at my ear. "Moan for me. Let me hear you."

Her fingers danced inside me, thrusting deep, caressing gently, changing tempo, changing rhythm, pulling me higher, and still higher as I urged her on with incoherent, breathless entreaties not to stop, never to stop, please *God* never *ever* stop.

"That's it. Talk to me, sweet Angel. Sing to me."

Then her free hand came up to tease and touch my swaying

breasts, pulling my nipples in time to her throbbing, seductive rhythm and I felt myself explode in a great screaming cry which echoed in my ears as the oncoming rush caught me from behind and swept me up with it. To go tumbling deep, ever deeper until I was lost and floating in an abyss filled not with darkness, but with points of sparkling brilliance, all calling me safely home and into the warm and loving nest of her arms.

And it could have stopped there, and I would have been satisfied.

But it didn't.

Still buried deep within me, she gently pulled us both up until I was on all fours and she was still pressed against me from behind. Her lower body moved away for a moment, then pressed back into my flesh, hot and wet, beginning a slow grind against my hip as her breasts trailed along my back.

Her breath came in low grunts with each forward thrust and her hair came tumbling down, long and wet, to tickle against my cheeks and ears.

She began to pick up the tempo, growling deep in her chest, her body driving itself against mine in strong, forceful thrusts, causing me to grab tight to the bedcovers in order to hold my ground beneath her coiled, primal strength.

Great, fat beads of sweat dripped down on me. Then her dormant fingers began to move within me once again, filling me, stretching me wide and open for her. My violently trembling arms gave out, landing me on my elbows. My head dropped between them as I used all the strength I had to press back against her sharp forward motion.

Her body moved against me, relentless, unforgiving, trapping me beneath the hard, strong weight of her, leaving only room enough for the frantic rocking of my hips as I felt myself once again near the peak of my arousal.

She paused just a moment, just a heartbeat, her lips pressed close to my ear. "I do so love you, Angel," was said on a faint breath of air.

And then she surged against me, a wild, untamed thing, howling as her fingers stiffened and spasmed within me, setting off my own intense release. Brilliant lights flashed and circled, then were dimmed as her body slumped down fully on my own, pressing me down into the mattress. Her chest heaved in great, heaving gasps and her fingers loosened and drew free from my body.

When she made to move off me, I went with her, gently guiding her to her back, my legs tucked in between her widely splayed thighs. I could feel her wet heat spread itself against my skin, and when her hips bucked once in unconscious reaction, I knew we weren't anywhere near done.

Reaching up, I kissed her deeply with all the tenderness that was within me to give. When she tried to take control once again, I refused, pulling away and giving her lips light nips until she got the picture and gave me her willing surrender, her eyes still dark and dangerous even within her seeming submission.

I kissed her again, exploring every heated inch of her mouth before quickly moving downward, both of our bodies giving me signals I couldn't help but obey. My tongue darted out to taste the salted sweetness of her muscled flesh. Her breasts were greedy for my touch and I paid each one homage in turn until I was urged, by my own body's wants, ever downward, over rippled muscle, strong, arching bone and soft, fragrant flesh until I reached my destination and took her into my mouth and tasted the essence of her as it exploded upon my rapturous tongue.

It didn't take long. She was much too ready, and so was I. Overcome with the need to fill her as she had filled me, I went within, feeling her grip my fingers in welcome. One thrust, two, three as my mouth continued to attend from above, and she stiffened beneath me, her long fingers threading themselves into my hair, anchoring me to her as she rode out the waves of her pleasure.

And when she relaxed and fell limp against the bed, I kissed her gently, then rested my head against her hip, still thrusting tenderly inside her welcoming warmth.

Her breathing evened out and became steady. Her fingers loosened their tight hold in my hair as a much-needed sleep caught up to her and took her over with it. Pressing a final kiss into her warm skin, laid my head back down on her belly, and when sleep came for me as well, I went willingly, a smile on my face and my fingers still clasped in a warm, velvet glove.

It was four days, seven hours, six minutes and thirty-two, make that thirty-three, seconds later. A bit obsessed with Father Time, you ask? Well, wouldn't *you* be?

True to her word, Ice called me every day, usually in the evening right before I went to bed. The funeral had gone, I guess, as well as funerals are supposed to go, which means not very well at all, but at least everyone got through it pretty much unscathed, except for the body, who I'm sure didn't have much of an opinion one way or the other on the subject.

The good news was that Pop was holding up well. The bad

news was that the reading of the will would probably be delayed at least a day, making it that much longer before Ice could return home. She hadn't had a definite answer in our last call because the probate lawyer was being obtuse, but she told me not to expect her until the end of the week, at least.

Which was still two days away.

For her part, Corinne did her best to be an engaging companion, even going so far as to apply for, as she called it, "assistant bed-warmer duty." I, of course, quashed that particular suggestion post haste, but in all other ways, she was wonderful, keeping me busy and helping keep my loneliness for Ice at least partially at bay.

And so there I was, sitting in the living room doing my best impersonation of a woman actually *reading* the paper that's sitting open in her lap, and not caring one whit about the clock whose hands had suddenly developed an inexplicable tendency to move backwards, when they moved at all.

Realizing my Rich Little days were far behind me, I gave up on the fruitless effort and instead pondered on the age old wisdom that said that closely examined cooking receptacles never simmered, and decided to tempt fate by doing the one thing, much as lighting a cigarette in a restaurant magically summons a waitress, that would almost guarantee a phone call, if nothing else.

"I'm gonna take a bath," I announced to a smirking Corinne as I laid the unread paper aside and came to my feet, stretching.

And not just an ordinary bath. Oh no. The god in charge of *telephonus interruptus* wasn't about to be enticed by a simple "just a quick dip to get cleaned off" sorta bath.

If one wanted to guarantee one his special attention, one had to make the effort to prepare a special sort of bath. With candles. And bath salts. And aromatic soaps that smoothed as they softened.

And, of course, bubbles.

Lots of bubbles.

That way, when you found yourself standing naked and dripping on the freshly waxed wood floor, trying to convince the nice man on the phone that you really, honestly and truly, had no need for a nose hair clipper with fifteen variable speeds and racing stripes, that God could get his chuckles at your expense as your water slowly cooled and your champagne bath suddenly became a flat glass of grape juice.

Does it sound like I've done a bit of research on the subject?

Well, after five years of enforced bath deprivation, let's just say I'd become somewhat of a connoisseur on the subject and leave it at that.

So off I went, accouterments in hand, to set the stage in the hopes that Ice would be overcome with the sudden and overwhelming need to hear my voice that very instant.

My bath drawn, I slipped into the steamy, fragrant waters and eased down until just my chin and the tops of my knees shone wet above the water.

Ahhh. Bliss.

I felt my eyes slip closed, but resisted the urge to do something one might do in a sultry bath when one is missing one's lover who is far away, figuring there was no easy answer to "So, Angel, what have you done with yourself today?" if I gave into the temptation.

Besides, if my libation was accepted, Ice would probably call just before I got to the really good part and I'd be left even more frustrated than before.

So instead I just let the hot water work its customary magic on my stiff muscles and let my mind wander where it would. The bathroom was well insulated, but I didn't fear missing a phone call because of it. Corinne would knock when it came.

Minutes passed, measured by the slow drip of the faucet.

Bubbles popped and the water grew tepid and I finally faced the fact that my offering hadn't been quite good enough.

Refusing to give in to my disappointment, I stepped out of the tub and toweled off, then pulled on the clean clothes I'd brought in with me. After a last, critical look at myself in the mirror above the sink, I turned away and opened the door, immediately assailed by the cool air of the cabin as it brushed against the heat-flushed skin of my body.

Stepping out from the tiny alcove that hid the guest bedroom and bathroom, I took one stride into the cabin proper, and froze, my eyes darting around as my heart skipped several beats in rapid succession, then made up for the loss by working triple-time.

A group of men, six at my counting, filled the living room with their dark-suited presence. They all looked to be of a type, big, broad, clean shaven, wearing regulation haircuts, plain ties, and shiny shoes.

My first thought was the FBI. But when my eyes landed upon Corinne's statue-like form, that thought immediately flew out the window. Unless I was terribly wrong about things, FBI agents didn't normally hold the business ends of semi-automatic pistols to the temples of unarmed elderly women.

The rest seemed unarmed, but I spotted the telltale bulge

beneath the suit jacket of the one nearest to me and knew that that could change in an instant. My empty hands raised in an unconscious, yet familiar, gesture as my mind desperately attempted to free itself from the fog it was trapped in.

"What...what's going on?" I hear myself ask as if from far away.

"Where's Morgan?" the man standing closest to me asked, his voice almost warm.

"Who are you?"

He smiled. It wasn't particularly cold or cruel, but it wasn't exactly welcoming either. "Answer my question, please. Where is Morgan Steele?"

"She's..."

Whatever lie I might have thought up faded quickly from my brain when I heard Corinne gasp as the man holding her tightened his arm around her throat and thrust his gun harder against her temple. An incentive, I suppose, to get me to spill my guts.

I looked back at the speaker. "Please. She's just an old woman. Please tell him to put the gun away. I'll tell you anything you want to know if you just do that."

After a moment, he nodded and turned toward the man holding Corinne hostage. "Put the gun away, Frank."

"But..."

"Do it."

With a fair amount of grumbling, Frank did as he was told, slipping his gun back into the holster beneath his shoulder.

The man turned back to me, smiling once again. "Tell me where Morgan is." His face hardened. "Now."

Trying desperately to think up a convincing lie, my peripheral vision was caught by the sight of Corinne slowly reaching toward the stand where we kept the fireplace tools. My heart sunk as I saw her hand wrap itself around the handle of the iron poker, jerk it free from the stand, and lay it hard against her onetime captor's face.

Blood spurted from the cut she'd made, and Frank went down screaming, his hand clamped reflexively over the gaping wound.

Bearing her teeth in a wild grin, she held the poker up like a sword, daring the rest to come at her with one beckoning hand.

Oh, Corinne. No.

Noticing that my questioner's attention was diverted, I closed my hand into a tight fist and launched it at his belly.

It was like hitting a brick wall. Pain lanced up my arm, but I couldn't afford to pay it any mind as he turned back to me, all traces of mildness gone from his face.

Committed to the fight, I kicked his arm away before he could reach for his gun, then went low and managed to sweep his legs out from under him.

Bet ya never expected that! I mentally taunted, gathering myself on the balls of my feet and waiting for his next move, adrenaline surging its way through my body.

Two went for Corinne and two went for me. Corinne more than held her own, managing to get in several devastating blows with the business end of the poker, spilling blood and dropping bodies where they stood. Her laugh sounded almost insane to my thundering ears, but I didn't have much time to think on that as I was soon occupied with bodies of my own, coming at me with fists and feet.

I used my "low center of gravity," as Ice had called it once, to my advantage, ducking underneath most of the blows launched my way. Such was the state of my mind that I didn't even really feel the few which landed as I tried to fight my way back toward Corinne, who was perilously close to losing her weapon.

A strong blow to my head temporarily stunned me, and as I shook it off, still trying my best to defend myself, I saw Frank rise up from the floor, his face the deep, dusky red of anger. His huge, trunk-like arm lifted—I could see the seams of his jacket stretch almost to breaking—and with one blow, he disarmed Corinne, then followed through to crack his fist hard against her cheek.

She went down as if pole-axed, unconscious before she hit the ground, her glasses breaking and flying from her face as blood oozed out from her ear.

Without a hitch in his movements, Frank reached again for his gun and brought it out, aiming for Corinne's unprotected head.

"*No*!" I screamed, pulling myself out from beneath the pile of men who had landed on top of me, punching and kicking for all they were worth.

Two steps, and I launched myself across the room, landing in a protective sprawl above Corinne's limp body, placing myself between her and the gun. "*No*!" I screamed again as I heard a round chamber in the weapon.

Things seemed to slow down then, as they often will when you're forced with a danger beyond your wildest nightmares. The center of my vision focused on the gun pointing directly at me. It seemed huge, staring at me with a dead, malevolent eye.

I saw his finger tighten on the trigger and I sent out a last, desperate prayer to Ice, asking her to remember the love I had for her and to keep it close after I was gone. *Dream of me,* I whispered in my mind, then closed my eyes for what was to come. *I love you, Morgan.*

The sharp report nearly deafened me, and I waited for the pain that was sure to follow.

So, this is what death is like, I mused. *It's not so bad. Didn't even hurt.*

But then my ears cleared, and I realized that unless a dead person could hear, I was still very much in the land of the living.

Because I could suddenly hear things. Roaring things. Tearing things. Screaming things.

I opened my eyes to an abattoir; the bloody killing field of a tiger let loose from its cage and preying upon the villagers who had caused it so much torment.

The tiger bore a woman's face, and her name was Ice.

Her raven hair flying out from her brow, her face frozen in a spasm of rage, she was all feet and fists and unadulterated fury. Men went down like tenpins, screaming and clutching parts of their bodies which were suddenly broken, or gouged, or just not there anymore.

Our eyes met briefly before she turned away, grabbing one of the still-standing men around the neck and twisting. The sharp snap which followed sounded even over the screams of beaten and bleeding men, and I felt my stomach lurch.

I had just seen Ice kill for the first time.

Her face had an almost sexual joy in it as she let the dead man drop to the floor, his body slumping against her legs before she kicked it away.

And I think that first kill would not have been the last, had the fight lasted even one second longer.

But it didn't.

I felt an arm press tight around my own neck, and the cool steel of a cocked and ready gun pressed itself against my head.

Looking up, I saw a second gun, this one in Ice's sure hands, pointed at my captor's own head.

"Let her go, Carmine. It's me you want."

"Put the gun down and I will, Morgan."

Ice smiled. "Oh no. I don't think so." A booted foot lashed out, and the man who'd been trying to sneak up on her from behind flew half the length of the room before coming to land, stunned, against the sturdy dining room table. "Let her go."

"I can't do that. I don't want to hurt her, Morgan, but I will if I have to. You know that. So just put down the gun and I'll do as you ask."

A standoff ensued. I made sure not to move a muscle, even to blink. My heart pounded hard in my ears. I tried to catch her eyes, but the only thing she was seeing was the man with his gun to my head.

"Drop the gun, Morgan. I know you're thinking about shooting me, but can you really guarantee I won't put a bullet into her head when you do? Think about it." His voice was very calm, very reasonable.

When I saw her begin to waver, I couldn't help but speak up. "Don't do it, Ice. He'll kill me anyway. You know he will."

"I won't, Morgan. You have my word on it. And you know my word's always been good."

Her eyes latched onto mine. Her face softened.

My heart sunk further. "Ice, please. Don't do this."

Her arm slowly lowered.

"No! He'll kill us both! Don't do this! Please!"

Her body followed, laying the gun on the floor at her feet.

"Good," came the satisfied voice of Carmine. "Now push it away. Slowly."

"Ice, no!"

Her eyes still locked into mine, she pushed the gun away, then slowly rose back to her feet.

In my peripheral vision, I saw one of the other men step quickly up behind her, and with one strong blow with the butt of his gun to the back of her neck, he dropped her, unconscious, to the floor.

His hold loosened at the same time I tore myself out of his grip and crawled over to her, grabbing her lolling head between my hands. "Ice? Ice? Wake up! Damn you, wake up!"

That was all I could get out before I was grabbed again and dragged away. I screamed and twisted in a fit of insane grief and rage, but was powerless against the greater strength holding me steadily.

"Get her out of here," Carmine ordered.

"Are you nuts?" one of his cronies replied. "The bitch killed Tony! Let's fuckin' do her now and get it over with!"

"No! It was his own damn fault for getting in her way. Dump him in the trunk and get her in the car. Move!"

"*No! Ice!*"

As I struggled, I saw two men come painfully to their feet, then bend down and grab my lover's ankles and start to drag her unresisting body the length of the room and through the shattered remains of the door she had exploded when she ran into the room. Her blood-covered hands left grisly trails along the polished floor as she was dragged along.

"*No!*"

When she was gone from my sight, Carmine put me down and turned me to face him, still holding tight to my shoulders. His face was filled, strangely enough, with sorrow and compassion. "Stay here and look after your friend. You won't be harmed if you do what I say."

Gritting my teeth, I slapped his arms away and lifted a savage knee into the space between his slightly spread legs.

With a lightning quick move, he evaded the worst of my attack, then twisted me again, pulling my arm up hard behind my back and forcing me onto my toes to relieve some of the intense pain in my shoulder. "Stay here," he repeated, his lips close to my ear. "I gave Morgan my word, but if you try to intervene, I *will* kill you."

"Do you think I care?" I snarled back, jerking my head away from his mouth. "Do you think I care what happens to me after you murder her?"

"Maybe not, but I do think you care about what happens to your friend over there. She looks pretty bad off. Do you think you could just leave her there to die?"

"Try me."

And suddenly I came to know exactly how Ice felt when her tone softened to the exact pitch that was now coming out of my own mouth. Peaceful, somehow. All the rage has washed out of me, leaving only a firm purpose behind.

I also realized, in that one moment in time, that I was fully capable of deliberately taking a human life, and could, in fact, relish it.

"I'd rather not," he replied. "You pack a pretty mean punch and I don't doubt that you'd kill me if you could. But you know I'm not gonna let that happen. So please, do us both a favor and stay here. Morgan is beyond your help. Accept that. And do something for the person you *can* help."

"Alright," I said finally in that same cool, remote tone I'd used earlier. "Let me go so I can help her."

"Don't try anything funny."

"I wouldn't dream of it, Carmine."

He gave me a healthy push and before I could stop myself, I collided with Corinne's still unconscious body and sprawled across her as I fell to the floor. When I pulled myself up again, I found myself looking down the barrel of his gun. "Be smart. And for what it's worth, I'm sorry."

Corinne moaned as I watched him slowly back toward the door. When he was gone, I looked down into a pair of dazed brown eyes. "Angel?" she whispered.

"Hang on, Corinne. I'll be right back. Just hang on for me."

Then I was up and running, almost tripping over the lengths of splintered wood that were all that was left of the door. Running out into the courtyard, I was temporarily blinded as the car started up and the headlights caught me square in the face. Throwing an arm up to shield my eyes, I ran in the direction of the car, wincing as huge clots of dirt pelted me as they flew from beneath the large sedan's rapidly spinning tires.

Still charging, I managed to grab one of the door handles, yanking the door open just as the car pulled away. I was jerked off my feet, my arm a shard of blistering agony, as I trailed along beside the car for a few feet before I was finally forced to let go.

Jumping back up yet again, I tore after the retreating sedan, not feeling the rocks and pinecones as they imbedded themselves in the tender soles of my bare feet and tore them to bloody shreds.

All too soon, the car disappeared from my sight, the briefly flashing taillights the last thing I saw as it made a sharp left turn and left the road for the forest beyond. A great cramp seared into my side and I was forced to come to an abrupt halt or risk fainting.

My breath came out in sobbing pants as my legs gave out and I fell to the ground, pounding the dirt with my fists and screaming out Ice's name.

"Who's there?" came a high, tremulous, panic-laden voice as I drew in yet another gasping breath with which to scream out my grief.

"*Ice!*"

"Tyler? Tyler, is that you?"

"Ice! Come back! Don't leave me!"

The voice came closer. "Tyler, it's me, Ruby. What's wrong? Are you hurt? Do you need me to call the police?"

That word again. That damnable, hateful, spiteful word. A huge part of me screamed inside. "Yes! Call the police! Now! They've taken Ice!"

But a smaller part, a more rational part, shied away from the idea they way a skittish colt rears away from an unexpected movement. "No!" I finally managed to yell through a throat raw with screaming. "No police!"

Pulling myself up to my feet, I looked through tear-swollen eyes at the rapidly advancing figure of Ruby. "Call an ambulance!"

She stopped, head tilted to one side. "Are you hurt, Tyler?"

"Just call an ambulance, Ruby, please. Hurry!"

"But..."

"Hurry!"

With small satisfaction, I watched as she looked at me a moment more, then abruptly turned and started quickly walking back up the small rise to her house.

My pain was beginning to catch up with me; my feet ached like rotting teeth and my shoulder, still sent up blazing jolts of electric agony with each breath I took.

With one last, long look in the direction I'd last seen the car, I too turned for home where Corinne lay injured and waiting.

Limping into the house, I spied her laying exactly where I'd left her, sprawled in an untidy heap on the living-room floor, a small pool of blood shining wetly in the dim lighting of the room. She was frighteningly pale and for a moment I was sure that her chest had stopped moving.

Running to her, I went to my knees, again cradling her head in my hands. "Corinne? Corinne, can you hear me?"

After a long moment, her eyes fluttered open, still dazed. "Angel?"

I couldn't help sagging with relief. "Oh, thank God. I thought I'd lost you, too." Tears were very close to the surface then, but I couldn't afford to let them fall. If I gave in to my nearly overwhelming grief, everything would be lost.

And I couldn't let that happen.

Still staring at me, her eyes narrowed. "Too? Who did you lose, Angel? What happened? Where are all those men?"

"They're gone. They got what they came for and left."

"What did they come for?"

Teeth clenched, I swallowed hard. My lips refused to move; refused to help utter the word locked tight inside my throat.

"Angel?"

"Just...just keep still, Corinne. Ruby's calling an ambulance. It should be here soon."

"Answer me, Angel."

I looked down at her, knowing she would see the answer in my eyes.

Her own widened. Her face became slack. "Oh, Angel," she breathed. "Oh, no."

I tore my gaze away from the utter grief in her eyes, knowing that it was only mirroring my own. "Pop."

"What?"

"I've gotta call Pop. He'll know what to do. I'll just call him." I could feel my hold on sanity begin to slip as I rose from Corinne's side as if in a dream, almost watching outside myself as I walked to the phone which was perched on a stand in the library. "That's it. Pop will help. He has to. He's the only one who can. Oh...*God.*"

With an almost clinical detachment, I watched as my fingers stabbed at the buttons by rote, then pulled the phone up to my ear. Two rings, then three, then four, and I almost slammed the phone back down in frustration, before Pop's sleep-blurred voice came over the line. "Yeah?"

"Pop, it's Tyler. Please, come quick. I need your help."

"Tyler? What is it? What's wrong? Is Corinne sick? Did Morgan get home alright? I know she left the truck here, it was runnin' kinda...."

"Just come. Please. And Pop?"

His voice was wary now. "Yeah?"

"Bring your gun."

Then I closed the phone on whatever answer he might have given, feeling my arms wrap around myself as my eyes darted around the library. The book Ice had been reading on our last day together sat neatly on one of the tables, the engraved silver bookmark I'd gotten her for Christmas shining from between the pages. Reaching out a trembling finger, I traced over her initials, remembering the look of quiet happiness that had come over her face when she'd opened her gift.

No, Ice. Please. Please.

"Angel?"

Corinne's soft voice penetrated the thick fog in my brain, and I turned, realizing that I'd almost totally forgotten about her. "Corinne... I..."

She smiled slightly. "It's alright, Angel. It's alright."

"No, Corinne. It most definitely is not alright. It'll never be alright again." My hands came up to my head and, like great wrenching claws, latched onto my hair, pulling and tearing. "*Noooooooo!*"

"Angel!" Corinne's voice was cutting, sharp, even given her head injury. "That's enough. You're a strong woman. We both know that. So start acting like one. I need that from you. And so does Ice."

Whirling, I stared down at her, my hands still in my hair. "Ice is *dead*!"

"You don't know that for sure, Angel. If you did, you wouldn't be calling Pop in to help. Some small part of you hasn't given up hope yet. Use that to snap yourself out of this. You need to, or she really *will* be gone."

Inside, I could feel myself reacting to her words. That damnable flicker of useless hope straightened and grew stronger, much as the rest of me wanted to snuff it out for good. It was stupid and impossibly naïve for me to even think to believe that Ice had a chance in hell of getting out of the trap she was forced into. The odds were higher than high that she was dead already, laying somewhere, cold and lonely, waiting for the beasts of the forest to make a feast of her lifeless body.

And yet...

The sounds of tires skidding to a halt outside the cabin made my decision for me, and after a quick, thankful glance toward Corinne, I ran back out the door in time to see Pop clamber out of his truck, rifle in hand, his hair sleep-tousled and his clothing hastily donned.

"Got here as fast as I could, Tyler. Now what the hell is goin' on, eh?"

"They've got Ice, Pop. They've got her and we need to get her back."

"Who? Who's got her?"

"Does it matter? Come on! We need to go after them!" I started for the passenger's side of the truck, only to be halted by a firm hand to my elbow.

"Hold on just a second there, Tyler. Might not matter to you, but it matters a whole lot to me. Wasn't born yesterday, and I ain't near ta bein' naïve enough ta think that those idiots Millicent's payin' ta do her dirty work could get the drop on Morgan even if she was tied up and blindfolded. And since you told me ta bring my gun, I'm guessin' that these guys got balls enough ta kill if they've a mind to. So if I'm gonna have my ass blown clear off, I'd kinda like ta know who's doin' the shootin', eh?"

Looking into his shining eyes, I knew I was trapped between a rock and a very, very hard place. The seconds slipped by, taking Ice ever farther from me and taking my hope with her. I honestly didn't know what to do.

Pop's eyes softened. "Tyler, you known me a long time, since you were a little kid. Not as well as ya do now, course, but well enough, I hope, ta know that anything ya tell me in confidence ain't gonna go no further than my brain. Whatever it is ya gotta say, it won't go nowhere else."

Being trapped with nowhere else to turn makes for strange bedfellows, as sure someone has said before me. It wasn't that I didn't trust Pop. To the contrary, I trusted him with my life.

The question was, could I trust him with Ice's life as well?

I didn't really have a choice. Lies were too hard to think up and he deserved to know the truth.

"Who are they, Tyler?"

I hesitated a second more, then threw all caution to the wind. "The Mafia."

His eyes widened. "Like in the *Godfather*? That Mafia?"

I nodded.

"What do they gotta do with the price of tea in Tibet?"

"Do I have your word?"

"You got it, Tyler. Cross my heart."

"Ice is...was...a Mafia assassin."

"Father God and Sonny Je-sus," he whispered. "I knew she wasn't no small-town mechanic."

"No. She's not. Six years ago, she was convicted of murdering a witness, which she didn't do, and put in jail." I took in a deep breath, then let it out slowly. *Make or break time, Angel. If he bales, take his gun, hop in his truck, and drive.* "That's where I met her."

His eyes widened still further. I would have laughed at the picture he presented, if I had it in me. "Prison? Were you a guard or somethin'?"

"No. I was a prisoner, too."

"You?! Naw. Yer havin' me on, Tyler."

"No, I'm not. Listen. Can we continue this on the road? We need to get going!!"

The sirens of the approaching ambulance could be heard drawing nearer, and I relaxed slightly, knowing Corinne would soon be in good hands. Ruby appeared as if from the night itself, her face a huge question mark. "It's Corinne. She's hurt. Can you go to the hospital with her and make sure she's alright for me? There's something Pop and I have to do."

She looked about to argue, but something in my face must have changed her mind, because instead of words, she gave me a brisk nod and headed into the house.

I turned back to Pop. "Please?"

Shaking himself as if rousing from a dream, he blinked, then released my arm. "Right. Let's go."

Nodding, I ran to the other side of the truck and jumped in. Pop started it up with one hand, while grabbing his CB mike with the other and shouting some terse directions in it before racking it again. "Got us some help," he bit off before gunning the accelerator and sending us off in a cloud of dust. "Hang on, Tyler. We got some assholes ta find."

We headed off into the woods, with me pointing the way (or what little of it I knew) as Pop concentrated on driving. The trail was, at first, pretty easy to follow. The sedan had gone fishtailing into the forest for several hundred yards before getting back out onto the road again, heading south.

We chased the truck's headlights down that road, both with our eyes glued to our respective sides of the road to see if the car we were tracking had made any other sudden detours.

My eyes caught a sudden flash, and when I looked up, I could see the fast approach of at least two trucks pulling up behind us. "Pop?"

He glanced in the rearview mirror briefly before returning his attention to the road. "The Drew boys. They're about the best trackers in these parts. Ain't shy 'bout getting into it, either, if it comes ta that."

We continued for another few miles in silence until the road intersected with another, running east and west. "Which way?" I asked.

"Did they say where they was goin' with her?"

"No. They didn't say much of anything at all, except that they wouldn't kill her in the house." I wiped angrily at the tears which started to fall again, blurring my vision. "Big of 'em, huh?"

"Think they'd try to get back to the States with her?"

I shook my head. "I don't know. Are there any roads that cross the border legally but aren't patrolled?"

"Not around here, there ain't. And tryin' ta cross through the woods in a car is plain suicide. Tear the wheels right off before ya got a mile in. Some rough country around these parts."

I could feel myself slump down into the seat. "So what do we do?"

Pulling the truck to a stop still some distance from the intersection, Pop hopped out and walked up slowly to where the roads crossed. As I pulled myself from the cab, I heard the other two trucks pull to stops behind us, doors open, and the heavy tread of the two brothers as they hopped from their own cabs. Together, we joined Pop, who was looking down at the blacktop. "How many in the car?"

I thought for a moment. "Six. And one in the trunk."

He looked up at me. "Morgan?"

I shook my head. "No. She...um...she killed one of them. They put his body in the trunk. She's in the car with them. I think."

Pop grinned, as did the Drews. "Damn good for her." He looked down at the road again, which was bleached a pale, bone white by the brilliant beams of three trucks' headlights. "Big car, then. Probably goin' pretty fast, at that."

John Drew walked across the intersection, then squatted down on his haunches, examining something in the southeast corner. I squinted hard, but couldn't make out what had caught his interest. He stood up, dusting his hands on his trousers and looking over at us. "Looks like they turned east," he pronounced.

Pop nodded. "Makes sense if they're goin' for the border."

"How can you be so sure?" I asked.

"There's a deep track where a car took this turn pretty sharply. No skid marks, but the gravel's sprayed out in a pretty representative pattern."

I looked at him. "Are you a police officer or something?"

Behind me, Tom snorted, which helped put me more at ease. A little, anyway.

John grinned. "Nope. Used to be a bounty hunter, though."

Wide-eyed, I looked over at Pop, knowing I was giving much too much away, but unable to do anything else. Pop grinned. "Sometimes he liked the bad guys better'n the good guys. Damn near got him in trouble more'n once." He gave me a covert wink and I finally relaxed fully, accepting his judgement on the matter.

I turned back to John. "What if it wasn't them, though? What if it was some other car? Or truck?"

"Oh, it was a car, alright. A truck couldn't have made the turn that fast."

"Yeah, but I'm sure there's been more than one car that's made that turn since..."

Pop put a hand on my arm. "So far, it's the best lead we've got, Tyler," he said, softly.

I sighed. "I know. It's just...I don't want to give up any others that might be out there just to go after this one alone. The longer we go without finding them..."

Tom stepped up to us. "How about this? You and Pop go down the most likely trail. There are about a million unpaved fire and logging roads as you head east, and it'll take awhile to search them if it looks like the car might have turned down one of them. I'll continue on south and John can go west for about twenty miles. If neither of us sees anything likely, we'll turn around and come out to meet you and help search along this road. If we *do* come across anything, we'll give a shout. Sound good?"

I smiled at him gratefully, surprised I had it within me to smile at all. "Yeah. That sounds great. Thanks."

Grinning, he clapped me briefly on the shoulder. "Let's go then."

Chapter 14

The sun had been up for several hours as we came at last back onto the smooth blacktop of the eastbound road we'd been exploring all night. My head pounded abysmally from the abuse it had suffered while we bounced down one rutted, unpaved logging road after another, hunting for clues that just weren't there no matter how hard I tried to will them into existence.

As night faded into day, my hopes faded right along with the setting of the moon. Every blind alley, every negated lead pushed me further and further into a well of despair I began to think I had no hope of ever leaving.

My mind insisted on showing me images of Ice's lifeless body laying still and alone, lost forever in the endless blind maze of forest which surrounded us.

Still worse were the pictures of Ice, bleeding but conscious, dying by slow inches and unable to move as the beasts of the night made their way closer to her, attracted by the scent of her spilling blood like sharks to an injured whale.

I savagely told my mind to shut up, to shut off, but the more tired I became, the more hours we spent in fruitless searching, the more it insisted on playing these images in a continuous loop, each more graphic and heartrending than the last, until it was all I could do not to scream and pound the dash until my fists were bloody.

The Drews had joined us halfway through the search, having come up empty in their own explorations. Having two more sets of eyes made the search go more quickly, but in the end, it made absolutely no difference at all.

Coming back to the present, I rubbed my gritty eyes as I mentally prepared myself for yet another trip down yet another road with yet another series of holes large enough to hide entire houses within. It was then that I noticed that we were heading to the west, away from the rising sun and the next road down the line. My heart sped up. "Where are we going?"

Pop didn't look at me. His unblinking eyes stayed fixed on the road. He was beyond pale, beyond tired, beyond old. "Back home for a bit, Tyler. We need a break."

"No!" I yelled, grabbing the steering wheel and almost turning us into the drainage ditch which ran parallel to the road on both sides. "No! We can't give up!"

He gently pulled my hand off the wheel and straightened the truck back out again. "We ain't givin' up, Tyler. Johnny an' Tommy'll keep searchin' till they can't go no more. I need ta get to a phone and call in some more help. There's just too much land out here fer only three groups ta search. And you need some sleep. I ain't gotta look at ya ta see you're about one step from goin' down deep and never comin' out."

"You don't understand!"

Coming to a halt by the side of the street, he finally took his eyes off the road to look directly at me. His expression was one of infinite sadness. "I understand better'n you think, Tyler. Lost my own daughter out here when she was seven. Her and a friend took off when they was supposed ta be fishin', and got lost. We found em two days later. The friend survived. My daughter didn't." He looked back toward the road again, his eyes shiny and dark, hands gripped tight to the wheel. "Musta tripped in the dark, near as anyone can figure. The friend couldn't say. We found them both at the bottom of one of the ravines. My daughter's neck was broken."

"Oh God." I closed my eyes for a very long moment. "I'm so sorry."

He looked back at me again. "I thank ya fer your sympathies, Tyler. Happened a long time ago, but sometimes it still hits pretty hard. 'Specially when yer not lookin' for it." Reaching out almost hesitantly, he gently touched my cheek with his weathered, work-roughened hand. "I ain't much for platitudes. Find em pretty useless as a rule. But I been around enough to know one thing. And that's that givin' up hope is the worst thing a body can do. I been around lots, but I ain't met many people like your Morgan, Tyler. If anyone can make it outta this almighty mess, I'd lay my money on her, if I was a bettin' man."

"And if you're not?" I asked through my tears.

His smile was sweet and kind and filled with compassion. "I'd lay it down anyway. She's a special one. So are you. I heard her call you 'Angel' once, and I reckon you're as close to one as these eyes are ever gonna see. So you just keep her alive in your heart, and alive she's gonna stay. Ok?"

After a moment, I gave a short nod against his hand, smiling a little. "Ok."

"Alright, then. Let's haul ass home and get some more help on this search. And when we find her, remind me I got a bone ta pick with 'er fer makin' me lose s'much sleep on her account, eh?"

I almost laughed at that. "You're on, Pop. I'll even hold her down while you pick that bone. Just leave one for me, ok?"

With a nod, we were off again, my soul seeming infinitesimally lighter for our conversation.

It's amazing what a powerful drug hope really is.

I sat on the bed, facing the headboard and staring sightlessly out the window. Though I'd been more than thirty-six hours without it, sleep was an elusive, useless thing. Though my mind and body craved it with a deep, abiding ache, my soul shied away from its implied comfort, knowing it for the sham it really was. Sleep wasn't the oblivion I needed; it would only bring about nightmares—or worse, happy dreams from which I would awaken only to die all over again when the realization of my living hell came down to visit once again, hitting me like a sucker punch hard to the gut.

No, better to stay awake and wrestle demons I could control, than to fall asleep and give up that control to the vultures who waited just beyond my conscious sight.

The sounds of Pop's gentle snoring floated up to me from the living room below, where he lay sprawled out on one of the couches. I smiled a little, thanking God for putting that man in my life. He'd managed to call in a great many markers from friends near and far. Friends who were as close-lipped and hardheaded as he was and could therefore be entrusted with the delicate and dangerous task set before them.

Ruby had called just as we'd arrived back at the cabin—I had ceased thinking of this place as home. My words came back to haunt me. Where Ice was, home was. Where she wasn't, it could never be—to share with us the good news that Corinne, though grievously injured, was expected to make a full recovery.

She had what Ruby called a subdural hematoma, which she explained as somewhat like a very bad concussion. The doctors had placed her on some strong medications to both calm her and decrease the swelling in her brain. It was expected to resolve on its own without surgical intervention, for which I was profoundly grateful.

Before hanging up, Ruby let me know in no uncertain terms exactly what she expected to be told when all this was over. If it was ever over.

I answered in like tones, promising her I would tell her everything I could.

If I could.

Turning away from the window, I sat with my back against the headboard, my eyes darting around the room, looking at anything, everything, save for the pillow laying so close to me. A pillow I'd cradled for the past four days—or was it five? Six? Time was the enemy once again—in lieu of the woman I wanted to hold. Her scent was still there, I knew, trapped within the fabric, offering comfort, offering peace.

But for how long? Long enough to last a lifetime without her? Long enough to soothe a chasm of empty nights and broken dreams?

Tears welled up again, and this time, I didn't bother trying to stop them, still denying myself the succor of her scent. Ice couldn't help me now. No one could.

Curling my arms around my body, I felt myself begin to rock, slowly, back and forth, back and forth in a primitive attempt at self-consolation. My tears continued to fall and I continued to let them, knowing they were just the beginning of a vast ocean of grief being held back by the most broken-down of sea walls; my quickly fading inner strength.

After a very long period of time, true to their purpose, my tears slowed and left me feeling, if not better, at least cleansed. The grief was still there, a roiling black tide, but it was just a little easier to tame for having found an outlet, however shortlived.

And with this newfound—if temporary—feeling of peace came the strength to realize that I couldn't go it totally alone. Reaching out, I grabbed the pillow and buried my flushed face into it, absorbing the cool fabric and Ice's exotic, comforting scent deep within me, helping to fortify walls beaten down by grief's relentless torrent.

My mind played back images of happier times, and I allowed those images to lull me into a much-needed sleep, the pillow still clenched desperately against my body.

When I next awoke, it was to that blind, heart pumping

relief that someone gets when they realize they've just been rescued from the clutches of a brutal nightmare.

But then I looked around.

And realized the nightmare was still there and worse than the most horrid of my mind's dark fantasies.

When it finally filtered through that the room was nearly pitch dark and I'd been allowed to sleep the day away, I gritted my teeth in anger and jumped from the bed, almost collapsing to my knees as the agony that was my feet made its presence known. Clinging to the bedpost, I took several deep breaths and willed my legs to support my body no matter how much they hurt.

After a long moment, they finally listened.

As I limped down the stairs, my pain lending strength to my anger, I chanced to look up at the clock on the fireplace mantle, and noticed that instead of sleeping the day away, only two hours had passed. When I finally made it to the bottom floor, my anger had abated somewhat, leaving more than enough room for my ever-present grief to begin encroaching once again.

Pop, his face gray with exhaustion, was in the process of hanging up the phone as I entered the downstairs living area. "Any news?" I asked, very much afraid to hear the answer.

A slow shake of his head. "No. Helluva storm's brewin' though. Gonna wash whatever tracks there are right away."

I followed his gaze out the huge picture window that covered most of the wall. The sky was an ominous black with roiling clouds from which lightning flashes passed, one to the other to the other like a baton in a relay race run by Zeus and his family.

It wasn't raining yet, but the world outside seemed poised for it: still, silent, waiting. I turned back to him. "Looks like we'd better get going then, huh?"

For a moment, it looked as if he wanted to say something, but whatever it was died on his lips and he nodded instead. "Yeah. Let's go see what we can do."

The storm hit just as we stepped outside. Instead of rain, however, hail the size of golf balls started to fall, hurtling toward the ground with amazing speed and evil intent.

"Let's just wait this out, Tyler," Pop said from beneath the overhang of the back porch. "Too dangerous ta go out in this."

"No. If you don't want to go, then give me the keys. I'm not staying here."

"Tyler..."

"No! I won't leave her out in this, Pop. I can't." Pictures of hail battering her defenseless body came to gory life in my mind, ice filling her dead, staring eyes like some grisly horror show special effect. I shut them savagely down. "I just can't.' So either come with me or stay here, but I'm going. With you or without you."

Then I grabbed the keys from his hand and took off toward his truck, not even feeling the hail as it pelted down on me.

And with a muttered "aww hell" that I could barely hear over the storm's fury, Pop ran out to join me, snatching his keys back and shoving me toward the passenger side as he opened his door and slipped into the cab.

Within seconds, we were off, our ride accompanied by a grisly tympani of hailstones as they pounded off of the truck's body and windshield, making it nearly impossible to see, let alone drive.

The hail soon changed into a driving rain that turned the logging roads into quagmires greedily sucking at tires as they passed in a spray of mud. More than once, the winch on Tom Drew's truck was called into service to rescue a truck sunk door-deep into the muck.

But still we went on; driven on by the news that one of Pop's friends had received from one of *his* friends who just happened to be on the Border Patrol. Impossible though it seemed, no black sedans had been reported crossing the border into the United States within the last twenty-four hours.

So, unless Pop was wrong and there in fact *was* a way to get across the border in a car without crossing the patrolled routes, Ice was still in Canada.

Somewhere.

And so day turned into night once again, only acknowledged by the quickly advancing hands on the watch at my wrist. The storm continued on unabated, lightning freezing and illuminating everything in brief, freeze frames of time, as if a photographer with the world's biggest camera were taking a series of pictures documenting our search.

Then it was our turn to sink into one of the mud-pits and we both hopped out of the truck as Pop radioed Tom for his help.

"When he pulls us out, we're headin' for home, Tyler. We're just spinnin' our wheels as it is. We could be right on top of her and not even know it with the storm the way it is. We need to wait for it to calm down some."

"I'm sorry, Pop, but I just can't do that. You can go back if you want to. I'll go on on foot."

"You can't do that! You'll get lost sure as hell!"

"I don't care. I can't stop searching, Pop. I just can't. I'm sorry." And with that, I started away, soaked to the skin, night-blind, and more than half insane with the need to find my lover's body.

"Don't do this, Tyler, damnit!"

I turned back, seeing the oncoming lights of Tom's truck as they approached. "Let Tom pull you out, Pop. Then go home. I'll be alright."

And with a sense of utter calm, I waited for the next lightning flash to illuminate the area, then stepped off the road and into the woods hearing the shouts behind me but not bothering to give them any acknowledgement.

I made my way blindly forward, feeling wind-driven branches whip at my face and body and not caring. When the next flash of lightning came, I found myself staring into emptiness, but was unable to stop myself as I stepped off a precipice and tumbled down a heretofore unknown embankment, feeling rocks and fallen branches jab and rake my naked skin and unprotected head.

My momentum was stopped, finally, by an uprooted tree. My body slammed into it, knee first, and pain exploded behind my eyes, making me cry out.

In that half-second of blessed oblivion, when the pain faded and I found myself looking out into nothingness, I thought *Good. I'm dead. Now I can finally find her.*

But then the pain returned and, with it, breath to my lungs and sounds to my ears. I heard my name being called and, painfully, turned my neck to see the backlit forms of Pop, Tom and John as they looked down the ravine into which I'd fallen. They were shouting something, but I couldn't make it out above the howling of the wind and the pounding of the rain.

It wasn't important anyway. I was still alive and Ice was still gone, and *that* was the only thing that mattered to me.

Slowly I pulled myself together and set about getting out of the trap I'd fallen into. Sitting up gingerly, I used both hands to pull out the leg that was wedged beneath the great, gnarled roots of the old pine I'd slammed into.

I nearly fainted when my leg finally tore loose from the tree's greedy hold and I saw the ragged flaps of skin where my knee used to be.

I wasn't about to let a little blood stop me, though, and, gritting my teeth against the agony, I hobbled back up to my feet and stood, swaying, as my body tried to regain its lost equilibrium.

I looked up again in time to see Tom and John slip-slide their way down the embankment, managing to keep their footing only by the slimmest of margins. Finally getting to where I was standing, Tom reached out to me, but I pulled away, my teeth set in a feral snarl. "Don't touch me!"

"C'mon, Tyler. You're hurt bad. You need to get back up top and get that leg looked at."

"The only thing I need, you bastard, is to be left alone."

"Tyler..."

"Cowards!" I yelled, some part deep within me shocked at this insanity, but the rest reveling in it. "That's all you are! Cowards! Go home, Tom. Get all warm and dry in your nice warm cabin. Kiss your wife hello and don't worry about me. Just...go home. I'll do this myself."

For that one horrible second in time, all I felt was hate. I hated them all, but I think, more than that, I hated myself.

"Tyler, please..."

"*No*! Leave me alone!"

He wouldn't, though, and grabbed me in a tight bear hold that I didn't have the faintest prayer of escaping, insane or no. Like some sort of trapped and wild animal, I fought for all I was worth, kicking and scratching and even biting, but he bore my rage patiently.

And when my rage turned to grief once again, he turned me in his arms, held me close and tight, and stroked my dirty, wet hair as I sobbed my sorrow into his massive chest.

"Is Pop ok?" I asked from my position on the couch, my badly damaged knee thoroughly cleansed and swaddled in several layers of towels and propped on two pillows.

Tom smiled slightly at me as he entered the living room from Corinne's room, where he'd taken Pop when we'd arrived back at the cabin. "Yeah. He was having some chest pain. From the tension, I think."

I sat up straighter. "He needs to get to a hospital then."

"Nah. He's stubborner than you about those things," he said with a pointed glance. "I gave him the medicine he takes for those attacks and he's resting fine now. A little sleep and he'll be better."

"Are you sure?"

"Yeah. It's happened before. Doc Steve checked out his ticker and it's ok, for the most part. Just relax. He'll be fine." He crossed the room to stand beside the couch. "How're you?"

"I'm ok."

"You really need to get that knee checked out, Tyler. I'm not a very good nurse."

"You did just fine. And I will. Have it checked out, I mean. Later."

He chuckled. "Peas in a pod, you are." Then he looked out the window. "I just checked with John on the CB. The rain's setting to clear and we're getting ready to go back out again."

"Ok."

Smiling, he reached out and ruffled my hair before turning to leave.

"Tom?"

He turned back. "Yeah?"

"I just want you to know I'm sorry for what I said back there. I didn't mean any of it, you know?"

"I know, sweetie. Grief makes us do some crazy things. Just remember, Morgan's my friend, too. And I'm not gonna stop until I find her. None of us are."

Suddenly shy, I looked down at my hands. "I know," I mumbled, yet again on the verge of tears. "And that means the world to me, Tom." Then I lifted my chin and looked him dead in the eye. "I need for you to believe that."

"I do, Tyler. Believe me. I do."

❖❖❖❖❖❖❖❖

Several hours later, Pop shuffled out of the bedroom, his hair a corkscrew of tangles, his eyes red, his face pale and drawn and stubbly with a couple of days' growth of beard. "How ya holdin' up, Tyler?" he asked, voice rough with sleep.

"I've been better. You?"

"Same." He yawned and stretched, then sat down in the chair next to the couch upon which I was lying. "Any news?"

"No."

He nodded, then looked out the window. "Weather's cleared up. That's good, at least."

"Thank heaven for small favors." It sounded sarcastic and, in truth, it was. I was hanging on by the tiniest, most frayed of threads, but more determined than ever not to again give into my anger and sorrow.

And, indeed, the night had cleared beautifully. The breeze seemed gentle as it swayed the pines and the stars and moon formed a beautiful tapestry across the sky above. Tom had opened the windows before he left, and the air was cool and fragrant as it brushed against my skin.

We sat for a while in companionable silence, listening to the chorus of frogs as they chirped for their mates.

Then they went silent and I looked over at Pop, who'd also noticed and was rising slowly from his chair, his face set in stony lines.

"What is it?" I whispered.

"Dunno. But I aim ta find out. Them bastards don't stop unless there's danger about."

"A bear, maybe?"

"Maybe. Or somethin' else." Going to the corner of the room, he grabbed his rifle and threw back the bolt. "Stay here. I'll check it out."

"Not on your life," I replied, easing myself off of the couch and placing my bare feet on the warm floor.

"Tyler, ya don't need ta be getting up with yer knee like that."

"I'll worry about it later. Let's just see what's out there."

Willing myself not to collapse as the sharp spears of pain drove up my leg and into my gut, I put some weight on my leg, nodded once with teeth clamped hard enough to draw blood from my lip, and hobbled across the floor, putting my hand on Pop's narrow back as we continued through the dining-room and out to the rear of the house.

We both scanned the darkness seen through the screens of the back porch, seeing nothing save for the gently rustling trees. "You ready?" he asked me, rifle held securely in his hands.

"Yeah."

With one foot, he pushed open the door and stepped out onto the patio with me close behind.

The eerie silence continued, broken only by the rustling leaves and the hum of the wind through the trees.

"I don't see anything," I whispered.

"Me neither. That's what's got me worried."

I was tempted to shrug it off, but the tension Pop was giving off wouldn't let me. I stood as still as I could, willing the pain in my leg to recede, if only for a brief second's respite.

Then I saw something; a movement in the bushes Ice had planted between the edge of our property and the road, a movement that was not caused by the wind. I stiffened, my heart racing anew, the pain finally forgotten as a new danger presented itself.

Next to me, Pop, also aware of the movement, raised his rifle slowly, socketing it snug against his shoulder. "I ain't in the mood for playin' games, whoever you are. So do us both a favor and c'mon out before I start shootin'." His voice, though low, was steady and strong.

The rustling continued.

"Do it, now, or I swear to God I'll pull this trigger and ya won't be doin' anything again."

After another moment, a white rabbit, fat with summer's bounty hopped from the bushes and twitched his impudent nose at us, his eyes red in the porch lighting.

I sagged against Pop in relief but he remained steady, rifle not moving a millimeter.

"What is it?"

"Rabbit's got blood on it."

"Oh shit." The tension in me redoubled and my eyes searched again the dark night.

"Last warning! C'mon out!"

A figure rose from the bushes like a beast from a nightmare, blood-covered and ragged and holding a pistol aimed directly at Pop.

My gasp of horror was loud in my own ears.

But something as close to a premonition as I'll ever be blessed with again reached in and grabbed my soul and sent my arm out pushing the rifle away a split second before Pop would have fired. "No!" I screamed. "Don't shoot!"

"Get back inside, Tyler," Pop ordered, bringing his rifle to bear again. "I'll handle this."

"No!" I yelled again, grabbing the gun with desperate strength. "Don't shoot! It's Ice!"

"What?"

"Look, Pop! It's Ice! Don't shoot! Please!"

His eyes squinted as he looked at the gore-covered apparition who was still standing, gun pointed at him. "Morgan? That you?"

"Step away from her, old man. Step away before I kill ya."

"Do it, Pop! Put your gun down and step away. Please."

"But..."

"Please!"

Slowly, he lowered his gun and took three careful steps away from me, his eyes still glued to Ice's savaged body and glittering, deadly eyes. Her gun was rock steady as it tracked his progress.

Standing alone, I slowly raised my hands. "Ice? It's me. Angel. Please put the gun down, ok? I'm fine. He didn't hurt me. Please put the gun down."

The gun swung back to me, her expression unchanged. If the Angel of Death had form and face, I was looking at it right now. "Please, Ice. Put it down. No one's gonna hurt you, love."

Her stance wavered for a brief second as her eyes closed,

then opened again. "Angel?" she whispered.

"Yes, sweetheart. It's me." I tried to smile through my tears. "Welcome home."

As if hit by a strong blow from behind, she seemed to crumple. The gun fell from her hands and she dragged herself from the bushes. I almost screamed when I saw the damage that had been done to her. Most of her clothes had been torn clean away, and she was bleeding heavily from more than a dozen wounds, including two obvious gunshots to her left thigh and right side, just above her hip. Her face was covered in blood from a heavily bleeding wound just above her eyebrow. The skin of her arms and legs were scratched and torn and covered with mud from where she'd no doubt fallen many times during her journey.

I hope I'll never live long enough to ever experience the massive strength she needed just to move those few feet separating us.

I rushed out to meet her half way, crushing her in a hug that would have killed a mere mortal.

"I killed 'em, Angel," she whispered into my ear, her voice husky and raw. "I killed 'em all. They won't hurt you ever again."

And then she collapsed against me, unconscious, bearing me to the ground with her as her desperate journey home finally ended.

"Holy mother a'god," Pop swore as he materialized beside me. "I wouldn't a believed it if I hadn't seen it with my own eyes. I'm *still* not sure I believe it."

"Help me get her in the house, Pop," I returned, pulling my body from beneath Ice's and cradling her head in my hands. "Please."

"Alright. You get 'er shoulders. I'll get 'er feet. Let's see if we can do this without droppin' her."

On three, we lifted her carefully. Dead weight, she felt almost impossibly heavy, and my knee was seriously considering retiring from the business. I took a few shuffling steps backward before I had to stop, my leg trembling too violently with pain to bear the additional weight. Ice's head lolled between my arms.

"We've got to put her down, Pop. I can't..."

"Alright, Tyler, alright. Lay her down nice an' easy. We'll figure out somethin' else."

Just then, headlights shown in the driveway and a truck came to a skidding halt a few feet from us. Tom jumped out, his face flushed with excitement. "Pop! Tyler! John just found.... Jesus Christ! Is that Morgan? How in the hell...?"

I looked up at him. "Tom. Please. Help. We...I...can't..."

"I've got it." Pushing me gently out of the way, he bent down and lifted Ice easily in his massive arms, cradling her gently against his chest. "Where should I take her?"

"Can you carry her upstairs to the bed?"

"No problem. Get the door."

Pop grabbed the door, holding it wide for Tom to pass through carrying Ice while I concentrated on dragging myself back to my feet.

It was funny, though. My leg didn't seem to hurt all that much anymore. My joy in seeing Ice alive coupled with the sure knowledge of what she went through to make her way back to me in the condition she was in made my own injury pale to less than insignificance.

I found myself, therefore, almost flying through the door which Pop courteously held open for me, dashing across the hard wooden floors, and taking the stairs two at a time to arrive just in time to see Tom lay Ice gently on our bed. The look on his face was a curious mixture of sorrow, amazement, and utter worship.

I suspected the same look was on my own face as well.

Noticing my presence after carefully arranging her arms and legs in a comfortable position atop the sheets, he stepped out of the way, giving me room to lower myself to my knees beside the bed and gently grasp one of her hands, holding it up to my cheek as my eyes played over her battered, blood and gore covered face.

I didn't see any of that, though. Not then. Not yet.

Instead, I just allowed myself to drink in the sight of her, alive and breathing and as beautiful to my eyes as the day I first saw, seemingly an entire lifetime ago.

"We need to get her to a hospital," Tom said finally, breaking the silence which had fallen over the room.

"No," I said immediately, looking up at him. "No hospitals."

"If you're worried about the cost, Tyler, don't. We'll..."

"No. It's not that. It's..." I took a deep breath, attempting to gather my thoughts. "She's been shot."

He looked me as if I'd suddenly regressed back to diapers. "Yeah, I know. That's why we need to get her to a hospital."

"You don't understand."

"Obviously, I don't. Mind filling me in?" There was just a touch of anger in his voice. Justified, I thought, given what he'd gone through to search for the very woman who was now lying, grievously injured, on the bed.

"First thing them docs'll do, Tommy," Pop said, coming into

the room, "after they stabilize her is ta call the cops."

"So? That's a bad thing? Those guys kidnapped her and tried to murder her! I think bringing the police in is a *good* thing right about now!"

"Won't help nothin', Tommy. They're dead already."

Tom turned to Pop, his eyes wide with shock. "What?"

Pop gestured to the bed. "She killed 'em."

Tom looked down at Ice, then over at me, his jaw slack. I nodded. "*All* of them?"

I nodded again.

"Jesus Christ," he whispered. "But...she could claim self defense, right?"

"Sure," Pop replied, "after they was done askin' her why them Mafia boys had such an interest in her."

"Oh."

"Yeah. Oh."

Reaching out, Tom laid a hand on Ice's brow. His eyebrows drew together in a pensive frown. "Well, whatever you guys are gonna do, it'd better be soon. She's burning up."

And suddenly, I could feel it as well in the limp hand I was holding. Always a warm furnace, Ice's body radiated a heat that was unnatural, even for her. I looked over at Pop, my fears plain on my face.

"I'll go downstairs and wet down some towels. That'll help cool her off for a start till we figure out who ta call."

"What about Steve?" Tom asked.

"Pretty fair country doc, but I don't think he's got the skills we need, Tommy."

Then he turned and walked back down the stairs, leaving us alone. Reaching out with my free hand, I gingerly touched the sweaty, dirty and bloody bangs on Ice's pale brow, carefully trying to avoid the myriad of cuts and scrapes gouged into her skin, a task which was nearly impossible. There didn't appear to be an unmarked inch of skin anywhere.

The tears were there. I could feel them burning at my eyes, demanding release, but I didn't let them fall. Time enough later, when she was out of the woods.

Needing to get my mind off of the sight my eyes were seeing, if even for a moment, I looked up at Tom. "When you came over here, you acted like you had some news?"

My friend startled, as if pulled from a dream. "Oh! Yeah! John found something about thirty miles down that road we were searching yesterday. We probably missed it because of the storm."

"Did he say what it was?"

"No. They were just getting ready to head down. Whatever it was, it had him pretty excited, though." He scratched at the heavy growth of stubble on his cheek. "Which reminds me. I'd better get back out to the truck and see what it was. Not that it makes much difference now, thank God."

"It might."

"Might what?"

"Make a difference. If she left the...um...bodies laying around."

"Damn," Tom replied, rubbing his forehead. "I didn't even think about that." He shook his head. "Lemme get downstairs and figure out what's going on."

Pop came into the room, heavily laden with wet towels, as soon as Tom left. "C'mon," he said, laying them on the bed and turning to me, "let's get 'er outta what's left of 'er clothes and lay these towels on her. Might help ta bring the fever down a little, at least."

"Alright." Struggling up to my feet, I worked on the upper half of her body while Pop worked on the lower. There really wasn't much left of the simple button down shirt she'd donned and her bra was another lost cause, having been ripped to shreds somewhere along the way. I didn't have to try hard at all to divest her of the tattered remnants hanging from her battered body.

"Oh, Ice," I whispered, looking down at the body bared to me. Her breasts were bruised and bloody. Several long cuts could be seen beneath the liberal coating of blood and mud which painted her skin. Her ribcage on the right was oddly shaped, and I guessed that she had three or four broken ribs. There was a long open gash which drew a grisly line from just beneath her sternum and ran underneath the blood-encrusted jeans Pop was currently working hard just to unbutton.

And, of course, there was the bullet hole just above her hip, surrounded by swollen, angry red skin and oozing a constant bloody fluid.

With a satisfied grunt, Pop finally managed to pry open the button holding Ice's jeans together and with a quick, though gentle, tug, he pulled them off, together with her underpants.

Excepting the second bullet wound in her thigh, her legs seemed to have escaped the worst of the damage, though she did have several wicked gashes on her calves and shins and both knees were swollen, scraped and bleeding.

Working together, Pop and I soon managed to cover her with cool, wet towels from head to toe, hoping against hope we could put a dent in the raging fever she had. "Do you have any ideas?"

I asked him when we were finally done.

"Been thinkin' on it," he replied. "Got a friend up country some who's pretty fair with a scalpel and knows how ta keep his mouth shut. Might do for a start."

I could feel myself sag with relief against the bed. "Thank God. Are you going to call him?"

"Do it right now."

Just as he turned to leave, we both stiffened as the sounds of shouting filtered into the cabin. The words weren't easily discerned, but from the heated tone, it was pretty obvious that Tom was trying his best to keep someone outside, while that "someone" was trying just as hard to get in.

There was a loud crash and then I heard my name. "Angel!"

Which was strange, because no man in town called me by that name.

My first thought was Andre, but he was a French Canadian who spoke with a thick, if pleasing, accent. The man who called my name carried no such accent.

"Angel, are you in there? It's Bull! I need to talk to you right away!"

"Bull?" I rose slowly to my feet. "Tom, it's alright! Let him in! He's a friend!"

I walked over to the wooden railing as Bull burst through the door, Tom hard at his heels, their faces still flushed with heated anger.

"Angel! Thank God I'm not too late. Where's Morgan? I need to speak to you both. It's really important."

"She's up here, Bull," I replied, taking in the sight of a friend I hadn't seen in a year. He looked just the same; right down to the massive beard he evidently didn't bother to shave even in the heat of summer.

"Um, could you get her to come down here? Please?"

"I can't do that, Bull. Come on up here."

He took his cap off and twisted it in his hands, blushing slightly beneath his heavy beard. "Are you sure?"

I smiled a little. "Now's not the time to get all shy on me, Bull. Just get up here."

"Alright."

I could hear him take the steps three at a time as his huge body barely made it up the narrow stairway. He made it to the top, then stopped, face slack with shock and some deeper emotion. "I *am* too late," he breathed. "God damn it. No!"

Walking over to the bed, he stared down at Ice's unresponsive body, fat tears rolling down his bearded cheeks. "Dear God, Morgan, no. You can't...no."

I stepped up and placed a hand on his back. "She's still alive, Bull," I said softly in an effort to ease his grief. "They tried, but they didn't succeed."

He turned to me, his eyes shiny with his tears, his hands clenched in massive, white-knuckled fists. "Was it...?"

I nodded. "At least I think so. Cavallo wasn't with them. She seemed to know one of them, though. A guy by the name of Carmine. He seemed to be the leader."

He returned my nod, his face twisting into a snarl of anger. "Yeah, she knew him alright. Carmine used to be a friend of hers, before he turned belly up and became Cavallo's stooge. Bastard. When I find him, I'm gonna...."

"No need. He's dead."

Bull's eyes widened. "Morgan?"

"Yeah. She killed all of them, then managed to make her way back here, though I don't know how."

"You mean they took her away? Alive? But how?"

I sighed. "It's a long story, Bull. Suffice it to say for now that they're not a threat anymore."

"They shouldn't have been a threat in the first place, goddamnit!" I could hear his teeth grind in anger.

"Did something happen?"

"Yeah," he spat. "They managed to find Andre, though how, I don't know."

"Oh, God. Is he alright?"

"He's alive. They beat the holy living crap out of him, but he's alive."

"Did he tell them?"

"No. Andre wouldn't spill anything if you pulled his fingernails out by the roots. He's tough."

"Then who?"

"Andre's partner. He just couldn't take seeing him beaten up like that anymore. He managed to get Andre to the hospital, then he called me. I was up in the mountains and didn't find out about anything till just this morning. I've been driving all day, praying to God I wasn't too late." He wiped the tears from his eyes. "But I was anyhow."

I rubbed my hand along his broad back, trying to console him. It wasn't working. He was wound up tighter than a spring. "It's alright, Bull. You couldn't have known."

"I *should* have, damnit!" He wiped his eyes again. "I should have, and I didn't. And now Morgan is...is..."

"She's alive, Bull. She's *alive*."

After a moment, he reached down and clasped Ice's hand in his own. "I'm sorry, Morgan. God, I'm so, so sorry." Then he looked at me. "She's burnin' up with fever."

"I know. She's been shot twice and she's got a whole bunch of other injuries on top of that. We were just about to call in a friend to help."

"Let me. Please. I couldn't stop this from happening, but at least I can help fix her up." He turned to me, eyes intense and pleading. "I was a battlefield medic in 'Nam. Chucked it all and moved up here when my tour was over, but I've kept up my skills. I might not know a lot, but I do know how to treat gunshot wounds." Reaching out his free hand, he grasped my own, squeezing it tightly. "Please, Angel. Please let me help. I have to make it up to her somehow. I have..."

I gave him my best smile. "That's the best offer I've heard all day, Bull. Thank you."

"No, Angel. Thank *you.*" He turned then, and almost ran into Pop, who had been silently listening to the exchange. "Oh, I'm sorry. Um...I'm Bull."

Pop smiled. "So I gathered. Pop." The two men shook hands as Pop carefully appraised my hulking friend. "You known Morgan a long time, have ya?"

"Yeah. Since she was a kid. I love her like a sister. Always have."

Pursing his lips, Pop nodded, once. "Alright then. Got gear ya need brung up?"

"It's in my truck. I'll get it." After a last look at Ice, he turned and ran back down the stairs and out to his truck.

"Guess we got lucky," Pop commented.

"Yeah. I guess we did."

Thank God.

Chapter 15

Soon after Bull left to retrieve his gear, Pop left as well, ostensibly to get fresh water, rags and soap with which to wash Ice's blood and gore covered body so that Bull could do what he needed to do to fix the worst of her injuries.

Left alone with my lover, I crawled carefully onto the large bed, then stretched out beside her. Reaching out, I gently gasped a lock of her hair and ran it between my fingers, looking down at her battered, still face. "Hi, sweetheart. It's me." I paused. "Well, I suppose you know that already, don't you. You always seem to know when I'm around and I don't think now is any different, right?"

I stopped, then laughed a little. "Yeah, I'm rambling. Par for the course, huh?" I sighed, sniffing back my tears. "I missed you, Ice. I felt...I don't know...dead inside. Like someone had taken my soul and ripped it right out of my body. And when I thought you were dead..."

I let the tears fall for a moment before strengthening myself against their still-seductive lure. "Enough of that. You're not dead. You're alive, and we're all gonna make sure you stay that way, alright?"

Then I smiled, picturing that sardonic eyebrow lift in my mind. "Yes, you heard me right. 'We.' When you wake up, I think you're gonna be in for one hell of a surprise, my love. You, the person who believes she is incapable of being respected and loved, are loved by many more people than you think. You wouldn't believe the number of people who put themselves in deliberate danger just to hunt down those idiots who kidnapped you." I could feel my smile broaden. "You'd be proud of them, Ice. God knows I am."

Anything I might have said further was interrupted by the return of Bull and, right behind him, Pop. Bull was toting a large, green backpack with a red cross emblazoned across the front.

"Present from Uncle Sam," he said, grinning and lifting the pack when he saw me staring at it. "I heard you talking. Did she wake up?"

I blushed a little. "No. I was just ...talking to myself, I guess. Telling her I missed her and stuff like that." I shrugged.

"Good."

"Good?"

Laying the pack down on the bed, he nodded. "Yeah. Whatever place she's in, she knows she's safe. But it's good to be reminded of that sometimes. Especially when you're hurting." Smiling slightly, he put one large hand gently down on her shoulder. "Whatever she went through, it wasn't pleasant. She needs to hear your voice to remember that it was all worth it in the end."

"You think she can hear me, then?"

"Oh, yeah. Even if she isn't responding right now, she hears you. I'm sure of it. So don't stop talking on my account. It can only make my job easier." He grinned crookedly. "Especially if she wakes up while I'm still working and decides my face would look better completely rearranged."

Remembering what she had done to the poor doctor who had tried to shove a tube down her nose when she seemed unconscious, I couldn't help but laugh. "Then I promise to do my best to keep your face looking as handsome as it does now."

Oops! In the year that had passed, I'd completely forgotten about the crush he had on me.

Bull's blush could have set fire to the lake outside.

Then Pop laughed, which caused Bull to scowl, and then everything was alright again.

Or at least as alright as it *could* be.

"C'mon, Tyler, let's get 'er cleaned up some so this lug c'n do what he came here ta do."

And so we did, each of us using towels and plenty of soap and water to tenderly minister to her torn and swollen flesh. The going was slow, at first, especially as I was trying my best to be gentle with her, not wanting to cause my already horribly injured lover any further pain.

But when Bull told me—rather sternly I thought—to put some muscle into it, I began to clean her more thoroughly and, by necessity, less tenderly, wincing every time the cloth swiped over the angry, swollen redness that circled her cuts like an obscene brand.

She wasn't wincing, though, or even twitching. Not even when Bull used his washcloth to clean the edges of the bullet hole in her thigh, probing it to loosen the encrusted blood and dirt which had fouled it.

I looked up at him, sure my expression of worry was showing easily on my face.

After a moment, he dropped the dirty rag to the floor and came up to the head of the bed, bringing with him a small penlight he'd liberated from the depths of his army issue backpack. Using his huge hands tenderly, he felt around her skull beneath the thick and tangled mat of her hair, frowning once or twice as he did so.

Then he pulled back each slack eyelid in turn and flashed the beam from his penlight into her eyes several times before lowering her lids once again and tossing the light back with the rest of his gear.

"Well?" Pop asked before I could voice the same question.

"She's got a couple pretty good sized lumps on the right side of her head, and her left pupil is a little sluggish, so I'd guess she's got a pretty nice concussion to add to the mix." He turned to look at me. "Did she seem okay when she talked to you?"

I thought for a moment. "Well, she didn't seem to recognize Pop at first, but then again, he had a gun pointed at her, so I'm sure she could probably be excused for that one. And, for a minute there, I don't think she recognized me either, but when I called out to her, she lowered her own gun and came to me." I closed my eyes, remembering. "She told me that she'd killed them all and that they wouldn't ever hurt me again. Then she passed out."

He nodded. "That's good, then."

"So, is the concussion why she's not showing any response to pain?"

"Partly. Add to that a good dose of sheer exhaustion and we've most likely got our answer."

"Most likely?" Pop asked, his bushy brows knit low over his eyes.

Bull spread his hands. "I'm sorry. It's my best guess here. Only a CT scan could tell us for sure, and since the chances of sneaking her into one of those things without being seen are remote..."

Both men turned to look at me and I once again felt the

weight of the world settle about my shoulders as if planning to stay for a good long while.

Instinctively, I looked to Ice, searching for answers in that still, battered, beloved face. *What would you do in my place, Ice? Would you trust Bull's decision, or would you want to make absolutely sure?*

Then I laughed a little, causing my companions to look at me as if I had suddenly sprouted another head, a little off to the left of the first one.

I know what you'd do, my love. You'd get me to the hospital so fast, the tires would bleed.

I reached out once again to finger a lock of her hair, desperate to have some sort of link with her. A link that wasn't cold, or pale, or bloody.

But you're not me. And as much as I hate to admit it, you can't help me with this one, can you?

I sighed.

So, either I trust Bull and hope he's not wrong, or I take you to a hospital to be sure and run the almost guaranteed risk of seeing you carted back to the U.S. in chains.

That exact vision, the one that had haunted my nightmares for the past year, came into my thoughts, and suddenly, the decision wasn't a hard one to make at all.

Then I looked up into the waiting faces of my friends, meeting their eyes steadily and without hesitation. "I trust you, Bull. And I know Ice does, too." I smiled. "So, let's get this show on the road and put Humpty Dumpty back together again, ok?"

Grinning in return, Bull gave me a gentle slap on the shoulder and returned to his pack, which he opened and began pulling out amazing quantities of medical gear, like a magician pulling a dozen rabbits from his top-hat.

"What did you do?" I finally asked as all the gear was laid out on the table by the bed, "rob a hospital?"

"Nah. I got a friend down south who keeps me supplied." He shrugged. "No big deal."

"And you keep it all in your *truck*?"

He chuckled. "Well, when you take a group of great white hunters out on a trek and spend a night or two picking a load of buckshot outta someone's backside with nothing but a pair of eyebrow tweezers and a Zippo lighter, ya soon learn that the Boy Scouts have the right idea." Then he pulled himself back to his feet. "Lemme go wash my hands and then we can get started."

"What do you want me to do?" I asked.

He smiled tenderly. "Just...hold her hand. Best medicine in the world for her right now."

I nodded.

That I could do.

Several hours later, it was done.

Ice lay quietly in the center of our large bed, looking impossibly small and impossibly fragile beneath the vestments of brilliant white bandages which swaddled her from head to toe.

From beneath one such bandage, wrapped around her left arm, snaked a coil of IV tubing which was connected to a clear bag of fluid hanging from an impromptu IV pole, which doubled, in happier times, as our coat-rack.

Swabbing one of the IV ports, Bull injected another dose of Morphine into the line, then discarded the used syringe and stripped off his bloodied gloves, grunting in satisfaction and stretching his massive body in all directions. "That should keep her out for awhile," he said, twisting his neck so that the vertebrae popped noisily.

"Is there anything more we can do?" I asked from my position beside the bed. My knees were killing me, especially the injured one, but I wasn't about to complain.

"Nope. The rest is up to her. Give her time to rest and start healing. She'll come out of it when she's ready."

Struggling to my feet, I limped over to Bull and wrapped him in the tightest hug I could manage, tucking my cheek against his huge chest and hanging on for dear life. "Thank you," I said, my voice muffled against his shirt. "Thank you so much. I don't know what we would have done without you, Bull. You saved her life. I won't ever forget that. Ever."

He didn't say anything, but I could feel his acceptance of my thanks in the return squeeze I received before being lifted off my feet and deposited into the bed beside my partner. "Time to look at your injuries," he said, grinning.

"Oh, no. Really," I demurred as his hands reached for the towel still somehow wrapped around my leg. "I don't need..."

"Hush."

Surprisingly, I did.

Giving the man my best put upon expression, I crossed my arms over my chest and watched as he gently unwrapped my leg to reveal my injury. "Not bad. Someone did a pretty good job of cleaning it up."

"That was Tom," I replied. Then I looked up at Pop, who'd been mostly silent as Bull worked on Ice, lending help as needed but doing little else, his thoughts seemingly far away. "Speaking of which, where is he?"

"Talked to him a little while ago. Said he couldn't raise Johnny on the CB so he was goin' back out ta see what was goin' on."

I sat up straighter. "Is there a problem?"

Pop shrugged. "Nah. They was probably outta their trucks investigatin' whatever in the hell it was they found."

"That was quite awhile ago, though. Shouldn't someone have reported back by now?"

Pop didn't seem particularly worried. "Give 'em a little more time. They'll be alright."

Nodding, I looked back to Bull, who was staring at me with a large syringe in his hand and a grin that Dr. Frankenstein must have worn just before he threw the fateful switch.

"Wha—?"

"Oh, come on, Angel. It's just a little needle," he teased mercilessly.

"Little for *you*, maybe..."

"Alright," he replied, moving as if to put the syringe away, "but those stitches are gonna hurt a lot more without it."

"S-stitches?"

I heard Pop chuckle off to the side and I shot him a glare before returning my attentions to the big man with the big needle. "It's not that bad," I countered, flexing my knee to show just how bad it wasn't, and nearly biting my tongue in half when a bolt of pain shot up to my groin. "See?" I said through gritted teeth.

Bull grinned. "Oh, I see alright." Using his free hand, he gently pushed on my shoulder until my back was against the backboard. "Just close your eyes and think happy thoughts. It's just a little prick. You won't feel a thing."

"You know," I said when my jaw finally managed to loosen, "you're just lucky you're armed, Bull, or I just might be tempted to make an unkind remark to rebut that last statement." Then I smirked. "Or confirm it."

His face went blank for a moment as he internalized my threat, then he blushed again; a deep, fire-engine red. Pop coughed in the background, nearly choking when he, too, got the joke.

My own quiet laughter was quickly cut off at the feel of a sharp needle sliding beneath my skin, followed by an intense burning sensation as the medication spread through my tissues. "Ow," I said, scowling.

"Serves you right," came the unrepentant reply. "Now just sit still for a minute and give it a chance to work."

Though tempted in the extreme to let loose with a volley of expletives that would have curled his beard, I wisely held my tongue, choosing silence as the better part of valor.

At least as long as he had pointy objects close to hand.

A couple minutes later, he returned, suture materials in hand and, almost before I knew it, I was staring down at a long row of neat stitches where a gaping cut had been just a short time before. "Thanks, Bull. Sorry about giving you such a hard time."

He grinned, snapping off his gloves. "Don't worry about it. You were a hell of a lot better about it than a whiney hunter with a butt-load of buckshot, that's for sure." Then he looked at me, eyes narrowed. "Ya know, those circles under your eyes are gonna be asking for their own zip code pretty soon. When'd you sleep last?"

Embarrassed, I looked down at my hands, clasped in my lap. "I...um...don't remember."

"Thought as much. You need some rest. So just lie down next to Morgan and try to relax. I'll keep an eye out for both of you."

"You need sleep, too," I replied, noticing the large, dark circles under his own eyes.

"Yeah, but I'm in one piece." Then he smiled and I could almost smell an ulterior motive brewing. "Besides, I think Morgan'll sleep easier knowing you're close by, don't you?"

"You're a devious man, my friend."

He shrugged, laughing. "It worked, didn't it?"

"Yeah."

"Okay, then." He tipped a wink at me. "Pleasant dreams."

My payback list had officially expanded.

Some time later, I was awakened from the depths of a profoundly exhausted slumber by something I didn't at first recognize.

Then it came again and this time, recognition was swift.

Ice twitched, then moaned, as if in pain.

Galvanized, I moved quickly away, horror dawning on my face as I realized that, sometime during my sleep, I'd unconsciously adopted one of my favorite positions, curled up on my side, my head on her shoulder, my arm tight about her waist, and my good leg thrown carelessly over both of her own.

"Oh my God, Ice. I'm so sorry! I didn't realize...."

"Angel...."

"I know. I'm here. I'm sorry, sweetheart...." I reached out to touch her, then realized that her eyes, far from being open and pain filled, were instead darting ceaselessly about beneath tightly closed lids.

"Ice?" Her entire face was literally bathed in a heavy sweat.

"Angel! No!"

One long arm blasted out from beneath the covers. The IV tubing stretched, then abruptly came free as blood and IV fluid sprayed across the bed. "Let go of her, you bastard!"

"Ice! Don't!" Reaching out, I grabbed her arm, but she pulled it away savagely as both legs powered up, kicking the covers free.

"Let her go, Carmine. That's right, let her go, or I'll rip your heart out and feed it to ya."

"Ice... please..." I wanted to reach out to touch her, to reassure her that I was alive and in no danger, but there wasn't a place on her body that I could do that without hurting her. Instead, I laid back down and put my lips as close to her ear as I dared. "Ice, I'm ok. I'm alright. Carmine isn't here, sweetheart. You're just having a bad dream. That's all it is. Just a dream."

"Angel?"

"Yes, sweetheart. It's me. You're ok. We're ok. No one's gonna hurt us. I promise."

And for a moment, her body went absolutely still, and I breathed out a silent sigh of relief.

"Angel! *Nooooo*!"

She stiffened beneath me, then began thrashing violently, as if within the depths of her fevered delirium, she was being held by chains of the strongest steel from which she was desperately trying to break free.

As I watched, horrified, her face twisted in a snarl of black rage while, from beneath tightly clenched eyelids; a stream of tears began to pour.

"Ice," I whispered into her ear, taking care not to be hit by her thrashing head, "it's ok. I'm alright. Please, it's ok." I put my hand down below her chest in an attempt to calm her, then pulled it away quickly. It was red and slick with blood.

I forced myself to stay calm in the face of this new horror, knowing that my agitation could very likely seep into whatever fevered state her mind was in and cause things to become worse than they already were. Lifting my head carefully, I tried to peer over the railing to perhaps catch a glimpse of anyone who might be on the first floor, all the while wondering why they hadn't come running when they first heard Ice's agonized shouts.

She stiffened, then thrashed again, arms and legs jerking as she snarled out her rage. One arm came free from whatever hold her nightmare had on it and flew out, hard, narrowly missing my head as I ducked beneath its killing strike.

When she lashed out again, I jerked away, sending myself tumbling over the edge of the bed to crash gracelessly onto the hard floor. Quickly gathering my legs beneath me, I stood and jumped back on the bed, calling out for help as I did so.

Fresh red bloomed beneath the pristine white bandages, the stains growing ever larger as she continued to thrash atop the bed.

Sounds of booted feet filled the house as I continued to try and calm my lover down without touching her, knowing that any attempt at restraint would be quickly and harshly thrown off.

Then I found myself airborne once again as Tom pulled me off the bed and set me on the ground behind him before moving to grab Ice's flailing arm and pin it to the bed. Pop did the same with her other arm, and John, the largest of the men save for Bull, grabbed her legs.

Snarling and snapping like a trapped animal, Ice brought all her strength to bear against this new threat, flinging the restraining hands from her as her body bucked and twisted violently. Men stumbled and swore at her immense strength before jumping back into the fray once again, trying to hold her down long enough for Bull, who was frantically searching in his magic bag, to do something to calm her down.

Pulling out an already loaded syringe, Bull stepped between Tom and the window. "Alright, hold her down. I need to...shit!"

The syringe flew past my head, followed by a backwards-stumbling Bull, who almost took my legs out from beneath me as he crashed into me, his arms pinwheeling wildly for balance.

"Hold her down, damnit! She's ripping all her stitches out!"

"We're trying our best here! Damn woman's stronger than a bear!"

"*Angel!*"

Something about the timbre of her voice struck a chord deep within me and I desperately tried to slip past the tight press of bodies surrounding the bed. "Ice!"

"Angel!"

I saw her hand reach out, trembling, and I tried to grab it, only to be pushed out of the way by Bull, who was wielding another syringe. I tried to slip past him, but he grunted as he thrust his hip out, preventing me from getting near the bed as he shouted orders to the other struggling men. "Turn her over, damnit! I need to get..."

He took a half step backward to avoid a blow and, seeing my chance, I slipped into the space he'd created and threw myself on the bed next to my wildly thrashing lover. "Enough!" I shouted. "Back off! Now!"

Four men looked at me, shock plain on their faces, but, to a man, they obeyed.

Then I turned toward Ice, finally confirming that my supposition was true.

She was awake. Her eyes were wide, grief-stricken, and brimming with tears. "Angel?" she asked in a tone of desolation so unutterably sad that my heart shattered beneath its blackened, lifeless weight.

"I'm here, sweetheart. I'm here."

She reached for me again, pulling her fingers back just before they made contact with my face. "I'm sorry. I'm so, *so* sorry. I tried to save you. I..."

"Ice! You did save me! I'm here! Right here!"

But she didn't hear me. Just kept speaking as if looking at a voiceless ghost. "Please forgive me, Angel. I couldn't..."

It was then that Bull, no doubt taking Ice's sudden calm as the perfect opportunity, reached past me, bared Ice's hip, and plunged his needle into her bruised flesh, depressing the plunger quickly, then removing the needle and stepping back away.

Her eyes flared in anger, then became almost dead as whatever drug he'd used spread through her weakened system. "...couldn't save you...," she mumbled as her eyes finally closed and her head lolled to the side.

I turned to Bull, my own eyes blazing in anger. "Why did you do that?" I demanded, feeling my fists ball tightly with the urge to lash out. "Why?"

"She needed to be sedated, Angel," he said reasonably. "Those stitches need to be tended to."

"You idiot! She thinks I'm dead! And when whatever dope you've shot her full of wears off, how do you think she's gonna react? There's nothing for her now! Nothing!"

His eyes grew huge as the realization struck him. "I'm sorry. I didn't..."

"Of course you didn't! You didn't think! You didn't trust me! You didn't do anything!"

"Angel..." Tom tried to break in, so I turned my anger on him as well.

"She's not a dangerous animal that needs to be tranquilized, Tom. She's a woman who thinks her lover is dead. How would you feel if it were you?"

Unable to hold my gaze, he looked down at the bed, not answering.

I turned to the others. "Well? Any of you?"

"You called fer help, Tyler," Pop finally said. "It ain't exactly like any of us has ever done this before. Maybe we made a mistake, but it was an honest one."

I could feel the anger bleed out of me at his words. I sighed, unclenching my fists. "I know, Pop. I just wish I could have had a little more time with her, that's all. I wish...well, that doesn't matter now." I turned to Bull. "I'm sorry for lashing out on you like that, Bull. I know you were only doing what needed to be done."

He smiled, putting a hand on my shoulder. "Don't worry about it. Next time, I'll trust your instincts, ok?"

"Let's just hope there isn't a next time." I smiled to take the sting out of my words.

He nodded. "Fair enough. How about if you help me undo the bandages and we can take a look at the damage, huh?"

"Sounds good."

❖❖❖❖❖❖❖❖❖

As it turned out, the damage wasn't as severe as it first seemed. Though she'd torn some stitches from the long, deep cut in her belly, the other wounds had just been aggravated and, with a little pressure, they stopped bleeding relatively quickly.

Her fever remained the biggest danger, at times soaring so high that Bull feared seizures from it. We bathed her with cool water to hold it down as best we could until the antibiotics he'd loaded her system with could do their job properly.

When things had calmed down somewhat for the moment, I finally had the presence of mind to realize just who had come to my call for aid. From my position on the bed next to Ice, I looked up at Tom and John, who looked profoundly out of place now that the immediate danger had passed.

"Did you find what you were looking for?" I asked.

John nodded. "Yeah. We found the car. What was left of it."

I sat up straighter, pulling Ice's hand into my lap and clasping it tightly. "Where?"

"'bout thirty miles or so southeast of here, off of one of the logging roads we'd been looking at. Less, as the crow flies, of course. It...went off the road and into a tree. Pretty damn fast, too."

I could feel the blood drain from my face as I grasped Ice's unresponsive hand tighter. "What happened?"

John looked at Tom and Pop before returning his attention back to me. "The driver died instantly. He ...um ...he had a steering-wheel through his chest."

My stomach turned and I swallowed back the bile that threatened to come forth. Without really knowing why, I nodded for him to continue.

John scratched his heavy beard, then sighed. "The guy on the passenger side, near as I can tell, flew through the window and smashed into a tree. He probably died pretty quick, too."

"And...the others?"

"They survived. The accident, anyway."

As I waited for him to continue, John again looked at his brother and Pop. The three men fidgeted, obviously not wanting to say anymore on the subject. "Please?" I asked. "I have to know."

Pop came forward and laid a gentle hand on my shoulder. "Tyler, the men who hurt Morgan are dead. 's best ta leave it go at that."

I wanted to. I probably would have given a king's ransom not to hear what was coming. But, in the end, I just couldn't let it go as Pop asked. I had to know what happened. Ice, I was sure, would never tell me, and the hole that it would leave would, in time I was sure, become much larger with each passing day. "Please tell me. Please."

More furtive glances were exchanged before Tom decided, apparently, to step forward and take the figurative male bovine by its bony head appendages. "It was like...." He raised his hands, palms up, searching for the right words, "like a pack of wolves had had at them or something. It was," he swallowed hard, visibly paling, "bad."

"How bad?" My voice was so soft, I was surprised anyone heard me.

"Bad."

"Maybe wolves *did* come? After, I mean?"

Tom and John shook their heads. "No," John said. "Corpses don't spill that much blood."

"Before, then?" I asked, determined to find a way to make things fit, other than the obvious, which I wasn't prepared to believe. "Maybe she left them for dead, and *then* something came and finished the job?"

Both men shook their heads again. "I'm sorry, Tyler," Tom said, "but that's not what happened."

"How do you know?"

"Because they all had bullet wounds to the head. Two of

them behind the ear. One to the temple. He bore the brunt of the savagery as well, for some reason."

Oh, I knew the reason. I knew it just as well as I knew who it was who'd been killed by a bullet to the temple.

The same man who had put his gun to *my* temple.

"Carmine."

"What?" Tom asked.

"Carmine. He was the one who made Ice drop her gun or he'd kill me."

Bull, who'd been listening quietly, nodded his head. "Add to that the fact that he used to be her friend. He betrayed her. She's never taken kindly to that. Roll all that up in a ball, add in those idiots taking shots at her, and I'm surprised she left enough of them lying around for you to find."

The nausea that was threatening from the start of the conversation finally hit. My stomach cramped hard, and I dove for the side of the bed.

Bull reacted instantly, steadying me and shoving a basin he'd used to clean Ice's wounds under my open mouth. There wasn't really anything in my stomach to expel, but it didn't seem to realize that right away. I gasped and sobbed, trying desperately to catch my breath as the vision of Ice and the men she'd killed played through my mind in an unending stream, causing my stomach to cramp over and over and over again without pause.

When my muscles finally, blessedly, relaxed, I slumped down on the bed, barely feeling the cool rag that Bull used to wipe my face and forehead. "You ok?" he asked, using almost the exact same tone of voice Ice had used in similar situations.

"I'm not sure," I replied as honestly as I knew how.

And, more importantly, would I ever be again?

That Ice had killed those three men wasn't really an issue with me.

While it might very well have been once upon a time, during Ice's capture and my subsequent search for her, I'd come to learn a deep, dark, and not particularly appealing secret about myself.

And that was that if I could have, I would have killed them all without a second's pause for taking her so violently away from me.

No, it wasn't *that* she'd killed.

It was *how* she'd killed.

Noticing Bull was still staring at me, one hand on my shoulder, I pulled myself together and moved away from him a bit, straightening my aching legs.

"What's going on, Angel?" he asked in a gentle tone.

I swallowed hard and manufactured a smile from somewhere. "I...um...I need some air, I think."

"Oh." Frowning slightly, he straightened back up to his full height and looked down at me.

I forced my smile to broaden. "Honestly, Bull, I'm ok. I just...you know...need to get out of here for a couple minutes." To lend credence to my words, I slipped from the bed, standing and stretching. "I'll be right outside. Down by the water. Call me if she wakes up?"

He looked as if he was going to say something, but after a moment, I could see his shoulders sag and he simply nodded in acquiescence. "Ok."

"Great. Thanks."

As I came to the bottom of the stairs, I saw Pop putting the phone back down in its cradle. I looked at him with questioning eyes.

He smiled slightly. "Ruby," he explained. "Corinne's been sprung. Gonna go up and get 'em both 'n bring 'em back home."

The smile, which spread my lips this time, was genuine. I would welcome them both back home with open arms, particularly Corinne, who I sensed just might have some of the answers I was so desperately seeking in my mind. "Thanks, Pop. That's great news."

"Yup." His eyes narrowed as he looked at me. "You sure you're gonna be alright, Tyler? Don't seem none too good to me right now."

I felt myself nodding, my lips moving to form the lie so naturally falling from my tongue. "I'm fine. Really. I just need some fresh air, that's all."

The look he gave me let me know in no uncertain terms that my lie wasn't in the slightest believed. After a moment, though, he shrugged. "Do what ya gotta do, I guess."

I nodded. "Thanks, Pop."

Chapter 16

I found myself on the little, green dock, not really aware of how I'd gotten there, only grateful for its cool, silent, and non-questioning peace.

My head was a jumble of conflicting emotions; my heart, not far behind.

Lowering myself down to the weathered wood of the dock, I trailed my feet in the water, watching the crescent moon play tag with the wavelets stirred up by the freshening breeze as I leaned my back up against one of the posts which anchored the dock to the shore and disappeared beneath the shallow, glistening water.

Ice had spent long winter days trying to teach me the skills needed for meditation. I called upon those skills now, clearing my mind of all intrusive thoughts and concentrating on the air as it entered and left my lungs, never really realizing when I'd fallen asleep between one breath and the next.

I found myself standing on a dirt road deep in the middle of nowhere. For reasons known only in dreams, I was in nothing save a white sheet, which twisted and rippled around my body in response to the wind circling through the grove in which I found myself.

The night was bright with stars which, as I watched, wheeled themselves over my head in a ballroom's stately waltz to music known only to them.

I tried to turn my body, to move, to look around, but I seemed to be rooted to the ground. A ground that was neither warm nor cold, wet nor dry; a ground which simply was.

Looking down at my feet, I saw them hidden, enveloped in a soft white ground-mist which covered the forest floor like something out of a fairy tale.

Though perhaps I should have, I didn't feel any fear. Just a sense of anticipation, knowing my mind had brought me here for a reason, and further knowing I probably wasn't all that far away from finding out just what that reason was.

My reverie was broken by twin spears of bright lights which lanced through the misty forest glen like a white knight on a charging steed. As I continued to watch—having no other choice but to do so, might I add—the lights coalesced into the high beams of an oncoming car. A car that was headed, at a very high rate of speed, down the very road upon which I was currently rooted, unable to move from its onrushing path.

My mouth opened wide in a silent scream as my legs ignored the desperate messages my brain was sending to them.

At the very last second, the car veered sharply left and headed down a small embankment and into the forest proper, where it was halted, suddenly, violently, in a scream of tearing metal and breaking glass, by the massive trunk of a very old, very sturdy tree who hardly shook at all with the tremendous impact.

Then the forest was silent once again.

I looked on in horror, knowing that no one could possibly have survived the carnage of that wreck. Still, I needed to run forward, to be sure, but my cursed feet remained rooted to the ground, refusing even the most forceful commands to move.

Then, to my amazement, one of the rear doors opened, and a blood-spattered figure stumbled out, collapsing on the ground and groaning as he—and I could definitely tell it was a man—cradled his head with both arms while rocking his massive body side to side in pain.

A second man followed the first. This man somehow managed to stay on his feet, though his face was a grisly mask of blood, which literally sheeted down from the gaping cut to his forehead and nose.

Then a third figure emerged, and this was one I recognized easily, immediately though she was battered, bruised, and as bloody as her two predecessors.

"Ice!" I yelled out to her, my heart beating quickly in my chest.

She didn't hear me, though. Didn't even lift her head to look my way as she stepped over the body of the first man, almost colliding with the second as she did so.

As I watched, she looked at the man she'd almost run into, a brief flare of rage lighting her pale eyes. Then it abruptly died out and she pushed past him, heading in an unsteady walk back toward the road where I was standing, her lips moving in a silent litany I would have paid a king's ransom to hear.

It was then that the third man pulled himself from the wreckage, and this also was someone who I immediately recognized, having had an up close and personal interaction with him just days earlier, when his gun was pressed against my temple.

"Carmine," I spat. I could feel my lips twist in revulsion as I watched him casually brush the broken glass from his still pristine suit, as if he hadn't a care in the world.

Smirking slightly, he carefully reached behind his back. When his hand came back into view, it was holding the same gun which had been pushed against my head earlier. With an almost careless grace, he lifted the muzzle and aimed in Ice's direction.

"Ice!" I screamed, jerking my entire body in an attempt to move. "Ice! Get down!"

But of course, she didn't hear me. Just kept walking toward the road, her hand occasionally going to the back of her head where the butt of a pistol had come down and knocked her unconscious, an almost distracted look on her face.

"Ice! Please! Get down!"

Almost as if she'd heard me, she turned, but it was too late.

A pistol shot rang through the forest.

Ice crumpled to her knees, her hands instinctively covering the wound just above her hip.

Lowering his gun, Carmine slowly walked over to Ice while in the background, his two goons managed to shake off their injuries and flank their boss, one to a side, like a pair of bloody bookends.

He moved forward until he stood just before her kneeling figure, his gun still hanging loosely at his side. "Mr. Cavallo wanted you brought to him so he could finish you off himself."

"He doesn't have the balls to finish off dinner," Ice replied, her voice jeering and cold.

Carmine tilted his head—in acknowledgement, I think—before stopping one of his goons from backhanding Ice for her insolence. Then he continued on in his even, quiet tone. "Since that now seems an impossibility, I really have no choice but to end this here."

Reaching out his free hand, he almost gently cupped Ice's chin.

She jerked it away, staring daggers through him, teeth bared in a snarl of pure challenge.

He tilted his head again, then removed his hand. "I'd say I'm sorry, but at this point, I don't think you'd believe me."

"Ya got that right."

"Anything you'd like me to pass on?"

I watched, panic-stricken, as she jerked her head back once again. A second later, a shining glob of spittle sprung from between his eyes.

Once again he prevented his cohorts from exacting revenge, then casually reached up and wiped Ice's gift away, smirking slightly and shaking his head. "Goodbye, Morgan. Despite how it now seems, it was an honor to know you."

Then slowly and deliberately, he raised his gun until the muzzle was just six inches from her forehead.

"No!" I screamed. "Ice!"

Again, my pleas went unanswered.

"This is just a dream," I whispered to myself, tears streaming down my face. "Just a dream. That's all it is."

To prove the point to myself, I pinched the tender flesh of my inner arm as hard as I could.

The vision didn't change.

Reaching down, I jabbed two fingers into the swollen skin of my lacerated knee.

Blinding pain tore through me, enough to wake up the stiffest corpse, and still no release from this nightmare.

Blinking tears of pain and grief from my eyes, I almost missed what happened next.

Almost faster than the eye could see, Ice's fist shot out, scoring a direct hit to Carmine's groin. The gun wavered, then dropped completely as he used both hands to cup himself. His eyes bulged and, almost in slow motion, he fell to his knees, mouth wide in a rictus of noiseless agony.

I found myself cheering loudly as the two remaining goons, in a universal empathy of men everywhere, winced and automatically reached down to protect their own private parts.

Which gave Ice time enough to roll away and come, more or less steadily, to her feet.

"Get her!" Carmine gasped, his face as pale as I'd ever seen a face become.

Gathering the wit they managed to share between them, the two goons began to lumber toward my lover. She grinned, then beckoned them closer. I could tell she was testing the weight of her injured side, trying, I imagined, to tell if it would hold her weight if she needed to lash out with her foot.

They came within range, both throwing wild, overhand rights that she managed to block easily, catching their fists, one to a hand, and propelling them backward several steps.

Unfortunately, the move also served to unbalance her, and

when she put all her weight down on the injured side, her leg buckled and she went down to one knee, teeth clenched tightly against the pain I knew was shooting through her.

"Come on, Ice," I murmured. "Get up, sweetheart. Don't let them beat you."

Forgoing whatever little finesse they managed to possess, the two men settled for using their greater combined body mass to tackle Ice to the ground, pin her there, and begin to rain blows on her unprotected body.

At first, she simply lay beneath the heavy weight, her arms instinctively rising to guard her head.

"Fight, Ice!" I screamed, stooping down and scrabbling around for any rocks which might be big enough to heft. "Fight, damn you!"

There was nothing, however. Beneath the mist, the ground was as smooth and unyielding as a varnished floor.

Having landed a particularly vicious blow to Ice's chest, one of the men rested his beefy weight back against her injured hip, laughing. "Ain't much of a challenge now, is she Tony?"

"Sure ain't," Tony agreed, displaying the IQ of a slug's slime trail.

"Nice tits, though," the first said, leering at Ice's chest through the gaping tear in her shirt.

"Not bad," Tony said, treating himself to a nice long look. "Think I like the blonde's better though. Now there's a rack!" He cupped his hands out in front of himself to illustrate said "rack" as I looked on, grinding my teeth.

"Oh yeah. I'd like a piece a that snatch!" Grinning, he looked down at Ice, threading blunt fingers through her hair and pulling her head up. "How 'bout it, dyke? Wanna watch when I fuck your little girlfriend senseless? Make her scream for me? Bet she'd like a little man-meat shoved up that tasty little cunt of hers, huh? Maybe in her mouth first? Wash the taste of pussy out of it?"

And as I watched, Ice's face, her whole body, seemed to change before my eyes. My racing mind likened the change to some werewolf movie I'd seen when I was younger—Michael Landon was in it, I think.

Her eyes, normally the palest of blues, darkened until they were almost black. Her face flushed, suffused with rage, and the tendons in her jaw and neck stood out in bas-relief. I could almost feel the dark energy radiating from her body as her muscles quivered and jumped, bunching up like a predator cat about to spring.

With one single thrust of her hips, she managed to unseat

the man atop her, sending him flying several feet up and back, to land on top of the still gasping Carmine.

Then she rolled, and as she did so, shot both hands out and grabbed Tony by his jacket, throwing him to the ground and pinning him beneath the weight of her own body. Sitting up, she reached down and grabbed his head and began bashing it down on the ground, over and over and over again without pause, guttural snarls coming from deep within her chest.

Even when it was obvious that Tony was well past the point of resisting, Ice continued to pound his head into the ground, her hands covered in his blood, her face and the remains of her shirt spotted with it.

The other two helped each other off the ground and plodded, limping, to their cohort's aid. Hearing them, Ice stood and whirled, unleashing her mindless fury on them both in a way I'd never seen before—and prayed mightily that I'd never see again.

I tried to remember that this was all a dream; likely my own mind's attempt to come up with a scenario for what had really happened in lieu of ever hearing it from Ice.

I tried to scream, to tell her and my mind to stop, but my voice was a tiny, insignificant thing, lost amidst the sounds of rage and pain which filled the night air to overflowing.

I tried to put my hands over my ears to block out the sounds, but they came through clearly.

I tried to close my eyes to the sights, but it seemed as if my eyelids were made of window glass, dooming me to stand silently by and watch as my mind turned the woman I loved into an animal.

She beat them bloody; beat them till they fell. And when they fell, she picked them up and beat them again. And again.

And again.

Soon, even Ice's reserves were spent, and the fight began to take on the look of a ballet attempted underwater.

A straight-from-the-shoulder right to the goon's face and he went down, only the whites of his eyes showing. When Ice took a second to catch her breath, bending over at the waist and putting her bloody hands on her knees, Carmine stumbled away and reached down for the gun he'd dropped when Ice had punched him earlier.

Turning, he lifted his arm slowly, as if the gun were made of the heaviest iron plating, the muzzle shaking wildly as he pointed it in Ice's direction.

Seeing him, Ice straightened and stared, absolutely no fear in the dark of her eyes. "Put it down, Carmine. It's over."

"Yes, it is," he said, his voice high and wavering. "For

you."

"Even if you kill me, Cavallo will see to it you're a dead man as soon as you set foot back in the states."

Carmine shrugged. "So, I won't go back then."

"Then why kill me?" Ice asked reasonably, using the opportunity to take a couple of steps closer to him when she noticed, as did I, the gun barrel dip just a touch.

"Because I gave my word."

"Promises can be broken."

"Not this one." The gun became steadier. "Goodbye, Morgan."

My scream and the gun's firing sounded simultaneously.

Blood sprayed from a newly bloomed hole in Ice's thigh.

But this time, she didn't go down.

Like a robot impervious to pain, she continued to step toward him as his eyes widened and a very real fear came into them. He lifted the gun again, but the only sound heard was the impotent click of the trigger.

Ice grinned. A terrible, horrible smile. "Ya should have taken my offer, Carmine."

One step closer. Two. Three.

More clicks sounded as Carmine continued to fire a gun which was obviously empty or jammed. In pure panic, he hefted the weapon again and, with the last of his strength, threw it at Ice, who batted it out of the way with an unconcerned, unhurried swipe of her hand while continuing her slow, deliberate advance.

With a gibbering moan, Carmine dodged left and hobbled as fast as he could to Tony, reaching down and grabbing the gun from the holster at the man's back.

Ice was on him before he could even think to turn around, her hand grabbing his wrist and wrenching the gun away.

Pulling an arm tight around Carmine's neck, she lowered the gun and gave a coup de grace behind the left ear of Tony, who was face down and moaning in agony.

Then she dragged Carmine with her as she moved over to the second thug, killing him in the same way as he struggled to get back to his feet again.

She dragged Carmine to the center of the clearing, then forced him to his knees as she followed behind.

She put the gun to his temple.

"Anything you'd like me to pass on?" Her voice was dark with intentional irony.

"Please. Don't kill me."

"Too late." Her finger tightened on the trigger. "Goodbye, Carmine. Tell the devil I'll see him soon, huh?"

"Ice. Noooo," I moaned.

But of course, she couldn't hear me.

A split second later and the deed was done.

Without any emotion whatsoever, she pushed his already toppling body over, then rose back up to her feet, her body swaying as the gun hung limply from one bloody hand.

After she had gathered what remained of her strength, she turned back toward the road and looked up. For a split second, I thought she saw me.

Her eyes widened.

Then she stumbled and almost went down.

Gritting her teeth, she began once again to move in my direction, as if pulled to my presence like a magnet to iron.

I held out my arms to her, calling her to me even as, within the very depths of my soul, I felt, for the first time, fear of this woman who was my lover.

She crossed the distance between us in a numb, shuffling gait, blood pouring from her many wounds, head down, gun swinging without purpose by her side.

And then, as I'm sure can happen only in dreams, she walked right through me as if I wasn't there at all.

And what I felt...God...what I felt as she passed through my soul...

Death.

A cold, empty void of the deepest rotting black.

And amidst the horrid darkness, the tiniest of guttering flames, one soft breath away from dying.

A flame that bore my image.

And seeing it, I screamed.

And screamed.

And screamed.

A hand came down on my shoulder, and in my terror, it felt cold and skeletal. I turned my head, half expecting to see Carmine's rotting corpse beckoning me to follow. Or—and God help me on this—an Ice who decided that as a witness to her depravity, I was just too much of a liability to let live.

Instead, it was Corinne's concerned, battered face which greeted me, an eon's worth of questions in her eyes.

"C-Corinne?"

"In the flesh, such as it is." She cocked her head, looking at me over the tops of her glasses. "That was quite a nightmare you seemed to be having."

"Nightmare?"

Her eyes narrowed. "Are you alright, Angel?"

Reaching out a trembling hand, I brushed the tips of my fingers against her arm. It was warm and solid and very much real.

That was all it took.

Launching myself forward, I threw myself into her arms, burrowing into the living warmth of her, letting it permeate the cold death which surrounded me like a slaughterhouse stench, too empty even for the relief of tears.

After a moment, she wrapped her arms around me and I felt a gentle hand stroke my hair as whispered words came softly to my ears.

A short while later, she carefully, gently disentangled herself and held me at arm's length, looking at me very intently. "Now, would you like to tell me what's going on and why you're down here having nightmares and not where I'd expect you to be?"

After several hesitant almost-starts, I finally gathered what remained of my wits and told her about my dream; everything up until the last, horrible, scene. That was something, I thought, I would never be able to tell anyone as long as I lived.

"Sounds rather plausible," Corinne remarked when I was done, her tone conveying no more surprise than if I had just told her I'd gone for a walk. "Is there something more?"

Confused, I stared at her. Where was the anger? Where was the outrage that my mind should conjure up such a horrifying image of the woman I professed to love?

After a moment, her expression changed. Her face became hard and her eyes narrowed. "Please tell me there's something more, Angel."

I looked at her, unable to say anything, unable to understand where this was going.

She sighed. "Angel, Ice was forced to watch you held at gunpoint, knocked unconscious, and dragged from her home to be executed. Did you just expect her to allow that to happen?"

"No. No! I just..."

"Just what, Angel?" Her dark eyes lit with a terrible pity and I felt myself becoming very defensive.

"Stop looking at me like that, Corinne."

"Like what?" she asked, her smile mocking.

"Like I'm some damn child who just got told Santa Claus doesn't exist."

"Perhaps when you stop acting that way."

"Corinne!"

"How many times has Ice told you she's a murderer, Angel?"

"What? I don't..."

"How many times?"

I could feel myself heating up as I looked at her, fists clenching and unclenching repeatedly. "I don't know."

"Once? More than once? Surely you'd remember something like that, Angel."

My teeth ground against one another. "Corinne..."

"It's a simple question, Angel. How many?"

"I don't know. A few," I allowed.

Smiling, she nodded. "And how did you respond? Did you tell her you understood? Did you run away screaming? What?"

"You know what I said, Corinne." I could hear my heart pumping in my ears.

"I don't know, Angel. But I can imagine. You told her you understood, didn't you?"

"I don't..." She looked at me. "Yes! Yes, alright? I told her I understood!"

She nodded, apparently satisfied. "But you didn't, did you?" she began, her voice soft with a compassion which burned rather than healed. "You didn't understand her, though you said you did. Didn't understand what it was like to have a heart so cold and dark that taking another person's life meant little more than taking a trip to the market. Didn't understand that when death means nothing, life means even less."

"Enough, Corinne!" I shouted, my words echoing over the flat expanse of the lake and setting a small flock of birds to startled flight. "Enough."

She smiled again. "Is it? I don't think so, Angel. In fact, I think it's as far from being enough as it's possible to get." Her expression gentled somewhat. "Ice is a killer, Angel. It may not be all she is, but it certainly makes up a great part of who she is. It shapes her thoughts, molds her actions. It's instinctive, like breathing." Her soft voice trailed off for a moment as she closed her eyes. When they reopened, they were full of a horrible knowing that I wanted to turn my face from, yet couldn't.

"Every day of her life, Angel, *every day*, she has to make the conscious choice to live another day without violence. Another day struggling against her own instincts. Another day of trying desperately to hold on to the thinnest and most frayed of cords tying her to this path she's chosen. And do you know why she does it, Angel?"

I looked at her, suddenly lost, suddenly unsure of the one thing in my life which had seemed bedrock. Ice's convictions. "Because she knows it's the right thing to do?" I hazarded.

The smile she gave me, sad and filled with gentle disappointment, wrenched at my heart. "No, Angel. Although it may be the 'right' thing to do, that's not why she does these things."

"Then why?"

Reaching out, she took my hand and clasped it tightly in her own. "She does these things because one day, several years ago, she met someone who, without even trying, reached inside her and grabbed hold of a heart she couldn't remember having. A person who, against all odds, captured her effortlessly and holds her close to this very day. And a person in whose eyes she can never allow herself to seem any less than perfect." She smiled again. "She does these things for *you*, Angel. Because she loves you. And because you've managed to do something no one else has ever done."

"What's that?" I asked, very aware of the hoarseness of my voice.

"You've made her see that she's worthy of being loved. It's what spurs her on, what dictates her actions now. It weighs heavy on every decision she makes, because no matter what, *no matter what*, she never wants to ever be seen as unworthy in your eyes."

Tears etched silent streams down the hills and valleys of my cheeks and jaw. Seeing them, Corinne grasped my hand more tightly, squeezing in comfort and, perhaps, understanding. "That's a heavy burden to place on anyone, Angel. I know that. Ice does as well. But when you told her, not once but many times, that you understood and accepted who and what she was, she felt it was a burden you both could share."

With her free hand, she gently brushed away my tears. "She's opened her heart and soul to you, Angel. The darkness *and* the light. That's a gift very few people in this world ever receive. A gift beyond price. And when she makes decisions that go against her very nature, like allowing Cavallo to live, all the while knowing instinctually that she'll pay for that decision later, she does so because she wants to be that person you see when you look at her every day."

A sob came up, unbidden from my throat, and I covered my mouth against its utterance. "She told me that very thing once," I gasped, only now understanding the true import behind the words she'd spoken. "That all she wanted to be was the person I saw when I looked at her."

Corinne nodded, her face kind, but grave. "She believes in you, Angel. She believes that you love her for who she is as well as the person she has the potential to be. But remember this. Her darkness will always be there. Just because she doesn't act on it doesn't mean it's gone, no matter how much either of you wish that were so. It's not a stain that can be washed away or a sin that can be miraculously forgiven like some penitent's confession to a black-robed Priest. It's a part of her as deep as her love for you. Neither can be erased."

Her gaze sharpened and I felt as if she were looking into the depths of my soul. "The decision is yours, Angel. Either you accept her for all that she is, accept that, given the life you two share, there will be times when she'll be forced to act on instinct because she's allowed herself to go against those instincts in the past and she must now pay restitution, or..."

I could feel the breath catch in my throat. "Or what?"

"Walk away, Angel. Quickly and far. Sever your ties with her and never look back. Bull tells me that she may think you're dead. If you can't be what she needs you to be, the one person in the world who loves her unconditionally, then please, for her sake, let her mourn your passing and be done with it. Don't hurt her more by allowing her to see the condemnation of her nature in your eyes."

After a long moment, she released my hand and stood up. "Think about what I've said, Angel. I'll be upstairs with Ice."

I stood as well. "I'm coming with you."

A touch on my arm was all it took to stop me in my tracks. "Have you even heard a word I've said, Angel?"

"Yes, Corinne. But I need to see her. To be with her. I need..."

She shook her head slowly, sadly. "No, Angel. This is something you're going to have to do without her. Ice can't help you with this."

"But..."

"No, Angel," she said firmly. Her eyes softened slightly. "Angel, I love you with all my heart. .You know that. But I love Ice just as deeply. And I won't see her hurt, by you or anyone else. So please. Stay here and think on what we talked about. Listen to your heart, Angel. It will tell you what you have to do."

I could feel my shoulders slump in defeat. Almost against my will, I nodded my acceptance of her request. A request that I well knew, knowing Corinne as I did, was more of a command than the simple asking of a favor.

She smiled slightly and, with a nod of her head, turned and stepped off the dock. I watched as she made her careful way back up to the cabin, my thoughts in utter turmoil.

When she disappeared around the corner of the house, I turned back and faced the dark water, not really seeing it for the tears blurring my vision.

The tears soon passed and I was left feeling weary, empty,

and very confused. I wanted so desperately to go to Ice. To see her, to hold her, to stroke her hair, feeling that somehow all the answers to my questions would rest with that simple, profound connection between us. A connection I could feel even with so much distance between us. Distance that I, in my fear, had caused.

I only thanked God, in all His mercy, that Ice wasn't awake to see it.

I also knew that Corinne was right. Ice couldn't help me with this. No one could, save for myself.

I wrapped my arms around myself as a chill wind blew off the lake, a harbinger of a winter not far away, even now, in the midst of a glorious summer.

As I looked over the lake as the wind swayed the trees, I forced myself to examine the hardest of Corinne's questions to me. Did I love Ice for herself? For the woman she truly was? Or did I, instead, love the woman I wanted her to be, an image I constructed in my mind; a white knight on a charging steed, with a pure heart and an untainted soul.

I snorted softly. Perhaps I'd gone a bit too far with the "Knight Errant" analogy. Ice had never been, even in the first moments of my knowing her, what anyone would consider pure of heart and soul.

But then again, who among us was?

Certainly not me.

So the question remained. Who *did* I love?

A real, flesh and blood human being? Or an image superimposed over that person to make her more palatable to my sensibilities, such as they were?

It would be so damned easy just to chuck it all and go with what my heart was telling me, which was that I loved Ice with everything in me, that she held my heart in the palm of her hand, that I trusted her in a way I'd never trusted anyone else in my life and that just the thought of not having her in my life made my guts twist inside.

But I also knew that to do that would be to do a great disservice to us both.

The dream terrified me more than I was willing to admit to anyone but myself. And until I figured out why, until I came up with an explanation that satisfied my need to know, I'd be no good to either of us.

And Ice only deserved the best from me.

How I went about giving that to her was another question entirely.

I heard myself groan as I once again lowered my stiffened

body on the chilled and worn wood of the dock. So many thoughts, feelings, emotions, and images ran through my mind that it was difficult to know where to start. Or, even, *how* to start.

"The best place to begin is often at the beginning," my mother was fond of telling me.

I shrugged to myself. Seemed as good a place as any.

A name came to my mind, and I went with it.

Cavallo.

The bastard who'd started it all. The bastard who'd almost ended it all.

From what I could remember of his history told to me in bits and pieces by Corinne, Cavallo was what was called a "mole." He'd risen up through the ranks of the Family Ice was attached to, the Briacci crime family, all the while snuggled deep within the back pocket of Briacci's largest rival. Hoping to plant the seeds of mistrust, he'd framed Ice, sending her out to kill an innocent man.

But, and this I'd almost forgotten in my terror over the nightmare I'd had, she'd refused to kill him.

"She refused," I whispered aloud, making it real, making it *there.*

Even knowing that such a refusal could mean her own death, she'd gone against orders anyway.

"Many of us have lines we draw in the sand and this was one of my lines. I never killed innocents and I never killed witnesses, no matter who they were testifying against."

I remembered those words as if she'd told them to me only this afternoon instead of five full years ago. They suddenly took on new meaning as the first part of my puzzle slipped silently into place.

When the man was killed anyway, Ice took the rap for it, to use prison slang for a moment, even going so far as to refuse the outstanding legal services of Donita, who very much cared for her and very much wanted to help.

And all because the Ice I met in the Bog that first time was a woman who'd acknowledged the light in her soul and though she wasn't guilty of the crime for which she'd been convicted, she was determined to pay restitution for the ones she *hadn't* been convicted of, even if it meant, as it seemed at the time, giving up her freedom as payment for the rest of her life.

Could I have done the same?

Well, in a way, I had. I was no more guilty of murdering my husband than Ice was of murdering that innocent man, but I, too, was willing to pay restitution because, whether it was murder or not, I *had* killed him.

So, in that way at least, Ice and I were very much the same.

Another piece added itself to the board.

My mind returned to Cavallo. Not satisfied with simply framing Ice, he wanted to twist the knife in any way he could, while still rising within the Family, intending, one day, to start a coup and take it over entirely. He'd set up Briacci's wife, a woman who'd been almost a second mother to Ice, had her thrown in jail, then had her murder staged for an audience of one.

My lover.

And though she was devastated over the death of a person she'd loved, and though I'm sure she had any one of a hundred chances to exact her own form of permanent justice on the man, she remained in jail, determined to pay for her crimes.

Another piece of the puzzle snapped into place for me as I began to view the events of five years of my life in an entirely new light, wondering, with a bit of shame, why I hadn't bothered doing so before.

Twisting the knife still further in her heart, Cavallo made a deal with the warden, condemning Ice to servitude by doing his bidding, stripping down cars which he then resold at a healthy profit. And when she'd finally had enough and refused to roll over any more, Cavallo, through his mouthpiece, Morrison, threatened harm to the one thing that was most dear to her in all the world.

Me.

Believe me when I tell you that I don't take that lightly, nor is it an enormous massage to my healthy ego to state such a thing so baldly. It is simply the truth as I knew it then and as I know it now.

Would a conscienceless killer have taken that threat lying down? Or would she have instead ripped the warden to shreds and caught the first hostage out of town on a mission to personally deliver Cavallo his very own death warrant?

Ice answered my question by her own actions.

She took it. She accepted the knife to her gut, not quietly no, but accepted just the same, in order to keep me safe, healthy, and whole.

And *still* it wasn't enough for Cavallo.

In a scene that still haunts my dreams and will continue to do so, I suspect, until I finally shuffle off this mortal coil, he came face to face with her—with a prison fence and a dozen fully armed guards between them, courageous man that he was—taunted her, and when she didn't rise to the bait to his liking, shot her in the back.

Quite against my will, the scene replayed itself in all its Technicolor glory.

With one last squeeze and a scream from Cavallo, Ice released her grip and held up her empty hands, grinning. Taking two careful, deliberate steps back from the fence, she winked at the mobster, then turned.

Our gazes locked as she completed her turn and the world began to spin in slow motion. From the corner of my eye, I could see Cavallo reach beneath his coat with his good, right hand.

"Ice!" I launched myself at her, aiming for her legs. "Nooooo!"

Her eyes widened in question.

The sound of a gun firing, oddly flat in the turbulent air.

The question turned to shock as a bloom of red stained the small, burned hole that suddenly appeared in the upper left chest of her jumpsuit. She looked down, then back at me.

Then her eyes went as empty as they were in my dream and she crumpled to the ground silently.

I landed on top of her, screaming.

I pulled myself away quickly, slapping at my tears as I turned her over onto her back. "Oh God, no. Ice, no. Please. Oh God."

Blood pumped out of the exit wound in slow, sluggish bursts. But that meant that she was still alive. Pressing one hand over the hole in her chest, I used my free one to stroke the hair back from her face. "Oh God, please wake up, Ice. Please don't die on me. Please. Don't do this to me. Please. Oh God. Oh God."

I was panicking, and I knew it. But I couldn't seem to stop. Blood welled up in the spaces between my fingers, painting me with its heated vibrancy. "Don't you die on me, Morgan Steele. Don't you dare die on me!"

The sound of running footsteps caused me to look up. The pale, scared faces of Sonny, Pony, and Critter stared down at me.

"Oh fuck!" Pony grunted, squatting beside me and pushing her own hand down on top of mine in an attempt to stem the bleeding.

"Get an ambulance!" I screamed, not even feeling the pressure of Pony's hand against my own. "Now!"

Nodding abruptly, Sonny turned and sped away, running back toward the prison in a furious burst. The shocked crowd parted easily to allow her passage.

"Are they gone?" I asked Pony, my rearward view blocked by her muscled body.

"Who?" Pony asked distractedly, her face grim as she increased the pressure on my hand.

"The warden and...the shooter."

My friend looked over her shoulder, still blocking my view of the fence and the area beyond it. "A car's peelin' rubber outta the parking lot," she grunted, returning her full attention to her task of slowing the bleeding pumping out of my lover with every beat of her heart.

"Thank God."

"What are you thankin' God for? That might be Ice's killer getting away!"

"She won't die. I know it. She can't."

"I wish I had your faith, Angel."

"You don't need it. I have faith enough for all of us."

Blinking, I wiped the tears from my face as my mind finally released its hold and allowed me to come back to the present.

"I kept the faith, Ice," I whispered. "And you didn't let me down."

And still, even after being shot in the back like a rabid animal, still she didn't go after him.

No, it wasn't until the final straw had been placed. A straw which had Morrison pay her a visit in the hospital and warn her that if anyone ever found out the identity of the person who'd shot her, my life would have been made a living hell, and any chance I'd ever see freedom again would have been flushed, like so much raw sewage, right down the proverbial toilet and, likely, my soul right along with it.

"I knew right then that I could never go back. I needed to...take care of things so that his threat would never become a reality."

It was only after that last straw had finally been laid upon a back overburdened did she finally lash out, not to protect herself, but to protect me.

Because she loved me.

And when she finally had the chance to take out all the pain, hurt, anguish, and rage upon the very man who'd caused her this grief, what did she do?

I closed my eyes, remembering.

"I wanted to kill him so badly I could taste it. My finger was on the trigger—just a hair's worth of pressure and it would have gone off, ending everything."

She tilted her head up toward the ceiling, her jaw working as she dragged her hands through her hair. "I couldn't do it," she whispered, harshly. "I wanted to, God, so badly. I wanted to end his miserable, stinking little life." She sighed, shaking her head. "But I couldn't."

Why? I could remember asking her.

"As I was standing there, watching him sleep, I thought about you." And here, her eyes came to rest, for the first time, on my face. She smiled slightly. "About that time when I had Cassandra's life in my hands. I remembered you telling me not to give up on my dreams, how she wasn't worth it. And I realized that if I went back to that person I used to be, the one who killed to get rid of my problems, that's exactly what I would have done." Tears sparkled in her eyes. "My dreams might not be much, but they were all I had. And I couldn't give them up. Not for him. Not for anyone."

"Oh, Ice," I whispered, much as I did then.

So many things made so much more sense to me now, when looked at through the distance of time. Ice's unswerving dedication to the changes she'd begun to make in her own life long before we ever fell in love. Her refusal to be baited into doing something that was becoming wrong for her until she was placed in a position where choices were non-existent.

I was finally beginning to see two very different sides to the part of Ice who was a killer. One killed in the heat of passion, to protect herself or those she loved. The other, diametrically opposed to the first, killed with the cool, remote disinterest of an assassin, which she had been for a very long time.

The first was an inherent part of her nature, a nature that had been shaped by the life she'd been forced to live when an innocent young ten-year-old woke up one morning to find everything she loved gone.

The second, I was beginning to see, was quite unnatural to her, though since she'd developed somewhat of a skill for it, and she used it as a tool much as the tools she used to fix cars.

Ice is, if nothing else, a woman of incredible passions. She has an immense, almost bottomless capacity for love. And an equally immense capacity for rage. Where love had always been reined in like a skittish and vulnerable colt, rage had been allowed to flourish.

And then, for some reason known only to her, Ice had decided to take a chance on revealing her heart and allowing love to sublimate the rage in her soul.

That decision came with a very large price, however. It was a price she was now paying. And it was a price that I, in my selfishness, never thought existed.

Until now.

Like Paul on his Damascus road, the scales finally fell from my eyes and I truly saw Ice's action of leaving Cavallo alive for what it really was.

A blind leap off a towering cliff with trust the only net she possessed.

Trust in herself, in her heart, that she was making the right decision. Trust in a justice system that had failed miserably to finally do the right thing. Trust in a merciful god or a kind fate to see her act of restitution and be pleased.

While a wise man once said, I think, that two out of three isn't bad, I'm sure he'd agree that one out of three is nothing short of abysmal.

Like a row of dominoes or a house of cards tipped over by a child's careless hand, that one merciful act set in motion a series of unstoppable events which led us to this place, where everything that could have gone wrong did and the proud, sure woman who'd made that leap now lay broken and bleeding in restitution for one act of kindness which turned against her with a vengeance.

I thought back to the night she'd received the phone call telling her that Cavallo had been set free and was after his pound of flesh. She'd wanted to keep the information to herself, but I'd poked and prodded, cajoled and whined until she opened up and laid her worries bare before me.

And what had I given her as payment?

Ridicule. Sarcasm. Moral high-handedness. I'd even had the gall to call her a coward. Accused her of using Cavallo as an excuse to run away from people who loved her. Threatened to attach myself like an unwanted parasite to her every thought, her every move.

When had I stopped trusting her instincts?

When had I started thinking that mine were somehow better?

I could feel my face flush hot with shame. The tender flesh of my palms protested as my nails dug themselves a new home beneath the skin.

All she'd ever wanted to do was to help in creating a safe space for me. A place where I would be happy, where I would be safe, where I would be loved, and where I would never want for a single thing. A natural leader, she'd sublimated that and instead walked by my side, lending her aid, her warmth, her strength, and her love to make sure that my dream was fulfilled to the best of her considerable abilities and far beyond my wildest hopes.

And what had I done with that freedom she'd given me? Taken it and run with it, effectively trapping her, placing her with my words into a cage whose bars were formed and shaped by the bond of love we shared.

A gilded cage, perhaps, but more of a prison, in some ways, than the Bog ever was.

"She's an adult," I told myself. "More than capable of making her own decisions. Don't take this away from her, too, believing that you somehow trapped her against her will. That didn't happen, and you know it."

"Maybe," I answered. "But did you ask? Did you even take a second to ask her if this was what she wanted instead of projecting your dreams and your needs onto her and calling it good?"

Did I?

I thought back to the conversation we'd had in that tiny hotel room Ice had taken me to right after our reunion. I remembered the musty smell of the heater as the air it feebly expelled ruffled the heavy curtains shielding the window from prying eyes. I remembered the stiff, shiny texture of the bedspread. Most of all, I remembered the expression on my lover's face, the look in her eyes, the tone of her voice.

"Damn it, Angel! If you stay with me, you'll only be putting yourself into yet another prison! Can't you see that?"

Yes, she was angry. But this time ...this time, I wasn't afraid.

"Ice, the only prison I'd be going back to is the one you'd put me in by refusing to let me make my own decisions over what I want my life to be. There wouldn't be any bars except for the ones around my heart. That's a place I don't ever want to go to. It would be a thousand times worse than the Bog could ever be." I grasped her hand and held it tightly, bringing our joined hands upward so she could plainly see them. "My life is with you, Morgan Steele. It has been since the first day I saw you. That won't ever change, whether you let me stay with you or not."

For the first time since I'd known her, Ice looked frightened. It wasn't a panic fright, to be sure, but she was scared. "I...can't..."

I put my fingers over her lips. "Maybe not," I whispered. "But I can."

And so I did.

And in so doing, I effectively, efficiently turned the tables on her. Cleaving myself to her despite her very valid and heartfelt objections, I took the decision out of her hands and bringing it into my own.

She tried to warn me—God, how many times?—that it would one day come to this.

And when it did, I gave her everything but what she needed the most.

My support.

She had done what she had done. Her actions, rather than stemming from within the murky depths of a blackened heart, were, quite simply, the only things she *could* do. No exceptions, no excuses.

She'd been pushed into a corner and had come out fighting.

If it had been me, I would have died in that clearing. So would anyone else I've ever known.

She lived.

And in the end, after the votes were cast and the results tallied, that was all that really mattered.

She lived.

And, just like that, all my doubts, my worries, my insecurities crumbled to dust and blew away. My shame still lingered and it would be something I would deal with for a very long time to come.

Right then, though, it didn't matter.

What mattered was that the woman I loved with all my soul needed me, perhaps more than she'd ever needed anyone before.

And come hell, high water, or a certain elderly librarian with an affinity for poisons, pokers and teakettles, I would try my damnedest to be for Ice what she was for me.

Everything.

A woman on a mission, I rose to my feet, barely conscious of the stiffness of my muscles and the throbbing of my leg. With determined steps, I walked off the dock, up the hill and into the house, ignoring the questioning glances thrown my way by the men and women who'd come to lend their support to a friend hurt and in need.

My face set in a stony mask borrowed temporarily from Ice, I ascended the stairs and entered the battlefield, giving Corinne a look that said, in no uncertain terms, that if she wanted war, she'd get it. I wouldn't back off until I'd won.

She read it well in those first silent seconds, her own eyes widening slightly before she relaxed back against the chair she'd pulled up beside the bed. She gave me a little smile of acknowledgement, tilting her head slightly in the direction of Ice, who was still in a deep sleep.

"Did she wake up at all?" I asked, fighting to keep the flush from coloring my face yet again.

"No. She's been resting quietly."

I nodded. Then I consciously softened my gaze. "I love her, Corinne. All of her. You can believe me or not, that's up to you. But I do love her, and I won't ever give her up." I swallowed, hard. "Unless she asks me to."

"And if she does?"

I took in a deep breath, let it out, and spoke the words written on my heart. "If she does, I'll let her go. Without question."

After a moment, Corinne nodded. Then she grinned crookedly. "Was there ever any doubt?"

"No. Questions, yes. Fears, yes. Doubt? No."

Her eyes twinkled. "Didn't think so."

I could feel my own eyes widen. "You didn't think.... Then why...?"

"Because you needed to sit down and examine things for yourself, Angel. Part of you was living in a dreamland for a very long time. And unless you gave yourself time to discover the reality of your true feelings, things would have continued to snowball until we were all buried in it. Ice doesn't deserve that. And neither do you." She laughed softly. "Ya done good, Angel."

I couldn't help but laugh in relief. "Remind me to hurt you later."

"Oooooh. Promise?"

Resisting the urge to smack her silly, I instead crawled up on the bed and curled up tight against the one person in the world who held my heart in the palm of her hand, and fell immediately into a deep and dreamless sleep, not noticing when her arm wrapped itself around my shoulders in an unconscious gesture of acceptance and love.

Chapter 17

When consciousness once again claimed me for its own, Bull's concerned face was the first thing I saw.

As his expression filtered its way through my slowly awakening mind, I sat bolt upright, grabbing his arm. "Is something wrong? What happened? Is Ice alright?" I demanded, too afraid to turn and view the object of my frantic questioning myself until I had a better idea about what I might find.

"She's fine," Bull replied quickly, making calming gestures with his hands, much as someone might who was trying to calm a frightened animal or child. "Just a little restless." Then he smiled, and I relaxed. "She woke up briefly, saw you, smiled, and fell right back to sleep. Didn't even have to give her a shot." Chuckling, he affectionately cuffed my arm. "Wonder if she'd mind if I stole you away for hunting trips. You seem to work miracles and it'd save me a mint in narcotics."

I couldn't help but grin at him. "Me? Alone with a bunch of sweaty men in an unheated cabin watching you pick ammunition out of someone's behind by candlelight? No thanks. Think I'll pass on that one, charming as the offer is."

Turning my back on his mock pout, I finally gathered the courage to look at my lover. Her face looked peaceful, smooth in a way it never did, even when she was sleeping. Her skin showed neither the high color of fever nor the waxen pallor I'd seen just prior to falling asleep. Reaching over, I laid a hand on her brow and found it cool and dry. "Her fever broke!"

"Yes," Bull replied, "a couple hours ago."

"That's good, right?" I asked, not taking my eyes off her.

"Well, we're not out of the woods yet, but yes, it's a good sign."

"It's a great sign," I replied, bending over and placing a kiss on her cheek. "She's tough."

"I won't argue with you there, Angel. She's about the toughest person I've ever known, and I've been around some real winners, lemme tell you."

I yawned and stretched, resisting the urge just to snuggled back down next to the woman I'd been away from for far too long. Looking at the clock, I realized that twelve hours had passed since I'd fallen asleep.

Bull must have read the question on my face, because he grinned in response. "You needed it," he said simply. Then he chuckled. "Besides, even if you were awake, there's not much you could have done anyway. Ice didn't seem very inclined to let you go for awhile there."

I turned to him. "What do you mean?"

"Just what I said. She was holding on to you like you were her Teddy Bear." He blushed. "Not that I was implying that Ice ever *owned* a teddy bear, mind you... She...uh... Aww crap."

I laughed. "I won't tell anyone if you don't."

He nodded, relieved. "Deal."

I heard the downstairs door open, followed by the sound of male voices speaking quietly as the men they were attached to entered the cabin. Bull glanced over the railing, then back at me, both eyebrows raised in silent question. "Sure. Have 'em come up."

He gestured, and I heard the men ascend the stairs, coming into the room and revealing themselves as Tom and John. Both were muddy and looked tired, but they also seemed very much pleased with themselves, sporting as they did identical smug grins.

"What have you two been up to?"

"Oh, a little of this, a little of that," Tom replied, bouncing on his toes like a young boy with a big secret—or a small bladder.

"Care to be a bit more specific?"

"We were busy getting rid of the evidence," John replied, elbowing his brother in the belly.

Evidence. My mind replayed the scene of my dream; the crumpled car, the savaged bodies, the guns...

"The gun! It's got Ice's fingerprints all over it!"

"Not to worry, Tyler," Tom replied. "We took care of that, too."

"How?"

The two men looked at one another.

"Just tell me, guys. Please?"

"Tell her."

Three sets of eyes widened and I turned to see my lover, very much awake and looking back at me.

"Ice?"

She smiled slightly, though her lips were dry and cracked and I could tell the effort pained her. "Hey." She reached up with her free arm and gently brushed the bangs from my head. "You don't look so good," she observed, her voice hoarse from disuse and the most beautiful sound that I believe I've ever heard, bar none.

Taking her hand gently, I kissed her knuckles, then cupped it against my cheek. "Maybe not, but I feel wonderful. Now. How about you, sweetheart?"

Her eyes closed for a moment as she appeared to take inventory. Then they reopened, warming me with the love in her gaze. "Not bad."

"Said the road pizza to the eighteen-wheeler," Bull joked, glass of water in hand.

No one in the room was more surprised than I when Ice allowed me to help her up to a half seated position against some pillows Tom shoved against the backboard. Of course, helping her to drink was out of the question. Accepting the water, she gingerly sipped through bruised and swollen lips until the glass was empty. "Thanks."

Handing back the glass, she then reclaimed my hand and urged me to sit beside her, resting up against the headboard. I complied with alacrity, grinning so broadly I was sure my face would fracture.

After I was settled comfortably, she turned her stare back to Tom and John, one eyebrow raised.

Both looked decidedly uncomfortable, but finally Tom stepped figuratively forward. "We ...um ...were wondering how to go about getting rid of the evidence. At first we figured we'd just stuff the bodies back in the car and set fire to the whole thing, but Pop said that we might just wind up setting the whole damn forest on fire and drawing more attention than we wanted to the whole thing."

Beside me, I could feel Ice nod her approval.

"So," John picked up the tale, "we just went with what we had and decided to make it look like a car accident/murder/suicide."

Ice snorted.

"Wanna explain that one?" I asked, perplexed.

"Well, all the pieces were there. The car accident was obvious. As was the scene of the fight. So, all we had to do is take the gun Ice had, wipe her fingerprints, put it in the guy's hand who had that shot to the temple and presto! Car slams into a tree, guy gets out of the car, beats the crap outta the other guys, shoots 'em in the head, then ends his own life with a bullet to the temple."

"We even wiped Morgan's trail away," Tom added, grinning proudly. I swore to myself that if the man had been born with a tail, it would have been briskly wagging. "Even Pop was impressed, and you know how hard *that* is to do."

"That makes two of us," Ice said, her voice warm, though still a bit hoarse. "Good job. Thank you, both, very much," she added.

Twin blushes brightened the faces of our friends as both shuffled their feet on the hardwood flooring, neither apparently sure of what to say to such a compliment.

Fortunately for them, they didn't need to come up with a response, because Ice fell back to sleep, slumping against me as she did so. I had a brief moment of panic, but the calmness in Bull's eyes relaxed me and together, we helped get her back into a more comfortable position on the bed.

That task completed, I looked back at Tom and John. "Is there something else?"

"Um, yeah," Tom said finally. "Rumor has it that those guys were in town for a couple days before they came calling. Seems that our good friend Millicent put 'em up for the weekend. Pop thinks that she even gave 'em directions to the cabin."

I vaulted off the bed so fast, my head spun from the abrupt change in position. "What did you say?" I demanded, grabbing Tom's huge arm. "You mean that bitch is behind this whole thing? Is that what you're telling me?"

"Calm down, Angel," Tom said, gently prying my fingers off his arm. "Right now it's nothing more than a rumor. No one knows for sure yet one way or the other."

"And how did this 'rumor' start?" I asked, fists clenched.

"Mary was fixing something over at the Silver Pine and she heard Millicent talking to some on the phone about the six charming men she put up for the weekend."

"Son of a *bitch*!"

"Angel..."

"What!?" I demanded, whirling around before I realized just whom I was yelling at. "Ice? Oh God, I'm so sorry. I didn't mean to wake you up."

"'s alright," she said softly. "C'mere."

"But..."

"C'mon," she beckoned, holding her arm out.

Unable to resist, I went to her, climbing back onto the bed and sliding into her tender embrace, taking care not to jostle her healing wounds. Giving me a little smile, she kissed my cheek, then settled me close before turning her head to look at Tom. "What does Pop say about all this?"

"He thinks she did it, but he doesn't think she knew exactly *what* she was doing. Or who the men were."

"That's no excuse!" I said. "She had no right to give complete strangers directions to our home! None at all!"

"It was stupid, I'll agree," Tom replied. "But being stupid isn't the same thing as deliberately setting someone up to be kidnapped and murdered, Tyler."

"This is *Millicent* we're talking about!" I countered. "The one who got someone to beat the crap out of Pop? The one who paid someone to firebomb his station? Am I the only one who sees this woman for who she really is?"

"Alright, Angel, that's enough," Ice said softly from beside me.

"Ice, it's not..."

"*Enough*, Angel. This isn't getting us anywhere."

I sighed, not willing to give up the fight, but realizing that there really wasn't any point in continuing. "When will somebody finally stand up to her?" I asked after a long moment. "Every time she's done something wrong, we've just turned the other cheek. And every time, she's just gone ahead and done something worse. What about next time, Ice? What if next time, it's...?"

I stopped there, but I knew she could read my thoughts on the matter. My biggest fear was that one night, our sleep would be shattered by the arrival of the police. That scenario was never far from my thoughts and continued to haunt my dreams.

As if sensing our conversation's deeper meanings, Tom cleared his throat, nudged his brother and together they grabbed an oblivious Bull and left the room. "We'll...um...be outside for awhile," Tom said as they descended the stairs and moved quickly away.

When we were alone, I turned back to Ice and laid a hand on her bruised cheek. "I'm sorry," I whispered. "I hate feeling helpless."

The soft skin of her face crinkled beneath my palm as one corner of her mouth lifted in a smile. "'s alright. I know this has been hard on you."

I gazed back at her, my expression serious. "Not on me,

Ice. On *us*. You and me." Pulling away slightly, I surveyed her from head to toe, tears filling my eyes. "Look at you, love. You've been beaten up, shot, almost sliced apart. You could have been killed."

"But I wasn't, Angel," she said simply. "I'm here and I'm alive."

"But for how long?"

A sob caught in my throat and I felt myself crumpling. Strong arms enfolded me, holding me close as a soft voice and tender hands soothed me. "Shhh. Don't cry, Angel. Please don't cry. Everything's gonna be alright. I promise. Everything's gonna be alright. Shhh."

I accepted her comfort, her love, for a long, much needed moment before attempting to pull away. When she wouldn't let me, I lifted my head. "I'm supposed to be comforting you. You're the one who went through hell and back. Not me."

She laughed softly. "Something tells me you went through a little bit of hell yourself, Angel." Reaching up, she tenderly cupped my chin, running her thumb over my lips. Though she was looking right at me, her eyes appeared far away. After several moments, she spoke. "After it was over, after I'd killed Carmine and his friends, the only thing that kept me from collapsing in that field was you, my Angel. Your smile. Your laugh. The sound of your voice when we make love. I needed to get back to you, needed to get back to the one good thing in this world that I know. Your light. Your warmth. Your love." Her hand trailed down over my face and neck to nestle against my breast, beneath which my heart beat strongly. "You."

Her eyes regained their focus and drilled into mine. "You say you're supposed to be comforting me. Don't you know you do that every day?"

I looked at her blankly for a moment, unable to fully process her words and their meaning.

Her face softened into a smile. "You do, Angel. Every day, without even thinking about it, just by being the person you are." Her voice became husky. "The woman I love."

Slipping her hand around the curve of the base of my skull, she used her implacable strength to easily draw us together, claiming my lips in a kiss filled with fire and passion and promise. I responded instantly, urgently, needing desperately to show her what she meant to me, this woman of fire and fury and boundless love.

Lost in the sensations of dizzying passion, my hands moved of their own accord, not even feeling the bandages that covered her many wounds. A soft grunt brought me back to reality quickly and I jerked my hand away from her belly as if scalded. "Oh my God, I'm so sorry! I didn't..."

"Shhh," she replied, pulling me close once again. "It's alright. I'm alright."

"You're hurt."

She captured me effortlessly in the power of her burning gaze. "I need you."

For those words, I would willingly sell my soul and damn the devil himself.

Grasping my hand, she brought it to her breast, laying it over her warm, firm flesh. "Touch me," she whispered.

I could hear myself moan as I closed my eyes against the exquisite sweetness of the feel of her beneath my trembling palm. When her body responded unmistakably to my hesitant touch, surging against my hand, I felt drawn up in a tide of overwhelming emotion that I was hard-pressed to contain.

"Let it go, sweet Angel," she whispered, using her free hand to draw our lips together again, tangling her long fingers in the short locks of my hair. "Just let it go."

Like a siren's sweet song, I allowed the sound of her voice, the movement of her body, to wash away the shame and the grief, the anger and the fear. Our lips met again, incendiary almost, and I just...let go.

I ran my fingers over her breasts, lightly at first, then with more urgency as the passion and the need for her flamed within me; a furnace with love and desire as its all-consuming, never-ending fuel.

I could feel her breathing deepen as I tasted her moan on my tongue. My hands moved with more surety, imprinting the silken feel of her flesh in my whirling mind with indelible imagery. Even the bandages, which swaddled her, ceased to be an impediment. Rather than hiding her wounds from sight, they became instead badges of her immense courage, her unbreakable will, each fiercely guarding the reminders of a battle hard fought and a war well won.

I laid gentle kisses to them all, imbuing myself with the strength of this wonderful, wondrous woman beneath me. The scent of her filled my senses; her taste, my sacramental wine. The sound of her voice was more beautiful to me than the music of a thousand choirs on a thousand worlds.

When I lifted my head from my benediction and my eyes were seared by passion-dark indigo, I felt the immovable, unbreakable strength of our elemental bond, its roots sinking ever deeper into my very soul.

And when my hand slipped down between legs which

opened to me and beckoned me to come nearer, to come inside, tears of joy ran anew down my cheeks as my fingers were welcomed sweetly home by the silken wet heat of her body.

"I love you, Morgan," I whispered, thrusting my fingers to match the tempo her own body had set. A curious combination of pain and ecstasy displayed itself on her beautiful features, but her eyes...

If love is a tangible thing, capable of being seen as well as felt, it is the look in her eyes when we make love. A look that says that I am the most precious and beloved thing the universe has ever created. That says that I am more wanted and more loved than I ever have even the hope of comprehending. That says that within me, the dream of the woman I love with all my heart, mind, body and soul, resides.

My fear tried to come back then; tried to remind me that I was far from being worthy of the gift she was giving me.

She saw it though, as she always did, with senses too foreign for me to comprehend. Surging upward even against the agony of her wounds, she pulled me to her, devouring my lips with her own, once again conquering my shame with the power of her love.

As my fingers continued to dance within her, hers trailed fire down my body and slipped past the insignificant barrier of my clothing, bathing themselves in essence newly sprung, painting me and arousing me with the evidence of my own desire before sliding deep within and filling me full.

Bodies merged by mouths and hands, we gave and took, advanced and retreated, gathering energy between us only to return it doubled and redoubled, our hearts beating loud, our breathing labored. Our souls twinned and separated, only to come together once again with the sounds of panting grunts and primal moans as each touch, each stroke, drove us higher and higher until, at last, the abyss was reached and we stepped off the peak as we'd climbed it.

Together.

And then we slumped together, bodies sliding against passion's sweat, riding out the last currents of incalculable bliss, shuddering with each small movement, until, at last, we became earthbound once more.

When enough strength returned for me to lift my head, I saw a single tear trail a path down her cheek. Her blinding smile told me all I needed to know, and, kissing the tear away, I laid her tenderly back down upon the bed we shared, returning the smile as I felt her face flushed and hot against the flesh of my neck, knowing the very second she slipped into the healing calm of sleep, her lips a gentle brand on my skin.

And, wrapped securely in a blanket of love and trust so strong and deep, I followed her into the shadows where nightmares didn't dare follow.

Blinking the sleep from my eyes, I tried to focus on the face hanging over me. "Corinne?"

"I'm trying for 'Louella, the tattooed Librarian' today," she responded, grinning. "Is it the right look for me?"

Looking at her closely, I saw for the first time the myriad of colorful bruises that lined the right side of her face and jaw. I felt a flush rising, ashamed that I hadn't noticed them before now. "How do you feel?"

"Pretty much as one would expect to several days after being pistol-whipped, I suppose," she said, her eyes twinkling.

I winced. "I'm sorry, Corinne."

She laughed. "For what? That was the most fun I've had since the demons of hell saw fit to release me from their little den of iniquity!"

"Our definitions of 'fun' seem to differ a little."

"But of course, Angel. You're merely a criminal wannabe, while I," she drew herself up to her full height, nose at a regal tilt toward the ceiling, "am the Black Widow."

Groaning, I rolled my eyes at her display of faux pomposity, then turned quickly to see if Ice was still asleep.

She was, her body and face relaxed, yet retaining that undercurrent of tension which was always present within her, save when she had been knocked out by the drugs Bull had given her. I could feel my face soften as I reached out and smoothed the sweaty tangle of her bangs.

Her face tensed momentarily, processing, no doubt, this intrusion into her personal space, then smoothed out into the soft planes of sleep once again as her breathing evened out and her body sank deeper into the nest of pillows surrounding her.

When I looked up, I saw an evil little smirk on my friend's face. "Not one word, Corinne. Not one."

Her eyes widened in mock innocence. "Moi? Surely you must have me confused with some other degenerate, Angel."

"Mmm. Hmm. Maybe we should start charging you for your nightly entertainment."

She pouted briefly, then grinned. "Would it help if I said I'd been moved to applaud a time or two? Or that I've been known to take notes on occasion?"

I could feel a whopper of a blush coming on. "More than I wanted to know, Corinne. Much more than I wanted to know."

She chuckled. "Then I suppose I shouldn't tell you about the times I..."

"Stop!" I commanded, raising my hand and burying my face into the pillows next to Ice's head. "Please."

"Oh, al..." The phone rang, mercifully cutting off her comment before it could be birthed from her lips. Before I could move, she was by the nightstand, lifting the receiver and cradling it against her ear, murmuring words I didn't really have the strength to listen to.

After a moment, she laid the phone back down and fixed me with a look I couldn't decipher.

"Who was it?"

"A certain septuagenarian who's a bit miffed that she wasn't invited to the tea party."

Oh shit. "Ruby. Damn, I forgot all about her. With everything going on, it just slipped my mind."

"Well, that's certainly understandable to one who actually *knows* what's been going on."

"You mean you didn't tell her?"

"Of course not, Angel. She simply was told what the doctors were told."

"Which was?"

"That I felt a bit of weakness and fell down, hitting my head on the table. They believed me. She didn't seem to, but she didn't push the issue at the time."

"She's pushing now?"

"Not in so many words, no. But I'm sure she'd appreciate some sort of explanation that didn't involve obfuscation." Corinne laid a gentle hand on my shoulder. "Ruby cares a great deal about you, Angel. She knows you're in pain, but she doesn't know why. All she knows is that you've seemed to shut her out for some reason. Perhaps a simple reassurance of your continued good health and good spirits would go a long way with her. She's worried, as I would be were I in a similar situation."

I nodded, convinced. "I'll call her right now."

"Don't bother. She said she was going away for a couple days to visit a friend. When she gets back, though, perhaps you could invite her over for a chat."

Sighing, I slumped back against the headboard. "Later it is, then." I smiled slightly. "At least one good thing came of this, though."

"And that might be?" she asked, giving me a very good "Ice" imitation, eyebrow and all.

"You two seem to be getting along better."

"We...understand one another," was all she saw fit to comment.

That conversation took place several hours ago, though gauging by how fuzzy my thoughts feel as they continue their unending journey through my mind, it could have been a week past, or a year. A quick glance at the clock tells me that another day has given its life so that a new dawn, now not far in coming, can shuffle forward, like the beast of Bethlehem, to be born.

Replaying the last year or so of my life has made me tired beyond telling, yet I can't seem to dredge up enough energy to lay myself back down on the bed and try for sleep. Or perhaps it's not energy I lack, but simple courage.

Where mostly pleasant dreams helped along many a lonely night in the Bog, nightmares rule the roost here, in the very place I'd thought to make those dreams come true.

By my side, Ice still rests, her breathing deep and even. *Do you dream?* I wonder, bringing the warm hand that still lays in my own up to my lips and brushing a gentle kiss across the knuckles.

She doesn't answer, of course. In all the years I've known her, it's one of the only questions I've never had the courage to ask.

Save for the tension which characterizes her even in this most peaceful of states (except, perhaps, for the afterglow of making love), she seems always to sleep the sleep of an innocent, unsullied by time and death and anger, all of which have been her constant companions for far longer than I've taken up cherished residence by her side.

Perhaps a peaceful sleep is her reward for wrestling down her inner demons and choosing to walk in the light.

Or perhaps she does dream; nightmares based on a reality that I can never hope to comprehend, only to understand and accept, which I do.

Perhaps they've kept her company for so long that her body no longer expends its energy reacting to them, choosing instead to conserve its power for when the darkness comes calling once again.

But in the end, I realize that it doesn't really matter. Ice's dreams are her own. That she chooses to share her life with me is the important thing, and something I treasure for the profound gift it is with every breath I take, waking *or* sleeping.

Experience has taught me the bitter lesson of ever taking that gift for granted.

When I told Corinne I would willingly give Ice up if I ever did that again, I meant every syllable. It's a promise that lives in my heart every day.

She's opened up so much to me in this past year; bared a soul filled with such brilliant light and such murky dark; been everything that I needed her to be and more.

So much more.

Perhaps spending a few hours going over everything that has gone wrong, and right, in the last year of our lives together has proven that better than anything else ever could. My body literally aches with the realization of just how deeply and profoundly I love her, how much of my soul she owns without trying, and how close I came to losing it all.

Shame still hides in my heart, no doubt biding its time, waiting to attack when I am most vulnerable. But I don't fear it anymore. Let it come. I'll fight it with the most powerful weapon in the world.

Love.

Looking out the window, I see that the rain has stopped, but the pregnant clouds paused over the somehow haunting darkness of the lake promise the cease-fire to be a temporary détente only.

My eyelids feel heavy, yet my body continues to fight sleep's seductive lure.

Until a hand detaches itself from my own and a long, lean body moves up to gather me into strong arms, cradling me tenderly as she lowers us both back down to the mattress. My hair is smoothed back from my brow, baring space for a pair of lips to linger.

"Sleep now," a resonant voice whispers, followed by the soft humming of a lullaby, which bathes me in its sweet serenity, sung by a woman with a heart and a soul more beautiful than the dawn that finally beckons from beneath dark clouds.

And if you wonder, as I do, what I've done to deserve such beauty and joy in my life, I'll answer you honestly.

I don't know.

But what I *do* know is that every day, in every way, I will make myself worthy of this gift beyond price.

It's the most fitting retribution I can think of for all she's given to me. Her heart, her soul, her body, and her spirit.

Her life.

Chapter 18

Five days have passed since that night. Days filled with a sense of peace and belonging that is unexpected, yet very welcomed, given everything that has come before. I suppose that being forced by danger to reexamine your life—foxhole theology, my father would have called it—really does put things into perspective. I'll have to remember that truism. As if I could ever forget.

Ice is well on her way to a complete recovery, as you'd expect, given everything I've told you about her so far. By the third day, she'd even managed to scatter the group of well-wishers gathered around the bed—deathwatch vultures, she called them—like a flock of frightened quail with one well-placed look and one menacing snarl added for effect.

I tried hard to stifle my laughter at the looks on their faces, but I'm afraid I didn't succeed very well. It felt good to be laughing again, truth be told.

The rains seem to have settled in, putting a somewhat premature cap on this year's tourist season. Though many of my friends make their living from the out-of-town visitors, I can't say that I'm at all sad to see it come to a close. The faster the summer ends, the faster I'll be able to put all the horrors the warm days brought with them behind me.

The added bonus of a shortened season is, of course, the early closing of the Silver Pine and the attendant loss of its proprietress, one Class A bitch by the name of Millicent Harding-Post.

I can assure you that the only tears I'm crying over that particular loss are tears of joy.

Ice says she has the beginnings of a plan to repay Ms. Harding-Post for all the kindnesses she's doled out to us over the year. She isn't ready to share it with me yet, but I'll be patient. She'll tell me when she's ready, this I know. And I also know that I'll enjoy every minute of it.

Bull left us a couple days ago. I was sad to see him leave, but, friendship aside, his healing skills really weren't needed anymore. Ice is a pretty good medico in her own right, and even if she weren't, he left us stocked with enough medical supplies to open up a clinic. And while the rains have chosen to visit us here in the lowlands, up in the mountains, snow is falling and he needed to get up to the hunting cabins while the roads were still passable to ensure they were properly weatherproofed and stocked for the harsh season to come.

Tom and John bid us their own goodbyes and went back to their families who were, no doubt, ready to tie yellow ribbons around old oak trees in the hopes of their eventual return. Even Corinne decided to give us some time to ourselves, choosing to spend several days in the company of Pop, who was feeling a bit under the weather after all the excitement of the past couple of weeks. I worry about him, for he's become someone whom I love dearly, but I know he's in good hands with Corinne.

The Black Widow seems to have lost her bite around Pop.

And, if I know Corinne half as well as I think I do, if he *does* wind up leaving this life, he'll go out with a smile on his face.

The rain let up just a bit this morning and Ice was outside before the last drop had fallen, determined to help along her rapidly regaining strength with a brisk walk through the woods. Tall and proud, with clothes to cover her bandages, anyone would be hard pressed to tell that she had even a scratch on her, much less two bullet holes and several long, deep cuts; even me.

I had watched in awe—and, truth to tell, no small amount of jealousy—as she washed and dressed and strode through the house without even a hint of pain while I lazed around on the couch, nursing my still sore knee and pouting.

With a smile and a kiss, she left to test her body the way those of us who must content ourselves with being mere mortals might test a cake to see if it is properly baked. Still, I couldn't help but return her smile and nod, knowing enough not to expect her until dark, at the least.

And that left me, of course, alone with only one thing left to do.

Call Ruby, who had come home last night, and invite her over for, as Corinne put it, a little chat.

It's something I've been dreading since Corinne saw fit to bring the subject up five days ago. While I very much want to see my long-time friend and mentor and explain things to her, I'm very much *not* wanting to see the look in her eyes once she realizes that pretty much everything I've told her since we've met was a lie.

I hate lying. It goes against everything I believe in. I'm not very good at it, as you've no doubt guessed by now, and every time I think I've succeeded, I turn around to find bite marks on my ass.

Still, the longer I put this off, the longer I let the truth hide beneath the weight of my guilt and shame, the harder the final truth telling will be for us both. As my mother always told me when I was young, pulling the Band-Aid off quickly was a whole lot less painful than ripping it off inch by slow inch.

Smart woman, my mother.

Ice finally got home an hour ago, drenched to the skin, but glowing with a vitality sorely missing over the past week or so, her eyes sparkling with good health and good humor. She refused to tell me what she'd spent the past half-day doing, figuring no doubt that I'd go all mother-hennish on her, but she *did* agree that perhaps a hot shower and a soft bed weren't such bad ideas after all.

It was good to know my powers of persuasion still worked. And even better to realize that after six years, I finally had a handle on them.

After a shower and a sandwich that I hastily threw together, she went right up to bed, where she sleeps even now, bundled up tightly against the faint chill in the air which lingers even after I've brought the fire up to a respectable roar.

Fall is definitely in the air.

And so here I sit, guts churning, waiting for the knock that will herald Ruby's entrance, replaying the words I'll tell her over and over in my mind until they're reduced to so much static, rendered all but meaningless by sheer repetition.

The knock finally came and I found myself rising to my feet, my knee sending out a warning twinge as I did so. I straightened my clothes and ran a quick hand through my hair, feeling oddly like a schoolgirl being sent to the principal, as I walked toward the door and pulled it open to admit my friend.

Ruby's smile looked rather forced as she crossed the threshold and into the house, allowing me to guide her into the cabin proper and to a seat in the living room. "Would you like some coffee? Tea?"

"No, thank you," she replied as she situated herself on the couch, not bothering to hide her frank head to toe assessment of me as she did so. Her eyes narrowed. "How are you feeling?"

"Better now," I answered honestly.

She nodded. "That's good to hear."

The conversation, what little there was of it, ground down to a halt, the crackling of the fire the only sound in the room.

Unable to stand the silence any longer, I took several deep breaths and turned to my friend. "Ruby, I'm very sorry I haven't..."

She raised a hand, her smile slightly more genuine. "It's quite alright, Tyler. I understand. I know what went on here."

Stunned, I looked at her. "You do?"

"Yes. I do. I had my suspicions at first, and what I've since learned has confirmed them."

I cocked my head. "Would...you mind explaining that, please?"

Her smile turned sad. "Tyler, I might be an old woman, but I'm not blind or deaf. Look at yourself, Tyler. You're bruised and battered. You've been beaten. And Corinne looks the same way. She says that she fell down and hit her head on the table, but that's not the truth, is it?"

I sighed. "No. It isn't."

She nodded sagely. "I know." Turning her body toward mine, she took both of my hands in hers. "I called your mother the other day, Tyler."

For just a moment, I forgot to breathe. "You ...what?"

"You heard me. She told me what really happened during your time in Pittsburgh. How you told her that your husband had abused you and how you said you killed him in self-defense. How you spent time in prison and were released on appeal."

Stunned was much too small a word for what I was feeling, and yet I couldn't help but nod, confirming her words, suddenly feeling very small and very young and very trapped.

"Your mother may not be the most warm and open person in the world, Tyler, but I do believe she really believes what you've told her. I know I do. You're not the type to kill someone in cold blood. That's just not within you. I know that."

I smiled a little, relieved that she, at least, believed in my innocence.

She returned the smile, squeezing my hands. "Tyler, I knew your father quite well. He had this cabin long before he married your mother and spent many summers here. I knew what kind of a man he was, and could only hope that your mother would calm him somewhat."

"I'm not sure I understand what you're saying," I replied, my mind trying hard to keep up with the twists and turns of her narrative and failing miserably.

"Your father could be a warm and loving man at times, Tyler. But he could also be worse than an enraged bear if something stuck in his craw. Many's the time I ached to step in when he took that anger out on you. To my eternal shame, I stood by and did nothing."

I stared at her, conflicting emotions warring for a place in my body. Shame for a long held family secret let out into the light. Relief that it was finally being spoken of. Confusion, still, not knowing where the conversation was leading.

"Before I married my husband, I was a teacher. And one of the things that I learned was that, quite often, daughters of abusive fathers unconsciously seek out the same in a potential mate. It's not uncommon, nor is it something to be ashamed of. I think you did that with your own husband. And I think you're doing that now with your friend, Morgan."

"What?" Tearing my hands from hers, I jumped to my feet so quickly that the room spun around me. Forcing down the dizziness, I stared at her, my eyes blazing. "I have no idea where you came up with this, Ruby, but you're wrong. Dead wrong."

"Am I?" she asked, her eyes blazing just as brightly. "Both you and Corinne were beaten to within an inch of your lives, Tyler. I came outside just in time to hear her driving away and you screaming for her to come back." Her face set in stony, savage lines. "Don't think me a fool, Tyler. I know what I saw."

"You *are* a fool, Ruby," I replied, feeling as deep a rage as I've ever known consuming me in red fire. "You put two and two together and came up with seven. I think you'd better leave before I do something we'd both regret."

"She's taught you well, I see."

"Get out, Ruby. Now."

"I know who she is, Tyler," Ruby continued, refusing to budge a solid inch. "I know who Morgan Steele is. I thought her name sounded familiar when we first met. When Millicent told me that those police officers had asked for directions to the cabin, I knew my hunch was right. So I spent the last several days going through old records until I found out what I was looking for. She's the Morgan Steele who murdered those children. The one who became a Mafia Assassin. The one who escaped from the very prison in which you were incarcerated. The one who tricked you into falling in love with her so that she could have a free ticket out of the country to escape justice. And the one who finally snapped under all the pressure she's heaped upon the both of you and lashed out with her fists like an animal."

I was paralyzed by her accusations, by a misunderstanding so great that it could not possibly have happened. My mind was screaming out to shut her up, to tear her limb from limb, or barring that, to pick her bodily up and throw her as far away from the house as I possibly could.

But my body was dipped in lead, unable to move.

Taking my silence for something it wasn't, her face softened. "It doesn't have to go on, Tyler. I couldn't do anything before, with your father. But I can now. I can, and I did."

That broke through. Stepping forward, I pulled her off the couch by the front of her dress, hearing the fabric tearing as I brought our faces mere inches apart. "What did you do, Ruby? *What did you do?!*"

"I'm doing what I should have done a long time ago, Tyler. I'm putting an end to this mess. The police are on their way. You'll never have to worry about her again. I promise."

"No." It was a whisper, but it carried the weight of the world behind it.

"Yes, Tyler. Yes. Finally. I'm doing this because I love you. Can't you see? I love you and I want what's best for you. So come with me. Please. You'll be safe when the police get here."

"*No!*"

Pushing her away from me as if she weighed less than air, I spun around and tore up the stairs, screaming Ice's name at the top of my lungs as I ran, tripping and falling and pulling myself up again.

She was already awake and on her feet when I bolted into the room. Turning away from the window, her eyes were shining and sad, her face set in a mask of bleak resignation.

"Ice," I said breathlessly, running up to her and grabbing onto her arm, "you've got to get out of here. Take the truck. Go up into the mountains. I'll find you when it's safe. You've still got time. Please. Run!"

Slowly, she shook her head. "It's over, Angel."

"It's *not* over! I won't *let* it be over!" I pulled at her, but it was like I was trying to move a mountain. "Damnit, Ice, move! *Now*!"

Gently prying my death grip from her arm, she raised my hand to her lips and brushed a kiss against my knuckles. "I love you, Angel," she whispered. "Never forget that. Never."

"No. Oh God, no. Please, Ice. Please don't do this." Seeing the blue lights of what looked to be a thousand police cars filtering through the trees, I shook my head in blind negation. "Please, Ice, don't. Fight, damn you! Fight!"

She smiled slightly, reaching up to cup my cheek. "I am fighting, my sweet Angel. For you."

Pulling me close, she kissed me, long and deep, before pulling away and grasping my hand. "C'mon."

Believing that she'd finally come to her senses, I followed quickly behind her as she descended the stairs and walked into the living room where Ruby, once again back on her feet and wiping blood from her lips, stared at her with an intense sheen of hatred blazing in her eyes.

And it doesn't shame me one bit that I wanted, with everything in me, to watch Ice wipe that look off her face forever.

Instead, my lover thrust me into Ruby's arms, then stared down at her with a look more searing than the sun. "Every word you said is true. I *am* a monster. I *am* an abuser. I brainwashed her and tricked her into falling in love with me so I could get a free ride. She was nothing more than my hostage. A ticket. And you'd do well to remember that when the police start to question you."

Ruby sneered. "You don't scare me."

Ice's lip curled, displaying her teeth. "Then you *are* a fool."

Then she stiffened, her head turning toward the back of the house. "Get down."

"You can't..."

"Now!"

Effortlessly, she pushed us both down onto the floor, hovering over us both in a stiff, protective stance, her head still cocked, honing in on whatever she was hearing.

The heavens opened up then, sending rain down in a deluge as lightning divided the sky and thunder cracked around us, shaking the house.

I heard it then; the sound of sirens as they closed in around the cabin. I struggled to regain my feet, but Ice pushed me back down, pinning me to the floor with her intense glare.

"Attention in the cabin! We have you surrounded. Come out peacefully with your hands above your head and no one will

be harmed! Attention in the cabin! We have you surrounded. Come out peacefully with your hands above your head and no one will be harmed!"

"Stay down," Ice said, giving me a last, long look before turning away and starting for the door.

"Ice! *No*!"

But she didn't listen. God damn her to hell, she didn't listen.

I struggled to my feet, nearly tripping over Ruby as she tried to restrain me and shoving her savagely back down to floor.

I ran after the retreating form of my lover, but by the time I got to the door, it was a lifetime too late.

The police swarmed over her, forcing her unresisting body to the ground and onto her stomach as they pulled her arms behind her back and cuffed them tightly, their guns drawn and pointed at her with malicious intent.

When they pulled her back to her feet, her beautiful face was stained with mud and blood. The front of her shirt, once a brilliant white, was painted maroon from the stitches which had torn open.

Like a man turned to stone by a vengeful god, I was doomed to stand and watch as my entire world was dragged off into the night.

It was cold. So cold.

And dark, like the bottom of a newly dug grave.

My whole body was numb; my heart, encased in a block of ice which promised never to thaw.

I could feel the rain around me, pelting down in almost horizontal sheets of stinging fire, driven on by the frenzy of an unholy wind.

A wooden shutter, torn askew by the power of the storm, slammed repeatedly against the weathered wooden siding, sounding a death-knell which rose even over the howling of the wind and the wailing of sirens. Sirens, which like the fog, crept closer and closer, not on cat's feet, but on dragon's bloody claws.

Lightning drew its spiky graph onto the sky, imprinting itself on my retinas.

Thunder cracked and rolled, pulling an inane thought to the forefront of my brain. *God's bowling with the angels again*, my father's voice said from somewhere beyond the grave.

And still I waited, blind and frozen like some immortal statue. Waited for the wind to cease its unending fury. Waited for the rain to part its opaque curtain.

Waited for a vision my eyes could not see. A vision my soul

could not forget.

As if drawn into the clearing by the force of my unvoiced plea, still more cars came, their churning tires flinging muddy fans into the air. Their powerful headlights broke through the cloak of mist, illuminating the scene I wished so desperately to see from my frozen perch on the porch of the home I'd helped to build.

A home, a dream, that I would willingly leave, never stopping once to look back upon it, if only someone would take these scales from my eyes.

If only.

She stood there straight and tall, backlit by the artificial lighting; my lover, my heart, my soul. Proud, back unbowed, head held high, eyes blazing fire.

Proud, yes. But helpless.

Not against the arms which held her, nor the cuffs which bound her strong arms, nor even the guns that pointed at every vulnerable spot in an otherwise invulnerable body.

No, not that. Never that.

Helpless, instead, against the weight of a past which had, once again, come home to roost.

Helpless against the weight of a love she had sold her very soul to nurture and cherish.

The look in her eyes is something I'll take with me to the grave. A grave that, God willing, will not be long in coming.

Anger at her past for intruding. Rage at the arms which held her, at the guns which nudged her with their hollow silver noses. Sorrow, that the chance we had had ended much too soon.

And love.

Always love.

Her full lips parted, and I strained to hear her words over the storm's redoubled fury. But even they were taken from me, just as surely as she would be, drawn away into the mist from which only endings came.

But still, I watched as those lips formed words only my heart could hear.

I love you.

And then a word came which shattered my soul.

Goodbye.

Available soon from

RENAISSANCE ALLIANCE

And Those Who Trespass Against Us

By H. M. Macpherson

Sister Katherine Flynn is an Irish nun sent by her order to work in the Australian Outback. Katherine is a prideful woman who originally joined her order to escape the shame of being left at the altar. She had found herself getting married only because society dictated it for a young woman her age, and she was not exactly heartbroken when it didn't take place. Yet, her mother could not be consoled and talked of nothing except the disgrace that she had brought to the Flynn name. So, she finds great relief in escaping the cold Victorian Ireland of 1872.

Catriona Pelham is a member of the reasonably affluent farming gentry within the district. Her relationship with the hardworking townspeople and its farmers is one of genuine and mutual respect. The town's wealthy, however, have ostracized her due to her unorthodox ways and refusal to conform to society's expectations of a woman of the 1870's.

As a bond between Katherine and Catriona develops, Catriona finds herself wanting more than friendship from the Irishwoman. However, she fears pursuing her feelings lest they not be reciprocated. And so the journey begins for these two strong-willed women. For Katherine it is a journey of self-discovery and of what life holds outside the cloistered walls of the convent. For Catriona it is bittersweet, as feelings she has kept hidden for years resurface in her growing interest in Katherine.

Coming Home
By Lois Hart

A triangle with a twist, Coming Home is the story of three good people caught up in an impossible situation. Rob, a charismatic ex-fighter pilot severely disabled with MS, has been steadfastly cared for by his wife, Jan, for many years. Quite by accident one day, Terry, a young writer/postal carrier enters their life and turns it upside down. Injecting joy and turbulence into their quiet existence, Terry draws Rob and Jan into her lively circle of family and friends until the growing attachment between the two women begins to strain the bonds of love and loyalty, to Rob and each other.

Vendetta
By Talaran

Nicole Stone is a narcotics detective with a painful past that still haunts her. Extremely attractive, yet reclusive, she has closed her heart to love and concentrates solely on her career. After someone tries to kill her partner in cold blood, she meets her partner's sister, Carly Jamison. An unmistakable attraction catches both of these women off guard. Can Nic protect her partner and Carly from the clutches of a ruthless drug lord bent on revenge and still open her heart to the one woman who could change her life forever?

Other titles to look for in the coming months from RENAISSANCE ALLIANCE

You Must Remember This By Mary A. Draganis

Staying In the Game By Nann Dunne

Blue Holes To Terror By Trish Kocialski

Full Circle By Mary A. Draganis

Bleeding Hearts By Josh Aterovis

Anne Azel's Murder Mysteries #1 By Anne Azel

Gun Shy By Lori Lake

High Intensity By Belle Reilly

New Beginnings By Mary A. Draganis

A Sacrifice For Friendship By DS Bauden

Sue is an RN who has been writing stories for about 20 years now. She lives in Atlanta with her computer, some books, a bunch of Xena stuff, and two dogs.

Printed in the United States
1578

9 781930 928244